TIME AND ELVIRA JONES

Marise Morland

TIME AND ELVIRA JONES

FICTION4ALL

A FICTION4ALL PAPERBACK

ISBN 978-1-78695-906-5

Fiction4All

Published 2025

Marise Morland

Unfathomable sea! whose waves are years,
Ocean of Time, whose waters of deep woe
Are brackish with the salt of human tears!
Thou shoreless flood, which in thy ebb and flow
Claspest the limits of mortality!
And sick of prey, yet howling on for more,
Vomitest thy wrecks on its inhospitable shore,
Treacherous in calm, and terrible in storm,
Who shall put forth on thee,
Unfathomable sea?

P. B. SHELLEY

Time and Elvira Jones

Chapter One

"Ms Jones, the Director will see you now," announced the receptionist.

Elvira Jones, blonde and statuesque, uncoiled herself from the depths of a settee. "Finally! Wish me luck, Charlene." An inner door opened and she disappeared inside.

"She's so beautiful," said the office junior enviously. "She could be a model."

"She's in marketing," Charlene explained. "The Simply Qubit division. She gets to show off our quantum products."

"And she wants to work *here* – underground?"

"It's cutting edge. And she's ambitious." Charlene paused. "That might not be enough to convince the old man, though."

Elvira, aware that the door had closed silently behind her, confronted three individuals seated at a long table. One vacant chair was positioned in the centre of the room. She took it, surveying her interviewers. An anonymous woman from HR; a security officer; and, the focus of her attention, the thin angular figure of CoherenceCo's exec, Rafe Bridgenorth.

The woman shuffled her paperwork. "Could you remind us please, Miss Jones – "

"Ms."

"*Ms* Jones. Can you tell us why you're seeking a career change from a secure, lucrative post to an as yet experimental branch of science?"

"Certainly. To be frank, quantum computing has stalled. Qubits are notoriously unstable. At the current rate of progress, we'll need decades before we can rival binary systems. Particle physics, on the other hand, has already transformed medicine and communications. The space industry has to be next. I'd like to be part of that."

"I value your enthusiasm," said Bridgenorth unctuously. "However, having considered your application carefully, I regret you have been unsuccessful on this occasion."

Elvira's cool expression didn't change, but inwardly she was seething. "Then with respect, Director, why bring me here? You could have said that in a memo."

"Because an unexpected matter has arisen, necessitating your presence. Your reply will be in confidence."

"Go on."

"We have offered the post of project leader to Clive Brightlingsea, and he has accepted, but has made an unorthodox request."

"Which is?"

"That you work alongside him as a senior analyst. We'd like your thoughts on this. How you would feel, for instance, working for someone younger than yourself? It would also mean a drop in salary."

The HR woman glanced at her watch. "What Director Bridgenorth is endeavouring to say is, has Mr Brightlingsea ever behaved in a way that would make it difficult for you to work with him? Such as innuendo, unwanted sexual advances – "

"No," Elvira interrupted. "Nothing like that." He knows what I'd do if he tried, her thoughts added.

Bridgenorth steepled his fingers. "Then do you wish to accept the offer?"

"If it's permitted," said Elvira carefully, "I'd like some time to think it over."

"Understandable. Would a week be sufficient?"

"Er … yes."

"Thank you, Ms Jones. I'll await your decision."

The trio rose and, without a backward glance, left via a private exit.

Elvira stormed back into the reception area, wishing she could slam the automated door.

"I assume that went badly?" inquired Charlene.

"Yes, but not in the way you might think. That self-serving little creep Clive's still trying to build his career on the back of other people's honest toil. He wants me as his subordinate, which means he'll take the credit for any success I might have."

"Isn't that a bit harsh?"

"No, it isn't. Clive's programs don't work. Do you remember Gwen Morrow?"

"Just about. Quiet and shy."

9

"And clever. When she was at Simply Qubit she wrote a paper challenging current thinking on entanglement. And suddenly there was Clive, cosying up to her, giving her the chat, taking an interest in her thesis. The next thing we knew, he'd laid claim to it. Even had the cheek to say she'd made a contribution. Gwen resigned."

"Did Bridgenorth know why?"

"Probably. But as far as he's concerned, Clive can do no wrong. I don't know whether to cut my losses like Gwen, or stay put and fight my corner. I've one week to decide, and since I've some leave owed, that week starts now. Bye!"

"Do you think she'll be back?" asked the typist.

"I hope she will," Charlene replied soberly. "We need women like her."

Elvira retrieved her jacket from its locker and approached a row of sturdily built elevators. One, she observed thankfully, was already at the lower ground floor, home to Simply Qubit. She knew from experience how long it took for the lifts to ascend from below. She presented her palm print to the scanner, noting – as she always did – the buttons marked Control, Basement and Sub-Basement. There were several other unmarked destinations. She had, of course, tried pressing them all, only to be told she didn't have clearance. Maybe that was about to change.

At street level was a covered parking area with an exit post manned by one attendant. It looked no different to any other industrial car park. Nearby was a small office block identifying itself as Bull and Bush Market Analytics. It was the type of building no-one looked at twice.

Elvira's silver Volvo halted at the barrier. The attendant was on his landline, and remained on it for over three minutes. She beeped at him impatiently, and at last he came to the window.

"Sorry, princess, that was Downstairs. Some particles got uppity and spoilt their experiment, and the CCTV – mine included – got messed up for the same few seconds. Did you see anything unusual?"

"Such as?"

He shrugged. "I'm not allowed to guess."

"I saw nothing and no-one, Max. Now stop interrogating me. I'd like to go home!"

"No kung fu tonight?" Max inquired.

"It's Mixed Martial Arts, and no. But I've time for a quick demonstration if you don't open that gate!"

He grinned and raised the barrier.

Elvira eased the Volvo out of the complex, accelerated, then braked a few seconds later. Someone was lying in the slip road. She pulled over and opened the door cautiously, suspecting a set-up. But there was nowhere for an accomplice to hide, and the fairhaired young man on the ground was genuinely injured. A gash over one eye oozed blood. Dazed and dishevelled, he flinched as she leant over him.

"Good lady, forgive. I was clumsy."

"What happened? Were you mugged?"

"I was running from bad people. To prevent them following I had to launch without a receptor."

11

"Receptor? What's that?"

"The entangled opposite. Time's ... forward ... arrow ..." A thin trickle of blood ran from his nose.

"Oh, great." Elvira contrived to sit him up. "Can I call anyone for you? Focus, dammit. Focus!"

He focused. "I need to find CoherenceCo. I know it's here. It has to be."

Elvira reached an instant decision. "Right, you're coming with me. We'll talk some more later. Can you stand? OK, I've got you. Now slide into the passenger seat." She rummaged in the glove compartment and found some tissues. "Here, use these, and try not to bleed on the upholstery. Seat belt on. No, not like that." She returned to the driver's seat, then ensured he was strapped in. "My flat's six minutes away. We'll get you sorted and then you can tell me all about the bad guys and what they have to do with CoherenceCo. Don't argue, that's an order."

"Your servant, good lady."

She wondered if he was being sarcastic, but thought it best not to ask.

Her flatmate's car was in the drive. Relieved, she parked alongside and called her. "Vivette, I'm home. Can you come down? *Now?* I've someone here who's in a spot of bother. His name's ..." She held the phone toward the young man.

"Paris Evason," he supplied shakily.

"Paris?" queried Vivette. "Nice. I'll be with you in a tick."

They bundled their mysterious guest up a flight of stairs to the first floor flat. "Hey, Paris," said Vivette once they were indoors, "before I allow you anywhere near my bespoke cushions you'll have to lose that overall. It's a mess. Mud all down one side and the sleeve torn open. Where's the zip? Buttons? Anything?"

Paris lifted his right hand fractionally, and the material parted from collar to waist.

"Magnets. Cool," said Vivette imperturbably. "Now off with the rest of it."

Disappointingly, he was wearing a plain grey vest and knee-length shorts. "Is this indecorous?" he inquired.

Vivette arched an eyebrow. "I think you could do with a make-over."

Elvira left her to her ministrations and went in search of a first aid kit. When she returned, Paris had been allowed to sit down.

"Why are you so woozy?" Vivette was asking. "Are you *on* something?"

"I swear I'm not, Face of Plessis."

She stared. "How do you know my surname?"

"Not now, Viv." Elvira came forward and began to clean the grit and congealed blood from Paris' forehead. "Make yourself useful and get him some brandy."

"But didn't you hear what - "

"Brandy! Move it!"

Vivette's annoyance lasted precisely one minute. Paris' look of pure gratitude was an ample

13

reward. She held the glass steady while he sipped, and gradually some colour returned to his face.

"So, mystery man," Elvira said gently, "would you mind explaining yourself? That was the deal."

"If you insist," answered Paris, avoiding her gaze. "Some criminals in my workplace were defrauding rich clients out of their money and then killing them. I tried to get evidence but I wasn't careful enough. As I told you earlier, I launched myself without a receptor, to avoid pursuit. I'm a time traveller, Ms Jones. From your future. Without a receptor, one's body weight displaces the continuum on arrival, and this creates a series of ripples which is disorienting – even painful – for the traveller. You don't believe me, do you?"

Elvira said nothing, recalling the energy burst that had cost CoherenceCo a day's work.

"*I* believe you," said Vivette. She'd retrieved the grimy overall. "This hole's busy repairing itself. And we all know that can't happen – yet. I insist on knowing how it's done!"

"I *will* tell you," he promised. "But first – what year is this?"

Vivette tossed a copy of Vogue at him.

He scanned the cover, then thrust it aside with an oath neither of the women recognised.

"Sounds like you screwed up," Vivette said impishly.

"You could say that. I thought I'd reached 2073, the year the Time Travel Institute was founded. Instead, CoherenceCo is still in its infancy."

14

"In-house experiments," Elvira confirmed.

"Forgive my ineptitude," Paris said dully. "If it's any kind of excuse, I was in fear of my life."

"If you were heading for 2073," began Elvira carefully, "what year are you actually *from*?"

"2584."

"Yet you still speak twenty-first century English."

"I'm speaking standard protocol 2000 London. Every TTI employee has sleep tuition in language variants. Time tourists have to blend in and we have to monitor them." He held out his glass for a refill – his second.

"Before you drink any more of that," said Elvira, "tell me when you last ate."

"Er .. oh." He summoned a grin. "Not since breakfast, and that was only Vegi-sim. Seven hours?"

"Just as well I asked. I'll order in." She readied her phone. "Any preference? Pizza, curry, fish and chips?"

"*Real* fish and chips?" he echoed.

Elvira didn't inquire what a fake version was like.

"Ladies," Paris said formally, "may I be permitted to bathe before the meal arrives? The launch set-up was messy and I probably smell of tungstron relay oil."

"Oh, so that's what it is," trilled Vivette, propelling him toward the ensuite. "Do you know how everything works? In the bathroom, I mean."

15

"I've read the history manuals," he responded through the closed door.

"Must you keep winding him up, Viv?" Elvira said reprovingly.

"He's kind of cute," said Vivette by way of an excuse.

"Yes, and he's also tired, hungry and scared. There's a lot more he needs to tell us, so enough of the teasing."

"OK," agreed Viv unrepentantly. "But let's see if we can dress him up a bit."

"In what?"

Vivette rummaged through a capacious wardrobe. "Some of Hercule's clothes."

"That waste of space! I wonder if he's still sofa-surfing?"

"Probably. Anyway, I'm confiscating these. Just the thing for our Paris – a new image. Geek chic."

Elvira continued to frown.

"And I'll let him choose," Vivette added.

"He might surprise you," Elvira said.

Paris obligingly chose an outsize Hawaiian shirt, drawstring linen trousers and ill-fitting white flip-flops. No-one commented.

The promised meal of cod, chips and mushy peas duly arrived. The women expected Paris to wolf it down, but instead he displayed exemplary table manners. After coffee he began to paint a vivid word-picture of CoherenceCo in the twenty-sixth century. The road where he'd landed so unceremoniously was in the same physical space as the time terminal which had dispatched him into the past. And that terminal was one of a vast array, serviced and maintained by technicians like himself. Beyond them was a ring of security; above, the plush reception areas where time tourists were processed and costumed; below, the particle accelerator which powered the complex.

"What about Strictly Qubit?" asked Elvira.

"It was sold off."

"All the more reason to switch careers, El," Vivette remarked. "Or is there something you're not telling us?"

Elvira reluctantly explained how her dream job had been hijacked by the duplicitous Clive. "I've a week to make up my mind," she continued. "I suppose I should put in *one* appearance, just for the chance to slap him."

A flicker of hope had appeared on Paris' face, only to disappear again.

"You want me to accept the terms, don't you?" Elvira asked quietly.

He looked away. "I'm sorry."

"Stop saying that! CoherenceCo's the only link to your time, isn't it?"

He nodded.

"And you need me to be your contact."

He repeated the nod.

"Be careful what you're getting into, El," Vivette advised.

"I intend to be. And that's why I need to know exactly how Paris discovered this crime syndicate and who's involved."

17

"And if they'll be expecting him to turn up again," added Vivette shrewdly.

"I promised I'd tell you everything, and I will," Paris said earnestly.

"We're waiting," said Vivette.

"First, you'll need some background. Have you heard of the Many Worlds Interpretation?"

"Yes," said Elvira.

"No," said Vivette simultaneously. Elvira went to make more coffee.

"Some theorists," began Paris carefully, "believe there are an infinite number of universes. And that when a time traveller interferes with the past – simply by going there – another reality is created. And it's the new version, with his visit included, that our traveller goes home to. Only, he doesn't. We at TTI have been time-conversant for hundreds of years, and in our experience people always return to their point of departure. So it's fair to say there's only one universe."

"And you're sure about that, are you?"

"There's no evidence to the contrary. But, the authorities don't take anything for granted. Every time trip has to be logged in, logged out, filed, checked and double-checked. We have statisticians who do nothing else."

"Figure - figure guys are a pain," Vivette remarked.

"Figure - figure *girls*," Paris corrected her. "And they're remorseless. That's how my involvement began – with a rant from the Stats department over a discrepancy. Over the course of

18

a month there had been three more departures than retrievals. Three, out of several thousand. But there shouldn't have been any. The error – or the collusion – was attributed to my section, and that angered me, because I'd done nothing wrong and I was sure my team hadn't either. I checked the manifests, found the identities of the three missing people, and realised I knew one of them, Gil Hannason. I'd studied alongside his son Eadwine, who was later to die in a skiing accident."

Elvira, in the kitchen, heard his voice begin to tremble and added a slop of brandy to his coffee.

"On an impulse I visited Jenufa, Gil's wife," Paris was continuing. "And I found he'd left her a message which couldn't be opened for another three months. She asked if I could override the program."

"Which, of course, you could," Elvira said, setting down the drinks.

"Of course," Paris confirmed with no trace of conceit. "The home AI did its best to stop me but I accessed the sub-routine that ran all the timers. And the message played. Someone at the Institute, someone at executive level, had claimed that a way into the multiverse had been discovered – a myriad different realities. In one of them, Eadwine had reputedly survived the avalanche. Gil had died on the mountain instead. The unknown exec was offering, for a massive fee to cover the energy output, to send Gil there to resume his interrupted life. The operation and others like it were still classified, so he was to tell no-one." He paused, remembering. "That poor man. So hopeful, yet so wretched. I think he knew he was being scammed but he'd have done anything if it meant seeing his son again."

"Only he broke the rules."

"He did. He couldn't simply vanish without telling his wife."

"And you're sure the multiverse project is fake?"

"Absolutely. I haven't told you how this ends. *If* it ends. Please be patient."

They waited. Vivette fidgeted.

"I went back to the Institute after-hours and retrieved Gil's metadata," Paris continued, forcing the words out. "They'd sent him to Point Nemo in the mid-Pacific, the furthest distance from any land. They'd sent him there *alive*. I felt sick. I tried to leave, but hadn't even accessed a conveyor buggy when I saw two strangers, a man and a woman. They weren't from security and wore no ID. The man's expression was cold, hostile; the woman seemed...almost amused. A synapsyn gun appeared in her gloved hand."

His listeners looked puzzled.

"Standard issue, to ensure compliance. Oh yes, we still have law enforcement. What world doesn't? The gun ejects a cloud of crystals – painless, non-lethal. But if any had touched me, I'd have given myself up."

"Just like that?" asked Elvira.

Paris nodded solemnly. "The arresting officer says, very gently, 'is there something you want to confess?' It's never failed. I'd have told my captors everything I knew, and begged them to forgive me. But, the woman didn't fire. It's breezy on the maintenance levels and she may have feared crystal blow-back. Anyway, I fled to the terminals, and fell into the nearest one while my pursuers beat on the door and tried to guess the locking code. I set the program too hastily. And here I am."

"How did they know you were onto them?" Elvira couldn't help asking.

"I'm not sure. They could have had eyes on Jenufa."

A car door slammed close by, and he jumped violently.

"It's only the neighbours," Vivette reassured him. "You're safe with us."

"I hope so," he said dolefully.

"Paris, thanks for sharing," Elvira said in an attempt to sound casual. "Let's change the subject. You were going to tell Vivette how you recognised her."

Paris brightened. "Yes, of course. Your face, Vivette – or maybe the face of a descendant – is all on the promotions for House of Plessis."

"You mean, our brand's famous? *Really* famous?"

"You diverted from boutique fashion to workwear. You designed functional, stylish, self-repairing clothes, firstly for industry, and then for the Moon and Mars bases. NASA offered you a lucrative contract."

"Oh, wow!"

"But first, you have to reverse-engineer my overall. Does any of your team have the necessary skills?"

Vivette wrinkled her brow. "Fabian has a chemistry degree."

"Then take it to him. You'll succeed – you *did* succeed."

"But, hold on. How did … *I* … invent your overall?"

"We need a cover story," Elvira said airily. "Let's create one."

"We need some more booze."

"Good idea." Elvira produced a bottle of Prosecco and three glasses. "Right, kids, let's brainstorm. Vivette can pretend she had a crazy old uncle who died and left her some weird inventions - "

"No good," Vivette declared. "Too many people know my only relatives are Maman in Amiens and Hercule, itinerant brother."

"They aren't really French," Elvira said to Paris in a stage whisper. "Hercule is Herbie. Maman is Mum in Ashby de la Zouch. And their surname's Plested."

"Amazing," Paris murmured. "We never knew."

"Just make sure it stays that way," Vivette warned. "So, let's invent a crazy uncle for Maman instead of me. When she goes to do the house clearance she finds endless notebooks with strange diagrams, plus actual gadgets that don't work - "

"Such as," said Paris, entering into the general frivolity, "a design for a laser which would focus on the moon and make it look blue."

"A cloak that whispers its brand name when you swirl it around," said Vivette.

"An eco-friendly interplanetary drive," suggested Paris, "consisting of a huge elastic band which is tautened over and over and then released."

The ideas grew more and more nonsensical as the level in the wine bottle diminished. Paris was now half asleep.

"Correct me if I'm wrong, Viv," said Elvira, "but didn't your mum teach you dressmaking?"

"She absolutely did."

"So, she could simply have found the overall in Uncle Bertrand's living room and tried to cut it up to make ..."

"Waistcoats," said Paris.

"Ugh," said Vivette.

"A raincoat, then," Elvira substituted.

"Wouldn't work."

"An anorak?"

"What's an anorak?" asked Paris.

"If your people have forgotten," Vivette intoned loftily, "then it would be a crime to enlighten them."

"Tote bags!" Elvira declared into a brief silence. "Your Maman was going to make tote bags for charity shops. And then, when the material started to move - "

"She got scared and called *me*," Vivette concluded. "Tomorrow, I'll brief her - "

On cue, her mobile buzzed discreetly from the coffee table.

"It's Cec," she announced. "Have to take this."

"Their photographer," Elvira whispered to Paris.

"What, *now*?" Vivette was exclaiming. "I thought that was last night. Oh, I see. Well, how will that publicise the new range? We'd just be silhouettes. Or the colour would be weird. Oh, all right, if you insist. I'll be with you at 2 am. And I've been drinking so I'll have to take a cab." She ended the call. "Cec wants to do a fashion shoot against the Northern Lights. I think he's wasting his time, but work's work. And it *is* rare to see them this far south."

"Rare? Not for much longer," said Paris sagely.

"I'd better get my things. And I'll see if I can crash at Fabian's afterwards. That means you can have my room tonight, Paris. We'll sort out the living arrangements properly tomorrow."

"About that," Paris was suddenly serious. "You do realise that because of my error with the date, I'll be dependent on your goodwill for an indefinite time?"

"Don't worry about it," Vivette said.

"We're not going to throw you out," Elvira added. "I thought we'd already established that."

"Nevertheless, my social background dictates that I make an offer to you," Paris continued. "My mother, Eva, was determined that I should make a good marriage - "

24

"Hold on," Elvira interrupted. "Your name, Evason. Eva's son?"

"That's correct. We denote the female line. Ours is a matriarchal society."

"This gets better!" Vivette murmured. "Tell us more."

"Mother enrolled me in a finishing school for young gentlemen. I studied for a diploma: Social Correctness and Comportment in the Company of Women. I was awarded a distinction. My society believe it's unseemly for a man to impose his presence on an all-female household when he has no means of paying for his keep. No means other than himself. The accepted thing for him to do would be to offer sexual services, and I feel obliged to do so now."

Elvira wasn't sure how to reply.

Vivette stared open-mouthed. "You're offering to pimp yourself out? As payment?"

"Exactly, yes."

"Well, that's very sweet of you, Paris, but couldn't you just clean the windows or something?"

"You've already given Viv the key to a brilliant future," Elvira reminded him.

"And you?" he inquired.

"I'll give it some thought."

"I'll – er – get my stuff," Vivette said, edging toward her bedroom.

"Wait," Paris said. "About the overall. I'm sure I've no need to tell you this, but – exercise discretion. Tell only Fabian."

"Got you."

"When he looks through a microscope, he'll see tiny hairs undulating across any hole you've made. Then another set will follow at ninety degrees to the first. The smart material grows back across this framework. Don't let him keep damaging it or it'll just stop working."

"Useful to know."

"And don't forget to file for a patent."

"No, no, of course not." Vivette tried not to look as though she *had* forgotten. "Er – what do I call this wonder invention?"

Paris smiled. "Vivlar," he said.

Vivette blew him a kiss and left the room.

"It's strange, Elvira ..." Paris began.

"What is?"

"I know exactly what Vivette will do with her life but I know nothing about yours."

"Why should you? We can't all be famous."

"No, but you *do* work for CoherenceCo, or you're about to. TTI is very proud of its pioneers. Your name wasn't among them."

"Then maybe I deck Clive next week, and old man Bridgenorth sacks me."

Paris gave a thin smile. "Do you have family?" he asked suddenly.

"Yes, both parents live about thirty miles north of here. I visit them sometimes. But if you want the truth - "

"Please."

"They're so much in love it's as if I'm intruding. I've always thought that. We don't quarrel, but they hardly notice whether I'm there or not."

"So your future's not with them." Paris tried to suppress a yawn. "Apologies. I must have been awake for sixteen hours."

"An eventful day," Elvira said.

"Slight understatement, but yes."

"Well, you can hit the hay as soon as Vivette's gone. What's keeping her, anyway? She always keeps her model bag at the ready. She's up to something."

Eventually Vivette reappeared, looking guilty. "Er … Paris. I've a confession to make. Well, *two* actually."

"What have you done?" asked Elvira ominously.

Vivette held up one of Paris' shoes to reveal a slice across the toe. "I did that with a steak knife. I wanted to see it regenerate. Only it hasn't."

"Because it isn't Vivlar," Paris said equably. "It's zugon hide, imported from Proxima B. Useful at TTI due to its anti-static qualities. But it doesn't self-repair."

"What's second on the list, Viv?" Elvira inquired coolly.

"Your vest and shorts, Paris. And the, er, thong that went with the shorts. I thought I'd launder them for you and, well, they've turned to a kind of soup. And the machine's clogged up. Couldn't you have said they were dry clean only?"

"Particle scrub, domestic version. Not invented yet." Paris tried to look severe, then dissolved into laughter. "Now I really *do* have nothing!"

"One shoe?" Vivette suggested. "Look, this is *my* bad and I'm sure I can get the other one fixed. There's a little shoe repair shop near Cec's studio, and the old chap who owns it reckons he can mend anything. I'll take it to him. It's worth a try."

Her phone sounded a text alert.

"That's my cab. You'll find a pair of Hercule's pyjamas on the bed."

Elvira grimaced. "Not the red ones!"

"The red ones." Vivette gave Paris a peck on the cheek. "Hey, no five o'clock shadow?"

"Perdurable epilation. Beards are unbecoming."

"Noted." Vivette seized her bag. "Laters, guys."

Elvira left Paris eyeing the detested pyjamas and went to prepare for bed. When she returned, in her sensible cotton top and leggings and carrying a mug of cocoa, she wasn't surprised to find him already asleep. She tucked the duvet more securely round him and, mindful of Vivette's designer pillowcases, checked to ensure the plaster on his forehead was still firmly adhered. Then she turned out the light and went to her own room. She drank the cocoa herself.

She slept badly, replaying the day's events over and over. Two hours later, therefore, she was instantly awake when a despairful cry sounded from the next room. Investigating, she found the duvet crumpled on the floor and Paris huddled miserably against the headboard, clutching a pillow.

"Nightmare?" she inquired.

28

"Sorry I disturbed you."

"Paris, you're like ice. Come on – back into bed." She retrieved the duvet, and after a moment's hesitation lay alongside him. "Just till you stop shivering. Don't put your cold feet on me!"

"I dreamt I'd been sent to Point Nemo," he said tonelessly. "Sea, endless sea. Implacable. Remorseless. My choice: to survive maybe another five minutes, or to give up, knowing that either way my killers had won. They still might."

"Listen to me!" Elvira shook him. "We're going to find those scumbags and shut them down. And the first step is for me to go back to CoherenceCo and get up close and personal with Clive Brightlingsea."

"Is that his surname? Brightlingsea?"

"It's the one he goes by."

"The Brightlingsea Principle is at the root of all time travel," Paris informed her. "It's required reading for every trainee. Now I *know* I'm meant to be here!"

"So he really does steal my work," Elvira sighed.

"*Our* work," Paris said, equally rueful. Elvira moved to sit up, but he caught at her sleeve. "Don't go! Stay till morning, *please*. I don't mean I want – unless you - "

"But you think the bad dream might recur. Of course I'll stay. Shall I leave the table lamp on?"

"That would be good."

"It'll be light soon anyway. Now try to go back to sleep. You'll need to be alert and clear-headed from now on, if you're to stand any chance of getting home."

***

Elvira woke just after eleven to find Vivette's go-bag placed discreetly in the living room, and a recent text which read: "Hi sleepyheads. Off to Primark to get clothes for Paris. Don't worry, they'll fit. Tell him he can thank me later."

"She took my shoe," said Paris, behind her. "The intact one."

"To be sure of the size, I imagine."

"And will she expect restitution?"

"She's teasing you. Take no notice." Elvira turned to face him. He was still wearing the pyjama top but had reverted to the linen chinos.

"The trousers wouldn't stay up," he explained.

Elvira couldn't repress a smile. "I'm sorry I missed that. Nice to see you so rested. Today's a bit of a write-off but I'll definitely ring CoherenceCo tomorrow morning. In the meantime, see what you make of *this*." She placed her laptop on a nearby table. "Try not to wreck it while I'm in the shower."

When she returned, he was gazing disinterestedly at a kitten video. "What's the verdict?" she asked.

"The word 'abacus' springs to mind."

"Hey, steady on. This is state of the art. And assuming I can remotely sign myself in as a particle physics student, you'll need to use it. I can't very well take you to CoherenceCo, can I?"

"I wish you could," he said, and meant it.

Suddenly the front door flew open to reveal Vivette, beaming, a Primark carrier bag on each arm. "Heads together in an IT threesome? I might have known. Paris, stop whatever it is you're doing and try these on. They'll transform you!" She glanced into the kitchen. "Elvira, you haven't even fed him! What were you thinking?"

"I had an energy bar," said Paris helpfully.

"You'll fade away to nothing. Let's grab a late lunch."

He looked wary. "Go out?"

"Just to a coffee shop. I want to show off the latest recruit to House of Plessis. That's *you*, silly!"

Later, with Paris relaxed and cheerful in jeans, loafers, a crisp white shirt and a baseball cap to hide the sticking plaster, Elvira had to admit Vivette had been right. He did look like a male model and was attracting some appreciative stares.

"You haven't once mentioned your father," said Vivette. "Do we have him to thank for your good looks?"

"My fathers? Sperm donor batch SOL3-GB-5-2558."

"Oh, I see." Vivette was suitably enlightened. "Pick and mix!"

"It seems to have worked," Elvira said more quietly. She wasn't exactly surprised. While sitting next to Paris outside the café she'd been covertly studying his flawless skin. She might have known it was due to 26th century genetics.

"Looks airbrushed, doesn't he?" Vivette remarked. "Paris, mon chou, you really ought to meet Cec. You'd look great in our new portfolio."

He smiled a little sadly.

Reluctantly, Elvira returned to the subject that was never far away. "So, Paris, I know you're impatient to get started on your rescue plan, but remember, I've never actually seen inside CoherenceCo. Until I find out what's down there we can't do much. Obviously they have a particle accelerator of some sort, though I've no idea what use they make of it. But thanks to Max, I do know their work was compromised by the interference your arrival generated. That has to be of some help to you, surely? Hopefully Clive won't have thrown out yesterday's results."

Paris was staring at her. "What interference? This is the first I've heard of it."

"You mean you didn't know?"

"I certainly didn't. There shouldn't have been any." He'd begun to look troubled once again.

Elvira repeated what Max had said the previous day. "Do you think the bad guys might have noticed?"

"If they had, they'd have been here before now. But anything that can disrupt a particle experiment *and* your security system is worthy of our attention. It might just be a means of alerting the future. Elvira – you *have* to contact CoherenceCo as soon as we get home. Ask to see them tomorrow at the latest."

"I will, I promise. And don't worry – I know exactly what to say to Clive. You'll get your information."

Chapter Two

Paris was at the front door as soon as he heard Elvira's car in the drive. It was after five- thirty. "I hardly dare ask," he began anxiously, "but – how was your day?"

"Much better than I'd hoped," she assured him. "Is Vivette not here?"

"She was. She brought a set of the Aurora photographs and said they'd be featured in Dazed and Confused. Is that really a magazine? I thought she was teasing me again. Anyway, she and Fabian have gone out to celebrate."

Elvira leafed through the prints. "These are beautiful! Eerie. Cec is so talented."

"And now he wants to photograph *me*."

"Without seeing you?"

"Viv took a sneaky picture at the café."

Elvira suddenly realised what was different about his face, and gently pushed his fringe aside. "No plaster. Did Viv get rid of it?"

He nodded. "She said the cut needed to breathe."

"It still looks a bit angry."

"Good. As long as it does, I'm safe from fashionistas with cameras."

"Why so bashful?"

"Because," Paris said a little ruefully, "my enemies might see the results. Magazine content's digitised and archived, and they're bound to run a search. That woman – the one at the time terminals. She looked at me as if ..."

"As if?" Elvira prompted.

"As if she were undressing me. She must have been a Streeter, a feral. Now can we please talk about something else?"

"Is food a safe topic? I don't want another of Vivette's lectures about not feeding you properly, so – fish and chips again?"

"I thought you'd never ask."

"OK. And once dinner's out of the way I'll give you chapter and verse about CoherenceCo. First, let me lose this straitjacket of a suit."

Once in the bedroom she let her composure slip a little. She was secretly relieved that Vivette wasn't around. That morning her flatmate had peeped into her room and caught a glimpse of Paris dead to the world – in a sleeping bag.

"He says the room's too cold at night," Elvira had said lamely.

Vivette's reply had been terse and to the point. "You two need to sort yourselves out!"

The meal over, and a pot of coffee at the ready, Elvira sat down at the laptop. Paris came to join her.

"Thank you," she said unexpectedly.

"For what?"

"For being so patient. I thought you'd be pestering me for news."

"Not patient. Fatalistic. Time's forward arrow, remember? I know what I need to do. I'm just not sure how."

35

"This might help." She placed a flash drive on the desk.

"Elvira – is this the data? From my arrival?"

"The same."

"And Clive just handed it over?"

"With no argument. And there's a very specific reason *why* he didn't argue – something I knew nothing about. Ready for something bizarre?"

"Go on."

"The CoherenceCo experiments aren't concerned with time travel. Clive's after the secret of instantaneous communication, ready for the first manned mission to Mars."

Paris' face was a picture.

"I know, I know. I probably looked like that too, when they told me. Everyone's aware that Clive's on a wild goose chase because nothing travels faster than light, string theory's a lost cause and tachyons don't exist. We're placing bets on how long Bridgenorth will go on financing him. Here's where the money's going.

"CoherenceCo has a secondary site in Chipping Norton, Oxfordshire. There's a disused railway tunnel, bricked up at both ends, and in it – or in the hill next to it – is a linear accelerator of modest size. Every day at 4pm – it takes that long to charge it up – a neutrino beam is fired toward the Bull and Bush complex. And every day at 3.45pm, we man the detector and look for anything that might arrive early. Of course, nothing does. Only a few stray spits and spots passing through.

"Clive's pretty cagey about the Chippy set-up: won't say who's working there nor what it looks like. But one of the techs whispered to me that there are several YouTube videos made just before security was stepped up."

"Made by whom?"

"Enthusiasts who like going into abandoned places. I haven't seen any of it yet, so we could watch later on when you need a rest."

"And I'll need one because …?"

"You'll see." Elvira readied the flash drive. "These particle tracks were detected on Tuesday at around four. The data analysts have been trying to interpret them ever since. Clive thought it was an attempt at sabotage, but after he'd bragged about his Grand Project I suggested that the anomalous readings might be someone's attempt to communicate. I also confided that I was willing to study the data at home for as long as it took, and share my conclusions with him."

"Clever girl!"

"Aren't I just. Go on, open the file. The image analysis still needs work, but maybe it'll make sense to you as it is."

Paris complied, then uttered one of his futuristic oaths. Elvira began to laugh, then stopped abruptly when she realised how shaken he was.

"It's bad?"

"It could have been. You're looking at my third narrow escape. I've outrun the assassins, hopefully; managed not to bash my brains out on a kerbstone, and, last but not least, avoided having my component atoms spattered all over Hampstead. What were the odds, Elvira, that a particle beam and a temporal shunt would converge on the same space at the same time?"

"You beat the odds," she said in the calmest voice she could muster. "You're a survivor, Paris."

"Not a very brave one." He gazed almost reproachfully at the random traces which could have spelled his epitaph. "Shall I let you into a secret? I'm terrified of time travel. The more I learnt the more I vowed I'd never subject myself to it. Ironically, I'm only alive due to TTI's safety measures."

"Care to elaborate?"

"As much as I can. Each traveller, plus their accoutrements, is surrounded by what's known as a brace. You'd call it a force-field. And before you ask, I don't know how it works. I'm just thankful it does."

"Did you just say accoutrements?"

"Sorry. Librarians wrote our training manual. Anyway, that brace knocked Clive's feeble offering sideways. Literally." He paused, gripping the desk. "Here's where you kindly offer me brandy."

"I think we're out. Will whisky do?"

"Please."

She poured a measure and added an equal amount of ginger. "Here. Make it last. We can't get pissed like we did the other day."

"No, absolutely not."

"So where were we? Oh yes. You were going to explain how you can make sense of particle data but not the technology that saved you."

"I'm not a physicist, Elvira. I'm a Grade 3 Time Tech. I keep the machines running. But I do know a lot about misfires – events beyond our control that can halt a time journey before it starts. We're trying to reduce them because there's nothing more ill-tempered than a time traveller all dressed up with nowhere to go. It can take hours to detect what stalled the process, then a day to reconfigure it. Solar radiation's a common cause. In fact …" He stopped, looking absent.

"Did you just have an idea?" asked Elvira.

"Maybe. I'm not sure yet. We need to make a to-do list." He grabbed a sheet of paper from the desk drawer.

"Hey, not on Vivette's sketches! She'll kill you!"

"Fourth attempt lucky?" Paris inquired with an unexpected smile. "Do we have notepaper and pen, Ms Jones?"

"We do, Mr Evason."

"Right. I'll talk and you scribble. Item one: secretive ventures like Clive's are dangerous. He could cause loss of life and never be aware of it. We, or rather *you*, have to halt the experiment, if only temporarily. He needs a diversion. Did you say CoherenceCo has its own accelerator?"

"A cyclotron, but it's not in use. I think Clive filched some of the workers."

"Item two, get them back and get the thing operational. Tell Clive you're planning to send a response and you can only do that from CoherenceCo. I'll simplify this data so even he can understand it. Then tell him that any particle stream from Chippy will fail, due to lack of power or the wrong alignment of the dynamic aperture – anything you think he'll believe. Imagine – no, don't write this down – CoherenceCo's output as I know it. Daily events, outward bound or incoming, always leaving or returning to the same location. Trips to ancient times or just a century or two ago. All from there. Every single one."

"Which leads us to Item Three. I want to devise something that mirrors the mess we've been looking at. Clumps of particles dragged every which way. If we keep disrupting the schedules, *any* schedules, someone's bound to realise the interference is manmade."

"But won't you risk harming your colleagues?"

"There'll be some frayed tempers, I daresay. Time transportation … takes time. First the destination's established, conditions checked, power incrementally increased. Then the receptor's placed and tested for stability. If the sensors detect an anomaly at any point in the process, a misfire's declared. The time tourists, meanwhile, are still in wardrobe."

"And I thought your job was exciting!"

"It has its moments. So, Item Four: we'll need powerful magnets. Dipole, quadropole, the works. Reinforce what's already there."

"Bridgenorth will provide them."

"I'm sure you're right, but does he have an efficient means of getting them to the site? They aren't exactly small."

"They'll arrive the same way as the rest of our equipment. Via the Northern Line in the middle of the night. The Northern Line runs close by our sub-basement. We can see the lights of the trains!"

"What else is down there?"

"Dark spaces, tracks that don't lead anywhere – I haven't seen much of it yet. It's still a work in progress. And it has decades-old history with the MoD, so questions just don't get asked about requisitions."

Paris surmised that one day it would be TTI's maintenance area, his workplace. "How strange this all is," he murmured.

"Right!" said Elvira briskly. "That's a plan and a half. Shall we take a break and watch those YouTube videos? I'll get some ice cream."

"You spoil me."

It didn't take long to locate the footage, and they watched in growing perplexity. The tunnel, accessed only by a high aperture at each end, was filthy and partly flooded.

"Are you sure this is the right place?"

"Apparently. I'll fast forward a little, see if our videographer reaches the far end ... and look what he's found. A section of recent brickwork with vents. Something's through there. A siding, maybe. That has to be where Clive's hidden himself."

"Where's the entrance?"

"Above, I bet. Let's see the other clip. This one's only a few weeks old. And – oh. No more exploring, then."

The high window, viewed from outside, had heavy iron bars across it. The young historian making the video noted the addition, then turned his attention to the industrial units above. Nondescript buildings, wire fences, no-one about.

"Well, there's a surprise," Elvira said.

"What is?"

"One of those units is identical to Bull and Bush Market Analytics. CoherenceCo's shop front. You've been there, but you weren't in a fit state to notice."

"Don't remind me."

"I've seen enough. Tomorrow I'll discreetly hint to Clive that he shouldn't be relegated to the sticks. He'll fall for it, you'll see."

"If you wear that skintight suit again he won't need any persuading," Paris remarked acidly.

"Don't worry – he won't have another chance to stare at my accoutrements. I'll be wearing a lab coat from now on. Can I ask you something?"

"Anything."

"What if your bid for escape had ended in a misfire?"

"I could have overridden it, used my maintenance ID. I'm not sure I would have, though. What's that saying of yours – between a rock and a hard place? That reminds me – tell your colleagues to keep a close eye on the detector. If there's any kind of reaction, however small, I need to know."

"Paris ... will this work?"

"Truthfully? I've no idea. But I can't think of anything else that might."

With an effort, Elvira refrained from asking him to give it up and stay in the twenty-first century. Because he couldn't. Time travel started *here*, with Clive Brightlingsea putting his name to it. And, the future authorities had to be alerted to the murders in their midst. Paris wouldn't abandon either cause.

Her phone pinged with a text. Vivette and Fabian wouldn't be back that night.

"Now I know we won't be disturbed by those two falling in the door," she said to Paris. "I think I'll turn in. I've had a demanding day and I'll need to be up early tomorrow. I have to see a man about some electromagnets."

"I'll stay up awhile and rewrite this data for Clive."

"Ok. I may be gone by the time you're awake. Feel free to raid the kitchen. You don't need to ask." She paused at her door. "I'll sleep better knowing you're here."

Later – and she was never certain of this – she thought he'd tiptoed in and kissed her lightly on the cheek. By morning she'd convinced herself she'd dreamt it.

***

Friday was confrontational. Elvira had begun to realise her studies at UCL had become outdated during the six years she'd spent in marketing. She was struggling to keep up with the team she was nominally in charge of. She learnt that the CoherenceCo cyclotron had underperformed earlier that year, and the same problem had reappeared when it was reactivated: chromatic aberration or particle drift. A sextupole magnet was the usual solution, and Bridgenorth had ordered one months ago, but it still hadn't arrived. At Elvira's request Clive had approached the Director; Bridgenorth had called in a favour and sourced a replacement from another facility. But he'd then reminded Clive that his project was vastly over budget. "I hope that young woman knows what she's doing," he'd said ominously. "For now, I'll give her the benefit of the doubt. There's something unusual out there – we've proof of that – and I want to know everything about it."

" ... and that was just this morning," Elvira continued dolefully. "Clive, of course, wasted no time in reiterating Bridgenorth's words and reminding me who'd picked me off the reject pile. But I haven't been demoted – yet. And the magnet will be delivered tonight and installed over the weekend. Did I do right?"

"You totally did," Paris assured her. "Today's readings are weak, random. TTI might find them a nuisance but they'd assume they were from a natural source. We need something much more robust, and hopefully we'll get it."

Elvira sighed. "I wish I knew where all this is leading."

"I'm sorry," he said automatically. "You're in a bad place and that's my fault. Would you like a hug? Might that cheer you up?"

"It would help." Elvira waited, then when he didn't move, put her arms lightly round him and leant on his shoulder. "I hope this isn't provocative."

"You're never provocative. Unlike Vivette."

"She does find you attractive."

"Only as a fashion plate. She thinks I'm still wet behind the ears."

Reluctantly Elvira released him. "I don't think Viv knows the real Paris any more than I do. Where is she, anyway? Avoiding me?"

"No, of course not. She's on her way to Ashby de la Zouch. It's her Maman's fiftieth birthday."

"Damn. I forgot. I'll send an e-card."

"She won't be back till Sunday," Paris added. "Which means we can do as we please tomorrow. I'd like to go out."

"You've changed your tune since last Wednesday."

"I'd like to go out with *you*."

"Are you inviting me on a date, Paris?"

"I'm asking you to rescue me from these four walls. We could find a café as before, or go for a walk. Or – anything."

"All right, it's a date. So, what are we eating tonight?"

"Vivette made a casserole. It just needs reheating, she said."

Elvira, feeling upstaged, decided the impromptu date would be memorable for all the right reasons. She opted for a stroll on the Heath, and soon knew she'd chosen correctly. Paris was calm, companionable, and appreciative of his surroundings. "Beautiful! Just what I need to get my head straight."

"Is the Heath still there – in your time?"

"Yes! Well, not as extensive. I'm finding it strange to look at the horizon and not see massive buildings on all sides. But I suppose I'll see them again soon enough - and everything else that spoils the view."

"Do you think you'll be treated as a hero once people know what crimes you helped prevent?"

He grimaced. "Hardly! I'll get a chewing over from the personnel department for disappearing. And then I'll have to face my mother's wrath. She doesn't like it when I misbehave or do something unconventional. She says it reflects badly on her."

"You mean she thinks she chose the wrong DNA?"

"That's the inference. I always retaliate by saying it's fifty percent hers."

"But she worries about you, surely. Especially now."

"I doubt she even knows I'm missing. She's off-world, on Procyon 4. A cultural exchange. Her counterpart runs the finishing school I attended."

Elvira was vastly intrigued. "So we did make it to interstellar space?"

"Well, er, no. The Morii contacted *us*. They'd infiltrated Earth centuries before, but wouldn't make contact until matriarchy was established. Principal

Rayah told us her people studied elephants and wild horses initially, and these societies showed such promise they thought there was hope for humanity. But we men did invent time travel. Somehow!"

"And have there been any wars since the girls took over?"

"No," he admitted. "But it isn't all sweetness and light in the big cities."

Elvira remembered the feral women he'd mentioned, but prudently decided not to reintroduce the subject. She suspected, wrongly perhaps, that his idea of feral didn't match hers. On an impulse she asked a middle-aged lady walking her Pekinese if she'd take their photo. Paris didn't voice an objection so she handed over her phone before he could change his mind. The passerby dutifully took the picture, returned the phone, then unexpectedly said:

"Young man, you need to smile more."

They watched her diminutive figure striding confidently into the distance, the little dog scampering to keep up.

"She's right. I don't smile enough," Paris said.

Elvira inspected the photo. Her best Simply Qubit marketing grin contrasted tellingly with Paris' profoundly serious gaze. "You don't mind if I keep this?"

"Keep it, please. Just don't put it online." Paris hesitated a moment. "I'd like to buy you something."

"Such as? Bearing in mind I'll have to pay for it?"

"When we were at the café, I noticed a second-hand bookshop. I thought if I chose one, I could write a dedication and give it back to you."

"I know the shop. So yes, let's do that. Promise you won't choose any first editions!"

"Promise. You'd better warn me if I pick one up. But I still want you to have something special."

"Anything you've chosen will be special. Now I don't know about you, but all this walking's made me hungry. How would you like fish and chips for tea? I thought you might. There's a takeaway in the same parade as the bookshop. Or would you rather finish off Vivette's vegan stew?"

"No thanks. It was dreadful."

"Did it put you in mind of Vegi-sim?"

"Not really," said Paris, always literal. "Vegi-sim is a breakfast cereal. Small green pellets that half-dissolve in water."

"You're not selling it to me, Paris."

"I wasn't trying to." The smile transformed his face. Elvira couldn't decide between taking another photo or kissing him. In the end she did neither.

The interior of the bookshop was small and dusty and made Paris sneeze, but he soon found what he wanted: a slender volume of selected poems by Shelley. "We studied the Romantics at school, though I found the original English difficult. You won't have that problem, of course."

"Do you want to pick something for yourself? Something more recent, perhaps?"

The shopkeeper was heading in their direction.

"Let's pay and leave," Paris said hastily. "I'll explain outside."

When they were a short distance from the emporium, Elvira halted abruptly. "What was *that* about?"

"I'm sorry. I just didn't want you wasting your money. I'm not allowed to take anything with me that could be construed as antique. It's forbidden."

"Spoilsports!"

"No-one minded at the outset, when it was only souvenirs. But gradually a whole import industry evolved – jewellery, automata, artworks – and an illicit trade in weapons. Swords, cutlasses, flintlocks. That's when the authorities put a stop to it."

A few stray raindrops eddied past. On the horizon the sky had turned indigo. Paris tucked the book inside his jacket.

"We'd better make tracks," Elvira said. "That faux suede blouson isn't going to keep the rain off. Vivette should've bought you a hoodie. You head for the car, I'll get the fish and chips and catch you up. The shop's right there. Hello? Earth to Paris?"

"Oh … sorry. I've never seen a thunderstorm this close."

"You'll do more than *see* it if you don't get a move on. Here, take the fob. Let yourself in if I'm not back."

The chip shop had only just opened, and there was a small queue. When Elvira returned to the car, just ahead of a cloudburst, she saw Paris standing, key fob in hand, looking puzzled.

49

"And this is the ace mechanic who builds time machines!" she laughed. "It's *this* button. Commit it to memory. Now in you go before you get drenched."

They barely made it. Seconds later, the heavens opened. Rain sluiced down the windows and drummed noisily on the bodywork.

"I'm not driving in this," Elvira declared. "It'll soon blow over. We can eat here." She unwrapped the layers of paper. "I've got gherkins this time. Eat up before it gets cold."

Paris was scandalised. "With my fingers?"

"I don't see any knives and forks around, do you? Come on, it's an old English custom. When I was little they used actual newspaper to wrap it in. So the newsprint was all mixed up with the vinegar. Yum."

He didn't move.

"Good grief. Those 26th century schoolmarms really went to town on you. Right, I'll sort this." She proffered a chip. "Open your mouth. That's right. Now a portion of fish. There, that wasn't so bad, was it? So am I going to coax you as if you're a two year old, or are you going to do as the natives do?"

"I'm - "

"If you're going to say sorry yet again, don't. It's your tutors who should be sorry."

Paris picked up a chip between thumb and forefinger. "I'm not very adaptable, am I? You'd manage a lot better if *you* were the time traveller. You're a natural. You'd improvise."

50

"I'd like to put that to the test one day," Elvira said wistfully. "Not that I'll get the chance. Now eat!"

"You're leading me into bad habits."

"Good. Tomato sauce?"

"Excellent. And now, I shall feed *you*. It's only fair. Keep still or this next chip goes in your ear. Or down your neck."

"You wouldn't dare. Paris ... !! Right, you've asked for it."

"That's very bad manners, Ms Jones. Very ... bad ... manners!"

"Might I remind you, Mr Evason, that I'm combat-trained?"

"And I, Ms. Jones, am extraordinarily inventive."

Not long afterwards, a truce was sensibly declared.

When the rain had slackened Elvira took a circuitous route back to the flat, giving Paris a chance to see more of the neighbourhood. His keen eyes missed nothing, but in another of his mercurial mood swings, he remained silent. As soon as they were home he disappeared into the shower.

Elvira, also introspective, looked again at the photo taken on the Heath. In the short time since that image had been captured, she'd discovered he was capable of fun, hilarity and downright silliness. She also knew it would take more than a food fight to see off the deeper issues that plagued him. But as for the lesser problem, countermanding the teachings of his governesses, she'd just had what she hoped was a brilliant idea.

"Paris," she said when he finally emerged, cleaning his fingernails, "how would you like to see what Regency England was all about?"

"Whatever you'd like to watch," he said absently.

"No, listen. This is where your school gets its ideas from. Girls tended to be vapid and undereducated and had to make a good marriage. Your society took those values and flipped them. I'll find you a box set of Jane Austen's novels, adapted for TV. I think you'll be intrigued."

"Jane …?"

"Austen. Haven't you heard of her?"

"No, but if she wrote of women as inferiors, she may be a proscribed author."

Elvira settled him in front of Pride and Prejudice, then retrieved an assortment of vinegar-stained garments from the bedroom floor, loaded them into the washing machine and set it running. She then took an unhurried shower and sat down to blow-dry her hair.

After the noise of the domestic appliances had died away she became aware of some odd sounds from the living room, and fastening her robe, went to investigate. She found Paris convulsed with mirth, scarcely able to speak for laughing. "Thank you, thank you, *thank you*, Elvira, for recommending this comedy. Delightful, silly women!"

"Well, I'll – leave you to watch the rest of it," she said, and retreated. Her phone was on the bed where she'd left it, displaying a missed call. Incuriously, she picked it up.

"Hi, it's Liam from Bull and Bush etcetera. Sorry to interrupt your weekend, but there's something I'd like to run past you. We've got the magnet, no worries there, but we were just minutes ahead of the bailiffs so couldn't hang about. I saw this interesting little cabinet just dumped near the accelerator – storage for accessories maybe. No-one could get it open so we brought it with us. Finders keepers! Give me a bell tonight if you know what it might be. We'll be working on the upgrade tomorrow, so no mobile contact. Photo attached. Bye!"

Elvira studied the item: rectangular, clean classic lines, possibly rosewood. The only thing odd about it was its presence in a high-tech facility. None the wiser, she turned the phone off. Paris was happily entertained for once, and she wasn't about to drag him back to anything work-related. The box, whatever it was, could wait.

***

Vivette, arriving home on Sunday afternoon, couldn't believe what she was hearing. "What on earth …?"

"Yes, it *is* Paris. He's binge-watching Jane Austen."

"And he thinks it's a sitcom?"

"Apparently."

"Well, I won't disturb him. Come and help me unpack. I want all the gossip. What's new at CoherenceCo? Any more time travellers? And what did you get up to yesterday?"

Elvira told her, including the fish and chip battle.

"Good! He's thawing out. Well, where's this photo then?"

"Here. But please, don't copy it. He made me promise not to share."

"Just as I thought," said Vivette, studying it. "Brilliant."

"Hardly the word I'd use. He looks so sad."

"No, silly, he doesn't. He's looking *blank* – and that's exactly the reason he'd be perfect for a photoshoot. People put their own interpretations on what they see."

"So I assumed he was sad?"

"Obviously. And we all know why. Hey, what's this? Next to him in your photo store. It looks like a sewing machine case. Vintage. Surely you weren't thinking of buying one? Elvira, the world's worst seamstress?"

In the next room, the TV had fallen silent. Paris knocked Vivette's door lightly. "Can I do anything to help?" he began, then halted, staring at the phone and the picture it displayed.

"Paris, what's wrong?" asked Vivette. "You look as though you've seen a ghost!"

"Do you recognise this?" Elvira added more quietly.

"May I see? Please, just give me the phone."

She handed it over and he pinch-zoomed the image, as he'd watched her doing many times. "There's a logo on the top. All the proof I need."

"You've got sharp eyes."

"I knew what to look for. The angle's wrong but you can just make out three intertwined letters: N, P, B. I've seen this box over and over, in TTI's museum of time artefacts. It's one of the first, if not *the* first, receptor modules. Now please, Elvira – who sent you the photograph?"

"Liam. From work. He left a voicemail too." Elvira played it, then ventured an apology. "I know I should have mentioned this last night, but I'd no idea it would mean anything to you. It looked so old-fashioned."

"It's all right," Paris said swiftly. "You don't have to tell *me* you're sorry, though I was enjoying the novelty. And I'm not having another of my meltdowns. I was just astonished to see it here."

"Do you know how it works?"

"I know how it *should* work. Let's get Vivette settled and then I'll talk you through it."

"Never a dull moment with you, is there, Paris?" Vivette said sweetly. "I believe I might have something for you in my case." She produced a bottle of cognac. "From Maman. To thank you in advance for my future career. And here's a home-made Victoria sponge for all of us. Now scat, both of you. Go and make coffee while I see to my toilette."

Banished to the kitchen, Elvira took one more look at the receptor module. "Should I ring Liam? He might be home by now."

"Only if he knows who built that thing."

"He doesn't. None of us does. Bridgenorth keeps his investment projects under wraps. Except … I'm friendly with his secretary Charlene, and she complained he was in a foul mood the other week because one of his proteges had let him down. An inventor, brilliant but with no head for business. Bridgenorth advanced him money he couldn't repay, and worse, he kept asking for more. So the old man bankrupted him."

Paris carefully wielded the cake slice. "So that's it then – another dead end. Unless someone can get a name out of Bridgenorth."

"Admit his poor judgement? No chance. And what do you mean, dead end?"

"We still don't know the true originator of time travel. History says it's Clive. *We* know it isn't. Consider this: why would anyone build a receptor when there's nothing to transmit? Exactly – they wouldn't. Your missing inventor had a prototype time machine and now he's run off in it. Or maybe he died trying. You won't find him."

"How do you know?"

"Because *no-one* found him," said Paris succinctly. "So, how to open the receptor. The box is slightly elevated by a wooden block at each corner. Reach under the gap at the right, not too far, and you'll find a recessed lever. Familiarise yourself with it by moving it away from you in a ninety degree arc. It will return to its start position when you let go. Are you with me so far?"

"Just about."

"There's an identical lever at the other end. You and a colleague must turn the keys in sync, three times. If done correctly, the lid will release."

"So our missing genius had a confidante?"

"I hadn't thought of that. I suppose he must have done."

Another conspiracy? Elvira wondered. But she kept the thought to herself. Paris was having enough difficulty coping with the original one. "So, what's inside the box?" she asked casually.

"In the early days before the time brace, engineers employed inert metals to avoid transfer fragmentation. The museum exhibit has been stripped clean but expect to find a layer of gold, silver or platinum."

"That explains where the money went. What's next?"

"This is a device from *your* time, not mine! Look for a USB port, plug it in, charge it. When fully charged it should wait on standby."

"Wait for what?"

"To receive something. If conditions are right."

For a moment Elvira thought she saw regret in his eyes. Or was she again seeing what she wanted to see? She wished Liam had never stolen the damn box.

She had similar thoughts the next day as she watched Liam and Freddy, a burly co-worker, lug the receptor out of the goods elevator and into the main lab. "What's he got in here – house bricks?" muttered Liam as they set it down. Clive, meantime, stood nearby with his arms folded.

Elvira mentally rehearsed the only piece of acting required of her. To adopt the necessary position she had to undo several buttons of her lab coat above the knee. Clive watched with interest.

The lever, the one she could reach, was just as Paris had described. She called Liam to help with the second one and then recited the instructions carefully.

"How do you know all this stuff, Elvira?" Liam asked.

"From my grandfather, a clockmaker. This is an example of a Geneva Stop Mechanism. Now concentrate!"

On the second try, the box opened.

"Bloody hell," said Liam with fervour. "No wonder the poor sod went bust!"

The interior was liberally lined with gold, every surface embellished with delicate gold leaf.

"Guys," said Elvira apologetically, "we'll have to move this again. Unless anyone has a really long extension lead?"

"And we need one because …?"

"Because I've just found a USB port near the right stop lever. We need to charge the box to find out what it does."

"Supposing it goes bang?" asked Freddy.

"It won't. As I was saying, we need a charging lead and a thirteen amp socket."

"You'll find them in my office," said Clive unexpectedly. "And I think I can locate a platform trolley, too. Wait there."

"What's got into *him* all of a sudden?" Freddy whispered.

"The sight of all that gold's gone to his head," Liam murmured back. "Have you no idea what kind of research we're looking at, Elvira?"

"No, but wasn't there a theory – something about converting photons into electrons by firing them at a gold target? Maybe this is some kind of receiver. Light into matter."

"Impossible."

"Well, we'll see what happens in an hour or two. Here comes Clive. Now don't you gentlemen have a cyclotron to buff up?"

It was another three hours before she found herself rooted to the spot in Clive's office, staring down at the enigmatic box. And Clive, with no facetious comment to fit the occasion, was equally nonplussed. Each gold leaf was stirring as if in a slight breeze. In unison they rippled and paused, rippled and paused. Elvira couldn't quite focus her eyes on the activity.

"What's it *doing*?" Clive muttered.

"I don't know," Elvira said irresolutely. "Idling? Scanning?" Then, inspired: "We should leave it running as long as we can. You wanted a new mode of communication. This might be it."

"You mean – the other scientist was working on it too?"

"Only a guess. But it would be typical of Bridgenorth to hedge his bets. Can I leave this with you for now, Clive? I want to inspect today's particle data and see if the new magnet's helped."

"Oh. OK," Clive sad abstractedly, already in a self-aggrandizing daydream.

Elvira made her escape. As soon as she could she hurried home, impatient to hear what Paris had to say about the day's events. "I've brought the data but no image analysis yet. They'd hardly started it. As for the receptor ..." She described what she'd seen. "It ran out of charge in about four hours, and just stopped."

"It's working correctly," Paris confirmed. "A simple receptor scan – one second back, one second ahead. When it detects an incoming brace it will begin to draw in air, second by second, and store it until the transfer's complete."

"Transfer?"

"A small amount of printed or digital information. No-one from this era will attempt to send a person for another forty years or so. Officially, that is."

"Is there anything else I can do before tomorrow evening?" Elvira was stoically trying to be helpful. "Assuming the data team's up to speed I could send more of today's analysis via my student login."

"That could help. But quite honestly, if the future's ignoring an active receptor, I'm out of options."

"Already? It's been running for less than a day. Tomorrow could make all the difference. Clive's even planning his welcome address!"

Paris brightened up momentarily. "Is he really?"

"Yes, and he's no idea he's *meant* to do that!"

"Interesting. This is the first indication that things are starting to align."

Elvira forced a smile. "Remember to check my inbox around lunch time. I'll send a link to the data."

"Elvira ..." he began helplessly.

"What? What's wrong with you today? I understand that you don't want to get your hopes up, but you've just begun to look scared again. And if you don't tell me why, I'm going to be cross with you!"

He sighed. "Maybe I'm overthinking this, but I'm worried."

"There's a surprise!"

"While we were trying to create misfires it would have been technicians who investigated. It's what they do. But a receptor's an open invitation to any traveller."

"You said it could only receive small packages."

"For the next half-century, yes. But as its signal's from such an early time, someone may decide to send an alert up the line. In which case, *anyone* could turn up."

"We've tripled our security. Clive may be a creep but he isn't stupid."

"Even so, you need to be wary. Promise you will."

He twisted his fingers together anxiously and she gently placed her hands around his.

"I can take care of myself. Trust me. And whatever happens at CoherenceCo I'll be thankful you're safely at a distance. Nobody knows you're here."

Chapter Three

Paris, in a tussle with the laptop's idiosyncrasies, was suddenly aware of a cold draught eddying past him. He knew its signature only too well. A twenty-sixth century receptor field. He had enough presence of mind to slam the laptop shut before turning toward the newcomer: a woman with cold amusement in her eyes, standing in the middle of Elvira's living room. Paris had last encountered that mocking gaze in the lower levels of the Institute, just before he'd fled into the past.

"You've given us quite a runaround, Paris Evason," she remarked.

"How did you find me?" he asked wearily.

"Your shoes," came the knowing reply. "Zugon hide. Highly regarded and subject to counterfeit. It carries synthetic DNA markers – where farmed, place of manufacture, vendor, batch number. Not that we needed all that detail. There's no other alien DNA on Earth. Not in 2023, anyway."

The synapsyn gun was in her hand.

"Please," said Paris, "not that. You know what I discovered, and why I ran. You don't need anything else from me."

"Actually, I do," she contradicted. "You interest me, Paris. By the way, my name's Despina. I'll permit you to cry it aloud, later."

"Why would I do that?"

She didn't answer immediately. "Do you realise," she said, "that when we cornered you in the tunnels, you were staring at me for two whole minutes? We could have overwhelmed you. Norvus could have beaten you insensible."

"Then why didn't he?"

"I ordered him not to. You see, I know why you stared. From fear – and desire. Yes, desire. Did the frisson of fear arouse you, or did you want to enjoy a bad girl? Or, were you half in love with easeful death?"

He recognised the quotation. He was surprised she knew it.

"You thought I was Street. How crass of you. We'll need to put that right."

"With Norvus' help?"

"I'll manage. I've sent him on a little errand – which will give us time for a catch-up. Judging by the décor, this is an all-female household. Your clothes are new and contemporary. In short, you're a kept man. According to the pattern of life profiling for this decade, your benefactresses probably think you're exceptionally polite, modest, appealing but inexperienced. Did you make the standard offer of sexual services for your keep?"

"What difference does it make?" he asked, increasingly confused.

She waved the gun. "Answer the question."

"Yes, I offered. Both women declined. I'm doing housework instead."

"So you didn't mention how your fancy finishing school gets its results?" She came close to him and drew a teasing finger along his mouth. "What a naughty boy. Lies by omission. May I

64

quote from your school prospectus? 'There is nothing more disappointing for a bride on her wedding night than a confrontation with a nervous and inept bridegroom. We guarantee that all our graduates are thoroughly coached in the performance of their matrimonial duties.' I also have reports from three of your ex-tutors - "

"They're meant to be confidential!"

" – Dora, who says you displayed energy and enthusiasm. Betty, who praises your sensitivity and solicitude. And Lani - "

"Enough, *please*!"

"And Lani, who simply writes 'Paris gives good head.' I'm not altogether sure what that means. Care to explain?"

The front door abruptly crashed open and Vivette's voice called: "Hey, Paris! I've got your shoe. Some weirdo outside the shop followed me and I had to pepper-spray him. Paris? Who's she? What the hell's going on?"

Paris made a grab for the synapsyn launcher. "Run, Viv!" he yelled.

She ran. Back to her car, the shoe still in her hand. Then she drove frantically to CoherenceCo, cursing the afternoon motorists and skidding to a halt at the barrier.

"Max! Max!"

He peered cautiously out. "Where's the fire?"

"It's Viv, Max. Elvira's flatmate. You have to get her up here *right now*. There's a hostage situation at the flat. Please, hurry. Tell her it's about Paris. She'll know what I mean."

Max made the call, appearing to dawdle; then his attitude swiftly changed. "She understands. She's on her way up. She said no police."

"Of course not. She can deal with it."

"I do believe she can," Max opined. "She'll be at least another five minutes though. Those elevators take their time."

"I'll move my car." Vivette backed it away from the exit. "Come on, Elvira. Come *on*!"

The lift from the sub-basement took six minutes. Elvira managed to ask Vivette just one quick question as Max raised the barrier. "Who's with Paris?"

"I think it's that woman, the one he talked about. She was wearing a gold metallic mini skirt, long boots, and - "

"*Viv*!"

"And she had a gun."

"Right. You stay here."

"But -"

"Stay here, Viv. I mean it."

Paris' clumsy attempt to seize the synapsyn gun had failed miserably. The canister had ruptured, shedding its icy contents on his face, neck and hands. Unable to keep his balance, he was currently on his knees before Despina.

"You damn fool," she said, almost fondly, and ruffled his hair as he leant drunkenly against her. "You've overdosed. You've absorbed enough to subdue six people! Stay still. You need the antidote."

"It's all true."

"What is?"

"What my tutors said. I promise you the best sex ever, if you agree to let me live."

"Paris, Paris. If I thought you could deliver, I might be tempted. But synapsyn depresses the system, so at the moment you have nothing to bargain with." A tiny inhaler appeared in her hand. "Before I administer this, you need to tell me about Eadwine Jensson. You claim to have studied with him but he was never on the Academy roster. What was the real reason for your visit to Jenufa?"

"That *was* the reason. Commis … commiseration." Paris was doing his best to slide to the floor. "Eadwine wasn't at the Finishing Academy. He was with me at TTI's training college. For time … technicians …"

Despina swore under her breath. How could her handlers have got the facts so skewed?

"Are you going to kill me now?" Paris asked, smiling hazily.

"I'll save you for later." Despina touched a communicator patch on her inner wrist. "Norvus, respond. Target is clean. I repeat, target is clean. Find the women and rendezvous with me *now*." Then, to Paris: "Here, take the inhaler. Breathe in. Deep breaths. Just breathe …"

"Get away from him!" Suddenly Elvira was there, seizing Despina and hauling her across the room. Paris crawled aside, found a table leg to lean against and watched beatifically as the two women fought.

***

"I should go after her," said Vivette as the Volvo disappeared from view.

"No, you shouldn't," declared Max. "We both know she can handle herself. You'd just get in the way." A beeper sounded from the gatehouse. "That's Downstairs. Be right back. Stay put."

Vivette leant on her car, still undecided.

"Miss Plessis?" said a baritone voice.

"*You* again!" She scrabbled for the pepper spray, knowing it was probably empty.

"My name's Norvus Maysson," said her presumed stalker. "I've just heard from my colleague at your flat. It seems your friend Paris was targeted in error. Now may I please inquire what you're doing with his shoe?"

Vivette took a more detailed look at him. Six feet tall, well-muscled, dangerous good looks. "Ever thought of being a model?" she asked.

"Do you always answer a question with a question?" he countered.

She explained about the shoe and he laughed uproariously.

"I'm sorry about the pepper," she added a little hesitantly. "Would you like to use my twenty-four hour sparkle drops for seductive eyes?"

"I had a remedy to hand, thank you. Although your product sounds interesting."

"Viv! Viv!" Max shouted from the gatehouse. "Come here, quick! Something amazing's happened. Elvira should have been here!"

"This wouldn't have anything to do with a gold-lined box, would it?" Vivette inquired.

"Is *nothing* secret anymore?" expostulated Max.

"I'll deal with this," said Norvus, marching into the tiny control room and propelling Max outside. "Does this speaking tube actually work? Anyone there? Isn't there a woman I can talk to? Oh, never mind. I'm your first contact authenticator. I presume you'll have received a wallet-shaped document via your prototype receptor unit. To conform with our security protocols, please open the wallet and read out the serial number on the inside flap." He paused briefly. "Thank you, The year 2073 has just acknowledged you. In approximately two hours you will receive a visit from an official of the Time Travel Institute. Stand by."

"Time travel?" repeated Max in hushed tones.

"That's what he said."

"Did Elvira know about all this?"

"Oh yes. She knew."

"What's he doing now?" Max peered past her at Norvus.

"Talking to his hand." Vivette tried ringing Elvira. It went to voicemail. "Now I *have* to get home!"

"I rather think you do," said Norvus.

***

Elvira soon found her MMA training was only half effective against Despina, whose fighting skillset was unknown to her. Also she was furious, which contravened the most basic rule of martial arts: stay calm. But she couldn't be calm when she hadn't even checked on Paris, spaced-out and helpless. What had she interrupted? An interrogation, a kidnap attempt? Several minutes passed before she managed to pin Despina to the floor, face down.

"Who sent you? Who's your boss?"

"Santa Claus." Despina dislodged Elvira and rolled sinuously upright, aiming a kick. Elvira seized her foot and toppled her over. The struggle resumed.

"Elvira, Elvira, stop!" Vivette rushed in and tried to grab her. "Stop fighting! These aren't Paris' bad guys. And – you'll never guess - "

"Then who *are* they?"

Norvus, looking every inch the hitman, lounged in the doorway. "We're from GTC Special Ops. We're hunting the same people Paris is so scared of."

"What's GTC?"

"Galactic Time Controllers. Our intel concerning Paris was faulty, and we apologise for mistreating him."

"Galactic …?" repeated Elvira, mystified.

"Earth isn't the only planet with time travel capabilities."

Despina helped Paris up. "How do I know you're GTC?" he asked suspiciously.

70

"Strictly speaking, I'm not. Despina Psamathe, mercenary. But don't take my word for it. You'll be able to verify it soon."

"That's what I've been trying to tell you!" Vivette elbowed her out of the way. "The future made contact, Paris. They sent a module."

"Did you call it in?" Despina asked Norvus.

"All done. They'll be making the regulation visit soon."

Despina and Elvira found themselves side by side. They glared at one another.

"Excuse me," said a new voice.

Elvira sighed and tried to smooth her tousled hair. "This is Colin from the downstairs flat," she announced to no-one in particular.

Colin looked embarrassed. "I – don't know what's going on here, but do you realise how much noise you've been making?" Then, unexpectedly, he rounded on Paris. "And it all seemed to start when *you* arrived!"

"Sir," said Paris with great dignity, "these ladies are rivals for my affection. I can't help it if they fight!"

"Do you want to make something of it?" asked Norvus.

Colin left.

***

It seemed a recipe for disaster to appoint Clive, whom Elvira had once described as an oil slick on the road of life, as CoherenceCo's representative.

71

But, with Bridgenorth mysteriously absent and everyone else in varying states of confusion, he was the only remaining choice. Amazingly, he performed his role to perfection – probably because he needed to be creative with the truth.

Initially, the spectators experienced the miniature whirlwind they'd now come to expect. And then, a second or two later, a gaunt middle-aged woman appeared in the main cyclotron hall. Her supercilious expression and gimlet gaze reminded everyone of their most feared headmistress.

"I am Clovis Trell, Liaison Officer with the Time Travel Institute. Who's in charge here?"

Clive stepped forward. "That would be me. Clive Brightlingsea, CEO of this facility."

She responded with a curt nod. "You have successfully achieved time transference and accordingly will be admitted to our organisation. This of course means you will be subject to our regulations. These are contained, in full, within the folder we sent you."

"We shall follow your instructions to the letter," Clive assured her.

Clovis turned her piercing gaze this way and that. "Where is your launch device? I see only the receptor."

Clive hung his head. "The transport is missing, along with our esteemed colleague, Nigel … Bonchurch." Mid-sentence, he remembered the initials on the receptor casing. "He said he'd made another breakthrough, but that's all we know. He disappeared days ago and we fear he's lost."

"Would this have anything to do with the numerous particle collisions you've been generating?"

"We were trying to create a beacon to guide him home." Clive continued to look tragic.

"You will cease these attempts at once," ordered Clovis. "You've been interfering with our daily commerce. We will maintain vigilance for your friend, although we offer no guarantee of finding him. From now on, use your cyclotron purely as an accelerator, with as few collisions as possible. You will find your interactions with us will evolve more speedily under such conditions. For now, of course, you will be restricted to modular exchanges. Have you any questions?"

"Not at present," said Clive, holding her gaze steadily.

"Then goodbye, Clive Brightlingsea. Welcome to TTI."

He moved to shake hands.

She vanished.

***

"They sent Clovis Trell?" echoed Paris. "O poor old Clive!"

"He rose to the occasion, apparently," said Despina. "Now stop fidgeting, stay on the settee and keep that car rug round you. I'm not leaving until I'm satisfied you've no synapsyn-lag."

"I've been asleep, haven't I?" said Paris, gazing outside at the lengthening shadows.

"You have. And I've been having an interesting chat with Elvira. There were a few things she needed to know."

Paris didn't immediately grasp the significance of this. "I'm hungry," he announced.

"That's a good sign," said Despina approvingly. "No greasy chips, though. Play it safe."

"I could make spag bol," Elvira suggested.

"Or, I could always dash over to 2584 and grab some Vegi-sim," Despina offered.

"Haven't you tortured me enough for one day?" Paris reproached.

"Spag bol it is, then," said Elvira. "Am I cooking for all three of us?"

"Please," Despina replied.

"I never thought I'd hear you say that." Elvira headed for the kitchen.

"Where's Norvus?" Paris asked.

"He and Vivette are visiting Fabian," said Despina. "He's having a spot of bother with the Vivlar fabric – the self-repair keeps stalling. So the GTC's decided to give the chemistry a little nudge. After all, we know Fabian succeeded. Now pay attention, you bundle of trouble. I've already run this past Elvira. When Norvus and me return to our own time, we'll prioritise the task of rounding up the Point Nemo killers. We have Jenufa and her cell, but as yet no others. The syndicate's very well organised."

"Can't you use synapsyn on the ones you've caught?"

"No use. Our detainees simply don't know anyone else. Nor do they know who the mastermind is. In view of this, we think you should stay here for now. I'll take your zugon shoes, just in case someone else attempts to trace them. Don't worry, Paris, you'll get them back. I'll return them personally."

"I'm sure you will." Paris' mind was racing. "How long did you intend me to stay? We both know that your investigation could take weeks, months, but you'd still be able to return here tomorrow if you chose."

"I'll negotiate something," Despina said quietly.

"If the GTC will listen. Just promise me this: when I have to leave, please don't snatch me away. Let me say my goodbyes properly."

"Properly. You mean like this?" Daringly, with Elvira only one room away, she leant forward and kissed him on the mouth. She took her time over it.

"You're shameless, Despina!"

She tweaked the car rug aside. The evidence of his arousal was all too apparent. "And you, sweetness, are back to your old self. Now set the table for Elvira. Best cutlery, place mats, shiny glassware. Go on! She says you've done nothing to earn your keep except load the dishwasher."

Paris obeyed, sighing. Later he endured the unwavering gaze of the two women as he made an art form of twirling spaghetti.

After coffee Despina left, first having exchanged a few cryptic messages with Norvus. Her departing words, before the mini-tornado took her, were to Paris. "Time to set the record straight, bad boy. No more dithering. Kiss kiss."

"She fancies you to bits," Elvira said.

"She's in lust with me," Paris admitted. "It's why she allowed me to run, initially. I ... take it she quoted my graduation report at you?"

"Chapter and verse. Oh, Paris, why didn't you tell me on Day One?"

"I assumed you'd think it morally wrong. Or just plain sleazy."

"No more sleazy than a Victorian gent taking his son to a brothel as soon as the lad was of age. And no more outrageous than the young men of your time offering sex for lodgings."

He took her hand. "Then let me disclose my true feelings. And please, don't interrupt – even if I blush, cry or say something foolish." He paused to assemble his thoughts. "After I'd had the nightmare, when you agreed to stay with me, I woke again at dawn. You had your arm round me, as if protecting me. I lay there for what seemed hours, gazing at your sleeping face and wondering how it was possible to fall in love so suddenly and so completely. I told myself I had to focus on my twin objectives – to establish time travel at CoherenceCo, and to stay one step ahead of the murderers. Today we solved the first challenge and the GTC are taking care of the second. So tonight, Elvira, I made a decision: the GTC owe me for my mistreatment and I'll tell them I want to stay here with you. I'll insist on it. I'm young and healthy and I can find work. I might even become Vivette's poster boy if that's what she wants." He faltered. "I only know that I can't lose you, Elvira. I can't lose you." Tears glistened on his eyelashes, but didn't fall.

"I love you too," Elvira said simply. "Everything about you. But I thought you were naïve and inexperienced. I also thought that one day very soon you'd vanish away and I'd have no hope whatsoever of seeing you again. So, I tried to keep a lid on my feelings. Because if I *had* seduced you, if you were what I'd assumed you to be, I'd have lived in your memory as your first embarrassing encounter. And I didn't want to be remembered in that way."

"Command me," he said.

She looked at him quizzically.

"I'm your kept man, your thrall, and I've done nothing to recompense you. Command me. It's your right."

"Very well," she said neutrally. He wanted her to take the lead. That wouldn't be too difficult. "Strip. Take off your clothes, every stitch, and prepare for my appraisal."

When he stood naked and unashamed before her, it was with the same composed, serious expression he'd adopted for the Hampstead Heath photo. She couldn't help remarking on it.

"Why are you looking at my face?" he asked indignantly. "Do I please you? Will this suffice?"

"You're beautiful," she answered softly, "and I can't wait to ... Paris, are you really going to fold your clothes neatly? *Now*? Yes, of course you are."

She undressed with somewhat less bravado, suddenly aware of her uneven tan and three or four bruises left by Despina. He kissed each one tenderly.

"You fought for me. I can never repay you."

"Yes you can, starting now. Bed." She led him there. "And don't forget, I'll be giving marks out of ten."

Even now, she half-expected awkwardness. There was none. What Paris brought to the love-act was confidence without flamboyance, experience without conceit. She guessed he had history other than the sex tuition, and couldn't help wondering how she compared with some uber-superior female of the future. One day she might ask him. But not yet.

Later, his duty discharged – as he phrased it – Paris struggled to stay awake. "Sorry," he murmured, when Elvira gently but firmly moved him over.

"Don't apologise. You've had a difficult day."

"It's bad manners to fall asleep first."

"I'll deduct one mark from your score, then." She smoothed some strands of damp hair from his forehead. "Your hair smells so nice. Like new-mown hay. Shall we pretend we've just made love in a cornfield?"

"I've never seen a cornfield."

"What? Why not?"

78

"Metro-London's vast. Remember the ring of skyscrapers I told you about? Every floor's a grainfield under its own artificial sky. The Harvester guild maintains it all. No outsiders allowed."

"Then tomorrow we'll get in the car and head out of town. I'll find you a field or several."

"What about work?"

"I'll pull a sickie. Now cuddle up and be quiet."

"Compliance."

"And Paris – I'm so very fortunate to have you."

Two hours later Paris was awakened by a piercing scream. The room was in darkness. Elvira hastily switched the bedside lamp on.

"Don't panic, it's only Vivette. She always lets everyone know when she's had a good time."

"Who's she with? Fabian?"

"No, it's Norvus."

Paris blinked sleepily. "Wow. She's not frightened!"

Elvira laughed. "Maybe Norvus should've been. He'll have some interesting love-bites in the morning!"

But when morning arrived there was no sign of Vivette and Norvus – although Vivette had scrawled "Yay!" on the kitchen memo. Despite the overcast weather, Elvira was still intent on finding Paris a cornfield. They set out after lunch, Elvira first asking if he was at ease with motorways. He answered yes, thinking of the flyers which criss-crossed the upper heights of MetroLondon at reckless speeds – albeit locked into invisible lanes. Without reference to the sat-nav Elvira took the North Circular for a few minutes, then the Western Avenue, then the M40.

"You know this route," Paris observed. "Let me guess, your parents?"

"Same general direction, yes, but a few extra miles. I hope you're not going to suggest calling on them?"

"Let's get our own situation sorted first," he said to her relief.

"Agreed. They're always abroad anyway. They're archaeologists. They'll have employed a house-sitter."

He didn't comment further. His relationship with his mother was all too similar.

"Why did they call you Elvira?" he asked with a partial change of subject. "Am I allowed to know that?"

"They both love Mozart operas, especially Don Giovanni."

"The so-called seducer of women?"

"That's the one. Elvira's the one who forgives him. And before you comment on that, don't. Tell me why you're called Paris."

"From the Iliad, of course. Mother named me after Paris, Prince of Troy, lover of Helen."

"Oh. Another seducer."

"Men don't seduce," Paris insisted. "Women choose."

"In *your* century, perhaps. Now stop being pedantic and watch the scenery. Who knows when we'll be back this way?"

The roads were getting narrower and narrower. A straggle of woodland kept pace with them, plus an isolated home or two, and neat white signposts pointing the way to oddly named villages: Bolter End, Skirmett, Fingest. The woods gradually gave way to undulating fields, bordered by tidy hedgerows.

At last Elvira stopped in a lay-by and turned off the engine. Silence. She opened the window a fraction. More silence. "That's a shame. I thought we might hear a skylark. Well, here are two cornfields for your delectation. One next to us, and one across the road."

"And people make love there?"

"In haystacks, traditionally, and you won't see those till after harvest. Which is around six weeks from now. Hey, look, the sun!"

Above, the grey clouds had formed rags and tatters. Glimpses of blue appeared, and one stray sunbeam spotlit the ripening corn. Paris regarded it with his usual seriousness.

"Please tell me this hasn't all been swallowed up by MetroLondon," Elvira begged.

"I don't think so. The city extends east and south, to the coasts."

"You don't sound very sure."

"I've never been out of MetroLondon, save for two interplanetary trips from Heathrow Spaceport.

I'm so glad you showed me this, Elvira. I feel privileged."

The sun blazed down; the colours of the countryside grew more vivid.

"I'm glad the weather's decided you're worth it." Elvira kissed his cheek. "Before we head back, I want to play you some music. We may not have heard a real skylark but this will make up for it."

The CD was already in position: Ralph Vaughan Williams' The Lark Ascending. Paris, whose musical education hadn't been best served by the Academy's focus on etiquette, was enraptured. He leant back in his seat and closed his eyes, holding Elvira's hand.

Five minutes later, someone knocked on the glass next to his ear. It was Despina. Paris, outraged, fumbled for the window button. "What are you *doing* here? You said I could have several days!"

"You asked. I don't recall saying yes." She glanced at the CD player. "Nice tune. Now if you'd just rein in the drama for one second: I was indeed going to leave you alone as requested. Only something urgent has come up."

"You took his shoes. How did you find us?" asked Elvira, more calmly.

"Remember all that fuss I made about the table settings? I stole your wine glass. DNA."

"But why would you want *my* DNA?"

"Regulations," said Despina briskly. "I have here a message from Paris' mother, all the way from

Procyon 4. She's finally been apprised of his adventures and has a proposition for you."

"For me?" Elvira repeated.

"That's what I said."

"And I suppose you've brought a hologram of her?"

"How very Star Wars of you. Do you know how cumbersome a holo-emitter really is? I've converted the recording into something compatible with your devices." She slid into the back seat. "Home you go. Quick as you like."

The return journey was conducted in near-silence. Paris stared mutinously out of the window. Despina maintained an air of mystery. Finally, via the laptop, Elvira had her first glimpse of Eva Mariosa. A strong, handsome face, reflecting the dignity of her position, but also revealing an imperious nature.

"Ms. Jones, I'll get straight to the point," she began without introducing herself. "As you will know, I am a diplomatic envoy based on Proxima 4, and news about my son has been slow to reach me. I'm now aware of the crimes he unwittingly uncovered and how he fled into the past to save himself. I also know that you took him in when he was hurt, gave him shelter and worked with him to contact his people. And –" She paused for emphasis – "I also note you are proficient in unarmed combat. Therefore, I wish to make you an offer. Since I cannot watch over him personally, I would like you to accompany Paris to his native time and become his bodyguard. I believe I raised him to be too gentle, and it would set my mind at rest knowing he had the protection of a dependable woman. If you are interested, Despina Psamathe will make the arrangements."

The screen blanked.

"Peremptory as ever," Paris remarked.

"To be fair, the GTC kept her waiting for three Earth weeks till the scrutineers finished their work," said Despina.

"And?"

"And you'd already noticed that Elvira's name wasn't on CoherenceCo's staffing list. We too found no record of her there. In fact, there was no digital or documentary evidence of her anywhere after this year. The GTC doesn't grant transfer requests lightly, but in Elvira's case they concluded that it had to happen. But as for you, Paris, and your dream of staying here: they'd never have allowed it, so it was best I didn't ask. You're too high profile. I'm sure you haven't forgotten the endless forms you had to complete when the TTI recruitment team came to your Academy. All work for the Institute is deemed vocational. It's why your mother couldn't get your appointment quashed. Oh yes, she tried. Did it never occur to you that a leading diplomat wouldn't want her only son working as a grease-monkey?"

"Do you mind?" Paris said indignantly. "Being a time tech takes skill and dedication. I take a pride in my work. We all do."

"And you're never short of a girl or two."

"We're quite popular," Paris admitted reluctantly.

"So popular that some young men of the town smear tungstron oil on themselves and pretend to be TTI's finest," said Despina with a knowing smile. "Luckily you'll be on hand, Elvira, to keep this one on a leash."

Paris suddenly looked distraught. "Elvira – I haven't asked if this is what you want. Is it? Please say it is!"

"It'll be a challenge," she answered. "But I'd be mad to refuse. Oh, Paris, don't cry. I've just said yes! You were so self-possessed last night – don't fall apart *now*!"

He took no notice but sobbed uncontrollably, holding onto a fistful of her tunic.

"He's been living on his nerves, poor petal," said Despina, sympathetic for once. "I don't suppose you've got any tranquillisers?"

Elvira shook her head. They settled for hot milk laced with cognac. After Paris was persuaded to drink it he finally quietened down, his head in Elvira's lap.

"Eva was right – she *did* raise him to be too gentle," Despina observed. "Can you do without me for a while, Elvira? I have to see Norvus about a few things but I'll be as

quick as I can. Be assured, we won't rush you into leaving – but maybe you should think about putting your affairs in order?"

"I'll make a list," Elvira said casually. "Hand me a pen, would you?"

***

"Well, Norvus, what kind of time tangle are you in this time? I heard the scriveners are baying at your heels again."

"It's a dichotomy. A *bad* one, Despina. I don't think I caused it but they're always quick to blame the throwback male, aren't they?"

"Tell me what happened," Despina said patiently.

"Vivette's future has a duality. Till yesterday it was just as always – the Face of Plessis, the amazing success of Vivlar, the NASA contract. Paris told her all this on the day of his arrival. There was no doubt in anyone's mind that it was a done deal."

"Until you had sex with her."

"Will you stop blaming *me*? I couldn't shake her off, the little wildcat. She was ecstatic. Her success was assured. And then I got called to the scrivener interface. Suddenly, Viv had an alternate future – an unremarkable one. She marries Fabian, but they don't have any kids because he's shooting blanks. The Vivlar product is lucrative enough for them to be comfortably off, but the NASA contract doesn't happen. I swear to you, Despina, this is not my doing. But I've still been tasked to fix it."

"I'll pay the scriveners a visit. Quite often there's some nuance that the shortsighted old dullards haven't picked up. I'll speak to Viv too, if you like."

"Oh, I *like*," Norvus said. "This needs a woman's touch."

The nearest interface, unsurprisingly, adjoined the TTI Stats Department. Despina related her errand, took her place in the allocated cubicle and waited, quite expecting to be told to report back in days or even weeks – not that it would have inconvenienced a GTC agent. But there were no attempts to stall her. Instead, the inner partition slid up to reveal a translucent info-screen.

"You are Despina Psamathe," stated a mellifluous alien voice.

"I am," said Despina, trying to hide her amazement. If the Morii had intercepted her enquiry then Vivette's future must have greater importance than she'd realised.

"You are here to resolve the Vivette Plessis duality," said the Morii. "How should I proceed?"

"Please display the percentage probabilities," said Despina. The screen lit in a pattern of numerals, showing a seventy/thirty split. As she watched, the secondary future gained two percentage points.

"Compare the Plessis family trees for the next two hundred years," Despina continued.

As Norvus had told her, the marriage between Vivette and Fabian had produced no offspring, and neither had the son they'd adopted in later life. In the recognised timeline, now under threat, Vivette had one daughter, Amelie. Amelie had followed her mother into the fashion industry, campaigned hard to popularise Vivlar, and married an astronaut.

"I take it he's the link to NASA?" Despina inquired.

"Indeed. And *their* daughter is Musette, who will make first contact with the Morii. Hence our interest in this matter."

"Of course," Despina murmured to herself. What was missing from the downbeat new future was the Plessis dynasty – the generations of motivated businesswomen who had achieved worldwide success for their company.

"Can you display visuals of Amelie?" she asked.

"At what age?"

"Let's try five and twenty-five."

The screen showed a darkhaired, lively little girl hand in hand with Vivette's mother. Then, Amelie at twenty-five. Despina smiled. The resemblance to Norvus was unmistakable.

"You appear to have your answer, Despina Psamathe," said the Morii.

"I will, as soon as I know her date of birth," responded Despina.

"The first of May, 2024."

"Thank you, Madam Morii. I know what to do now."

There had been no-one in the other half of the cubicle, of course; the alien woman was probably at the Morii Residence near the spaceport. But that did mean a skilled operative like Despina had been able to help herself to on-screen data – which, unsurprisingly, was not permitted. She was in no doubt that the interface clerks knew what she'd done. No-one stopped her on the way out.

***

"It doesn't take long to unpick a life," Elvira said ruefully.

"A week and a half," Paris answered pedantically.

"I don't think I've missed anything. All accounts closed, personal documents shredded, contents of laptop deleted. Vivette can have the device – hers is ancient."

"What's on your agenda for today?"

"Some clutter-clearing girls will take my bagged-up clothes to a charity shop. Then just two tasks are left: resigning from CoherenceCo, though after this unscheduled absence they've probably guessed I've quit. I'd like to leave it the way it is, but I really should tell Clive never to mention me."

"Is he likely to?"

"Probably not, but after what nearly happened with Vivette I want to guard against accidental change. I need to stay out of CoherenceCo's history."

"And what's your last to-do item?"

"The most difficult one. Telling my parents. I'll have to write a letter, and hand-deliver it to ensure it gets there. But I still haven't a clue what to say."

"Give me the notepaper," said Paris. He then proceeded to write rapidly for a couple of minutes. "Here. How's this?"

Elvira took it and read: "Dear Mother and Father: As you know, I've been an employee of the Ministry of Defence for several years, and of necessity haven't been able to share details of my work with you. This is to inform you that, with immediate effect, I have been appointed to the security staff of a very significant person. This will entail going wherever he goes, at very short notice. I'll try to stay in touch, but obviously it will be much more difficult for me to do so. Nevertheless, I still am, and will remain, your loving daughter Elvira."

She put down the paper and stared at her lover.

"Is that what you want?" he asked.

"I think," said Elvira, "that I'm going to employ you as my ghostwriter whenever the need arises."

"I aim to please," he replied, with one of his beautiful smiles.

"You always manage to surprise me. I thought you'd be all antsy this week."

He raised an inquiring eyebrow.

"Impatient to get away," she clarified.

"I am, but ever since I've been sure of our future, I'm happy to wait peaceably in the era that nurtured you."

She kissed him on the nose. "I'll copy this masterpiece out, and tomorrow we'll deliver it. Fancy a last look at our cornfield?"

"I would. Without Despina."

"Oh, but we'll *need* her. When we're good and ready."

And so, Paris and Elvira delivered their letter by taxi, then proceeded to Fingest Lane. They wandered into the cornfield, where the crop was now waist-high and ready for harvesting, and put on the bracelets Despina had issued to them on her last visit.

"Paris, hold my hand," Elvira said.

"Don't be nervous. It's a supervised transfer. All set?"

"Bring it on."

The wheatsheaves curtseyed in a sudden breeze.

***

"Hello, you!" said Vivette.

"Is it safe to approach?" asked Norvus. "You won't unsheath those wicked little claws?"

"Of course not, you knucklehead. Come here and give me a hug!"

He did so, very gingerly, as if she were made of bone china. "How far along are you?"

"Four months. And no problems. Don't worry, Norvus, I'm going to take very good care of this little one. I couldn't believe it when Despina told me what almost happened. Did you know she came charging in like a maniac, prised the morning after pill from my hand and threw it down the loo?"

"Despina likes to make an entrance. She didn't have to leave it till the last second. But why take it at all, Viv?"

"I didn't want to! Believe it or not, I was only trying to keep *you* out of trouble. I heard her telling you off for getting involved. Something about the GTC scribblers. Sorry I got it so wrong."

"But are you happy? Is there anything you need?"

"I'm fine. More than fine. Fabian often talked of getting married but we both knew he was infertile. He was worried I might resent that eventually. But it's different now. He actually approves of your inspired intervention, as he calls it. And Maman's over the moon – she's always wanted a granddaughter and she's selling up and moving down here. She doesn't want to miss a moment."

"Sounds like you've got it all sorted. Why did I ever think otherwise?"

"Well – there is *one* thing you could do."

"Name it."

"Paris chose this book of Shelley's poetry as a gift for Elvira. After he knew he could take her with him, he wrote a lovely dedication."

Norvus took it and read: "Leave the troop which errs and which reproves, And come and be my guest – for I am Love's. Your servant, Paris."

"Well?" Vivette asked eagerly.

"What's the troop that errs and reproves?"

"CoherenceCo and its ungrateful bosses, of course. She only went back for Paris' sake. Please,

Norvus, it's just one little book. Can't you sneak it to her? It would mean so much."

"How could I refuse you?" he answered.

She hugged him again. "You're nothing but a big softie, Norvus Maysson."

"Only where you're concerned. I'd better be on my way now. Sorry about the flying visit. I'll come back when I can and hopefully stay longer, but do bear in mind there will be times when I simply can't make it."

"I understand," Vivette said steadily. "One thing more. I want you to promise me something."

"You'd better tell me what it is first."

"Don't ever visit me when I'm old. I don't want you to see me old. Now scat. Tell Elvira – no, don't tell her anything. She never listened to my advice. She'll be all right. She'll be amazing."

Chapter Four

The scene shifted imperceptibly. Before Elvira could think about being somewhere else, she *was* somewhere else. A place with subdued greenish lighting, a metallic odour – and a dozen exuberant young men who, amid cheers, hoisted Paris on their shoulders and carried him off.

"His workmates," said Despina at her elbow. "Word got out and he's their hero. They couldn't quite believe that someone so genteel managed to foil a conspiracy."

"Aren't I supposed to be shadowing him?" asked Elvira.

"He's hardly likely to come to grief in the company of such strapping examples of masculinity," Despina remarked. "I must visit this sweatshop more often. And before you ask, the reason they didn't grab you too is because I pulled rank on them and told them to leave you alone."

Elvira wrinkled her brow. "That conspiracy isn't *completely* foiled, now is it?"

"Well, no. The mastermind's still eluding us. But our most recent investigations indicate that he's based in the past. Not *your* past, but an earlier time than this."

"So Paris launched himself *toward* danger, not away from it?"

"It seems so," Despina said noncommittally.

"Dammit, Despina, you can't tell him! He'll have another meltdown!"

"My lips are sealed," she promised airily.

Elvira looked around. "Is this the exact place his journey started?"

"Right first time. It was quicker and easier to bring you both here. You'll need to be acclimatised and the TTI has all the right resources. I'll be with you till the essential stuff's out of the way."

"Essential? Do you mean some kind of decontamination?"

"Nothing so crude. That was all done as you arrived. The next thing we have to do is update your language status and maybe add an overview of recent history. Then we'll get you a change of clothes. You can borrow some of mine in the meantime."

Her attire presently consisted of boots, gold leggings, short, flared skirt, form-fitting gilet and elbow-length fingerless gloves.

"Perhaps something less - flamboyant?" Elvira suggested.

"This is no time for modest dressing," admonished Despina. "You'll be under scrutiny while you're in the news. Work on your image. Paris will appreciate it."

"I think he likes me as I am."

"Always room for improvement."

Despina escorted her to an elevator, remarkably like its 21st century equivalent in appearance, although its mode of transportation doubtless wasn't. They ascended one floor only.

"Welcome to my pied-a-terre," said Despina, unlocking a featureless green door, the first in a long row. "Rooms for economy class tourists," she elaborated. "They're right above the brace generators so things can get a bit rackety around noon. I'm not often here at that time, though. Excuse me while I check my messages."

"Answering machine?" Elvira asked. "Surely not?"

"Not. It's a link to an off-world server." She tapped a code on a tabletop panel. She had one new message, the contents of which she found risible. Elvira could only discern a few words of standard English. The rest consisted of unknown terms and GTC jargon.

"Trouble with some of the sperm banks," Despina translated for her. "Mothers pay all kinds of money for designer choices and sometimes leave most of the batch unused. It's tempting for employees to sell the leftovers instead of having them destroyed."

"That doesn't sound like a job for the GTC."

"It depends. Some of the samples can find their way into the past. But, as you rightly assumed, these investigations are half clerical and half tedious legwork. Now I've earned a reputation for success I can pick and choose my jobs, and I think I'll pass on this one." She opened the door to the kitchenette. "Want coffee?"

"Yes please. White, no sugar," Elvira said automatically, then added: "However strange 2584 turns out to be, there's still coffee. That's reassuring. I'm still trying to process the fact that 2023's gone. Just – blinked out."

"It's still there," said Despina comfortingly. "All of time is. Time doesn't move, *we* do. And thanks to science, that movement doesn't have to be linear."

"And where does the GTC fit in?"

"Time Controllers *is* a slight misnomer. We can't, unsurprisingly, control time itself. Our remit is to keep track of all unlicensed travellers, stop them accidentally harming themselves or others, and deal with affiliated crime such as smuggling. Nothing challenges the universal picture, but a lot of local disorder can result when people attempt changes – even if they mean well." She paused. "It's a lot to get your head round."

"Especially when I can't speak the lingo." Elvira directed a meaningful glance at the messaging panel.

Despina frowned. "You aren't still worrying about the sleep programming? Believe me, it's painless and it works. Before I came to Earth I couldn't speak a word of English."

"You're from off-world? I thought you were Greek."

"I am. I'm from New Sparta, a colony of Greek ex-pats on Epsilon Eridani 3."

"Is that where you learnt to fight?"

"Correct. I competed in the Pankration from an early age." Despina brought in two mugs of coffee and two slices of bougatsa. "Me? Cook? She added, anticipating Elvira's next question. "Waste of my talents. There's a nice little Greek deli on Level Five, and I patronise it shamelessly." She touched the tabletop again and a wall info-screen lit to display the restaurant, Rhodos. "This viewer isn't interactive, so you can't talk to it and vice versa. Economy, as I said. It's just a travel guide to the city – what's where and how to get there. Here's something that will interest you. The Plessis Tower."

The image shifted, this time showing a tall, elegant building with "Plessis" blazoned across its upper storey. And next to the sign, the smiling face of Vivette.

"That's wonderful," Elvira breathed. "I wish she could see it."

"Knowing Norvus, he'll have found a way to show her. We agents all have bio-enhancements, as you've seen, to keep in touch with our partners in the field. But portable devices were limited to retrieval bracelets and synapsyn – and then only when making an arrest."

"You said *were*."

"We're now permitted certain small accessories. No weapons, no anachronisms. Just – this type of thing." She fielded her belt bag from the couch and retrieved a 25mm dice. "Norvus has one as well."

"I assume this has nothing to do with gambling?" inquired Elvira.

"Nothing whatsoever. Watch." Despina raised the innocuous-looking dice and aimed its one dot at the image of Vivette. Then she held the object firmly and twisted it in half. Inside was a tiny square of film with a rapidly developing image. A miniature Vivette beamed up at them.

Elvira stared at it, perplexed. "A Polaroid? You're still using Polaroids?"

"Very handy for evidence-gathering. Inadmissible of course - too easily faked - but enough to dissuade petty crooks, or unfaithful spouses using time travel for loved-up getaways. Having got our pictures, we just give the culprits a good talking to and that's usually all they need. Now, your body language suggests you're getting anxious about Paris. Shall we go and rescue him?"

"I'm just worried they'll get him drunk."

"And you haven't?"

"That was different," Elvira said defensively. "Won't he need to go back to work tomorrow? *I* won't be bringing anything in, will I? And I still haven't seen where he lives. I assume I'll be moving in with him?"

"Questions, questions," Despina said in mock weariness. "I daresay Paris will want to resume his work as soon as possible, but not tomorrow. He hasn't been debriefed yet. Secondly, there's no way you can both live in his apartment."

"Been there, have you?"

"No, but I've seen others. I imagine Paris keeps his neat and tidy but it's just a place to sleep, not to live in. Which is why I'm offering you the tenure of this flatlet until you get settled. It'll be close to Paris' work, for which he should be grateful, as his pals tell me he often oversleeps. Take it, Elvira, I insist. I've other places I need to be. Don't worry, I'll still be around tomorrow. And, if I may drop a substantial hint, you also needn't worry about an income. And that's all I'm saying at the moment."

"Is Eva planning to pay me?"

"Later, I said!"

"Shall we go and collect Paris, then? Feed him maybe?"

"Of course. After you ditch that silly Bo-Peep dress. It's fine for cavorting around in cornfields but from now on you need to look more combat-ready." Despina touched a lever and a section of wall swung round to reveal two rails packed with clothes. "Choose."

Elvira tentatively selected a jumpsuit in shell pink.

"No, no, no. Not with your English rose complexion. Hasn't flat-sharing with Vivette taught you anything? If you wear that you'll look as though you couldn't fight your way out of a paper bag. Here, try this." She held up a military-style khaki two-piece. "You can't fight in high heels, either, but they'll have to do for now. My shoes would fall off you."

"Where *is* Paris? Is it an easy walk away?"

"The boys will have gone to the Timeweavers' Arms, close by. They don't serve food but I can recommend a nice little bistro on the next level – Hera's tits, I nearly forgot. Contraception."

"What? Oh."

"Quite. My instructions were to transfer you safely with your immediate needs catered for, and I wouldn't be doing my job too well if I forgot *that* little detail, would I?" She rummaged in her bag again.

"A lipstick?"

"A spray. Give me your left arm."

Elvira folded her arms tightly. "Not until I know what's in it."

Despina sighed. "I took the leaflet from your pills and made sure this matched. Use it nightly. Replace after a month. And if that's too much faff, we'll get you an implant. Now stop dawdling and get changed. You have a choice of the extremely small hygiene area, or asking me to look the other way."

Elvira, from curiosity rather than modesty, chose the former: she placed the hormone spray on a shelf, then wriggled free of her cotton dress and threw it out of the compartment. She couldn't see any faucets, so rightly assumed the odd-looking shower was a particle scrub. She'd have to ask Paris about that later. The rest of the plumbing looked reasonably normal.

When she emerged, Despina inspected her attire and gave a nod of approval. She handed her a turquoise cape to complete the outfit. "We're not in a domed city yet. It still rains!"

They walked.

"So the male contraceptive pill never materialised?" Elvira asked after a moment.

"The science did, but not the psychology," Despina said. "There were many complications – everything from dishonesty to performance issues. And later, after we'd bred much of the aggression out of our men, it just wasn't feasible to meddle with their reproductive status. What would we have had left?"

"Not a lot," Elvira conceded.

Despina paused by another elevator. "It's the lazy way, but kinder to your feet," she remarked, with a second disparaging look at Elvira's shoes. "I'll add boots to your shopping list."

"We're going sideways," said Elvira, a few seconds into the ride.

"What of it?"

"If an elevator goes sideways it shouldn't be called an elevator, should it?"

"Gods of Olympus, you're starting to sound like Paris. Modern English lesson number one: this is a multi-cube. Or just cube."

"Thanks. Nice to know."

As soon as the doors opened Elvira heard the unmistakeable sound of a tavern in full raucous voice. Once inside the crowded Timeweavers' Arms she saw Paris surrounded by the same dozen cronies, alternately guffawing, shoving him and shouting in his ear. He caught her eye, and his frantic look almost screamed "get me out of here." She promptly barged her way to his side, elbowing his friends and several other drinkers out of the way.

"Into mischief again? I can't leave you alone for five minutes!"

Behind her, Despina seized two of the brawniest engineers and pinioned them against the bar. Whatever they'd just said had infuriated her.

102

Elvira assumed it was sexual innuendo and prepared to deliver a few slaps.

"Elvira! Bring him! *Now*!" Despina yelled. "They're planning a Street incursion, the idiots. Get him out!"

Elvira grabbed Paris and almost carried him outside. Despina led the way back to the multi-cube. The doors rolled shut, cutting off the whoops and laughter.

"I do hate running from a fight, but we couldn't risk injury to you," Despina said apologetically to Paris. "Use English 2000 for now. Elvira will get her updates tomorrow."

"The lads didn't mean any harm," Paris said unhappily. "They were just partying. I tried to calm them down."

"Unsuccessfully," Despina observed.

"What were they planning to do?" asked Elvira, confused.

"The feral girls stage mock fights for their trusted patrons. Invitation only. No-one gets seriously hurt so the city enforcers turn a blind eye. But if any of those boys had shown up, the Streeters would have been livid. And you can guess the rest. I think I managed to sabotage the plan, but I'll call Enforcer HQ just in case."

"I don't know the venue," said Paris.

"The enforcers always know."

The cube, after several vertical and horizontal course changes, came to a halt.

"Here we are. La Chanson d'Amour. Go on in. I'll join you after I've sent this alert."

Elvira chose a window seat with a scenic view across Metro-London. The early evening sun burnished the outlines of the distant grain towers. Far below, treetops dappled the Heath. "You're very quiet," she said to Paris. "Are you OK?"

"Yes. Sorry. Today's been a bit much."

Despina was back in a few moments. "Right, it's sorted. Have you been here before, Paris?"

He shook his head.

"Well, I hope you like crepes. They're the best in town. My treat."

Elvira, despite the strangeness of the day, found she had a good appetite. But Paris just picked at his food.

"Paris, this isn't like you," Elvira said gently. "Something *is* wrong. Please tell me what it is."

"Those young men back there," he began hesitantly. "My friends, my workmates. I've known most of them for years. But now they seem so childish, so vacuous. Everything's so different. I thought *you'd* be out of your depth, Elvira – but you're not, are you? I look at the skyline out there and I feel almost homesick for your time."

"Your adventure's changed you," Despina said soberly. "I thought it might. You're losing your roots at last. When do you reach your majority?"

"Another five months."

"Have I missed something?" asked Elvira.

"In five months, I shall be twenty-eight, the age when men attain their majority. I'll then be able to vote, borrow money, and get married."

"Right," Elvira said slowly. "You make it sound like an impending responsibility. But it needn't be. Coming of age can be fun. And I'll be with you to help you enjoy it!"

Paris gave up his struggle with the crepes. "Despina, I'll need to go back to my own apartment and spruce up. I can't present myself at Human Resources dressed like this. They'd see it as irresponsible. Can Elvira stay with you tonight?"

Despina lifted an eyebrow. "Why?"

"*Why?* Can you imagine what those drunks would do if we both turned up? They'd be listening at the door, playing pranks - "

"All taken care of," Despina said soothingly. "The enforcers will have sobered them up and given them secure accommodation for the night. They'll be given a meal tomorrow, Vegi-sim probably, and released in time for work. You'll have the whole block to yourselves till morning. I just need a few more hours in my apartment to re-route my inbox, re-stock the kitchen and ensure you have some clean laundry. After that, it's all yours."

"You're too good to us, Despina."

"We got off to a bad start. I haven't forgotten that. Tomorrow, early, you'll receive a continental breakfast courtesy of the GTC. We have a busy day ahead so you'll need more than Vegi-sim to kick-start it. Now I must love you and leave you. I assume you can find your way home from here?"

"Of course!" he said indignantly.

"Excellent. I'll see you at nine. Be ready!"

***

Despina had planned the next day's activities like a military campaign. First on the itinerary was delivering Paris to TTI's human resources department, in an assumption that he'd need her support; but she was pleased to find him nonchalant and unconcerned. He pointed out to his assessors that they'd failed to spot corruption in the ranks, and insisted on being paid for the days he'd missed. If they refused, he was minded to quit. And probably half his team would follow. Aware of his current hero status, the panel had little choice but to authorise his wages. The entire interview had lasted only twenty minutes.

Next, he and Norvus were due to attend the debriefing at GTC headquarters, Greenwich. Norvus had yet to detail his involvement with CoherenceCo, and Paris would be expected to give a full account of his time in the past. Again, he seemed untroubled by the prospect.

Despina rounded up Norvus, handed Paris over and hurried back to Elvira, who was examining a pocket e-reader she'd found at her lover's bedside. "I can't make much sense of this at the moment, but it seems to be a romance."

Despina spared the text a quick glance. "Nothing strange in that. Men read romances. FYI, this download pre-dates his time trip. It'll be interesting to see if he finishes the story."

Once the two women were on their own in Despina's apartment, the older woman relaxed a little. "Sorry about all the secrecy yesterday, but the alternative would have meant your keeping a secret from Paris. I'm still not sure how he'll react when he knows."

"Knows what?"

"That Principal Rayah-Nova of the Excelsior School for Noble Gentlemen has asked to meet you today. Paris had far more respect for her than for his mother, and I'm sure he still does. But, she's sent for you alone, and I didn't want him dismayed by that. He's still annoyed with his teammates, and that worked well for him today."

"His teacher sounds intimidating."

"Believe me, she isn't. But before you meet her, we do need to get your English up to scratch."

"She's told you why she wants to see me, hasn't she?"

"Yes."

"And you're not telling *me*."

"You'll know soon enough. Now, under the circumstances I think we'll resurrect your cotton dress. It isn't too crumpled. And ... you'll need these." She handed Elvira a lingerie bag.

"Is that mine? It *is* mine! My new knickers! Really, Despina?"

"One hundred per cent cotton and anti-static. Perfect for your language induction and much better than the paper ones they'd offer you."

"I can't believe you stole my knickers."

"I didn't steal them, I repurposed them – at the same time as I was inspecting your Pill supply."

"You're incorrigible."

"Yes, I am. I'm also in a hurry. So step into your cotton finery and let's go."

"Where exactly?"

"The spaceport. You'll be meeting *two* people there today. The second one works there. If we leg it we can catch the turbo-link returning empty from depositing today's tourists."

"What's that vibration in the air?"

"The brace generators powering up. It's 11.30. And you're booked into the Orientation Suite in half an hour. Oh, don't pout! Paris may like it but my Spartan upbringing detests it. Onward, Ms Jones. You'll soon be a new woman!"

Still with a myriad questions unanswered, Elvira threw on her borrowed cape and followed Despina through the warren that was the TTI.

***

One hour later, Elvira walked resolutely away from the hushed quiet of the Orientation Suite and sat down on the bench where Despina waited. "It hasn't worked. I'm sorry."

Despina raised a quizzical eyebrow. "What do you mean, it hasn't worked? Did you take off your shoes and hosiery when directed, and lie on the recliner? Did you fall asleep?"

"The AI said I'd sleep for a short while and dimmed the lights. And then it told me to get up. I hadn't slept."

Despina grinned. "Are you sure about that? You've just been speaking 26th century English with a very natural London accent."

"But I can't be!"

"This is your default setting, to coin a phrase. When you've learnt to focus better you'll be able to hear your native version keeping pace like a backing track. Don't try and analyse it for now, just talk! And before you launch into a soliloquy, you'll be pleased to hear that Paris impressed the debriefing committee with his modesty and politeness. I've just been speaking to Norvus. I thought we could all meet for a meal later."

"At the spaceport?"

"Yes, but don't get too excited. There won't be any huge rockets taking off. The passenger liners and the freighters don't make landfall, only planet hoppers, and sometimes not all that many. Ours isn't the only spaceport in the world!"

Elvira, still bemused, looked about her. "Why's there no-one around? Did you tell everyone to keep away from me?"

"Hades, *no*! Why would I do that? We're still on the edge of the TTI here, and that means everything's being run like, well, clockwork. Today's intake of tourists will be in wardrobe now. If any needed orientation they'd have been and gone before we arrived. There's plenty of hustle and bustle elsewhere. You'll be sorry you asked! Now, are you ready to meet the Principal?"

"As ready as I'll ever be."

"Right. Let's do it. Just one more cube-trip to the Morii Residence. Er – you do realise that Rayah-Nova is Morii?"

"Yes. Paris told me."

"What a paragon that boy is," Despina said with a small sigh.

Surely, Elvira told herself, Paris' Morii mentor couldn't be that intimidating, given the affectionate way he spoke of her?

She was not mistaken. Her first impression was of a benign, smiling academic. Only then did she notice the woman's golden skin, lustrous amber eyes and midnight blue hair in a long plait. Rayah offered a traditional handshake. She had six fingers.

"Welcome, Ms Jones. I wanted to thank you in person for your kindness toward dear Paris, and your unstinting attempts to return him home."

"He's a wonderful young man," Elvira said carefully, "and a credit to your school."

"To be honest," said Rayah, "I was amazed at his resourcefulness. I knew he'd developed a social conscience but he's surpassed my expectations. This is why I chose not to meet with him today. He's a little too fond of looking back on his schooldays and I didn't want to encourage that. He's taken a definitive step into maturity and he needs to move forward now. And so, Ms Jones, to the business of the day. I wish to give this into your safekeeping." She handed Elvira a small key of traditional design. "This opens a safety deposit box in a long-established bank in Metro-London,

Thetamora Sol UK. Your flatmate Vivette bequeathed some shares in House of Plessis to you. The company she founded is now a multi-million pound organisation, so ownership of these shares will ensure you never need to earn a living – unless you choose to. You're wondering, are you not, how I became custodian of this key. Is your history overview in good order? It was included in your orientation."

"I – haven't had a chance to use it yet," Elvira said hesitantly.

"Do so now. Search your memory for knowledge of our banking system."

And instantly, Elvira knew that all financial institutions were run by women. She knew that pounds, shillings and pence were once more legal tender in Britain, instigated by the Morii and their twelve digit hands. Men were not permitted to enter the major banks, either as employees or customers. They had their own credit unions. The international – and interstellar – exchange medium was the ECU or Earth Currency Unit.

"Vivette entrusted the shares to Norvus, as you might expect," Rayah was continuing. "You'll now see why he couldn't safely retain them. Despina's itinerant lifestyle wasn't best suited either. So, she asked *me*, Paris being the connection between us all. Remember, when you attend the bank, an associate will need to be present with a second key. They have your DNA on file already so you'll be able to open an account that very day, if you want. And now for my final surprise."

"Another one?"

"You'll like this one. I think you'd benefit by having a friend your own age, to show you the town and help you amass some possessions."

"Girl stuff?"

"Girl stuff. Fortunately I know just the person. Her name is Saranna Sefora and she's a ground hostess here at Heathrow. She'll be joining you, Paris and your two GTC friends for dinner."

"Supposing we don't get on?"

"I'm certain you will. She's Vivette's direct descendant. Now I must return to my duties. Perhaps, the next time we meet, I should introduce you to my Novettes, my trainee teachers. They'd be fascinated to meet you and hear your story. Ah, here's Despina. Off you go. And don't lose that key!"

They dined al fresco on a high balcony overlooking a network of roads, warehouses and depots. No launch pads, no gantries, just landing circles for the hoppers. A huge hotel was visible in the distance.

Elvira finished a second slice of pizza. "Despina," she said, "do you know of anywhere I could continue my martial arts classes? I'm going to put on weight otherwise!"

"We can't have that, can we, Paris?" Despina answered teasingly. Paris grinned and started on a third portion.

Saranna was late. When she arrived, hurrying in breathlessly, Elvira immediately saw the facial likeness to Vivette: dark hair, mischievous eyes, retrousse nose. But the resemblance ended there. Saranna was as tall as Elvira and her stride owed more to the parade ground than the catwalk. Elvira, who'd had in mind the uniform of a 21st century air hostess – fitted jacket, knee length skirt, high heels – was surprised to see Saranna in a dark green loose-fitting tunic, cargo pants and sneakers. A jaunty cap carried the spaceport logo.

"Grovelling apologies, gentlemen and ladies. I was delayed by a nitpicking bureaucrat from Altair. He's here on a research tour of our libraries. Can you think of anything less exciting? Anyway, enough about him. Elvira, I'm so looking forward to our trip to the shops. Forget the mega-stores – I know some amazing boutiques on Thatcher Boulevard."

"I'd like to see what House of Plessis is selling," Elvira ventured.

"Then you'd look like everybody else," Saranna declared. "But, it's your choice. Before you decide, see what's trending. I hear Street style's the in thing this autumn."

Paris scowled.

Saranna, undeterred, beamed at him. "You should come with us. Vivette never had the chance to dress you up but it isn't too late to put that right."

"Does anyone *not* know my life story?" he asked plaintively.

"Let's face it, Paris," Norvus said, "you're an urban myth. Your idiot friends at the TTI made sure of that."

"But surely there's no harm in taking him shopping?" Saranna persisted. "Elvira will be there."

"What about the mis-" Norvus began, but Despina silenced him with a look.

Saranna launched into an enthusiastic description of the young men of the town and their fashion fads, ranging from the bizarre to borderline obscene. Paris continued to look unimpressed.

"I hope you don't still have communal changing rooms," Elvira said, trying to move the conversation on.

"We don't have *any* changing rooms," Saranna reassured her. "It's all virtual now. You can choose up to a dozen outfits you think will suit you, and the AI will generate a hologram of yourself in your chosen garments. You can accessorise, add jewellery, shoes and so on, as long as they're in the database. Then, when you've narrowed your choice down to three, your clothes are delivered by pneumatic despatch or by an obsequious member of staff, depending on how upmarket the venue is. You then go into a private mirrored cubicle and preen to your heart's content."

"Paris, didn't you *know* that?" Elvira asked him.

"I don't do high-end fashion. I order my work attire and leisure wear via an info-screen. It usually fits."

"That," declared Saranna, "is the saddest thing I've heard this year. You'll admit next that you've never had dancing lessons."

"The Gentleman's Excuse Me Two-Step."

Marise Morland

Saranna sighed. "Just when I thought it couldn't get worse."

"I can't dance either," Elvira pointed out. Saranna was about to add something scathing when Despina said:

"People, that skimmer's heading straight for us. Could be trouble."

Saranna groaned. "Oh, *no*. It's him. Agarad the Second. Agarad the entitled. He's lost his servant and he blames *me*."

The skimmer pulled up alongside the balcony, the canopy opened, and a querulous voice said: "Saranna Sefora! We had not concluded our discussion."

"Yes, we had," Saranna contradicted.

A gaunt elderly humanoid, brow furrowed, directed an ice-pick gaze at her. "I am still without a page-turner. You agreed to find a replacement."

"As I understand it," Saranna said with exaggerated patience, "you're scheduled to visit many libraries, and only the British Library presents a problem."

"Correct, Saranna Sefora. I cannot peruse archival volumes unaccompanied."

"Then visit all the other repositories first, starting with the smallest and working up. That means your first port of call is a library based in the last surviving red telephone box. Its location is - "

"I *know* where it is."

"Your second," Saranna went on remorselessly, "is with the cataloguing department of the Bountiful Women's Literary Guild, Upton Snodsbury. And so

115

on. If you follow this schedule, you should reach the British Library in one year and six months. I guarantee to have a page-turner ready to accompany you by then. Will that suffice?"

"It will have to. I will contact you on my return to this vicinity. Good day, Saranna Sefora." Agarad raised one hand to close the canopy, and everyone save Saranna smothered a gasp. Agarad the Second of Altair 3 had improbably narrow, strangely elegant, webbed hands.

"Now do you see why he needs help with rare books?" inquired Saranna. "The British Library insists that all researchers wear sterile cotton gloves, and he can't. His world's part maritime, part aquatic. The people have an oral tradition and little use for paper. Agarad will memorise as much as he can and incorporate selected texts into their lore. They hope one day to be part of the Consortium of Planets under the Morii." Saranna stopped lecturing. "Agarad may be a pain in the backside but he's still something of a genius."

"You seem convinced you can find him a page-turner," Norvus remarked.

"I'm not at all convinced. Hopefully someone suitable will put in an appearance. We get a lot of footfall in the course of a year."

They talked, ordered drinks, then talked some more before the gathering broke up. Despina promised to escort Elvira to the bank the next day.

"And then I shall leave you to Saranna's tender mercies," she concluded. "Don't spend all your windfall at once!"

Finally, Elvira and Paris were alone in their borrowed apartment. They stood in its centre and held one another close for several minutes, saying nothing.

"That," Elvira said at last, "was manic."

"I never want another day like that," he murmured. "I just want to sleep it all away."

"Is that *all* you want?" she teased.

"Not quite all."

"Then we'd better sort out the bed-settee."

"It flips over. Standard design." Paris demonstrated. "Do you know where Despina keeps the bedding?"

"In her wardrobe. I saw it earlier." Elvira retrieved a duvet set in pale peach, one of Despina's favoured colours. "You do the honours while I make us some hot chocolate. I saw that earlier too."

Paris finished first and came to join her in the kitchen. "So," he said, "what's your opinion of Saranna?"

"She's a bit full-on but I think she'll be indispensable while I'm getting used to things. Er – you don't mind coming on this shopping trip of hers?"

"I do, but I'll make an exception. I hope I'll enjoy putting clothes on you as much as I enjoy removing them."

She gave him a playful punch. "Have you been keeping score?"

"Oh yes. Tonight will be the eleventh time."

"Patience, lover. I haven't finished my nightcap."

Elvira expected Paris to deliver a languid, gentle performance and then doze off. Instead he found a new reserve of energy and was demanding, insistent, near insatiable. And then, in a moment, asleep. The following morning, he reverted to his usual apologetic self.

"Elvira, I'm sorry, I'm sorry. I was rough. I didn't hurt you, did I?"

"No, silly. I'm used to being thrown around. But I wasn't expecting such a marathon. What happened?"

"Despina's perfume happened. I lost control."

"What perfume?"

"Couldn't you smell it? On the duvet, the pillows, everywhere. I've noticed it before, on her."

"I've never noticed it. Maybe it's pheromones, something to attract men. Though I wouldn't have thought she needed any chemical help. Stop fretting. We'll leave the bed made up, run the air-con and the scent will soon disperse. I know what you're going to say – that it's bad manners to be over-zealous."

"It's also exhausting."

"I'm sure it is. So this seems an appropriate time to remind you that Despina's taking me to the bank today. Relax, she won't be here till ten. So you've ample opportunity to report for work and be elsewhere when she arrives."

Paris hurried off to the shower and Elvira permitted herself a secret smile. Despina's parting words to her had been: "I've left you a special treat." At the time, she hadn't a clue what it might be.

***

Banks, Elvira decided, would never change, and Thetamora Sol UK was no exception. The interior was neutral and bland, the air conditioning a notch too high. Despina had lent her a coat-dress in pale emerald, suitable for the occasion but not a garment she would normally associate with the fiery Spartan. It was, Despina had explained, reserved for GTC committee meetings.

While they waited, Despina used her bio-communicator to locate martial arts groups and send the results to the info-screen in Elvira's lodgings. It would now be down to Elvira to find one to her liking.

The safety deposit box was eventually opened and a proportion of the shares cashed in. It would, the attendant sniffily informed Elvira, take three working days for the funds to become available.

"Oh, ignore her," Despina said airily as they left. "You're a Plessis shareholder. No-one will refuse you credit, so you can hit the shops straight away."

"Saranna will be pleased."

"Before you start in earnest, take her advice and spend some time in a tourist café like Regardez. It has one-way glass so you can gawp at passers by without annoying them. See what they're wearing and how they carry themselves. Otherwise you

119

could make some wrong choices. Can't you take Paris along? He hasn't the fashion sense he was born with."

"His team won't like it if he keeps having days off."

"I rather suspect," said Despina, "that they won't *be* his team for much longer. He's outgrown them."

***

"They know they're being watched," said Elvira. "Look at the body language. Everyone who passes this window is self-conscious or self-important. Or downright provocative. Him, for instance."

A youth of around eighteen, dressed as a medieval minstrel, paused to adjust his codpiece.

"But no-one knows *precisely* who's in here," Saranna returned. "Sometimes, dress designers sit in this very spot and look for inspiration. See anything you like?"

"The calf-length fringed gowns would suit me, but would I suit *them*? I'm supposed to be Paris' defender. I couldn't fight in those!"

"Something street-related, perhaps?"

"Ripped leggings and tattoos? Paris would be appalled."

"I'd like to see him in that minstrel outfit," Saranna said reflectively.

"No chance."

"Not the *real* Paris. The holographic one. In-store."

"Oh, I see."

"You *will* see. I think I know just the shop. Not too trendy but with a certain edge. It's called Leisure 4 Lovers."

Elvira was suddenly pensive. "All these women have one thing in common. Classic beauty. I can't match that."

"But you *could*!" Saranna leant forward conspiratorially. "You don't think they were born that way, do you?"

"They can't all be designer babies."

"Of course not. That's exorbitant, unpredictable – and it's always what the parents want, not what the offspring eventually wants."

Elvira had to agree.

"I'm talking about sculpture by Ace My Face. Its creators work on a single premise: nobody likes their own face. Forget plastic surgery, forget Botox. They're ancient history. You've had the memory grafts, haven't you, and they work perfectly. Ace My Face changes the memory your face has of itself. At least, that's what the ads say."

"Ads will say anything."

"Then don't believe them. Believe what you've seen walking past you. You could be stunning, Elvira!"

"Have *you* tried it?"

"A few tweaks here and there. It helps in the hospitality industry. But first things first. I promised Rayah that I wouldn't swamp you with info. Clothes first, OK?"

"OK."

The next day the trio duly presented themselves at Leisure 4 Lovers. Elvira began by requesting customised blue jeans for Paris and herself. Saranna yawned. Paris indulgently permitted his holographic self to be garbed in the minstrel outfit, noting a momentary glitch in the image which somewhat spoilt the manly effect. Subsequently he left Elvira to make the choices for them both, and settled down to read a TTI technical manual.

Despina, elsewhere on a case, was startled to see an alluring image of Paris projected onto an entire side of an office block. She guessed which influencer was to blame and hastily searched her device for a commentary. She soon found it.

"Hello again, fashionistas, Street Grrls and gossip addicts. Welcome to more of Metro London's hidden secrets, courtesy of my roving eye-spy. Before I return this pop-up channel to its rightful owners – sorry, Level Seven Traffic Monitors, you need to up your security – I have something special for the ladies. Paris Evason, crimebuster and time traveller extraordinaire, is back with us, along with his 21st century warrior squeeze Elvira. I tracked them both to the boutique Leisure 4 Lovers, where they were updating their outmoded threads. Just for a few precious seconds I hacked their holo-catalogue and retrieved this image, now displaying on your nearest wall map. Out beautiful Paris, larger than live, attired in azure crotch-revealing tights and a tabard whose hemline fails to cover his assets. Girls, isn't he just *minty*? Catch more like this on my usual portal. This is Nimue Pamina, your gossip gadabout. Keep watching the walls!"

"Damn, damn, damn!" Despina muttered. "I hope he didn't see that. I hope his dim-witted friends didn't either."

Nimue's followers would have already moved on to the next piece of trivia. Other people, however, had longer memories.

The new clothes were delivered, on a rail, by a uniformed courier.

"Where are we going to put all this stuff? Elvira asked.

"Just shove Despina's things closer together," Paris suggested. "I'll take mine to my apartment tomorrow."

"We need to get one larger home," Elvira continued. "I'll ask Saranna how to go about it - unless you know of someone? It can't be too far from the TTI, of course. What about the Stats girls? Where do *they* live? Paris, you're not listening! Have you still got your nose in that workshop manual?"

"Er – yes."

"Oh, I'm sorry, angel pie. I sound like a nagging wife!"

"You could never be that. As for this - " He waved the e-reader – "there's something I need to run past you."

"Oh?"

123

"You know that I haven't been getting along with my workmates recently. They were driving me crazy yesterday with their endless silly jokes. And, well, I've decided to put in for a transfer from maintenance to construction. It looks fascinating. Instead of endless repairs, I'd be building a time machine from start to finish – except for the brace. That's the physicists' territory. I'd even get my name on the finished item! And, more importantly, my co-workers would be older. TTI doesn't normally assign under-28's to that department, but as I'm nearly of age, they said I could apply."

"When's this happening? Tomorrow?"

"The preliminaries are. There's a short written exam and some practical tests. What are *you* doing tomorrow?"

"Checking out some MMA clubs and seeing more of the city. Is it all right if I bring Saranna back for tea? She won't stay long. She's on nights this week."

"You don't have to ask my permission," Paris said soberly. "I'm still your thrall."

"I'm not at ease with that situation," Elvira said, gently imprisoning his hands. "Maybe we should announce our intention to marry. It's the real reason I came here, after all. What's the next step? Do I propose on bended knee, buy you an engagement ring?"

"Both are optional," Paris said. "But we could let it be known we have an understanding."

"Then let's do that. And now for option one."
She dropped to one knee. "Paris Evason – do you
have a middle name?"

"No such thing any more."

"Paris Evason, would you do me the honour –
the very great honour – of becoming my husband?"

"I would. With the greatest of pleasure." He
raised her up and held her admiringly at arm's
length. "I can't believe my good fortune. I wish we
could marry tomorrow!"

"What are the formalities, when the time
comes?"

"We book the nearest registry temple, or a
location of our choice. I wear white. You, as the
bride, have no dress code. Before any of that, you'll
have to seek my mother's approval. But please don't
let's talk about *her*. Not tonight!"

***

Saranna bounced in, made a quick circuit of the
apartment and pronounced it too small. "I'll
certainly keep my eyes peeled for something more
generous," she promised, " but as you can imagine,
Elvira, flats are at a premium in this region. Houses
even more so."

"There's no immediate rush," Elvira said. "Not
unless Despina wants this back, and even then she
wouldn't just throw me out. But – and you're the
first to know – Paris and I have decided to marry as
soon as he's of age."

"Brilliant!"

"So, we'll need a proper home in about five months. I don't suppose you're an expert wedding planner?"

"Afraid not. But I know a few people who – hello, what's this?" Saranna had picked up the book of Shelley's poems. "An artefact! How did you get it through?"

"Norvus arranged it. Vivette insisted."

Saranna read the dedication. "Paris, you're such a romantic."

"I try," he answered. Then, unexpectedly: "This portrait of Shelley doesn't do him justice. I saw him once."

Elvira was astonished. "When? How?"

"About three years ago, Lake Geneva in the summer of 1816 was in the top ten of TTI destinations. Many clients – mostly women, it must be said – wanted to see Byron, Shelley and their party arrive at Secheron. And regarding Byron, some wanted …" He paused, seeking a euphemism.

"A piece of him," Elvira suggested.

"Quite. So our usual monitoring services didn't suffice. GTC personnel were on the spot to ensure every traveller kept a respectful distance. If they didn't they'd be fined on their return – all of which played havoc with our schedules. As team leader I complained about the disruption and was shown some of the GTC visuals."

"And that's when you saw Shelley? What was he doing?"

"Standing apart from the others, looking introspective and remote. And undernourished."

126

"Fashionably thin," Saranna corrected. "How about being a time tourist, Elvira? I can see you're interested. Is there still a waiting list for that trip, Paris?"

"It doesn't work like that. The attraction's worn off now, but the original travellers will still be there."

"I must say I'm intrigued," Elvira admitted.

"Then let's do it!" Saranna clapped her hands. "You too, Paris."

"Absolutely not!" he said emphatically. "I'm never going into the past again!" Then, less forcibly, "but I'll supervise if you want. In fact, I insist."

"Then that's settled," Saranna declared.

"It would be reassuring to know Paris is monitoring us," Elvira said more quietly.

"You do remember what I told you about the delays?" he asked. "The costuming, the endless checks, the misfires?"

"I remember."

"We know all that," Saranna said impatiently.

"I can't do anything tomorrow. Exam results."

"The next day, then." Saranna was not to be put off.

Paris sighed. "I'll make the booking and confirm it with you. They'll have the program stored so there won't be any prep."

"And then what?" Elvira asked.

"Then you report to wardrobe at 10 am. You'll have a lot of waiting around for a trip that only lasts fifteen minutes."

"Not a very good salesman, is he?" Saranna remarked.

"I don't need to be. We're at capacity."

Elvira, sensing the beginnings of a spat, hastily dispatched him to the kitchen for tea and pastries. "Saranna," she continued, accosting her friend before she could follow him, "we have a free day tomorrow so what's on offer in theatres? Do you even have them any more? I'd like to see a play or a musical or a lunchtime concert. I haven't heard a note of music since I've been here, except the ambient sounds they were playing in Leisure 4 Lovers."

"Well spotted with regard to the music. TTI has a complete opt-out because it interferes with the brace resonances or something. Ask Paris. A mere century ago, a city-wide survey showed that most people wanted to chat quietly when eating, not have to shout above music. So, now, restaurants have to opt in if they want to play any, and ensure customers know in advance. Yours was a particularly noisy century, Elvira. You're bound to notice the difference. But rest assured, the theatres and concert halls are operating normally."

"I'm glad to hear it."

"As for what's on, let's see if the city info yields anything interesting."

To Elvira's delight, one of the arthouses was performing "The Immortal Hour".

"I *must* see that! We sang bits of it at school. I can't believe it's still in the repertoire."

"The Morii encourage us to cherish our myths," Paris said, handing out cakes, cake forks and mugs of fragrant tea. Elvira and Saranna continued to chat happily about the shows on offer. Only when Saranna – once more oblivious to the passing time – had suddenly rushed off, did Paris again voice misgivings.

"My love, you mustn't let Saranna railroad you into doing things you'd rather not. Are you totally in favour of this 1816 trip? It doesn't seem like you."

Elvira picked up the book of poetry, held if reverently. "It might not have been my preference before you said Shelley's portrait was unflattering. I've read these poems over and over, *really* read them, and they're wonderful. I just want to see what he's like."

"I do understand. And you'll probably think I'm worrying about nothing as usual. But *I* had a friend once, a reckless friend. We were inseparable. And it's easy to be caught up in things you later regret."

"What friend? What was his name?"

"Eadwine Jensson."

Elvira stared. "The boy who died in the avalanche?"

"The same. As I said, reckless. I'm talking about almost a decade ago. I was shy, unworldly, and he did much to put that right. Mostly by getting both of us into scrapes. On one particular occasion we took flyers to level ten, the top, and were racing one another. Something went wrong with my aircraft." He paused a moment. "If a flyer loses

129

power it will find the nearest exit point and drop one level, to a lane which supports a lower speed. If the fault persists, it will repeat the process until it can halt safely. To this day I still don't know what caused mine to fail, but it dropped lower and lower and didn't even halt at level one, the final lane. It just pancaked on down and smashed into the ground on level minus three – the Streeters' zone. An airbag protected me from the impact but I'd no defence against the ferals. They were all over the crash site immediately, stripping the flyer of usable components."

"Did they hurt you?"

"I assumed they were about to, and just froze. They thought I was in shock, hauled me out of the wreck and into a lock-up, and threw an old blanket round me. They'd decided to ransom me, or attempt to. They detailed the youngest among them - Kizzy, they called her – to find out if anyone would pay. I explained where my mother was, and how to contact her. No reaction. But when she heard I worked for the TTI, Kizzy looked delighted, drew a knife and began to cut my clothes off me. She slashed them to ribbons, and yet that blade never touched my skin. Her skill was amazing. Eventually I confessed I'd been off duty and wasn't wearing anything that would self-repair. She laughed and said in that case we should move straight onto proving I was alive and well. You know the drill, she added. One DNA sample. Not blood, as that would infer injury."

"You don't have to tell me the rest if you don't want to," Elvira said quietly.

"I must. I don't want us to have any secrets. No-one else knows, Elvira. Not my mother, not my employers. Eadwine knew, of course, but kept quiet to hide his share of the blame. Anyway: I was so shaken up I could do nothing. I thought I was finished – that Kizzy would get mad at me and use that knife. Instead she got rid of it, gave me some booze, squeezed onto the bunk next to me and pulled the blanket over us both. I still don't know if she was being kind or just following instructions. Maybe she thought it was my first time. At last my body remembered its training, she got her sample and was gone. Disappeared. I never saw her again.

Eadwine, meanwhile, had alerted the enforcers and they turned up in a suss bus with smoke bombs. They had me out of there in seconds. No-one accused me of trespass because the evidence of the flyer crash was there in front of them. I insisted I didn't need a medical check, so they put an oversized detention uniform on me and told me to be more careful in future. They hadn't even asked my name." He stopped speaking and brushed away a stray tear. "Sorry, I'd no idea that episode still carried such an emotional charge. It took me a while to recover and I never forgave Eadwine."

Elvira rested her head on his chest. "My poor love, keeping all that to yourself. And that poor girl, too. What kind of life does she have?"

"It's a harsh life, but the Streeters aren't destitute. The Morii wouldn't let that happen."

"And your friend – wasn't it his father who …?"

"Fell victim to the fraudsters and made me a time fugitive. Which kind of brings us full circle, doesn't it? Here we are."

"Here we are. Together."

He nuzzled her neck. "Now, about Saranna. All I'm saying where she's concerned is, don't acquiesce. You don't know this era. Sleep tuition isn't the same as experience. Oh, by the way -"

"What?"

"I sang in The Immortal Hour too. The Song of the Sidhe. My voice is indifferent but Rayah said I looked like an elfin prince. Maybe I did, then. No muscles on me."

"You wouldn't have a photograph, I suppose?"

"I would not."

"Then sing it to me. The Song of the Sidhe. Sing it!"

"That wouldn't be in my best interests. At the moment you think I'm absolute perfection – yes, you do! – and I'm not going to ruin that by singing. Tomorrow you'll hear it sung as it should be."

"Fair enough, muscle-man." Elvira hesitated a moment, then again broached the subject of Eva and the all-important message to Proxima 4.

"My best girl, I *know* you're impatient to make this official but could you bear to wait another week until I'm settled in my new post? Then we'll have *two* pieces of news and she might actually approve of my career change. Let's just enjoy ourselves first. You've got your musical to look forward to, and then you make your trip to Geneva - "

"I wish you were coming with me."

"You won't even think of me once you're there."

"This is all routine to you," Elvira persisted, "but I don't even know what a time machine looks like! This brace you keep mentioning. Does it enclose us? Is it claustrophobic?"

Paris retrieved his e-reader from under a cushion. "You can't *see* a brace. This is what you'll see – the standard duo model for couples or two friends. So, yes, you *are* enclosed, by interlaced circuitry, but you can see through the gaps."

Elvira studied the image. "That's so elegant! Not what I was expecting at all."

"We call it a lattice. And, there's no soundproofing. You can speak to the people outside your cubicle, as well as see them. Nothing to panic about. But before all that you'll have had your costume fitting, and I'm not allowed in that section. You might find it a little more hands-on then Leisure 4 Lovers!"

Chapter Five

The immaculately displayed costumes extended into the distance, forming a gentle arc as they neared the vanishing point. Elvira guessed they encircled the entire Heath on one of the TTI's upper levels. Every era was represented. A group of teenage girls, probably a school party, were choosing 1960's outfits with an air of great solemnity.

If they can't lose those expressions they'll stand out a mile, thought Elvira.

"You're the 1816 party?" inquired the wardrobe attendant assigned to her and Saranna. "Just one moment please." Two rails of dresses moved soundlessly toward them on a conveyor. "I'm afraid the choice is a little restricted today. Some items are still on loan."

"Are they originals or imitations?" Elvira asked.

"Originals. And if you're wondering how we avoided the artefact ruling, it doesn't apply here. These garments have only one destination – the time of their manufacture. Otherwise, they remain here. I assume neither of you has made this trip before? I thought not. I'll briefly explain the function of each item and leave you to familiarise yourselves with them. Your single undergarment, a shift, is made of linen. It has drawstrings at the back, so you'll have to lace one another up. The outer garment is free-flowing with a high waist,

134

fitted bodice and puff sleeves. Both items are ankle length. There is one pair of knee high stockings with garters, one pair of slippers, and an optional bonnet, shawl and reticule."

"Don't we get any boots?" asked Saranna. "Those slippers look like ballet pumps."

"All boots from this era are in circulation at the moment, or in for repair. The scriveners have just placed strict limits on what we can source. The popularity of this venue was left unrestricted for too long, which explains why we've had to ration visits to fifteen minutes. Three years ago, you could have stayed for much longer." She glanced at the nearest chronometer. "My next clients are due. When you've changed, leave your own clothes in the lockboxes provided, and affix your ID." She handed the women a tag each. "Do you require a zone of privacy?"

"Er ... er ... yes."

"I will set it as I leave. It's optical only and will deactivate when you step through it. Your escort will meet you in the main reception area."

"Just a moment," said Elvira. "Something's missing. Knickers? Pantaloons?"

"They didn't wear any. Pantaloons belong to the Victorian age. You should have done your homework, Ms. Jones!"

A shimmering effect similar to a heat haze sprang up, encircling the two novice travellers. The outlines of the chamber beyond were blurred and diffused.

"Well, shall we?" asked Saranna.

"They didn't wear much, did they?" Elvira said dubiously.

"Maybe they expected some chivalrous gentleman to put his greatcoat around their dainty shoulders," Saranna replied with a smirk.

"Pah!" said Elvira expressively. "I might just keep my knickers on."

"Maybe you should. It won't be very warm where we're going. The year without summer, remember? Volcanic rubble in the atmosphere."

"I was forgetting," Elvira admitted. "I hope this is going to be worth it."

"We're bound to be indoors," opined Saranna. "It makes the spotters' job easier."

As arranged, Paris met them in person to escort them to the lattice hall. He took one look at Elvira and smothered a grin. "Sorry, sorry! You look exactly like the women in that comedy. How did it go again? Oh, Miss Bonnet. Oh, Mr Bingle. Er, why have you brought that silly little handbag?"

"To put her knickers in if she decides to take them off," Saranna said mischievously.

"I'll pretend I didn't hear that," said Paris, still grinning.

Elvira thrust a ringlet out of her eyes and marched past them to the cubicles. This was all beginning to seem like an expensive mistake. But despite her doubts, or perhaps because of them, there were no technical issues nor misfires. A breeze sprang up, she drew her shawl more tightly about her, and looked around at the Hotel d'Angleterre, Secheron.

"Bit of a dump, isn't it?" said Saranna, beside her. "See that gaggle of women over there, looking squeaky clean in the boots we should've had? They've got to be our time tourists. And Byron must be in the middle of them. And – well, would you believe it! What were the chances of that?"

"What?"

"Those men on the edge of the group aren't husbands or lovers – they're GTC, keeping Milord from being molested. Look at the gent on the left in the frilly shirt. It's Norvus!"

The agent looked across and caught Elvira's eye momentarily. "He didn't know me," she said, puzzled.

"Of course he didn't! He's three years younger than he'll be when you meet him. Where's Shelley?"

"By himself with his nose in a book," Elvira said, pointing.

"Right. Now here's what we'll do. I'll fight my way through those hangers-on and try to grab Byron. The spotters will be distracted and that'll allow you to have a very short conversation with Shelley. Of *course* he won't ignore you. He's a man of breeding. I know you want to talk to him, so *do* it!"

She rushed off, and Elvira, eager now, approached the solitary figure leaning on a pillar. "Excuse me. Mr Shelley?"

He looked up. Two beautiful blue eyes, not sky blue like Paris' but deep indigo, regarded her with polite interest.

"May I beg a moment of your time?" Elvira went on hurriedly. She hadn't had tuition in Regency English, since it was assumed she wouldn't be speaking it, so she kept her sentences formal and hoped for the best.

"Of course you may," he responded, thrusting his book into one of his many pockets. "How may I address you, Miss …?"

"Call me Helen." She'd already chosen her alias. Helen – and Paris. He wouldn't be best pleased with her but she could always blame Saranna. "I've been reading your poetry, sir, and simply had to tell you how wonderful it is."

"I'm pleased my humble efforts have found favour with someone. May I enquire where you purchased them?"

"From a quaint little bookshop in Hampstead," she replied truthfully. "In Queen Mab, your description of a voyage to the stars was … amazing. I believe such things will be possible one day."

"Let us hope so," he answered seriously.

"May I ask a personal question?" she went on, very aware of the seconds ticking soundlessly past.

"Assuredly."

"The poet in Alastor – is that you?"

"The suffering outcast?" He smiled ruefully. "I can see why you think so, given my recent history. I assume you're acquainted with it?"

"Yes," she began. A commotion across the hall interrupted her.

"Lord Byron's entourage. Don't be concerned – he's used to it. My brave Mary is presently attempting to extricate her sister from that mob."

Several people, including Norvus and a reluctant Saranna, had broken away from the crowd.

"Here comes my companion with our guardian," Elvira said dolefully. "I'm afraid our conversation has to end."

"It need not. When not besieged by devotees, Byron hosts literary evenings for his friends. Please seek us out. You seem in need of like-minded company."

Norvus paused to obtain new instructions. A second GTC agent seized Elvira's arm, none too gently, and marched her and Saranna toward a nearby arboretum. "I have them," he reported. "Clear for retrieval."

Instinctively Elvira hitched up her skirt and aimed a kick at him, just too late. 1816 dissolved in a swirl of meadowsweet.

The two friends almost collided on their return to the TTI cubicle. Saranna was flushed and grinning from ear to ear.

"What happened?" asked Elvira. "I heard a lot of laughter and cheering."

"I elbowed my way up to Byron and gave him a big smacking kiss," Saranna related gleefully. "And then I said, 'oh, beg pardon, Milord, that was too forward of me!' And he replied 'not at all, m'dear. Do it again!' I would've, too, but an agent manhandled me away. Did you speak to Shelley?"

Elvira outlined the conversation. "He's intriguing," she concluded. "But I knew he *would* be."

The cubicle door slid back and a GTC representative beckoned them out. "Ms Sefora, you physically interacted with a denizen. Standard fine, fifty pounds. Ms Jones, a caution: you spoke with a denizen, but you kept your distance and observed propriety." He handed over two penalty slips and was gone.

Paris, initially silent, walked them back to the costume floor. "You were only supposed to *look* at him," he reproached Elvira after she and Saranna had retrieved their own clothes. "Was that your doing, Saranna?"

"I caused a diversion. She made her own mind up," Saranna said blandly. "Listen, lovers, I have to dash. Got a 4pm start today, freighter reschedule, and first I want to go home and scrub my feet. That arboretum mud went straight through those silly shoes."

"Next time, get some chivalrous gent to throw his coat over the puddles," Elvira said lightly.

Paris was briefly waylaid by an elderly colleague, thus giving Elvira a chance to add a hasty whisper: "Don't forget what we talked about just now. Send the details to Despina's city guide."

"Will do," Saranna promised. "See you in two days. Can't wait!"

"More girl stuff?" asked Paris.

"Yes, as it happens. It's my birthday the day after tomorrow."

140

"Elvira, why didn't you mention it sooner? Thursday's going to be my first full day in Construction. I can't request any more leave."

"It's fine, you don't need to. What's happening tomorrow? I take it you passed the exam?"

"Why wouldn't I? It was foregone. I was just speaking with one of my supervisors, Cyprian. To begin with he's going to let me practise assembly, using bits and pieces and leftovers. Then I start my first proper assignment."

"And you're looking forward to it, aren't you?"

"Very much. Now let's get out of here before someone asks me to repair something."

"Aren't you going to ask how old I'll be?"

"And get a slap?"

"I won't, I promise. Would you believe twenty-eight?"

"*No!*"

"Yes."

Paris kissed her in full view of the technical staff. "In that case, since I can't be with you on the day, we'll mark the occasion *now*. I think I can find my way back to La Chanson d'Amour, with that lovely view of the Heath – and I'm sure I can do justice to the crepes this time."

"You spoil me."

"Only because I love you."

Later, gazing at the landscape which was both familiar and unfamiliar, Paris said: "Do you think I'll ever stop feeling nostalgic for the life I nearly had?"

"Only you can answer that," Elvira replied.

Paris nodded in agreement. "Maybe we should take a trip back there one day. We do have some unfinished business with a cornfield! Now, tell me all about 1816."

Elvira did so. "Once Saranna had pointed it out, it was obvious who the time travellers were," she concluded. "They were too neat and tidy. Their hair, their crease-free gowns, everything. You don't look like that after rattling along for miles in a post-chaise!"

"And thus, we have proof that the future informs the past," Paris said, instantly serious. "Byron quit the hotel because he was sick of being spied on and stared at. He rented the Villa Diodati – and we all know about the famous ghost story evenings and the origins of Frankenstein. None of that might have happened if it hadn't been for a bunch of nosey time-travellers."

"And they didn't even realise what they'd done." Elvira matched his mood. "Doesn't that prove there's still a way to make benign changes without screwing things up? Every moment I was speaking with Shelley I was thinking that this perceptive, gifted man had only six more years to live."

"At school we often debated the immutability of time," Paris reflected. "The consensus was, things had to *appear* to stay the same. Not quite the same thing as unchanging. The GTC scriveners doubtless have their eyes on it all, but unfortunately neither you nor I have eyes on *them*."

"True," Elvira said slowly, "but maybe Despina does. Before she puts in an appearance, I'm going to read all I can about Shelley's death by shipwreck. Maybe there are anomalies. I have to find out."

"Well, it'll keep you out of mischief, I suppose," Paris said indulgently.

***

"And are you sure this can all be concluded today, Saranna?"

"In your case, yes, because you know the result you're after. I've seen people dithering over catalogues and holograms for days on end, but you're not a ditherer."

"Thanks for the vote of confidence." Elvira stared across the softly lit vestibule with its arc of flowing script above: "Ace My Face."

"Having second thoughts?" Saranna inquired.

"No. Honestly. I just don't want you to be hanging around all day."

"It's your birthday! I'm not going to leave you on your own. Anyway, you won't be here all day. Here's the running order: you'll tell the clinician exactly what you want, namely, more emphasis on eyes, straight bridge to the nose, more prominent cheekbones. She'll raise a hologram accordingly. And you'll hate it, because those changes don't add up to a whole. Then she'll show you the effect you're really after. These women know what they're doing. She'll focus the enhancer, start the program, and you'll simply relax into it."

143

"And it isn't uncomfortable?"

"It feels like someone's gently stroking your face. Pretend it's Paris."

"This is all *for* him," Elvira said a little too vehemently.

"And to impress his mother," Saranna remarked.

"That too. Er – if you haven't had the treatment how do you know how it feels?"

"Hearsay," Saranna said unconvincingly, and they both laughed. "Also, I did want to look a bit more like the Plessis poster."

Elvira straightened her shoulders. "Right, let's do this. Where do I check in?"

Saranna was absolutely right, of course. Elvira's initial idea of a new look was nothing like the regal, dignified woman who strode out of the processing booth that day.

"Oh, wow," Saranna said, for once lost for words.

"You shouldn't have waited," Elvira scolded. "You'll be late for work."

"I'm *always* late. Are you getting a new coiffure to match?"

"Not now. I've an MMA session booked. Don't worry, my sculptress Adelaide assured me that this face can tolerate the odd whack or two – better than the previous version could. I'm off to find out!"

"See that pretty young lad waiting to pay?" Saranna whispered as they strolled past endless mirror images of themselves. "I was talking to him

144

before he went in. He's a budding actor, trying to impress his lady love."

"I'm sure she'll appreciate it. He looks like Narcissus."

"True. But his girl's over there by the door – and he hasn't once taken his eyes off *you*! Watch out, he's coming over."

The newly beautiful young man fixed an adoring gaze on Elvira, and declaimed: "Is this the face that launched a thousand ships, and burned the topless towers of Ilium?"

Saranna suppressed a giggle.

"Young sir," Elvira said severely, "you haven't introduced yourself."

"I'm Nestor."

"Nestor, I have no claim on you. Go to your lover. She's waiting."

Nestor didn't budge. "Here will I dwell, for heaven is in these lips, and all is dross that is not Helena!"

Nestor's other half approached quizzically. Thinking quickly, Elvira put on her Simply Qubit all-purpose smile. "Good day, Ms -?"

"Deltress Paige."

"Deltress, I'm Helen Adelaide, customer feedback. I've just asked Nestor a few quick questions about his experience today. He's graciously awarded us a vote of excellence. Would you, as his partner, care to give your opinion on our work?"

Deltress seized Nestor by the chin and inspected him. "You've done well with such

145

unpromising material. Eight out of ten. Come on, you."

Nestor trailed unhappily behind her toward the exit, pausing to look back a couple of times. Saranna was still trying not to laugh.

"Do you think he was sincere?" Elvira asked her.

"He looked as though he was."

"Oh dear. I wasn't expecting that."

"Well, full marks for defusing a tricky situation. Better than having an Elvira-style punch-up in Ace My Face's foyer. Now let's leg it. Otherwise we'll *both* be late!"

***

Elvira arrived home, showered, put on one of her new dresses and waited for Paris. At last he arrived, grimy but happy.

"Did it go well?" she asked.

He halted, letting go of his shoulder bag and staring at her in dismay. "Elvira, your face! What have you *done*?"

"I thought you'd like it," she faltered.

"Was this Saranna's idea?"

"Not this time. It was mine."

"Then why didn't you tell me what you were planning?" he demanded.

"Why are you so upset?" she countered. "What's wrong with my new face?"

"Nothing. It's beautiful." His voice trembled slightly. "But it isn't the face I fell in love with. Please tell me you remember."

She remembered, then. How could she have forgotten any detail of that first eventful day? She'd scraped Paris off the road, taken him home, clothed and fed him, soothed his nightmares and, tired out, had dozed off next to him in her appalling passion-killer pyjamas. And he, waking in the dawn light, had watched while she slept and fallen in love with her face. The face she'd just discarded.

Impulsively she hugged him, unmindful of the smears of relay oil transferring themselves to her dress. "I'm sorry, I really am. I just didn't think."

"My best and only girl," he said gently, "I'm at fault as usual. I shouldn't have reacted like that. You have an indomitable will, my love, and I'm sure there'll be other times I'll try and oppose it. I'll always lose, and rejoice in my defeat."

"You'll make me cry in a minute," Elvira said. "Where did you learn to make such pretty speeches?"

"At school, of course."

"Along with the sex?"

"Uh-huh."

"Does that mean I'm forgiven?"

"I suppose so. Here – let me show you a sample of today's work." He undid his bag and drew out a strip of circuitry, just a few inches long. "This is a segment of the frame that surrounds all time travellers. It -"

147

The tiny system glowed feebly red for a moment.

"Should it have done that?" Elvira whispered.

"In situ, yes. Not in isolation. It must be picking up stray emanations from the next floor down. If it becomes fully active at midday when the system comes online – if it glows gold – then ..."

"Then what?"

"It means I could in theory build an entire time apparatus here, with a borrowed power source." He laughed, breaking the spell. "Just daydreaming. It probably picked up some random discharge from something shutting down for the night. Look at it now. Dead as a doornail."

"Shouldn't you find out what happened? It might do something you can't handle."

"No such thing. And even if there were, I can't access the generator floor. Physicists only. If anything else happens I'll report it. Now, let's go and scrub up. I think we can both fit in there - "

"If not, we can have fun trying."

"- and then we'd better order some supper. What would you like?"

"Fake fish and chips," Elvira said promptly.

"No, you don't want that. You really don't. Pick something else."

"What happened to all the cod?"

Paris sighed. "Fished to extinction. We ate them all."

"Couldn't someone have gone back in time and grabbed some more?"

"We ate those too."

Elvira deliberated. "All right, we'll order a meze from that Greek place Despina likes."

"Rhodos? They don't do deliveries, just meals to go. And much as I adore you, Elvira, I'm not in shape for a solo expedition to Level Five."

Elvira gave up. "TTI canteen?"

"TTI canteen. At least their chips are edible."

When they returned, after a surprisingly tasty all-day breakfast, they immediately noticed a flashing amber light on Despina's coffee table messaging system. "Well, it's either *for* her or *from* her," Elvira said, slightly apprehensive. "Better play it. She might want to crash here."

She almost trod on the mini circuit board and was sure she'd noticed a fading red glow at one end. Before she could alert Paris, Despina's voice said:

"Hello you two. If my calculations are correct, and they always are, today's when Paris' time circuitry displays an anomalous power signature, here in this room. It'll happen again and he'll want to notify someone. It's essential that he doesn't. I can't divulge details at this point, but present patterns suggest you'll be involved in a timeline restructure. You know how these things work; I can't give you guidance. Things just have to play out. Paris, this has nothing to do with the Point Nemo killers. You're in no danger. Elvira, congratulations on the new face. You'll find it will open many doors. I'll stay in touch."

The message ended.

"Cryptic," Elvira remarked. "I wonder what she's getting us mixed up in?"

"I'm sure it's nothing we can't cope with," Paris said cheerfully. "No danger means just that."

No danger to *you*, Elvira thought. She kept the thought to herself.

Pari's first week at Construction swiftly turned into a fortnight. Two scholarly Stats girls, whom they'd met in the canteen, offered to show Elvira what was left of the old London. In return, Elvira treated them to a Covent Garden ballet: Giselle, which was still in the repertoire. As one of the earliest examples of girl power, this wasn't surprising. Then, on his first weekend off, Paris braved his lingering fear of flying to accompany Elvira on a three-seater flivver tour of the city.

But at last, Elvira made a solitary trip to the spaceport and its booths for interstellar communication. There she mingled with returning MetroLondoners and visiting off-worlders, all recording variations on "down safely, missing you already." When it was her turn she composed herself stoically and, error-free on her first attempt, told Eva Mariosa that she and Paris were in love and that she intended to marry him as soon as he was of age. She remembered to cite his promotion at work as a sign of maturity and reliability. "Please give us your blessing," she concluded. "It would mean so much to him."

The tiny digital drive was then packaged, sealed and sent on the first stage of its journey to Proxima 4. Paris joined her in the evening for dinner at the MetroLondon Space Hilton. Saranna sent champagne to their table.

In the fortnight or more before Eva's reply was expected, Elvira and Paris exchanged rings, spent a fun evening at Rhodos, went to several concerts and walked the city in a kind of euphoria – prompting Nimue Pamina to enquire, via her wall vlog, whether the gods of Olympus had returned to Earth. The loved-up couple didn't notice, and Saranna, for once, said nothing.

Paris radiated contentment, and Cyprian praised his diligent work. While he was busy at Construction, Elvira visited the nearest British Library terminal and began her research into Shelley's fateful sea journey. She found more questions than answers.

At last, the scheduled transport from Proxima 4 emerged from the Morii hyperway and nudged itself ponderously into Earth orbit. With exasperating slowness, shuttles and landing hoppers began transferring good and passengers to various locations on the globe. Paris and Elvira waited impatiently in the al fresco café where they'd first met Saranna. She was supposed to be placing an announcement on the main info display when their item was ready for collection, but to their surprise Despina appeared, in person.

"Eva seems to think I'm her personal courier," she said, trying not to look jaded. "She marked this message high priority and told me it wasn't communal booth material."

"Mother can be such a snob sometimes," Paris muttered.

"So," said Despina with uncustomary patience, "where shall we play it? There are several discreet GTC venues near here."

"The nearest, then. As long as people don't think we're being arrested."

"I don't understand," Elvira said, frowning. "It was just a courtesy message. Nothing to do with the GTC."

"*Anything* involving you is a GTC matter," Despina contradicted. "Now let's get this done. I'm in the middle of a case."

Eva Mariosa looked tired. "My dear Elvira: if I'd known, when my son was still a child, that he'd one day secure a proposal from a strong wealthy woman such as you, this answer would be very different. But today I can only say, with regret, that I cannot approve this match. Your wedding cannot go ahead because Paris is, in effect, already married – or he *will* be. As soon as he is of age, a contract I made sixteen years ago will mature. He is in an arranged marriage with Lelza, only daughter of Bryony Dawn. At the time I authorised this, the finances of House Mariosa were in a parlous state and it made sense to unite with House Dawn. Bryony ensured that Paris had a good start in life. I attach an electronic copy of the marriage contract and the address of my attorney, should you wish to explore the possibility of contesting it.

Paris – I assume you're hearing this - I may have been remiss in not keeping you informed. I wanted you to enjoy your youth unencumbered by responsibilities. I regret you had to find out this way."

Paris had turned so pale that Elvira thought he might faint. In fact, he was white with anger. "How *dare* she! How dare she sign away my future! I'll have nothing to do with this Lelza."

"I'll pay her mother off," Elvira said promptly.

"You can't," Despina told her. "Don't get your hopes up. You'd have to be related to either family, by birth, before they'd consider a settlement."

"Then what about Paris' debt of honour to me? He's made that very public."

"That, and his thrall status, ends as soon as he's of age."

"I'll renew it," Paris declared.

"It wouldn't carry any weight."

"Despina, does this bombshell have something to do with the strange message you left us a month ago?" Elvira asked suspiciously.

"Nothing. I'd no idea that Eva had done this. She kept it very very quiet. As for the message, just follow my instructions, Paris. The TTI doesn't need to know about the circuit phenomenon."

He nodded, still fuming.

"Regarding Eva, the best advice I can give you at the moment is to avoid kneejerk reactions. Let's concentrate on your strengths."

"Do I have any?"

"I can think of two straight away. Your work upgrade is even more vocational than before, and you can't be forced to give it up. You can retain some of your old life. Build on that. Secondly, any marriage can be annulled if there's no consummation."

"There won't be."

"What I don't know is, how long you'd have to wait before applying for an annulment. It could be years."

"I don't suppose there's any point in talking to Rayah?" ventured Elvira.

Despina sighed. "I was just thinking that myself, but the Morii don't involve themselves in personal disputes. It's always the bigger picture where they're concerned. They maintain the hyperways, govern the Consortium of Worlds, provide finance, keep tabs on the scriveners and educate our men."

"Then at least have this attorney look into House Dawn's background."

"She's probably done that already. If there was any mud to be raked up, she'd have found it."

Elvira switched her attention to Paris. "What about *your* family history? Any dirt there?"

"None that I know of. And I'm sure House Dawn would have been onto it if there were. But you've just given me an idea."

Elvira scrutinised him, worried. His anger had subsided but now he was too calm, his eyes bright with sudden inspiration. "What?"

"What if *I* suddenly became disreputable? What if I – " he glanced at Despina – "aid and abet illicit time journeys, for instance?"

154

Despina caught his drift immediately. "That might be the way to go. We at the GTC were wondering what would set you off. You were always such a punctilious individual."

"Boring, in other words," Paris said lightly. "A man can change. You'll see."

The wall chronometer pinged discreetly. It was midday.

"Might I suggest," Despina said, "That you hurry back to your – or should I say *my* – apartment? You might find a light in your darkness. And don't lose Eva's message chip. You'll need that to spur you on. Elvira, be strong."

"I will," she asserted.

"Excellent. Now go."

They stumbled breathlessly into the apartment to find it suffused in a golden glow. Elvira immediately thought of CoherenceCo and the receptor box. The circuit strip lay where they'd left it, shining gently and reassuringly.

"She knew," Paris said. "Here's what's going to happen, and I'm afraid it will mean the end of our social life for the foreseeable. We have three months and two and a half weeks left before my birthday on February the 26th. During that time, I'll be working all the hours there are, evenings and weekends too, until I've completed my own time machine here. Here, where we're standing. I'll acquire everything I can from Cyprian, and if he can't supply all the components I'll help myself from the TTI reserves. Piecing together Despina's hints about a time restructure, I'd say that I provide the tech and you, Elvira, have all the adventures. Without interference from the GTC."

"Adventures? Alone?"

"It seems that way. I imagine I'll be here, monitoring you. Do you want to see Shelley again? It looks as though you'll have the chance."

"A chance to alter *his* timeline?"

"Maybe. Too early to say. It's what you wanted, isn't it?"

Elvira looked flustered, unusual for her. "Paris, slow down. If we do any of this, and it looks as though Despina wants us to, then it needs to be done *carefully*."

"When executing this venture, I'll be ultra-careful."

"So I should think. Before you start on this work-fest we need to see Eva's attorney. Together. And is there anything on social media about this Lelza? What does she look like? Does she live alone or with her mother?"

"Elvira," Paris said warningly, "social media isn't the free-for-all it used to be. Nothing's anonymous. Check your history program! As soon as we investigate Lelza, she'll know, and I'd rather not rattle that particular cage just yet. But by all means let's see what the attorney can tell us."

***

Two days later they nervously kept an appointment with Aurelia Neve, LLM, at her chambers in the Grays Inn Road. Elvira hadn't expected to be seen so promptly, but to her surprise found that Eva had already been in touch, explaining that she now had doubts about the match, and instructing Aurelia to give every assistance to the devoted young couple. Aurelia had accordingly cleared space in her diary.

"You must really have impressed my mother," Paris whispered as he and Elvira were being shown in.

"I think *you* might have had something to do with it, " Elvira whispered back.

"No. Never me," Paris said.

Aurelia Neve, pint-sized and middle-aged, was as sharp as a tack and determined to fight for her clients. "Your mother is quite correct," she told Paris, "in stating that your vocation takes precedence over any plans Lelza has for you. I've re-examined the original document because, as I'm sure you both know, a minor slip in the wording can often invalidate all or part of a contract such as this. I'm pleased to inform you that there *is* such a loophole. Perhaps you'd care to examine the text for yourselves."

The screen aligned itself to face them.

"There is no restriction on the number of hours Paris can work, save that paragraph b3 of Section 10 specifies that he must consort with his wife no less than one day, twenty four hours, per week. Consort, in present legal parlance, simply means being in one another's company. The word no longer has a sexual or marital definition, and thus has been wrongly applied here – possibly by an AI."

"What *is* the correct wording?" Elvira asked curiously.

"I'd have to confer lengthily with my colleagues to be sure of that. At the moment it doesn't even say the married couple have to be alone! But, perhaps, 'live in connubiality'?"

Elvira winced.

"Suffice it to say, I'd never have allowed a document like this out of *my* office! Paris will have a generous amount of independence – which I'm sure wasn't House Dawn's intention. The bad news is, Paris' best and probably only hope of an annulment is if he refrains from consummating the marriage."

"So we've been told."

"I hope your informant mentioned willpower. For believe me, Paris, Lelza will do all she can to seduce you. Girls in her situation are relentless and many are successful."

"Do you have anything on file about her?" he asked, prompted by a nudge from Elvira. "Her address, her ambitions? An image?"

"Her age?" Elvira interjected.

"I do know her age, as her birthdate was appended to the original agreement. She's now twenty-four."

"Is that *all*?" muttered Paris. "Does she still live with her mother?"

"No. Lelza has lodgings in Barnet Heights."

"Is that prestigious?" inquired Elvira.

"It might be, if it weren't overshadowed by a grain tower. Lelza is studying plant biology."

"It sounds to me as if she doesn't want to *be* married."

"Oh, she does – but only to please her mother and her House. Here's the one photo I was able to obtain." Aurelia touched the screen and Lelza's image appeared. She was skinny and pale, with cold blue eyes, thin mouth and wispy shoulder-length blonde hair. She wore white, which didn't suit her pallor.

"She looks eminently resistible," Paris remarked.

"And no earthly use as a bodyguard," Elvira concluded. "Aurelia, in your opinion would I now have to step down from that position? After all, Eva hired me despite Paris' forthcoming nuptials, and I have the GTC's backing too. If I were to accompany Paris on his visits to Lelza – in my professional capacity of course – it would surely put a damper on her enthusiasm."

"I'll certainly look into it," Aurelia promised.

"A glimmer of hope?" Elvira inquired on their way home.

"I'm not sure," Paris said. "It's too soon to tell. For now, I'll stay focused on my work. I've just time for a quick lunch with you – in the canteen again, I'm afraid – and then it's back to being Cyprian's apprentice. What will you do? Meet with Saranna?"

"She's still involved with the sightseers on board that cruiser. But Janine and Petra from Stats are keen to meet up again."

Paris brightened. "Well, if they're around, tell them I'll look in later if I can. They're clever and sensible. I'm not trying to choose your friends for you, but - "

"You prefer them to Saranna." Elvira finished the sentence for him.

"Saranna has her uses. But at the moment I think we could do with some stability."

Making use of the e-message board in the canteen, Elvira arranged to meet with the Stats girls at 4.30, and spent the early afternoon tidying the flat and clearing as much space as possible for Paris to situate his project. She wasn't sure how large a time cubicle for one actually was, but she was guessing – rightly or wrongly – that it would be about the size of a 21st century telephone box. At least, ceiling height wouldn't be a problem – one advantage of having an apartment in the middle of a cavern. And this realisation led to a light-bulb moment: they could create a mezzanine level, for sleeping.

Pleased with herself, she continued with her clean-up, and at teatime went to the canteen. Petra greeted her with a conspiratorial grin.

"I hear you were given a caution!"

"Yes, on my first time-tourist trip," Elvira confessed, smiling also. "How did you know?"

"The TTI tattlegraph. Also, that jobsworth who gave you the ticket happens to be my brother. So, I know how your friend Saranna distracted the spotters and allowed you to talk with Shelley."

"It was an impulse on her part," Elvira said a little cautiously. "I paid her fine."

"Was it worth it?"

"To meet Shelley? Oh yes."

"Shall I tell her?" Petra asked Janine.

"Tell me what?"

"Fess up, girl," Janine advised.

Petra sighed. "Oh, why not? Eadwine must have bragged to Paris about it years ago, so there's no point in being secretive. Like you, Elvira, I booked a fifteen minute trip into the past. I was still at university, studying the piano and writing a thesis on the 19th century Romantic composers. It was my dream to see and maybe even speak to Franz Liszt. I was the only time traveller at one of his salon performances."

"And?"

"And his entire audience consisted of duchesses, countesses, princesses, et cetera. I couldn't get anywhere near him. I began to think he must be a colossal snob, but then realised one had to be titled, or at least wealthy, to be invited by the salon owner." Petra paused to sip her coffee. "At the time, I'd had a couple of dates with Eadwine Jensson. He was working in Dispatch in those days, not maintenance, and my brother introduced us. I was feeling so miserable at having wasted my money that I poured out my troubles to him, and he said he'd fix it."

Just then, Paris hurried up to the table. "Sorry to crash your girl time, Elvira, but Cyprian wants me to work till seven tonight. I begged fifteen minutes just to tell you I'll be late." Then, looking around at the slightly guilty faces: "Were you talking about me? Please say you were!"

"Petra used to date Eadwine," Elvira said.

"Who didn't?"

Petra blushed a little. "We knew you were friends. He never told you he'd taken me to see Franz Liszt? Illegally?"

Paris hastily pulled up a chair. "I'd no idea. I thought he'd never time-tripped, legally or otherwise. How did he go about it?"

"Does it matter?"

"It *might* do."

Petra resumed her tale. "He turned up with some flouncy dress and told me to put it on. *He* was wearing some silly military uniform, all braid and boots, filched from Wardrobe no doubt. Then we took a multi-cube to the lattice hall, where I'd been that morning. It was deserted and mostly unlit. Eadwine led the way to a little chamber at the far end where there were two cubicles, idling."

"Because they were on test," Paris said. "Surely he didn't ...?"

"He bundled me into one, made a few adjustments and crammed in after me. Then he gave me a recall bracelet, almost as an afterthought."

"No-one was monitoring you?"

"Well ... no. I thought it was a bit weird."

"Weird?" echoed Paris. "Downright dangerous. Three major safety infringements. I can't believe he *did* that!"

"Could we have been lost?"

162

"Lost, vapourised, you name it. Go on, what else did he do?"

"We materialised outside some mansion, not the one where the soiree had been held. It was twilight. A manservant opened the door and I saw a few coins change hands. Then Eadwine said 'see you later' and sauntered off."

"He left you there?"

"I just said so, didn't I? The flunky looked me up and down disparagingly and asked how he should announce me. I said, as honestly as I could without knowing the date, that I was Petra Rosalind of the London Royal Academy of Music. He ushered me through some double doors and there was Liszt, about thirty years older than when I'd last seen him less than a day ago."

"That must have been surreal," Elvira said.

"It was, all of it. I must have looked and sounded a complete idiot. But Liszt was so kind and courteous. He invited me to play for him, which I did. Two of the Consolations. He seemed pleased." Petra's expression softened as she remembered. "I finally summoned enough nerve to ask if he'd play one of his show pieces. He chose the Mephisto Waltz No. 1. Then *I* played La Campanella. And so on. The music took over and we just kept on playing. Until the manservant, Alfons, came in and said we were keeping the domestic staff awake!" Petra giggled. "I suppose they had to be up really early to clear the fireplaces or something. After that, we just talked. Alfons brought us hot chocolate."

163

"Where was Eadwine all this time?" asked Elvira.

"I never found out. Eventually he rolled up drunk and Alfons kept him outside. Then Liszt asked, very seriously, if I knew that my young companion had said I was a woman of the night, a present for the maestro, and had bribed Alfons to let me in."

Paris swore under his breath.

"I was so embarrassed I couldn't answer. Liszt calmly took out some monogrammed notepaper and inscribed a few sentences. 'I've addressed this to your Principal, endorsing your musical proficiency and saying that in my estimation you could teach piano to an advanced level,' he said. 'This should guarantee you a generous income. I suggest you dispense with that young man forthwith.' And I did, just as soon as I was back here. It took three attempts for the auto-retrieval to activate."

"Thank you for sharing," Paris said sombrely. "I always regretted ghosting Eadwine. Now I feel justified. Elvira, I'll see you tonight. *You* decide how much to tell our friends about Eadwine and me."

"Why did you give up music?" Elvira asked Petra. "Was it something to do with Liszt?"

"Well, yes. Seeing him young, and then – not so young. All that adulation, all those hangers-on, gone. The music industry's always been driven by the search for something new, and all the hard work I was putting in suddenly didn't seem worthwhile. Maths, on the other hand, is predictable and safe."

164

"So you went for stability." Elvira recalled Paris' description of the girls. "Now could either of you help me with something?"

"If we can."

Elvira outlined her idea for a mezzanine floor. "But," she concluded, "I need to know who owns the flat. They might object."

Petra and Janine conferred. "All we know is, the TTI flats aren't rented as such," Janine said. "They're assigned. Yours is designated tourist accommodation so it would be assigned by the spaceport. I'm sure Despina will have advised them that she's appointed you her guest."

"If it's owned by the spaceport, wouldn't Saranna know who to approach?"

"Worth a try, since Despina's not around. I bet Saranna could come up with some stylish ideas for it too."

Paris, when Elvira shared her plans that evening, was all in favour. "And it'll keep Saranna out of mischief for a while!"

"I ... didn't say anything more to the girls about Eadwine," Elvira told him hesitantly. "It didn't seem right."

"Did they ask?"

"No."

"Then that's my moral duty discharged, I'm happy to say."

"You still missed Eadwine, didn't you?"

"Until today, yes. We all thought him charismatic, adventurous. I wanted to be more like him. Now, after hearing Petra's story, I realise he

165

was selfish and dangerous, prepared to risk the life of a girl he hardly knew."

"I'm glad he's out of your system at last. You're going to need all your resilience to deal with Lelza."

Paris didn't answer immediately. "If Petra *hadn't* gone back in time and met Liszt, she wouldn't have changed careers nor met me. She wouldn't have given Eadwine his character and I'd still be lamenting him. Time plays its tricks on us all."

***

Saranna was delighted to be involved in the mezzanine project, and knew exactly how to get permission for the work.

"There's only one rule other than the usual regulations," Elvira said. "Make it as basic as possible in case Despina wants it changed."

"Or, make it so beautiful she doesn't want to change it!" said Saranna airily. "I've an idea. We're always extending the spaceport, and the only viable direction is downward. Just recently the contractors found the remains of an old cinema which they thought was twentieth century or thereabouts. Art Deco. Anyway, an interior designer called Albie Nellison, whom I happen to know, brought the excavation to a halt until he'd salvaged some artefacts. I'll find out what he's done with them. All right if I commission some designs?"

"Go ahead. I love Art Deco."

"Don't forget to tell him about the brace reverberation," Paris added. "It shouldn't be a problem if he uses the right materials."

The day after, Albie, tall and talkative, was hustled into the apartment by an enthusiastic Saranna. "Excellent ceiling height," he remarked. "You'll still have plenty of headroom on both levels."

He sent a self-guided measuring cube to record the relevant dimensions, then made some quick sketches. "I think I have just the thing. Saranna told you about the cinema? Wonderful find, perfectly preserved. To either side of the screen were two art deco trees with slender branches entwined. I was looking for somewhere to feature them and this is ideal. I can print reproductions quickly and easily. This is purely for decoration, you understand; the loadbearing joists will be further back. The floor can be mahogany with the interlaced effect continuing along the safety rail. The staircase could be a traditional spiral, discreetly to one side. And you'll need downlighters to offset the shadow beneath the structure. Crescent moons, I think. There'll be no furnishings up there except a bed, correct? I recommend a futon for less weight, and it'll hardly be seen from your leisure area. Or perhaps you'd prefer a curtain across?"

Paris and Elvira could scarcely keep pace with such a torrent of ideas. Albie promised some finished sketches on the morrow and loped away.

"One more thing," said Saranna before she followed him. "Assuming he's your choice, you'll need to move out while his team does the work. There are several tickets left for the next flight to the Polar Orbiter in three days' time. It's a luxury mini-break: no science, no astronomy, just dining and relaxation and looking at the Earth below."

Elvira sighed. "It sounds lovely, but Paris doesn't have any more leave due. We'll manage. We can sleep in his old apartment and have all our meals in the canteen. It's only for a couple of days, isn't it? While Paris is at work I'll go to the British Library or shop for some futons."

Paris looked less than happy.

"And if any of his ex-workmates try any nonsense I'll deal with them. Severely."

It was an uncomfortable few days. The TTI maintenance teams weren't being confrontational, but away from the bedrock everyday noise levels were raised, and Paris' contemporaries seemed to spend most of their leisure time running up and down corridors and banging doors. They all seemed to manage on a couple of hours' sleep. Paris, healthily tired every night, slept well enough, but Elvira resorted to lying in each morning once everyone was at work.

At last, on the fourth morning, Saranna appeared and announced that the mezzanine was complete. Albie, fidgety and anxious, was on hand to deal with any queries. There were none. His initial sketches had transformed themselves into an elegant, tasteful addition to the previously basic living space. He had added a few Alphonse Mucha posters to the main area, so its functionality would be less marked.

"It's perfect," Elvira said at last. Paris agreed.

"Great!" declared Saranna. "In that case, Albie has a favour to ask."

They looked at him inquiringly.

"Would you," he ventured, "permit me to photograph my work and use it in my latest brochure?"

"Take as many pictures as you want, as long as I'm not in them," Paris said promptly.

"I'd prefer not to be in them either," Elvira said after a pause. "Not without Despina's approval."

"Just one, to add perspective?" Albie persisted.

"I can do that!" Saranna chirped, and posed coquettishly on the stairs while he prowled about with various lenses.

"That should be enough," he said at last.

"Guys," said Saranna, "I've just had an idea."

"Not again," groaned Paris.

"Ingrate! Just listen. You wanted more background on Lelza, right? Without her realising it was you? How about if Albie were to deliver mailshots to her entire block? Brimstone Heights, was it?"

"Barnet."

"She's bound to be impressed. I reckon she'll at least want some makeover suggestions. Her mother's loaded, right, so no problem there. Then, if she takes the bait, Albie can say he needs some before and after photos. Even if there's no after,

you could still see what's there now. You can learn
a lot from a person's lifestyle."

"That's sneaky," Paris objected.

"Oh, come on, Paris! Don't be so *correct*!
Your wellbeing's at stake here!"

"Do it," Elvira said.

***

Over the next few weekends, the highlight of
Elvira's life was watching Paris as he worked. It
was a delight to watch him. She would lie on the
futon, chin resting on her arms, gazing fondly down.
She didn't speak; he probably wouldn't have heard
her. He was silent, intent, totally absorbed in his
task. His capable hands arranged and assembled the
lattice sections he'd been able to collect. The
apparatus began to look like a time cubicle.

Then one day, five weeks after he'd started, he
stepped back and said: "That's as far as I can take it
for now. Do you see what's missing? The broad
skein of circuitry across the top. Have you ever
heard the lads talk about Old Chronos' jockstrap?
Sorry. Indelicate. They mean our missing item. Its
official name is a brace tether, and without it this
contraption isn't sending anyone anywhere. There
are no second-hand tethers to be had as the burn-out
rate's colossal. Tomorrow I'll have to raid the TTI
reserve store and hope I don't get caught."

"Where *is* this store?"

"Transport level. Sub-basement. Near the
auxiliary cubicles."

"Not far from here, then. And what kind of security does it have? CCTV? AI's?"

" Real people mostly."

"In that case, go now. You're sweaty, scruffy and you reek of tungstron oil, so, you'll look as though you've every right to be there. Be an actor, Paris! If challenged, say you're doing emergency repairs. Or say some VIPs are travelling tomorrow and you don't want any misfires. A high burn-out rate, you said? Then take *two* tethers. It'll look more convincing, and if they fail *that* quickly, we might need a spare one ourselves! I assume you can carry two?"

"The new ones are coiled."

"Take your tool bag, then."

He fetched it. "I'm no use at bluffing. Can't you come with me?"

"How can I? It would look weird. Just get it over with!"

Resignedly, he went. Each section of corridor had a security door, and each door required a palm print. If things went wrong there was no way of pretending he'd never been there. "I *know* I'm going to screw this up," he muttered.

"No, you're not!" said a voice he recognised.

He turned, startled. "Norvus!"

"It's fine, Paris, just relax. I'm working a case and Despina thought you'd be the perfect ally. I've just had a quick word with Elvira, so I know the nature of your errand. Thanks for dawdling. It saved me running to catch up with you."

"How does Despina always know when to intervene?"

Norvus shrugged evasively. "Practice makes perfect, I guess. Right, we're here. Go in, keep that anxious expression on your face and be exactly what Elvira told you to be. I'll wait within earshot."

"I'm really not happy with - " Paris began. Norvus operated the door mechanism and gave him a shove.

An assembly of TTI components, each in its secure packaging, was displayed on movable racks. Two overalled menials regarded Paris stonily.

"And what brings you here on a rest day?" one asked.

Paris stammered out his request.

"Don't I know you?" asked the other attendant, squinting. "You're Construction's under-age recruit, aren't you?"

"I'm late with my initial project," Paris improvised. "I need to complete it by tomorrow."

"Course you do. Two brace tethers coming right up." He placed two sealed packs on the counter in front of him. "That'll be two hundred new pounds. One hundred each."

"What are you talking about? All these products are paid for by the finance department. You dispense them, that's all."

"It *isn't* all, not in your case. Designer boy, by the look of you. Rich mama? She'll bail you out, won't she? Of course, if you're unwilling to close the deal, these essential items go back on the shelf. Shame about your project."

172

"This is robbery," Paris objected, raising his voice a little.

"Take it or leave it," said the first attendant. "Got your payment tab memorised? Good." He produced a non-standard keypad and turned it to face Paris.

"Gotcha," said Norvus. "Norvus Maysson, GTC. Grayham Jean and Eben Myra, I'm arresting you for extortion. Get out of the way, Paris. I do believe these morons are going to rush me."

They tried. The attempt lasted ten seconds. Norvus dusted himself down and spoke briskly into his bio-communicator. Two GTC patrolmen appeared and removed the two dazed warehousemen. "Sorry you've been troubled," one of the officers said to Paris as they left.

"Well that was fun, wasn't it?" Norvus remarked. "We knew those two were on the take, but we needed proof. Don't worry, I won't name you on my report. Now pick up those tethers and let's go. Oh, before I forget: Despina sent this. One of her specials. She didn't want you rummaging around Dispatch in full view of everyone." He handed over a data chip. "It'll take Elvira to the Villa Diodati. A social visit, initially."

"What do you mean, initially?"

"Can't say."

"Then at least tell me my machine will work!"

"Again, I can't confirm that. But my guess is, you'll be naming your handiwork before tomorrow's out."

Paris said little on his arrival home, and Elvira thought it best not to pry. He remained in silent mode until the tether was in place and the equipment had responded with a soft radiance. All it needed to complete the process was a strong link with the brace emitters below, which probably wouldn't occur till the following day.

"So we just wait?" Elvira asked quietly.

"Not for much longer. I'll come back at lunchtime and ensure everything's lined up. And you'll need some Regency clothes from somewhere. You can't go near Wardrobe."

"Saranna's on it. She knows some theatrical costumiers."

"Of course she does," Paris said with just a hint of admiration. "In a way, I wish she were going with you. Trouble just bounces off her."

"I'd noticed," Elvira said wryly. "Paris – have you chosen a name for the device yet? Only we're going to be busy tomorrow. If there's any kind of ceremony maybe we should do it now."

"There's no ceremony. I just announce it before the first run. It has to be a woman's name and it should never be changed."

"Let me guess: it's bad luck if you do. It's the same with renaming boats."

"So it is. I'd forgotten that. Trust me, my best girl, you'll cherish the name I give her. You'll see."

Elvira gave him a gentle push toward the shower. "Then shall we scrub up and go out? There's still time. We could go back to La Chanson d'Amour."

174

Paris smiled wearily. "I'd love to, but I mustn't. Not today. If I were to see that enticing view of Hampstead I'd be tempted to escape into the past with you, and forget about timelines and Despina and my forthcoming, unlooked for, unwanted marriage. But we can't run, because Despina would find us. Maybe she'd be gently reproachful or maybe she'd smack us around, but she *would* find us. Because she's very very good at what she does. We have to play our part in this, whatever this *is*. So, yes, we'll scrub up and go out. We'll go to Rhodos, have an excellent meal and maybe smash a few plates. Then we'll come back here in a much happier frame of mind and … and this speech has gone on too long."

"Paris."

"What?"

"You're amazing. And you're right. Now please get in that shower!"

Chapter Six

"It's midday," Paris said. "The moment of truth. Keep your eyes on the lattice."

Elvira and Saranna did just that. The floor trembled very slightly under their feet. The brace lab below was at full output. For a minute or two the lattice maintained its normal, almost imperceptible glow. Then suddenly a bright zigzag traversed the entire structure, following every intricacy. It traced the complex route three times, then was gone.

"She's ready," murmured Paris. "Touch her, Elvira. She'll know you."

Elvira complied. A gentle tingle ran through her fingers. Paris placed his hand next to hers and spoke to the machine. His solemnity might have seemed amusing, but somehow didn't. "Your name is Hope. May you provide safe travel and an answer to all our endeavours." Then, to Elvira, "Do you agree with my choice?"

"Absolutely," she said. "Saranna, you were about to show me the accessories you brought."

"Coming up. You're going back to the year with no summer, right? So as well as that flim-flam you're wearing, I've provided some comfy boots, a warm hooded cloak in emerald green – which will contrast nicely with your hair and skin tone – plus some vintage coins."

Elvira put on the extra items and pocketed the money.

"One last detail," said Paris. "Your recall bracelet, made from an offcut of Hope's own circuitry. Either one of us can activate it. It will return you here and nowhere else. Ready?"

"As I'll ever be."

Paris inserted Despina's data chip into the Hope's integral reader. Immediately, the apartment's messaging system sounded an alert. Elvira, unsurprised, answered it. Despina's voice said: "If you're hearing this recording, Elvira, it means you're about to leave. Listen carefully. You'll materialise at dawn near the Maison Chappuis, Montalegre, close to the Villa Diodati. The cottage is occupied by Percy Shelley, his wife-to-be Mary and Mary's half-sister Claire Clairmont. You'll see a young woman hurrying through the mist: it's Claire, on her way back from a tryst with Byron. At this point in history neither Shelley nor Mary knows Claire is pregnant by Byron, nor that she's involved them in her pursuit of him. I suggest you befriend her, continuing to use Helen Adelaide as your alias. Remember that Shelley already knows you as Helen. This will secure your position in their company."

"What - ?" Paris began.

"Listen," Elvira said peremptorily.

"You, Elvira," Despina was continuing, "need to fulfil a specific duty resulting from your choice of alias. To preserve the relevant timeline you must act on my instructions as I issue them." Then, more informally, "Sorry about my haphazard methods but it was Shelley's fault. If he'd only stayed put geographically my task would have been much easier. You can replay this recording if you wish – but don't delay too long."

Elvira didn't feel she needed a reprise. She stepped into Hope's cubicle and waited.

"What was all that about?" demanded Paris.

"I honestly don't know."

"Why use a false name?"

"I'd broken GTC rules by speaking with Shelley and I didn't want to implicate him."

"Helen as in Helen of Troy. I get that. But why Adelaide?"

"She was my aesthetician at Ace My Face. I borrowed her name to avert some hassle from another client. Saranna can tell you more. Now are you going to throw that switch or not?"

He did so, with obvious reluctance. An eddy of displaced air swirled round him. Elvira was gone. He turned away, suddenly bereft.

Saranna patted his shoulder in an attempt at reassurance. "You mustn't get emotional. She's Elvira, remember? Any trouble and she'll put the boot in. *Both* boots. Why not focus on your creation? You must be very proud."

"I was. It's worn off."

"What I'm trying to say is, if the GTC know all about this and haven't shut you down, then they must have a solid reason for not doing so. This is scrivener territory. *Nobody* gets to do this!" She deposited Paris on the settee, still shrouded in its dust sheet. "Of course you're worried. She's your partner. But can I please ask you to focus on something closer to home?"

"Another problem?"

"Well, yes, and one I didn't want to involve her in. Not when she's got a timeline to fix. Albie did manage to get some photos of Lelza's place. I only hope he can persuade her that it's not a good environment for a well brought up young husband." She searched her usual collection of bags and retrieved a folio. "Look. Isn't this disgusting? Shelves full of bell jars, petri dishes, lichens, waterweed, fungus. She's trying to develop new food sources, or so she told Albie."

Paris wrinkled his nose. "As if Vegi-sim isn't bad enough."

"Albie suggested that once she has another resident to consider, she'll need a separate laboratory. She's thinking about it."

"A separate flat would be better," Paris remarked. "I have to get back to my legitimate job, Saranna, if I still have one. Please thank Albie for his intervention and ask him to keep up the propaganda. Something tells me I'll be glad of it later!"

**

The chilly morning air struck though Elvira's thin gown. She drew her cloak tightly about her and took a few steps along the track, unsure which way was the correct one. Stay here and wait for Claire, she thought. She'll be here. Despina's calculations are always spot on.

And here she was, bonnet askew, dark curls a-dance. Elvira stepped forward.

"Claire?"

"That's me."

"I'm sorry – you probably don't remember me. I'm Helen. I was at the Hotel d'Angleterre when those tourists mobbed Lord Byron. You were caught up in the crowd."

"And getting nowhere. Stupid doe-eyed matrons! I had every right to speak to Byron. We have an understanding."

"Have you told him yet?" asked Elvira, trying to establish herself in the role of confidante.

"Told him what?"

"About the baby."

Claire's eyes widened. "How did you know?"

"Just a guess. You have that look about you."

"He sensed it too. I think he was pleased, but one never knows with him. And now *I* sense you have a favour to ask of me."

They began to walk toward the Maison Chappuis.

"My guardian has business in Secheron which will occupy him for two days," Elvira began. "He thinks I'm at Evian-les-Bains, taking the waters."

"Go on," Claire prompted.

"While at the Hotel d'Angleterre I spoke with Shelley, and he invited me to one of Byron's literary evenings. Of course, he may not have meant it. Perhaps he was just being polite."

"When Shelley promises something he usually means it," pronounced Claire. "And I happen to know that Byron expects us there tonight."

"Then may I crave your hospitality in the meantime?"

"Of course. I insist. And while you're here you can tell me all the secrets of your spa treatments. You didn't achieve that beauty by accident! Oh, and don't mind Mary. She's being peevish. She didn't really want me on our tour. So it would help if we didn't wake Willmouse on our way in."

"Will -?"

"Mary's boy. Six months old. Elise looks after him most of the time."

"Elise?"

"Nurse. Shh, that's her window."

They tiptoed into the silent house. Claire's room was on the far side, overlooking the lake.

"Stay here. I'll see if Shelley's awake. He's up with the lark most days."

In less than five minutes she'd returned with Shelley in tow. Smiling, he darted forward and clasped Elvira's hands. "Helen, you look radiant! What's wrought this transformation?"

"When you last saw me I was tired from the journey," Elvira said, having rehearsed such an answer. "And I was worried about my friend."

"What friend's this?" asked Claire.

"You saw her kiss Lord Byron."

Claire giggled. "Oh, *that* friend! I've never seen L.B. look so astonished. Is she not with you?"

"Sadly not. She had to go home."

"At your guardian's insistence, no doubt," Shelley remarked. "I'm glad you managed to shake him off. Later, we shall discuss how to rid the world of such oppressors. But at present I'm in need of breakfast!" He disappeared as swiftly as he'd arrived.

"And I'm in need of some rest," Claire admitted, suppressing a yawn. "Can you do without me for a while?" And, kicking off her shoes, she threw herself backwards onto the bed and was asleep in seconds.

For the first time Elvira began to notice the complete absence of noise. During her last visit, inside the crowded hotel, there had been an excess of it; but out here, nothing. And thus Mary's voice was clearly audible through the walls.

"Really, Percy, not another itinerant. We can't subsidise anyone else!"

"It's just for a day or two. I invited her."

"And when was this?"

"She was at Secheron. She'd eluded her guardian temporarily and oh, Mary, you should have seen the way he treated her. He pinioned her arms and marched her off as if she were under arrest!"

"And I suppose she's beautiful?"

"You're missing the point."

"No, Percy, I don't think I am."

A door closed and the voices faded.

By the time Elvira ventured out, however, Mary had apparently put aside her issues with Shelley. Her manner was cautiously polite. "You've just left

Evian-les-Bains? I assume that means you're starving. I've made porridge for breakfast as the weather's so unseasonal."

"Thank you. I'm most grateful," said Elvira, and meant it. She'd been too on edge to eat lunch, only to face the prospect of a long hungry day. From noon back to six in the morning, then the whole six hours over again. Saranna had thoughtfully slipped a bar of chocolate into one of her pockets, but it wouldn't have helped much.

Mary was explaining that a delivery barge often moored at their inlet, to enable Lord Byron's many provisions to be carried in boxes and panniers through the adjoining vineyard to the villa. "His chef proclaims himself the best and demands only the best produce. Which bodes well for this evening."

"I thought Byron only ate potatoes."

"Not exclusively. And when he decides to, he still has to feed his servants – and his pets."

Still so young, her entire literary career ahead of her, she busied herself with pots and pans. Shelley hadn't reappeared. Claire would probably sleep all morning.

So, I've met them, Elvira thought. Tonight I'll meet Byron and Dr Polidori. And then what, Despina? Why am I doing this? She touched the quiescent recall bracelet, well hidden under her sleeve. No contact with Despina meant no further instructions, which in turn meant she was only there to observe and be observed.

At last, after a day of perpetual twilight, Shelley and the three women strolled the short distance to the Villa Diodati. Elvira soon discovered that this was *not* the time when Byron would announce his ghost story competition. Obviously, Despina hadn't risked sending her to such a well-documented meeting of minds. Tonight, less interestingly, the men were discussing ideal political systems, with frequent reference to the Ancient Greeks. An excellent wine, of a vintage she couldn't begin to identify, was making her drowsy, but she paid attention whenever it was Shelley's turn to speak.

"If mankind is to have a secure future," he said earnestly, "there must be extensive social reform. In another few centuries the world will see the abolition of marriage and the downfall of organised religion."

"And in the meantime you're applying these reforms to yourself," commented Byron. Shelley paid no heed.

"Who knows what such a society may achieve?" he went on. "Men will build great cities – towers of crystal which will shine with their own light. People will travel through the air and beneath the sea. Perhaps they will even journey to the moon and stars, and meet the beings which dwell there."

"Airy-fairy nonsense," Byron muttered.

"It's brilliant, and so accurate!" Elvira enthused, then hastily amended this to something safer. "I mean, I agree absolutely." Then she subsided, mentally cursing the wine and allowing Byron to

184

continue his speech about Utopia. No-one seemed to have noticed her faux pas except Shelley, who directed a quizzical stare in her direction. He continued to study her covertly, and, increasingly on edge, she overturned her almost empty wine glass. A servant glided forward and removed the glass and tray.

Suddenly Claire was at her elbow, whispering. "Helen, you're losing a stocking!"

Elvira gazed down at the wrinkled material round her ankle. "Oh, sh..."

"Your garter must be undone. Stand up, straighten your gown, and we'll walk out of the room in a slow dignified manner. Ready?"

They walked.

"Don't worry – I know my way around here, remember?"

They entered a rest room and Claire retied the offending stocking. "Had enough of reforming the world? I'll walk you back to the cottage if you like. I'm staying here tonight so you can have my room."

She disappeared briefly and returned with a lantern. Elvira followed mutely.

"I don't think Mary likes me," she said at last.

"Well she wouldn't, would she? You've beguiled her lover."

"I've hardly spoken to him!"

"And yet he couldn't take his eyes off you all evening. What did you say to him at Secheron?"

"I told him I admired his poetry."

Claire chuckled. "Excellent move." She held the lantern high. "Here we are. Shall I wait while you go in?"

"No need. You go. I'll just take the night air for a few moments."

Claire started back toward the villa, then seconds later, remembered something and turned round. "Oh, by the way - "

There was no-one else on the path.

***

"Paris! If you're in that shower, come out before I throw you out!"

"I'm here." He peered over the mezzanine rail. "Something wrong?"

"What do *you* think?" She disappeared into the miniscule shower room, catapulting her Regency gown out of the door some moments later.

Paris retrieved her cloak and boots from the floor next to the Hope's cubicle, and carefully removed some dirt from the interior with a hand-held vacuum. He then maintained a discreet silence until Elvira, in a housecoat, skin tingling from the particle scrub, came to join him. "I never want to see another earth closet," she announced. "And as for cheese-flavoured ice cream …!"

Paris grinned. "Welcome to time travel!"

"I still don't know why Despina sent me there. Did I really need to meet the whole gang?"

"*She* must have thought so."

"Well, I think I was the wrong person for the job. My cover story was weak, I had a wardrobe malfunction, and I'm just so *tired*! I have to sleep, Paris. I'm sorry."

"You do know it's after ten? Shall we both turn in?"

"That would be wonderful. I've missed you."

"What, even when hobnobbing with literary luminaries?"

"Yes. Yes! I just want to get back to normal. I do hope Despina leaves us alone for a while."

"There'll have to be a debrief, I imagine. Standard GTC practice for solo missions."

Elvira yawned. "Oh, OK. But after that I'd like some peace!"

Despina, who'd doubtless been aware that Elvira had cued the Hope's return protocol, deferred contacting her till late the following day. "I examined the original time displacement before and after your intervention," she said, "and was pleasantly surprised. You've already begun to shore things up."

"I've no idea how."

"By *being* there," said Despina, infinitely patient. "So, when we call on you next, your excursion should be no longer than two hours. Is that helpful?"

"Immensely. Just don't put me anywhere near cheese-flavoured ice cream."

"I'll do my best. There's more good news: the scriveners have decided that we can put off the next stage until after Paris is twenty eight. That means you can be together at Christmas and seven weeks after. And rest assured I'll redouble my efforts to liberate him from his marriage."

The TTI stayed open every Christmas. It was one of their busiest times, with people seeking the festive season as it used to be. This inevitably brought problems with tourists being drunk or rowdy or helping themselves to artefacts. Machine malfunctions and misfires escalated, and the construction team was routinely seconded to maintenance duty. 2584 followed this usual pattern. Paris came home tired, irritable and trying to shake the feeling that he'd taken a retrograde step.

Elvira had fared slightly better. She'd met with Saranna for drinks, only to discover that the rest of MetroLondon was underwhelmed by Christmas and New Year.

"That's because the official new year is May 1st," Saranna explained. "Wasn't that in your history programme? We celebrate the Morii Festival of Light. Renewal and regeneration. And we've incorporated the Iron Age Beltane festival of fire, fertility and rebirth."

"Fertility rites?" Elvira inquired, searching her memory enhancements.

"You bet! Such fun. Maybe in four months, if you've extricated Paris from marital misery, you two can be chief celebrants. And, regarding Lelza, I've a titbit of news that might just cheer him up."

"What?" Elvira asked resignedly.

"Albie's started work on Lelza's apartment and he's absolutely smitten with her."

"And how does she feel about that?"

"I don't know. Neither does Albie."

Elvira sighed. "Albie's the type to get a silly crush on any woman who offers a kind word. It won't amount to anything."

***

Elvira and Paris tried to make the seven weeks as memorable as possible. Saranna conjured up two more tickets to the Polar Orbiter, where they had their first view of a twilit Earth cradled between a sunrise and sunset. The sight, though beautiful, failed to lift Elvira's spirits. "A new beginning, or the end of an era?" she asked.

"We'll come back when I'm a free man," Paris answered staunchly, "and then it'll mean just one thing. The start of our new life."

Kindly Cyprian, aware of the approaching deadline, temporarily reduced Paris' hours. He also set up some fictitious wage deductions such as training fees, union dues and an hourly rate for Elvira's hire – in case Lelza should demand that Paris hand over his earnings. The clawbacks would be available for Paris to dip into at any time.

Elvira went, with Despina, back to Leisure 4 Lovers, where she commissioned a leading fashion designer to create a fight suit – something eye catching and formfitting, but protective in all the right places. For some undisclosed reason, Despina had insisted that she should have such a garment.

They again dined with Saranna at the spaceport, close to the arrival and departure terminals. All through the meal Saranna was trying not to look mysterious, and Elvira wondered what diversion was being planned this time. She pretended not to have noticed.

"There's something I want you both to see," Saranna said eventually, and used her staff pass to access a private multi-cube.

"Is this allowed?" Paris asked with a tiny frown.

"Yes, master of correctness, it is. But we *do* have to be quiet."

They emerged into a gallery where a row of sturdy white pillars presided, Parthenon-like, over the interior of a temple. A young couple were being married in a simple hand-fasting ceremony. A giant screen relayed a close-up to their assembled guests. The newly-weds accepted gifts of fruit and flowers before stepping into a coracle and, once seated, being wafted slowly into the distance by artificial waves. Dappled rays of golden light accompanied their progress. Alone on the viewscreen, a white-robed mezzo-soprano sang them on their way: "My soul is an enchanted boat which, like a sleeping swan, doth float upon the silver waves of thy sweet singing." The service ended.

"One day," said Saranna, "I hope to see you two married here. We're all rooting for you. Anyone know what that song was?"

190

"Yes," said Elvira, dabbing at a sentimental tear. "It's Asia's aria from Prometheus Unbound. By Shelley."

***

Finally, February 26th arrived. There was nothing to mark the occasion. The marriage contract was now in force. Paris and Elvira duly presented themselves at Barnet Heights and waited for the understandably indignant Lelza to demand the meaning of Elvira's presence.

"As you are doubtless aware," Elvira responded superciliously, "my client is here under duress. I believe he may be at risk of domestic abuse. Until you convince me otherwise, I cannot relinquish him into your care."

"It's our wedding day," Lelza said sullenly. "I've prepared a special meal. For two."

"May I inspect it?" Elvira asked in a tone which suggested that no was not an option. Lelza led the way into the dining room where an overabundance of dishes surrounded a cheaply produced bride and groom centrepiece.

"I'm sorry, Lelza, but I cannot allow Paris to eat any of this. You may be trying to feed him the uncertified results of your experiments with foodstuffs. Of *course* I've researched you! I take my work very seriously. Until I give you clearance you're not to feed Paris anything you've cultivated. You may put this meal aside for your own use."

"What do we eat, then?"

"You've two options. We can go out, or you can order in."

Paris chose Rhodos, where Greek dancers performed once a week. The live bouzouki music thwarted any attempt at conversation. Elvira lingered over her dessert as long as she could.

"Now," she began when they were back at Lelza's flat, "you do realise that Paris' mother didn't inform him of this arrangement and thus he's had no time to adjust. Tonight, Lelza, I'd like you to pretend you're on a first date. Polite conversation only, please. Don't forget your partner is a graduate of the Excelsior School for Noble Gentlemen and address him accordingly. I will be in the next room."

She went out, first having attached a short-range bug to the underside of the table. She then settled down with an earpiece to listen to the most awkward conversation she'd ever heard. Finally, however, Paris found his voice.

"I'm sure you must know, Lelza, that I neither wanted nor welcomed this marriage. I cannot and will not commit to it. Please don't embarrass me or yourself by trying to initiate intimacy, either now nor in the future."

Lelza was silent.

"Could you perhaps see yourself in a different relationship?" Paris went on more quietly. "Is there someone you'd like to encourage?"

Lelza sniffed. "Whether there is or isn't, I don't see what difference it makes. I promised my mother, and House Dawn in general, that I'd comply with their wishes."

"Then you'll be compliant in name only," Paris declared.

Later, when Lelza was disposing of the spoilt banquet, he accosted Elvira in barely controlled desperation. "I'm *not* staying overnight, not with her ladyship prowling around. I'd never sleep, even if you were with me. I managed to check the two bedrooms: one single, one double. There's no way to make that work other than the way she wants."

"All right, then – change of plan," Elvira said, thinking quickly. "The ruling was twenty four hours in a week, so we'll split it. Twelve now, which is nearly up, and twelve tomorrow. Or, six hours tomorrow plus an evening. She'll agree. I'll make it sound like a better deal."

"Make the offer, then. Anything's better than this."

"She's like a blank slate, poor girl," Elvira mused. "She's already copying one or two of your unconscious mannerisms."

"I wish you hadn't said that."

"We'll get through it," Elvira insisted. "We have to."

Paris risked a quick hug. "I wonder what the Albie situation is? I don't see anything that looks like his work."

"But those nasty little things in jars aren't here. Albie was creating a lab for her, wasn't he? Shame we can't ask her about it but we aren't supposed to know. Now shhh, she's coming back." Elvira gave

Lelza one of her 21st century saleswoman smiles. "Hey, there you are. We've been discussing how we can make better use of Paris' schedule. You both need to ease into this new situation. Sit down and I'll explain."

"Thank you," said Lelza unexpectedly. "Mama says I'm too caught up in my research. For her sake I want to make this relationship a success."

"Then let's work toward the best possible outcome," Elvira said, hoping her sales technique hadn't gone stale. She felt as if history were repeating itself. Paris was again relying on her to rescue him; and once again, she wasn't sure how.

***

The new arrangement with Lelza went better than they'd hoped, not only due to the staggered schedule but because Albie had made his presence felt. Initially he'd only installed a stud wall in the overly large kitchen. The adjacent room was now a temporary lab, still in need of plumbing work. His main task, which would require Lelza to move back with her mother temporarily, was to create a picture window with a garden effect. A floral arch and the illusion of steps, based on Le Jardin de la Javeliere, would lead the eye toward rose bushes and a water feature. While helping Lelza choose a theme, Albie had discovered they both had an obsession with the Fibonacci sequence and patterns of Nature in general. This helped to explain his undeclared fondness for her.

Paris, not wanting to encounter the formidable Bryony Dawn, had asked both Elvira and Saranna for fresh ideas to keep Lelza entertained. Saranna, of course, had tried to improve her sartorial choices – "not that they could be much worse," as she'd remarked to Paris. She'd also suggested a shorter, sculpted hairstyle and a makeover to temporarily improve the girl's pallid skin tone. Elvira, discovering that Lelza was not a ballet fan, took her to see a revival of The Arcadians. In between, there were lunches and dinners out, during which Lelza prattled endlessly about botany, landscape gardens and Fibonacci.

Three weeks went by before the obligatory return, albeit a brief one, to Barnet Heights. Albie had excelled himself. One could almost believe that Le Jardin de la Javeliere was just one step away.

"She could have achieved the same effect with an immersive hologram, at a fraction of the price," Paris remarked when she and Elvira were back at their apartment.

"I think it was a labour of love on Albie's part," Elvira said. "And because of that we know much more about Lelza. She needs a kindred spirit and it isn't you. Do you know what that rose garden reminds me of? The poem 'Patterns' by Amy Lowell."

Paris didn't know it.

"The narrator's lover has been killed in a war, and she's pretending he hasn't. She walks up and down a beautiful garden in her brocade gown, alone, seeing patterns in everything."

"Best not to mention that in front of Lelza," Paris advised.

***

"We need to have a little talk, Paris."

"I do know the facts of life, Despina."

"Silly! I'm referring to Elvira. No doubt you think the GTC has been exploiting her and you blame me most of all."

"I know you're a law unto yourselves, answerable only to the scriveners and the Morii. Do my opinions even count?"

"They do, to me. Will you hear me out?"

"If you insist."

Despina poured herself a drink. "About Elvira's strange rapport with Shelley," she began. "I genuinely didn't know where it was leading. The scriveners just fed me dribs and drabs of information, and told me to implement it. Until today, that is. I now know Elvira's precise role in the past, the nature of her link with Shelley, and what she must do next. Where is she now?"

"Gone to have her contraceptive implant renewed. But you know that, don't you?"

"I know that when she's at the clinic she won't be given a replacement, by orders of the GTC. She *will* be given a drug to kickstart ovulation. She won't know about the switch. And you, Paris, must give me your solemn word to forego penetrative sex for a limited time. She has to conceive Shelley's baby."

196

Paris, despairful, buried his face in his hands. "If I'm to lose her, at least tell me now. The truth, Despina!"

"You will *not* lose her. In fact she'll need you to be strong and supportive. She has a difficult time ahead."

"What? Conceiving a poet's child?"

"Leaving the child in the past for Shelley to adopt. That one little scrap of life is the cause of the anomaly we've been trying to resolve. The GTC had no idea who the mother was, whose identity Shelley was concealing, till Elvira invented that pseudonym for herself."

"Helen Adelaide."

"Yes. I suspect the scriveners made the connection before now, but chose not to enlighten me. Shelley named his daughter Elena Adelaide. Now do you see?"

Paris was silent.

"It isn't all bad news." Despina tried to lighten her tone. "Elvira doesn't have to give birth. We can supervise her until the embryo is established and then transfer it to an ectogenetic womb. She won't bond with the child, which should make it easier for her to hand it over."

Paris grew angry. "You're treating her like a lab rat!"

"Oh, stop being so dramatic. *You* were nurtured the very same way. You don't think Eva carried you to term, do you? You were delivered at Astrolabe Babes, in the rudest of health, screaming your defiance at the tech team."

Paris managed a grim little smile. "At least that explains why I've such a poor relationship with my mother."

"So, will you support Elvira through this? I can't emphasise enough that you *cannot* tell her what to do or say. To sustain the timeline, she has to have autonomy."

"I know the rules. When does all this take place?"

"In five day's time. Tuesday at twelve noon. Is the Hope serviced and ready?"

"Yes, but I can't be on hand for the monitoring. Not all of it, anyway."

"No problem. I'll see to it myself. In person."

It was the longest five days that Paris had ever endured. Not only did he have to maintain secrecy, but had to feign tiredness in the bedroom. All he wanted was to keep Elvira close, love and cherish her. And it had all been denied him. When Tuesday arrived he stayed in the background while Despina outlined the mission.

"Once again I'm short on objectives, but here's what I *do* know. Shelley's address is 119 Great Russell Street, Bloomsbury. The date is the tenth of March, 1818. In one more day he'll have left for Italy. This is the only time we could be sure he was alone. Claire, her infant daughter, Mary and her two children are presently with Mary's father, Godwin. Shelley is disillusioned with the impecunious Godwin and doesn't attend. They won't hurry back. If necessary, Norvus and his friends will stage a street brawl to ensure everyone

198

stays put. Bearing in mind the extended day we foisted on you last time, Elvira, we've chosen an evening arrival." Despina paused.

"Shelley is in need of a fresh start. There have been two suicides in his recent past – his estranged wife Harriet and Mary's half-sister Fanny. And, he's been denied custody of his and Harriet's two children. However, he doesn't lack resilience. I have high hopes for this meeting."

"I'll bet," Paris muttered.

***

With pinpoint accuracy, Elvira was conveyed to the entrance hall of the Bloomsbury town house. "Only two hours," she murmured to herself. "I have to make this count. Despina's orders!"

There had been more instructions. Surprisingly, Despina had issued her with one of the GTC's dice-cameras, telling her to "get evidence". For whom, and why, remained unclear. Even more surprisingly, she wore a mini-receptor disguised as a necklet. With this, she could summon Despina to her in the event of trouble. She was still piqued at the inference that she couldn't handle trouble.

Shelley's study door was ajar, and resolutely she ventured in. The room was warm and welcoming. A coal fire blazed cheerily in the grate. Shelley was scribbling in a notebook, oblivious to her presence. Would he even recognise her? For her, only a few weeks had elapsed since they'd met in Geneva. For him it was over a year and a half ago.

"You'll ruin your eyes," she admonished gently.

He looked up, startled, then smiled in genuine pleasure. "Helen. I'm delighted to see you. Claire said you vanished like a will o' the wisp, and now you've reappeared just as suddenly."

"The door was on the latch. Are you writing a poem?"

He laid aside his pen. "Attempting to. I hadn't realised it was so dark. Would you mind lighting that lamp for me?"

Disconcerted, Elvira attempted to do as he asked; but try as she would, the lamp refused to burn. The wick smouldered, smoked and went out. At last she gave up, only to find him watching her closely. She remembered that look from the Villa Diodati.

"Where are you from, Helen? If that's indeed your name."

"What do you mean?"

"Exactly what I said. I've just seen you defeated by an oil lamp. I've noticed your ineptitude on previous occasions."

"Thank you very much."

"But not," he went on, "because you're inept by nature. You're simply unfamiliar with the details of our everyday life."

"You're very observant, Mr Shelley," Elvira said, trying to discourage this line of questioning. "No-one else has noticed these … ineptitudes," she added, not quite truthfully.

Shelley took the offending lamp and lit it deftly. "Nevertheless, *I* have noticed. But where are my manners? Come, sit with me. May I offer you a drink?"

"You've seen what fortified wine does to me."

"This is harmless. Rhubarb and lemon cordial."

She took the glass he offered. "You require an explanation, and you shall have it. Where I come from, where I disappear to. Whether you believe me is another matter."

"Would this have anything to do with that ruffian who dragged you off at Secheron?"

"It would, yes."

"He acted disgracefully. Please, explain further. Whatever your secret is, I promise to keep it safe."

Elvira found his earnestness endearing. He didn't deserve to be embroiled in some GTC-driven plot, not with the other complications in his life. But she'd been given no alternative. "The truth, then. At the Villa Diodati you imagined the human race in the distant future, when we're able by our science to travel to other worlds. Can you also imagine someone travelling through time, exploring the past? Their disguise would have to be correct in every detail. They'd have to blend in. Maybe they wouldn't cope too well. Does that sound familiar?" She drew a deep breath. "My name isn't Helen, it's Elvira. Elvira Jones. And I'm a time traveller. I could give you a lecture about the changed world, who invented what, but it wouldn't convince because I personally haven't lived it. I'm going to tell you about *me*."

In a few lightning sketches she described her meeting with Paris, his rescue, her new life, time travel as a tourist industry. "I suppose you think I'm delusional. Perhaps you want proof." Her cloak was draped over the back of her chair. She located its only pocket, removed the dice.

"A throw of the dice will convince me?"

"This is no ordinary dice. Look this way. Smile please. Thank you." She peeled the miniature exposure from the camera. "Hold out your hand. Now watch."

He did so, with childlike fascination, as the image coalesced.

"Your likeness, faithfully reproduced by this little gadget. There are light-sensitive chemicals in the paper. Now burn it. Drop it into the lamp."

He obeyed. The film turned black, writhed briefly and was gone.

Elvira held the dice up as if admiring it. She hoped the secret selfie of herself and her companion would satisfy the GTCs requirements. "See? It's just a dice again."

"You're risking your liberty."

"Not this time. It isn't like our stolen conversation at Secheron. The GTC permitted me to relocate to a distant century on the understanding that they'd occasionally require my services. I'm what they call a character in play. They sent me here, to you, today, without explaining why. Maybe they wanted me to confide in you. Maybe I *shouldn't* have confided in you. Or … maybe I should just go." She stood up. He did likewise.

"Please stay, Miss Jones. Elvira. I haven't yet given my response to your story."

She waited. She'd had no intention of leaving.

"I'm convinced, but not by your clever science nor your apparent ability to walk through locked doors." He tilted her chin until their eyes met. "The truth is here, in your gentle face, in your every gesture, each time you speak of the lover whom you fear is lost to you. He exists – I know it as surely as if he were here now. And I know this also: that if you were mine, I would allow nothing and no-one to take you from me."

She knew he was impulsive but didn't expect his embrace to be so unequivocal, nor that the perfect Cupid's bow of his mouth could deliver an equally perfect kiss - or several.

He released her momentarily. Remembering the role of Helen of Troy in Dr Faustus, she said absolutely nothing. It seemed the right thing to do.

Assured of her compliance, he led her gently but insistently to a Grecian couch near the hearth. Then, with practised ease, he unlaced her gown. It rippled to the floor.

"You have enchanted me, Miss Jones," he murmured. "I fear the future you've shown me. I fear your kisses. But how can I not love you?"

Hastily and unselfconsciously, he unfastened his breeches. "Permit me to lay siege to your beauty."

I can't believe he just said that. Elvira, naked except for a thin chemise and a few oddments of lace, searched for a suitable reply. "You're wasting time," she said at last.

While he possessed her the room seemed full of dancing shadows. She'd never made love by firelight before. It was eerie, and beautiful. Further off, the oil lamp flickered sporadically. For a moment Elvira was uneasy, then refocused hurriedly. It wasn't a receptor field. These old houses were always full of draughts.

"Tired of me already?" Shelley asked teasingly.

"I thought I heard someone," she said lamely.

"What if you did? It's nothing they won't have seen before. In fact, the idea of being caught in flagrante is – immeasurably – exciting - " He shuddered against her.

"Sorry," she murmured. "I spoilt the moment."

"Indeed you did not. In precisely one minute, or two at the most, I shall return to the fray. I shall be merciless. You shall not escape." He seized both her wrists to demonstrate.

His right hand closed over the recall bracelet and there was a soft spat of static. Even in the uncertain light, she saw him blanch. "Elvira, what …?"

He was suddenly a dead weight in her arms. She swore profusely, eased him to the floor, then took off her necklet and jabbed furiously at the jewel. "Despina, I need you!"

It was less than five minutes till she appeared, but it seemed longer.

"What in Hades have you done?"

"Nothing! He had the tiniest of static shocks from my bracelet, and passed out."

Despina was instantly intrigued. "Very interesting! Well, his vitals are stable, so let's get him back on the couch. Do his buttons up, would you?" She rummaged among the various inkwells and pots in the bureau.

"What are you after?"

"Laudanum. There's bound to be some here somewhere. Ah, this looks like it." She unstoppered a small glass bottle, sprinkled some drops of the strongly scented opiate on Shelley's clothes and hair, then hid the bottle under a cushion. "I assume you told him quite a lot? Well, this'll ensure no-one believes anything he says when he wakes up. Now let's go."

Elvira, still troubled, emerged from the Hope's cubicle. Paris wasn't there, which, considering her dishevelled state, was just as well. Despina had somehow arrived ahead of her.

"What do you mean, you screwed up your assignment? Shelley's reaction to your bracelet means he's made a connection to the future – or maybe the future reached out to *him*. Either way, it puts us in an excellent position when we apply to the scriveners to extend his life. And you were absolutely on target with your seduction of him. All that sob stuff about Paris. Percy Shelley could never resist a damsel in distress. Well done. Exactly what we wanted."

"Why couldn't you have just *told* me?"

"Rules. Anyway, get tidied up before Paris sees you. I just have to make a quick sortie to check that Norvus has called off his roughnecks. Then I'll explain the next stage of your mission. And, Elvira: *don't wash.*"

Chapter Seven

"You knew," said Elvira.

"Yes," answered Paris.

"All of it?"

"Yes. I was Despina's captive audience."

"I'm not accusing you," Elvira went on quietly. "I know how difficult it must have been to hide the truth."

"You *should* be accusing me. I got you into this by telling you I'd seen Shelley on the GTC footage and that he was better looking than his portrait."

"I'd forgotten that!"

"*I* hadn't. So, I'm going to make the biggest ever fuss of you till this is over. Afterwards, too!" He hugged her appreciatively. "You smell gorgeous."

"Not to me I don't. Sweat, sex, chimney smoke in my hair."

"How long before you're allowed to scrub it all off?"

"Despina didn't say. I'll ask her when she's back."

"Don't hurry on my account. Where did she disappear to this time?"

"Great Russell Street, one day later. Shelley didn't have a chance to say goodbye, so he might have left a note in the empty house. Despina thought it was worth checking. We don't want any more anomalous situations." Paris gathered her closer. "So, what was he like?"

"I've already told you. Intense, eloquent - "

"Don't prevaricate, sweetness. What was he like as a lover?"

"That isn't a fair question! Shelley never had your ... advantages."

"So he didn't satisfy you?"

"Er – no. He got overexcited. And the bracelet incident ruined his second attempt. He kissed nicely though."

"Hmm," said Paris, moderately content.

"But what *happened* with the bracelet?" Elvira went on somewhat tactlessly. "I thought you'd know."

"I can't explain such an adverse reaction. But it's a prototype, just as the Hope is. I'm still on a learning curve."

They talked idly, both wishing they could do more than talk. Fortunately Despina came back before the temptation became too great.

"You found something?" asked Elvira eagerly.

"Yes. As I suspected, he'd left you this." She spread out a crumpled, singed sheet of parchment. "It's a poem. As you can see, someone threw it on the fire. We'll never know who, since neither of us can suddenly appear in the middle of a houseful of people and wait to see who's responsible. It could have been Shelley himself, fearing he might cause you trouble by writing it. Or it could have been Mary, annoyed that he was clearly unfaithful on the very eve of their new start abroad. Or it could simply have been the cleaner, preparing for the next tenant. As you can see, we've lost the beginning and a few lines in the middle. Fortunately the fire was nearly out."

Elvira held the edges of the parchment down. "Is this really his handwriting? This scribble? I can't read a word of it, can you?"

"Not much, but I can see your name."

"May I?" Paris examined the poem under the nearest light source. "Yes, I can read it. I'm becoming quite good at deciphering scrawl since I've been at Construction. We can't use e-notes as even their tiny output messes with exposed circuitry, so Cyprian leaves written memos everywhere. His handwriting's worse than anyone's. Shall I read this aloud?"

"Please," said Elvira.

"I can see 'radiant as summer' and 'a lady once was mine.' Then it continues:

I dared to love her, but the fragile thread
Which briefly bound us – with so much unsaid

Was riven, and I fell to nothingness;
I slept and dreamt again of her caress.
This room, this London, ashes heaped on dust,
I now abandon ..."

Paris paused. "The manuscript's damaged here. This is the last stanza:

Beloved! Angel! I will fly to thee,

Bestride the sundering years which shackle me,
Seek out thy wondrous cabinet and behold
Elvira, framed in bands of living gold."

"You read that beautifully, Paris," Elvira said softly.

He gave a mock bow. "Courtesy of the Excelsior Academy's elocution programme."

"Elvira," said Despina ominously, "Did you tell Shelley about the Hope, and what it looked like?"

"No, absolutely not. I spoke as a tourist. No science except the photograph you made me take. I didn't lie to you earlier."

"In that case," Despina conceded, "I was only half right. Shelley didn't just tangle with the future in some nebulous way. He's forged a very strong link to *you*, Elvira. No, Paris, I don't mean a romantic link. This is different, and beyond my experience - "

Paris feigned surprise. "Really, Despina?"

"Yes, really. Since I have to guess, I'd say we're looking at some kind of life-changing event."

Elvira was confused. "You mean – the baby? If there *is* a baby?"

"The baby belongs in the past. This is a future-oriented progression. Think of ... two arterial roads converging. That's a clumsy analogy but it'll have to do. Maybe it's too far off to make sense. Anyway - " Despina handed Elvira an e-documentation card. "This will admit you to the GTC's medical lab in seven day's time. They'll run the pregnancy tests."

210

"I thought I had to wait a fortnight."

"In 2023, possibly. A week's all we need now. And in your case we have the additional evidence of the corrected timeline."

"And then what happens?"

"We monitor you very closely to determine when we can transfer the foetus to the ectogenesis unit. Ideally we won't have to admit you before then but sometimes it's advisable. Paris, I haven't forgotten about Lelza. I'm hoping Saranna will be able to deputise for Elvira if the need arises."

Paris sighed, but said nothing. Decorum kept him silent.

"When can we resume intimacy?" Elvira asked, saving him.

"Theoretically, as soon as your pregnancy's confirmed," said Despina. "Follow your instincts. But be aware, you might lack enthusiasm. We never did find a cure for morning sickness."

**

Unsurprisingly the test was positive, and Elvira returned from the clinic with an information folder – which she didn't read – and some iron supplements which she didn't take. She didn't as yet feel nauseous, just lethargic. Paris reluctantly continued work after Elvira had assured him she'd summon him immediately if she felt worse. Saranna, the only person outside of the GTC to know the truth, brought ginger snaps and barley sugar and asked Elvira if she'd like a holovid projector to help pass the time. Elvira thanked her and declined. She simply wanted to sleep.

Janine and Petra came calling, believing – understandably – that Paris was the expectant father.

"No, he isn't," Elvira told them candidly. "And we don't want people thinking he is, as it would be seen as a futile attempt to scupper Paris' marriage."

"Then who's the real father?" inquired Janine. "Does he know?"

"It's not like you to be so careless," Petra put in. "Was it a one-nighter? Did your implant fail?"

"Yes, and yes," Elvira said. "I'd like to name my lover but I've promised him discretion. He's married, and he's agreed to adopt the baby if I forego all contact. So that's the plan."

"Is his wife on board with that?"

"No idea. That's for him to sort out." Elvira tried to sound dismissive. "Once this little one's in ectogenesis I can get my life back on track."

"That sounds like the Elvira I've come to know," Janine remarked.

The following weekend Saranna was unavailable, and after a third uneventful check-up, Elvira decided to go with Paris to visit Lelza. "You're not going without me. She'll only start haranguing you."

"But how do we explain your condition?"

"*Condition?* Don't be so Victorian. I'm allowed to be under the weather sometimes, aren't I? Tell her I ate something that didn't agree with me. Fake fish and chips maybe."

"Yes, that'd do it."

"Right. Now go and find your baggiest pair of overalls. You're not parading around in those tight jeans. No sense in showing her what she can't have."

He grinned and went to change.

Elvira tried to make herself presentable in a navy trouser suit and white shirt, but couldn't disguise her wan complexion. Hardly before she'd set out she began to wish she hadn't volunteered for the trip. The multi-cube ride made her feel queasy and the short walk to Barnet Heights was exhausting. To her relief, Lelza was quietly sympathetic and offered her green tea. Elvira didn't entirely relax. Lelza was, even in repose, like an entitled little kitten waiting patiently by a mouse-hole. Were there any mice in greater MetroLondon? Probably.

She hadn't realised she'd spoken aloud until Lelza said: "There are mice in the grain towers. The Harvesters simulate natural surroundings on some levels, then compare and contrast to obtain the best result. I thought about applying to join the Guild once, but it seemed too restrictive."

She went to refill her cup, and Paris whispered: "Mice, Elvira? What a weird question. You're in a strange mood tonight."

"I am. My mind's all over the place."

"Are you happy in your chosen career?" Paris asked Lelza when she returned, in an attempt to keep the conversation bland.

213

"As far as it's progressed, yes. Ideally I'd like to visit the regions my plant specimens come from. When I was younger I wanted to be a deep-sea diver and study coral reefs. Now, with my new responsibilities, that's no longer possible." She looked directly at Paris. "I could have sustained my work anywhere. You cannot. I do acknowledge your service to the TTI, although you may not think so." She paused a moment. "In just over a fortnight it will be May Eve. Beltane. I hope you'll be available then. I'm planning a small gathering here and naturally I hope to introduce you."

"I agree it's high time I met your mother," Paris said unenthusiastically.

"I don't mean her. Just … people our own age."

"In that case I shall be pleased to attend," Paris answered formally.

Elvira was looking so fatigued that Lelza herself suggested that she should be at home. Once they were on their way, Paris again asked the reason for her odd behaviour.

"I don't know. I just feel … adrift. I felt a bit like this when I first came to MetroLondon, but it soon faded. I'm just wondering: did Despina tell you that what's conceived in the past is drawn to the past?"

"Not in so many words, but I've heard the reverse said. What's conceived in the present needs to stay in it. We always give a safety warning to pregnant time trippers, namely, that giving birth in the past is *not* a good idea. They mostly take heed.

But there were one or two money-back demands after unborn children became distressed. Travel issues, always, but the TTI tattlegraph put its own spin on things. Did the babies sense they'd been removed from their original timeline?"

"Speculation? Superstition?" Elvira persisted.

"Pseudo-science. And almost certainly wrong."

At last they reached the corridor of tourist apartments. After they left the multi-cube he almost had to carry her the last few steps. Once inside, she disappeared into the hygiene cubicle and reappeared a moment later.

"Paris. There's blood. Call the lab. The card's … somewhere. I don't know where I left it."

When he couldn't find it he called Despina, who told him not to panic and dispatched two med-techs. With routine efficiency they placed Elvira in a stasis bubble and carried her off. Paris made to follow but Despina restrained him.

"You can't be with her. She's fragile and she's rejecting the child. Let the medics do their work."

"You're not leaving me here!" Paris said furiously. "If you don't take me with you I'll follow and kick the door in."

"You're delightful when you're angry," Despina said. "But you need to calm down. I know the perfect way to achieve that but I think we'd both be sorry afterwards. So please, take a few deep breaths and tell me what led to this deterioration. What did she do, what did she say?"

Paris recalled as much as he could. When he got to the part where Elvira had said she felt adrift in time, Despina interrupted.

"This is what's wrong. There are *three* timelines in play, the third being the pull of her old life. We have to counter it with something from 1818. Where's that poem?"

"Pressed lovingly between the pages of Shelley's better known works. I teased her about that."

"Fetch it. It could make all the difference."

Paris brought it to her. "I don't see how this can possibly help."

"Our forensics team will extract DNA, perspiration, hair particles, anything embedded in the paper. The paper itself, even the ink, has its own attributes. And don't worry, they'll only sample a small area of the document."

"And then what? Do you make a serum?"

"No, no. It's just like air. We'll introduce it into her bubble, let her sense it."

Paris, who'd never studied timeline quanta, had to be content with that. On arrival at the GTC's specialist facility, Despina escorted him to a basic, single bedded room usually reserved for agents injured in the field. "My colleagues want to sedate you, but I've assured them you won't be a nuisance. Don't prove me wrong."

"I'll sleep. I'm exhausted. But please wake me if you need to."

"I promise."

"Despina – if she miscarries, will she have to go through all this again? I don't mean her liaison with Shelley. He'll be kind to her. He adores her. I mean what happens after. *This.* Being a lab rat, as I said."

"Let's not get ahead of ourselves," Despina advised.

"That's a yes, then," Paris said resignedly. "Any chance of some cocoa? We always used to have cocoa. In Hampstead."

Despina gave him a tiny peck on the cheek, and left. There wasn't any cocoa.

In the morning she was back with somewhat reassuring news. The threatened miscarriage had been averted and there were no chromosomal abnormalities in the foetus. However, Elvira's stress hormones were off the scale. "We've been talking to her," Despina went on. "She's permanently despondent about Lelza. And, she's worried she won't cope when she has to surrender her child to foster care in 1818."

"Because she'll have bonded with it?" Paris queried.

"No, she doesn't believe she will. But she knows there'll be more unhappiness for Shelley when the baby dies at the age of fifteen months. I've offered to do the hand-over to the foster parents, and she's content with that. But – we'll have to keep her in. As you rightly said, she can't start over, so we have to ensure she doesn't have to."

"Can I see her now?"

"You need to eat. Our food's better than the TTI's. You can see her after breakfast." And to ensure these instructions were obeyed, Despina grasped his arm tightly and escorted him to the executives' café.

Elvira was looking better than he'd thought she would. She'd applied a little make-up and was wearing a pink bed-jacket borrowed from another expectant mother. "Hello, you!" she said. "I'm keeping you off work, aren't I? Sorry to be a pain. I assume Despina's told you what's what?"

"Pretty much."

"Now listen, Paris – there's something more immediate that's been bothering me. In a fortnight it'll be Beltane, this … sex festival. I'll still be in here and I don't like the idea of you entertaining Lelza without me. Not on *that* night. Saranna's told me how wild it gets."

"Lelza said she was having friends round."

"What friends? Why's she never mentioned them before? I don't trust her."

"Well, maybe Saranna can come with me."

"She's going to some spaceport bash. I've already asked Despina to step in, and she's agreed. She says it's safe enough inside the TTI's boundaries but there's no way she's letting you roam around Barnet on your own. And there's no way *I'm* letting you stay overnight at Lelza's."

"But surely," ventured Paris, "Despina has her own plans for May Eve?"

"She normally meets with some colonists from New Sparta. They visit Greece, not MetroLondon.

She also said she didn't mind skipping a year. Don't argue, Paris, please."

"I won't. I'll do as I'm told. But it goes without saying that I'd far rather be with you."

"Then, don't say it. Kiss me instead."

"Compliance," he replied, and they both smiled.

***

On April 28th, news arrived which overturned their careful plan. Norvus had been attacked while on an assignment, and had been rushed back to the GTC casualty unit. He'd received a penetrating stab wound and subsequent concussion when he'd struck his head on a stone floor. Crucially, he'd been in Venice in mid-1818, which meant that both Despina and Elvira could provide the right ambience to aid his recovery.

Elvira, of course, was already on site. Despina was ordered to stay close until Norvus was out of danger. In any case, she wanted to be at his side. Elvira and Paris had long suspected that the relationship between the two agents was more than just professional.

"I'm so sorry," Despina said to Paris. "I can't leave him. Please understand."

"It's all right. I'll manage," Paris assured her, though his heart sank at the thought of being alone with Lelza on May Eve. "But what in the cosmos *happened* to Norvus? I though he was invincible."

"I don't know yet. The scriveners are being close-mouthed as usual. But they did say I'd get my chance at retribution later, so I'll hold them to that."

On the morning of the 30th, she was less vengeful. Norvus had a robust constitution and the knife wound was healing well, thanks to bio-weft. He was in and out of consciousness and seemed lucid, but the clinical lead was taking no chances and had scheduled a brain scan.

"I'd like to stay for his results," Despina told Paris, "but he's making such good progress I don't need to abandon you completely. Remember the necklet I gave Elvira before we dispatched her to Regency London? She thought I was being over-protective, but she found herself in a situation. So might you. Here's a medallion you can wear under your shirt, or over it if you're feeling flamboyant."

"There's a chip in it?"

"Yes, sending a continuous signal to my comms badge. As long as it continues to operate I'll know you're well and happy. If you're in extremis, simply smash the jewel and I'll be with you stat."

"That's good to know. I'm grateful – although I probably won't use it. After all, what could Lelza possibly do to terrify me?"

"She might surprise you," said Despina.

***

It began fairly innocuously. Lelza had bought some snacks and a quantity of alcohol, which she stacked casually on the dining table. When no-one turned up she seemd genuinely upset. Paris didn't think she was a good enough actress to fake distress, which presumably meant she had a collection of fair-weather friends.

He did what he could to salvage the situation. He dined with her, watched holovid celebrations from Australia and New Zealand, then at midnight went with her onto the balcony to witness the local laser display. He hadn't realised how accurately the newest generation of lasers could depict copulation.

"That's tacky," he remarked.

"It's *life*," Lelza retorted.

Paris was startled. It was the first time she'd seemed fully engaged with reality. Below in the street, shrieks and ribaldry made themselves heard.

"And so it begins," he said dismissively. "Fortunately your apartment has good soundproofing, so we can opt out. I'm calling it a day. You should too." It went against all his careful upbringing to turn his back and leave her standing there, but he managed it. Then he retreated to the smaller of the two bedrooms, closed the door quietly and keyed in the privacy code. Then, after a pause, he randomised the code. Finally, reluctantly, he kicked off his shoes and stripped to his vest and boxers. He didn't think he'd sleep, but the room was warm, the bed comfortable, and he was mentally tired. Three hours passed.

Suddenly he was wide awake. The sound that had disturbed him was the quiet musical beep of the door release. He swore under his breath for failing to guess that Lelza would have had the lock tampered with. By Albie, probably. He switched on the overhead light as the door swung open.

Lelza stumbled in, barefoot, her night-robe askew. She had a half empty vodka bottle in her hand. "Where's that little mousey, hiding in my housey? *There* you are, pretty Paris. Don't be shy. Give Lelza a kiss."

"You're drunk," said Paris irritably. "Go back to bed."

"Aww, don't play hard to get. It's Beltane! Do your duty, Paris. Make our aged parents happy. Let's get your kit off …"

He seized her wrist. "Lelza, that's enough. It's not happening. Now clear out and sober up."

Her mood suddenly changed. "Don't talk to me like that. Just don't. Always putting on airs." She brought her face close to his, eyes like flints. "Sanctimonious pipsqueak. Designer scum! My mother says I'm useless, my workmates laugh at me, all because of *you*. You, you, you. I hate you!"

She stepped back and hurled the bottle at him. He dodged. It hit the wall and shattered.

The noise seemed to sober her a little. "I didn't mean - " she faltered. "I'll clear this up."

"Leave it," Paris said hastily. "I'll do it." But she was already trying to pick up the pieces. Before he could stop her she'd tripped on her nightie and trodden on a sliver of glass embedded in the carpet. Blook spurted from her foot.

Exasperated, Paris sat her on the end of the bed, tore a strip from the hem of her thin gown and tried

222

to staunch the wound. It continued to bleed. "Where's your first aid kit?"

"Bathroom."

"Right. Come on. Leave all this." He hauled her into the bathroom, sat her on the laundry bin and applied a coagulant spray to her heel. "We should get this looked at. There might be glass in it."

"No. Leave me alone." She brushed him aside, stumbled to her bedroom and slammed the door. After a moment he heard her sobbing, dejected and defeated. He might have felt justified, had his kindly nature permitted it. Sighing, he took the medallion from his neck, removed the jewel and crushed it carefully. Then he waited for Despina.

She arrived equipped with a first responder's medkit and an evidence bag. Paris stared.

"What on earth did you think she'd done to me?"

"It's called hedging my bets. There's never anyone on standby during Beltane, so I came fully prepared."

Sheepishly, Paris updated her.

"Well," she said when he'd finished, "that wasn't quite the scenario I was expecting."

"Maybe I shouldn't have called you, but she was inconsolable. I'm sorry."

"Don't be. I'll talk to her. In the meantime, get some booze down you. You look … odd. Pale as those virgin bedsheets."

"Don't."

"Back shortly." Despina used her GTC override on Lelza's door and went discreetly inside.

As promised, she soon reappeared. "I've given her the official chat, taken a fragment of glass from her heel and sedated her. She'll sleep, and hopefully forget a few things. Now, Paris, what's eating you?"

"Something I thought I'd forgotten," he said unhappily. "I was an anxious, needy child and Eva couldn't respond to that. I soon learnt that throwing a tantrum was the best way to get her attention. One day she got furious with me, held a hand-mirror in front of my angry little face and snarled: 'Look at yourself, you miserable brat. Is this what I paid all that money for? Is it? Aren't you ashamed?' Just minutes ago, Lelza's face was just inches from mine. She yelled every insult she could think of. Her eyes, Despina. Her angry eyes. It was just like looking into that mirror long ago. I couldn't believe how like me she was."

A look of pure surmise crossed Despina's face and she uttered some choice curses in New Spartan. Paris politely waited for her to explain.

"Just after I brought Elvira to this century," Despina began, icily calm after her outburst, "the GTC offered me a routine job which I turned down. I think that may have been a mistake. A stupid one. Where's that evidence bag?"

"Under your chair."

She retrieved it, grabbed a sterile pouch and deposited Lelza's bloodstained bandage into it. "One down, one to go. Your turn." She seized a wisp of Paris' hair between finger and thumb, and pulled.

"OW! What was that for?"

"DNA," she replied succinctly, inserting the golden strands into a small tube. "I have to get these back to the lab. I'll be as quick as I can, I promise. Don't go out. There'll be stragglers. Tidy yourself up and wait." She spoke into her bio-communicator and was gone.

Paris, annoyed at her extreme reaction to a mere domestic spat, helped himself to more whisky from the selection on the dining table. Since he couldn't go home, he'd at least make the waiting more bearable.

***

The GTC forensics lab was a haven of quiet after the late night revelry outside. Quiet, until Despina arrived.

"Stop whatever you're doing," she ordered the duty technician. "I need a DNA analysis of these two samples, urgently. Check for a half-sibling match."

"What's so important? We're thin on the ground tonight."

Despina bit back an epithet. "Last September I was made aware of an illegal trade in designer sperm batches. To my everlasting shame I didn't take the case. I now have reason to suspect Astrolabe Babes, and this DNA will confirm it."

"You still haven't explained the urgency."

Despina raised her voice an octave. "A troubled young couple in an arranged marriage are

225

at risk of committing incest. To prevent this we need to act *now*!"

"Why didn't you say so to begin with?" asked the tech girl mildly. "Two hours. Stay on site."

"I'll be with Norvus," said Despina. "Message me the instant you have the data."

Norvus was wearily pleased when she returned. "You look fired up. All well?"

"I'm hoping. Anything new with you?"

"Not since you left. But earlier – and I didn't tell you since you were so preoccupied – I was visited by a victim support worker, offering a paid leave of absence. I'm going to take it and spend some time with Vivette."

"Watch out. We don't want any more dichotomies."

He grinned. "As if! I'm thinking of later, when she's in her forties. She and Maman and Fabian will have relocated to Bouafle, near Versailles. Amelie's safely married to her astronaut."

"That sounds perfect. Go for it. And now, it's time I knew what put you in here. I assume you've been cleared to discuss it?"

"Discuss my failure, you mean," he said wryly.

"Well, spit it out!"

"My gentle Despina. Since you ask me so sweetly: I was supposed to prevent the murder of Lord Byron."

"*What*? But he doesn't die in Venice and he isn't murdered!"

"Quite. And you know as well as I do that if someone famous dies ahead of schedule, the

226

timeline breach can extend for decades. So the scriveners have ring-fenced the whole day. No-one gets in, no-one gets out."

"Who was the assailant? Some loser trying to make his mark on history?"

"No, some madwoman that Byron had installed in his palazzo and couldn't get rid of. I know, I know. I was complacent. She had a stiletto, I disarmed her, and missed the smaller knife she had in her shoe. I won't get leave to try again after a mistake like that."

"Someone will have to."

"That's the whole point of the ring-fence, isn't it? To make a measured, informed choice. Except – I heard some careless talk when they thought I was unconscious. They mentioned Elvira and a fight suit."

"I was told to commission that suit weeks ago. They surely don't expect her to get involved *now*?"

"It doesn't have to *be* now, does it?" Norvus pointed out. "Always one step ahead of us, our clever scriveners."

"Not always." Despina paced the floor.

"For Hera's sake, woman, stop prowling. Come here, sit by me and let me bore you with my photos of Vivette and Maman in Ashby de la Zouch. Oh, and mind where you're putting your left elbow. My midriff's still painful."

"Milksop."

Obediently she reclined beside him and viewed the snapshots, lovingly transcribed into a 3D holo-globe. Far from being bored, she was a little

227

nostalgic. "A simple life, but attractive. Just like Elvira's world. No wonder she misses it sometimes."

The holo-globe reached the end of its stored images and started again. The gentle dissolve from one scene to the next was peaceful and soporific. When her communicator shrilled, startling her, she was almost reluctant to answer.

"It's Vantine from forensics. Good news, Agent Despina. A fifty per cent match. Your unhappy young couple are half brother and sister."

Despina punched the air. "I *knew* it! I must tell Elvira - "

"Wait," Norvus said peremptorily. "You can't tell her yet. If you go public now, you'll have made two people very happy. But Astrolabe Babes will shut down their op before we've had a chance to nail them. Let's pool our imaginations, shall we? A spot of brainstorming? It used to work in the old days when we had a knotty problem."

"Just in the short-term, then," Despina conceded. "You first."

"Good girl. For starters, remind me again of our designer siblings' ages?"

"Paris is twenty eight, Lelza twenty four."

"So, what was trending thirty years ago? Sperm donors on the catwalk. Hunky lads eager to share their attributes. Donor house parties. Matriarchs and their daughters would have turned up their entitled noses at offerings that had been on ice for a week, let alone five years."

"I don't see where you're going with this."

228

"Patience, D. In essence, this is all down to money, isn't it? An employee defrauding the company. I'm not familiar with all this women's stuff, so talk me through the client-consultant process. Paris' mother confers with – who *does* she confer with?"

"A tech-visualiser. She tells him or her what she wants, a batch is formulated, and she books a date for the insemination."

"Same tech, same department?"

"Absolutely. Astrolabe Babes' ads all boast about continuity. It reassures the clients. Moving on, the pregnancy's achieved, Eva's tech takes the payment and the fee goes into the firm's accounts. As she bought exclusive use of the batch, the rest is destroyed."

"Except that it isn't," Norvus concluded for her. "Somehow the depleted batch is sequestered away until Lelza's mother comes in, and then our less than honest visualiser persuades her to accept it. She pays, but the money doesn't go near the firm's books. And no-one suspects."

Despina frowned. "This is where our hypothesis falls down. Neither of our redoubtable women would have accepted historic products, as you rightly said. They'd have wanted the best."

"Of course they would. Now this is a leap of faith on my part, but the more we dissect this the more I'm convinced I'm right. I believe there's only one perp, and that person is sending donor material back through time to himself, using the single packet relay."

229

"Does that still exist in our timeframe?"

"Indeed it does, mostly for medical emergencies. I was very glad of one earlier."

"So *that's* why you thought of it!" Despina said warmly. "Creativity out of catastrophe. I'm impressed. So, how do I put a stop to this malpractice?"

"You don't. You'll need the GTC auditors for that. They're the only people who can barge in without notice and demand to see all records. Don't worry, no-one will know they're GTC. They'll have a believable story ready. You'll have told them what to look for and that's what they'll do, while they're throwing things about. And, since you'll be passing my idea off as yours, you'll have the satisfaction of interrogating the culprit."

"Synapsyn?"

"Of course, what else?"

"Norvus, you're a star. What would I do without you?" Belatedly, Despina checked her login time. She'd been there two and a half hours. "Oh, Hades. I have to get Paris out of Barnet Heights before Lelza wakes up. He's not in a good place, in more ways than one. I can't believe I have to drag him back to the TTI."

Norvus surveyed her critically. "How long is it since you slept?"

"Too long. But I have to do this."

"Why? He's on TTI's retrieval list, isn't he? Didn't you transport him from 2023? Well then, grab a custody band from stores, add his ID and key it to your flat."

230

"But it'll go on record as an arrest!"

"A protective measure," he amended. "Now scat. You're dead on your feet."

***

Just before sunrise, Despina returned to Lelza's apartment. All was quiet, but Paris was not in his room. Recalling where she'd left him, she tiptoed into the dining room and found him fully dressed and asleep at the table, blond head resting on folded arms. An open bottle of whisky was close by, but it was obvious that he'd consumed no more than a measure. He'd simply been unable to stay awake for her.

Silently thanking Norvus' foresight, she clipped the plain brass circlet round his wrist and selected a frequently used destination from her bio-server. Her bracelet signalled its readiness. She touched it to the custody band, and a breeze swirled through the suddenly empty room.

At the moment of transference Despina seized Paris round the waist, and when they materialised near the mezzanine stairs she was able to lower him down gently.

"Wha …?"

"Its all right, Paris, you're home. I didn't wake you as I know how you hate time travelling – even a fifty second relocation. I'm sorry I was so late but it was very very worthwhile. I'll explain everything after I've had some sleep. I hope you don't mind me crashing here."

"It's your flat," he said reasonably.

"So it is. Come on, then." She manoeuvred him up the stairs to the futon, took off her boots, metallic skirt and hoop earrings, and subsided thankfully. She was asleep in moments. Paris yawned, removed his suit for the second time that day and lay down next to her, smoothing a quilt over them both. Their bodies didn't touch. There was plenty of room.

He surfaced at half past eleven to the welcome aroma of coffee and the sound of Despina speaking swiftly and urgently. "You're in position? Good. Just ensure that no-one suspects what, or rather who, you're really after. Contact me as soon as you have a name."

"What's going on?" Paris asked.

"Oh, just something Norvus wanted me to finish. The coffee's freshly made if you want some."

"I do, and then I'd better call Cyprian. There's always a high level of absenteeism after Beltane and I could still go in this afternoon if he likes."

Despina sensed something amiss. "You're mad at me. Why?"

"Why do you think? You took our DNA – Lelza's and mine – and then you slapped a suss bangle on me. Just because of a scrap and some spilt booze!"

"Oh, gods." Despina moved to put an arm round him. He didn't shrug her off, but stared at the opposite wall. "Paris, listen. Your record will stay unblemished. That wasn't why I took the DNA. I was protecting you both."

He gazed at her in confusion. He'd never seen her look so distressed.

"If I ignore protocol and take you into my confidence," she continued, "you won't be allowed out of here until this is resolved – even if I have to tie you up. Is that understood?"

"Perfectly."

"You provided the truth yourself when you told me about Eva's mirror and Lelza's eyes. I rushed the DNA to forensics and they checked for a familial match. You're Lelza's half-brother, which means your marriage is null and void. I wanted to shout it from the rooftops but Norvus stopped me. I haven't even told Elvira. Once we've caught who did this to you, we can tell the whole city. Correction: I'll tell Nimue Pamina and *she'll* tell the city."

Paris looked stupefied. "I'm sorry," he mumbled at last.

"Aren't you always?"

"Sorry for doubting your motives."

"You're forgiven."

"I'll never have to go near that dreadful apartment again?" he went on, half to himself. "Never have to see that infuriating girl again?"

"Not if you don't want to."

"And I can marry Elvira?"

"That's the general idea."

He focused at last. "Someone should contact Aurelia Neve. There's bound to be paperwork. But first – I'm starving. Ravenous. If the TTI canteen's out of bounds, can we order in?"

Despina resisted an urge to hug him. "You bet we can. How about crepes from La Chanson d'Amour?"

"Sounds perfect."

She'd forgotten how delightful his smile was. It was a long time since she'd seen it.

Later, after a generous serving of crepes and a lemon sorbet dessert, she began to wish she wasn't on duty. Yes, she wanted the case resolved, but any competent agent could handle an interrogation.

"Quiet, isn't it?" Paris remarked.

"Now that you mention it …" Despina had only just realised. "No brace generators. Absentee physicists! It must have been a totally manic Beltane!"

They relaxed with yet more coffee, and Paris – having rediscovered his tongue – chatted happily about the modest wedding he'd like, and how he and Elvira would have to settle for whatever Saranna foisted on them.

Finally, at around three-thirty, Despina had the call she was expecting. She put it on the table-top screen. "Jane Gwendoline here, senior auditor. Excellent news! We've got her. But she very nearly eluded us."

"*She*? I thought it would be a man. Someone resentful of the designer class."

"Wrong for once, Despina! Her name's Araminta Grace and she's been with Astrolabe Babes for decades. She must have known the game was up when we arrived, as she tried to do a runner. We caught her at the spaceport, about to board a shuttle. She was booked on a hyperway flight to Wolf 359, and I'm sure I don't need to tell you the Wolf 359 system's neutral, not part of the Consortium. We'd have had no end of trouble extraditing her." Jane paused. "I know you wanted to lead this interrogation, but there wasn't one as such. She confessed almost at once. She said the thefts had been on her conscience for years."

"Thefts, plural?"

"Two. She did it, she said, because she longed for designer daughters and couldn't afford them. Her girls are in their early twenties now and know nothing of their mother's crime. We'll be handing her over to a detention unit shortly, and they'll follow due procedure including a synapsyn-based reprise."

"Ask her about the other theft," Paris prompted.

"We have the details," Jane reassured him. "Fortunately, the offspring didn't marry anyone they shouldn't. The genealogy department's updating the family trees and we'll make a present of them to both families. It'll be a good talking point. But since you're there, Paris, there is *one* thing I ought to mention."

"What?"

"Despina and Norvus got the chain of events back to front. Bryony Dawn, Lelza's mother, was the first recipient of the shared batch. Araminta then sent the remainder five years into the past and sold it to Eva Mariosa."

Paris was suddenly silent, and Despina cast an anxious look at him. He'd turned away, hiding his face, and she thought he was about to cry. "I'll deal with this, Jane," she said hastily, "and catch up with the legal proceedings in due course. Thank you for a job well done."

"I suspect we'll be all over the news tonight," the auditor said. "There were scores of people at the spaceport. My apologies in advance."

The instant the screen blanked, Paris dissolved into helpless laughter. Not distress, as Despina had feared, but pure mirth.

"I was all set to comfort you," she said, somewhat disappointed. "I didn't think you'd find it funny."

"Funny? It's hilarious. Lelza got the pick of the crop and I got the rejects? I can't wait to tell Eva. A toast, Despina. Let's drink to avaricious Araminta and the new me!"

Accordingly, Despina poured two glasses of whisky and ginger. Paris accepted his with a flourish.

"All my life," he said more seriously, "I've had to put up with Eva ranting on about my pedigree and how I wasn't living up to it. I felt such a failure at times. But now I feel vindicated, if that makes sense. I was always true to myself. That makes me very happy, and it's all thanks to you and your amazing intuition. I could kiss you."

"I'll save you the trouble." Her kiss was lingering, determined, and arousing.

"You're not using those pheromones again, are you?" he asked when she eventually let him draw breath.

"No," she murmured. "This is all you. You've been too long without."

"Is that an invitation?"

"It might be."

He attempted a frown. "Despina, will you stop sparring with me and get up those stairs?"

"Finally!" She ran ahead of him with a whoop of anticipation. He followed, nonchalantly stepping out of his suit and leaving it in a heap.

"Don't undress," he ordered. "*I* want to do it."

"Whatever lights your candle."

He expertly removed her close-fitting top and breast banding. The mini-skirt had smart fastening and he paused, enjoying the moment. "I don't want the code. This delightful little skirt stays on."

"Because it fuels your fantasy?"

"You know it does. And as for what it conceals …" Throwing her down, he grabbed a handful of fabric and hauled with vigour. Something tore. Then leggings, underwear and eventually boots all disappeared over the railing in a glorious tangle.

"Now, lover," Despina murmured in his ear, "show me what they taught you at the Academy."

He was being tested. Of course he was. Well, since she wanted a performance, she'd get a superlative one. He was in the precise mood to deliver it.

***

"Hey." Despina shook Paris gently by the shoulder.

"Oh, sorry," he said automatically. "Was I sleeping?"

"Yes, and no wonder. Your sex tutors did an amazing job on you. They deserve the Freedom of the City for their exemplary work."

"Was I really that good?"

"Oh, you were. All three times. Anyway: I didn't want to interrupt your post-coital doze as you looked such a sweetie, but it's almost time for the evening news. I thought we'd best check it out."

"Back to reality." He scrambled off the rumpled bed. "Elvira's going to be furious with me."

"I don't think she will," Despina said quietly. "Not when she hears how elated you were with your status reversal. Anyway, she can hardly complain when she's carrying Shelley Junior."

"You *told* her to seduce him!"

"I told her nothing. She chose. Now let's not argue. I want to see what the paps managed to dig up."

The wall screen lit. "You're livestreaming City News on Percipient UK, bringing MetroLondon to the world and beyond. Today, GTC operatives made a lightning raid on Astrolabe Babes, Ealing, followed by an arrest here at the spaceport. Araminta Grace has confessed to selling exclusively formulated sperm batches twice over, and retaining the profits. We can reveal that at least one such illegal sale resulted in the marriage of a half-brother and sister. In addition, we are reliably informed that one of the recipients was none other than Bryony Dawn, one of the company's benefactors. Ms Dawn, may we approach you for a comment? Does this mean that Astrolabe Babes will no longer benefit from your sponsorship?"

"It does, and they're lucky I don't sue. Fortunately for them, my daughter interceded, and I bowed to her wishes."

"Well, *there's* a first," Despina muttered.

Lelza stepped nervously in front of the lens and began a prepared speech. "I agreed to go on camera today as there's someone I wish to acknowledge. I could have been trapped in a proscribed relationship had it not been for my assigned bridegroom's tireless efforts to free us. He showed the utmost forbearance and resilience in the face of an impossible situation, knowing instinctively that something was wrong. Thanks to him I can now propose to the man I love." She dragged a bashful Albie into shot. "Albie Nellison, will you marry me?"

"Yes," he stammered. "Yes, yes, yes!"

The crowd cheered.

"Staged," remarked Despina.

"Quite likely," said Paris, "but I don't think Albie was part of it. He's no actor, so if he looked taken aback, then he was. He's probably still working on that ancient cinema under the spaceport, and came up to see what was going on."

"Nice of Lelza not to name you."

"It was, but it won't keep me out of the news. I've been seen in public with her, so has Elvira, so has Saranna."

"Saranna can give as good as she gets."

"I don't doubt it. It's Elvira I'm worried about. I don't want the paps targeting her."

"They won't be able to while she's in the medlab. We don't even allow newsfeeds. But I suppose it's possible that someone might *tell* her you're off the hook, if they thought it would help her get well."

"That's just what I was thinking. That news should come from us, don't you agree?"

"From *you*," Despina corrected, "and not until you're squeaky-clean. Get to it. Then I'll relocate us. And Paris – no remorse. You can fess up later, if you must, but right now all she needs to know is that you'll be free to marry her."

When they reached the medlab they found some whispers circulating. One or two of the outlying departments had seen the telecast and linked it with the recent forensic work, but in the absence of the bridegroom's name had yet to make a connection with Elvira. Norvus had unsurprisingly said nothing. No rumours had reached the maternity unit.

"Well, there she is," Despina whispered, giving Paris a shove. "Off you go. And take that silly grin off your face or you'll spoil the surprise."

"Where will *you* be?"

"Elsewhere."

She lingered near the door long enough to see Elvira's face light up in pure joy. Having visited Norvus and dealt summarily with some intrepid reporters, she sneaked back for one more look at the lovers. Paris was sitting on the bed with Elvira leaning against him. She looked radiant. And on Paris' face was a look of perfect peace, his inner demons silent at last. Despina retired without being seen.

241

Chapter Eight

It wasn't all sweetness and light, of course. The annulment, in all its pedantic detail, took several weeks to process, hindered by the timelag in receiving Eva's instructions from Proxima 4. She was demanding compensation from Astrolabe Babes. House Dawn's solicitor was being deliberately obtuse, and Aurelia Neve was caught in the middle.

Elvira was unfazed; she knew she'd be married sooner or later and spent many days in Saranna's company, making and revising plans, drawing up guest lists and looking at wedding outfits. She'd finally been allowed home but remained remotely monitored. A tiny implant relayed the baby's autonomic functions to the medlab.

The media remained curious about the father's identity, but her reply was always the same: she though she'd lost Paris, so what was so unusual about taking another lover? She'd given Petra and Janine leave to tell what little they knew, which they did, enjoying the attention. Cyprian, at his belligerent best, kept all questioners away from TTI Construction. Paris himself, on the few occasions that he'd been cornered, pleaded ignorance. "I don't believe you!" said one very persistent young woman. Paris had responded with one of his dazzling smiles. "I'll let you into a secret. I don't believe me either!"

Nimue Pamina remained unusually silent on the matter, for the simple reason that Despina had threatened her with shutdown if she voiced any scandal. But Despina had also promised a forthcoming exclusive if she cooperated.

Elvira's pregnancy became less and less troublesome as the weeks went by. The baby was healthy but underweight, and the antenatal team decided to transfer it to ectogenesis at twenty weeks, where its growth could be assisted. Elvira was at ease with this, though she had to admit she'd miss what Paris called her "sweet little bump." Or maybe she'd just miss his fascination with it. At the clinic she was talked through the procedure, not all that different to a caesarean of her era; the main difference being that once she'd healed, an aesthetician would eradicate the scar and restore her figure to its trim proportions.

Then, while she was gently coasting toward these events, Despina dropped another bombshell.

"Time for our next assignment. Yes, I'm coming with you. We're to prevent Lord Byron's murder at the hands of his mad mistress. Norvus will acquaint you with the details."

"Norvus …?"

"And we must check if your fight suit still fits. You're a bit more roly-poly than when it was bought."

"You mean – I'm going like *this*? Why?"

"Because Shelley will be there too. He needs to *see* you pregnant, doesn't he? Otherwise you, or

243

rather I, could be taking him anyone's baby in another four months."

"Paris is going to freak out when I tell him."

Despina sighed in exasperation. "It's a timeline breach, and he'll know how essential it is that we fix it. Thanks to Norvus we have the whole attack on Byron mapped out. Here's a rendition." She inserted a holo-chip into the tabletop reader. "The green stick figure is Norvus. The red, Margarita Cogni, Byron's mistress. Watch."

The two outlines swirled, intersected, broke apart, recombined, halted. The green figure became an immobile dot. "She had *two* daggers. Here's my revised version. You and me, two against one. I relieve Margarita of her only visible weapon and floor her with a drop-kick. She mightn't be that easy to subdue, so I've omitted the resolution for now. You protect Byron, then, once I have Margarita pinned, remove the second knife from her left shoe. We can re-run this later."

"No," said Elvira.

Despina scowled. "Are you trying to back out?"

"No, I'm saying your plan won't work. *I* have to lead."

"What for? I'm the better fighter."

"You also bear a grudge. That woman almost killed Norvus. You'll confront her in anger and you'll lose. My MMA instructor, back in Hampstead, told me never to lose my temper with an opponent. If I did, I'd be giving them the advantage."

Irritably Despina turned off the display. "Point taken. We'll rehearse. If I think you're up to speed we'll change places. Oh, I don't believe I mentioned that you'll have another chance to see Shelley on his own. You know how difficult that is to arrange, but I've managed it."

"It doesn't *sound* as if we'll be on our own!"

"You will be. Byron's going to be so so grateful, and he'll sort it. And, if it isn't too much trouble for you, I'd still like to know why Shelley wrote that poem. What did your recall bracelet cause him to see?"

***

The fight garment, despite its Leisure 4 Lovers logo, was little more than a one-piece body suit, ankle length with a racer back. The one original feature was an iridescent band of Vivlar, flexible but strong, which encircled Elvira's torso and cushioned her baby bump in a way that no other material could. A traditional loose-fitting white jacket with a tie belt concealed the odd design. The latter was introduced at a late stage when Elvira complained that she looked like an insect. Despina, on the other hand, looked resplendent in a sea-green body suit with a pearl-strewn bodice.

After some practice bouts, it was agreed that Elvira could take the leading role against Margarita. "All you need to remember is to stay off your back," Despina warned. "Don't expose your stomach, however fleetingly. Arm locks should be a breeze.

You can throw the bitch over your shoulder if you want. In the event of any problems, the entire medical resources of the GTC will spring into action. The antenatal unit is already prepped and awaiting your return."

Norvus was somewhat dubious about the women's plan but knew better than to challenge it. Just prior to their departure, he talked them through the data he'd originally been given.

"This is the Palazzo Mocenigo. Vast, isn't it? And this, adjacent to the waterfront, is the place where everything kicks off. This is Byron's erstwhile mistress, whom he nicknamed La Fornarina. As you can see, she favours flamboyant dress, including ridiculous hats with trailing ostrich feathers. I assumed her attire would impede her mission, but be warned, it didn't. Oh, while I think of it, Elvira – don't expect La Fornarina or Byron to remember me. As far as they're concerned, I was never there."

"Don't they remember *anything*?"

"Always be mindful of the universal rule," Norvus said solemnly. "Time *is*. It doesn't move, *we* do. We leave our mark on it, but only superficially. When we interact with the occupants of a timeline they're rightfully creating, we work within strict parameters. We prefer not to be noticed. And if, as on this occasion, things go wrong, we can only retreat, reset and start over. The event never happened, so the participants have nothing to remember. Tabula rasa. What's the matter, Despina? Didn't think I knew the science? I wouldn't have qualified if I'd skipped it. Now get going, both of you."

***

Byron scanned the waterfront, having just yelled for his chief gondolier. Nearby was a valise containing the few effects he was permitting La Fornarina to keep. He was sending her back to her equally faithless husband, a local baker.

She hurtled out of a side corridor, screeching invective, stiletto held high, long black tendrils of hair streaming Medusa-like in the wake of her fury. Byron froze for what might have been a second too long. But Elvira was suddenly there, using La Fornarina's momentum against her, tripping her and forcing her arm back until she dropped the knife. Despina kicked it toward Byron.

"Here, take care of this a moment."

Margarita attempted to rise, but Elvira almost casually flipped her over one shoulder to again land on the tiled floor, more heavily this time. She then held her down while Despina straddled her knees, prised her shoe apart at the heel and found the second blade – small, serrated and deadly.

"Got that twine, Elvira? Then let's truss her up."

"With pleasure."

Duty done, Elvira turned to Byron. "I think this person belongs to you."

"Not for much longer." Byron managed a charming smile. "So, Miss Helen Adelaide, or,

Elvira – or perhaps I should call you Penthesilea? It seems I'm in your debt. Yours too, Pallas Athena."

"Despina Psamathe." She offered her hand and he raised it to his lips.

"Pray tell me how you happened along so fortuitously. But wait – here he is at last. Permit me to introduce Tita Falcieri, gondolier in chief."

Tita, a giant of a man, ambled in. "Si, signore?"

"I'm sure he heard me calling him, which meant he was either eating, sleeping or transacting some business of his own. Isn't that right, Tita?"

"Si, signore."

Byron continued in fluent Italian, and Elvira, who'd had no time for a language upgrade, asked Despina what he'd said.

"Tita is to take La Fornarina back to her husband. Byron was going to pay Cogni to keep her there, but now she's seen *us*, he doesn't think it will be necessary."

Tita hauled Margarita to her feet. She glared at Byron and spat a few words. Elvira raised a quizzical eyebrow, and Despina continued: "She says this place is accursed, and now that Byron has allied himself with the Furies, his soul is damned too."

Byron had followed Tita outside.

"Despina, I have to get rid of the Vivlar band," Elvira said swiftly. "It's making me itch."

"Go ahead. It's done its work."

Elvira encoded the release and stepped out of the garment. It rolled itself into a ball. Then she

248

retied her jacket, just too late. Byron had seen what she'd been at pains to conceal.

"Enceinte?" he inquired.

"It would appear so."

"And is this relevant to your presence here?"

"Your pardon, Milord." Byron's manservant had entered silently and unobtrusively. He showed no reaction to the strangely attired duo.

"What is it, Fletcher?"

"Mr Shelley has just arrived."

Byron's eyes narrowed. "Is Miss Clairmont with him?"

"He's quite alone, Milord."

"Then show him to the library and make him welcome." Byron continued to stare at Elvira. "Shiloh. Here. And somehow you knew. The child's his, correct?"

Elvira contrived to look abashed.

"So his cousin Tom was right," Byron continued. "I suppose you want me to believe you've never heard of Tom Medwin?"

"I haven't."

"Well, you should have. Because he's been spinning a tale of a beautiful rich English woman who follows Shelley from country to country, professing her love for him."

"I didn't *follow*," Elvira objected. "I got here first."

"Of course, we were *never* here," Despina interposed smoothly. "History will show that Tita or Fletcher – or maybe both – foiled the attempt on your life. I'll help you write the memoir if you like."

"Your offer is respectfully declined. My account of the incident will, as you assume, contain no mention of itinerant warrior women."

"I'm glad we understand each other, Milord. In return for our work here today, may I beg one favour on behalf of my friend?"

"Proceed."

"She needs a romantic setting to impart her news to Shelley. Would you lend them your best gondola, the one with the cabin, and your most discreet gondolier?"

"Consider it done. Mind you, I can't vouch for the discretion, as most of my gondolieri are Tita's brothers."

"We'll settle for Tita, then," said Elvira sweetly. "I'm sure he'll look after us."

"While you're making the arrangements," Despina continued, "might we be allowed a half hour to refresh ourselves and change our attire?"

"I'm afraid I can't furnish you with dresses."

"Our luggage is following and will be here directly," Despina said. Elvira looked puzzled. Byron, with an eloquent shrug, summoned another servant.

They found themselves in a suite that had probably been Margarita's. Gaudy robes and ostrich feathers festooned every available surface.

"I hope you're not suggesting I wear those?" Elvira asked frostily.

"Of course not. Wait." Despina spoke into her bio-communicator. "Saranna, are you in position? Got those two packages we talked about? Send them to these precise coordinates. Ciao."

Almost immediately a breeze ruffled the assorted feathers. The receptor delivered a sturdy young man, attired in 1818 shabby chic and carrying some vacuum-packed clothes over one arm.

"I remember you!" Elvira said. "You sang Midir in The Immortal Hour. Saranna introduced us – briefly."

"Gino Aglietti." He extended his free hand. "I'll be serenading you on your gondola trip." He proffered the clothes. "Saranna chose this outfit for you. She said it would complete the picture. Are you celebrating a birthday?"

"No, just a special occasion," Elvira said.

Later, Byron watched from the sidelines as Tita, wreathed in smiles, carefully lifted Elvira into the gondola before taking his customary place at the stern. Gino stepped nimbly on board and sat near the prow.

Elvira had been transformed. Her gown was rose pink and ankle length, with a scoop neckline and dainty puff sleeves. She looked as fragile as porcelain.

Shelley, in an outdated suit and ubiquitous open-necked shirt, was the last to arrive. He kissed Elvira passionately, unmindful of the spectators. "Why did you disappear?" he demanded shrilly. "I thought I'd lost you forever!"

Byron turned away, shaking his head in mock despair.

Elvira accosted Gino. "Could you please ask Tita to travel slowly and take the long way round, if there *is* one? I've some matters to discuss with Shelley so don't sing to begin with."

"Close the blinds when you're ready," Gino suggested.

Elvira now knew, courtesy of Despina, the reason for Shelley's presence – and why Byron had been so relieved that Claire wasn't with him. Claire was now the mother of Byron's daughter, Allegra. She'd been persuaded to give Byron custody, only to see him tire of the child and have her fostered. Shelley was trying to arrange visitation rights, which meant that Elvira's errand would inevitably strike a raw nerve.

Once they were in the cabin Shelley again embraced her, but with more restraint. "My dear Miss Jones," he began formally, "Byron has acquainted me with your difficulty. I can only beg forgiveness for having compromised you. What restitution can I offer?"

She took a distancing step back. "In the light of what brought you here today, this is going to sound cold and selfish. We don't have much time to ourselves, so please, just listen."

He remained silent.

"Time sets its own rules," she continued. "Not those imposed on us by any human agency, but something universal. In our case, the inescapable truth is, what's conceived in the past has to remain

252

in the past. I can't keep this child. If she has any chance of survival once she's born, I must entrust her to you."

He seemed about to speak, but forebore.

"There were problems," she went on. "I almost miscarried and the time specialists have been watching me like hawks ever since. When I leave here I'll be going back to that."

"Then aren't you risking her life now?"

"No, just the opposite. This is *her* time. I feel empowered. Fulfilled." She paused a moment. "She'll be born around Christmas. Can I rely on you to make arrangements for her care?"

"I'll do whatever is required. And I'll acknowledge her as mine."

It was the right response, and one which would generate yet more scandal. And, of course, she couldn't warn him. "I'm sincerely grateful," she said, inadequately. "We'll know where to find you when the time comes."

"Of course you will. It seems that nothing's impossible where you're concerned, Miss Jones."

She wanted to kiss him then, to smooth out the small frown of responsibility that had appeared on his brow. But as usual she had an agenda to follow. "I still haven't apologised for running off and leaving you that night in London. It was time that ran out – I'd only been allocated two hours. I sent for Despina after your adverse reaction to my bracelet. We couldn't wake you."

"Neither could anyone else. I slept for hours."

"What happened was unprecedented," Elvira continued. "We need to know more." She removed a piece of paper from her one small pocket. "It's a sketch. We didn't want to risk any more photographs. Is this what you saw? Your poem would suggest it was."

He held the picture near the daylight. "It's your time apparatus, isn't it? Built for you by your lover? You described it so well. The trellis-work, deserving of a garden setting. The shining ribbon which conducts the electrical charge. But – this wasn't the vision I had."

Elvira was taken aback. "Then what? I was watching you, Shelley. You looked terrified. What did you see?"

"A vast interior, like a theatre or concert hall. You, in a gold dress, with sunbeams all around you."

"Was I on a stage?"

"I'm not sure. It was just a glimpse. And then, a hammer blow. Ejected. Cast out."

"I need to know what scared you."

"That place! There was such foreboding. A malign presence …" He ran his hands through his unruly hair. "That was no help, was it?"

"I'll consult the experts," Elvira said. Inwardly she was disappointed. Shelley's hallucinations had resounded eloquently down the years. This was just another example.

He'd spied her unadorned wrists. "You're not wearing the bracelet today."

"I left it with Despina. I didn't want any more incidents." She closed the blinds with a snap. A soft twilight descended. "No more questions, I promise. They're not important. What matters is that we're here, alone, for the first time in months. One precious chance to continue what we started. Is that so wrong of me?"

"Wrong? Is love *ever* wrong? Pray seduce me, Miss Jones. I'm very easily persuaded."

"I *know* that," she returned archly. "Undress, then. Must I always urge you not to waste time?"

He shed his clothes rapidly, as if glad to be rid of them. Child of nature, she thought fondly, carefully removing her pink dress and coaxing him onto the narrow sofa. At a discreet distance, Gino's youthful tenor commenced a barcarolle. The water swirled softly.

"I will be gentle," Shelley promised.

The sofa had one coverlet, all satin and tassels. After it had slithered off them a couple of times, they left it on the floor.

Elvira, much as she tried not to, couldn't help comparing the physique of her two lovers. Paris, despite the aesthetic beauty of his limbs, was healthily solid. Shelley, thin to the point of emaciation, carried no surplus weight whatsoever. Apart from the rhythmic labour of his manhood, his physical presence was slight, almost elusive.

When he paused to rest, she suddenly said: "You remind me of Icarus."

"Icarus? Another failure? You certainly know how to compliment a poet!"

"No, listen. You're so wonderfully light that I can imagine invisible wings beating, beating, holding you above me."

"What else do you imagine? There has to be more!"

"I'm not much good at storytelling, but let's say that Icarus has just made his escape from wherever it was - "

"Crete."

"- and he's carrying a girl in his arms. The wings don't melt, at least not yet. Don't you get it? Ascending to freedom. Triumphant. Defiant ..."

He forgot about being gentle. She didn't mind.

Later, they drowsed in one another's arms and listened to Gino's beautiful singing:

Mi par d'udire ancora
Ascosa in mezzo ai fior
La voce sua talora
Sospirare l'amor.

"I don't know that song," Shelley murmured sleepily.

"I do. It's the Romanza from Il Pescatori di Perle – the Pearl Fishers. The opera won't be written for another forty-five years."

"Then I'll go and see it when I'm seventy."

Yes, Percy Shelley, Elvira thought. You *do* that.

The aria continued. Two tears, one from each eye, trickled down her face and landed on his shoulder. "Tears of happiness," she lied. "Don't forget the rest of the Icarus legend. The bit *everyone* forgets. Daedalus also warned him not to fly too low, to avoid the waves. Are you listening?"

No answer.

Silently she made a vow. He wouldn't die in another four years. When she got back to 2585 she'd create havoc with Despina, the GTC, the scriveners, everyone. She was going to save him.

***

"Mission accomplished!" Despina said cheerfully. They were back at the TTI flat, having said goodbye to Gino, Saranna, and the rose-pink dress which Elvira had grown rather fond of.

"One question," she said to Despina.

"Only one?"

"Why did you go to so much trouble to set up a lovers' tryst?"

"To cement the deal, stupid. I had to ensure that Shelley had some fond memories to reflect on. He has to *want* this child, not see it as a liability. And it's worked! I could almost *hear* the timeline falling into place, like the tumblers in a safe."

"I'm glad you're so pleased with yourself. Now could you please concentrate on keeping Shelley alive? Is it even going to happen?"

"Hold on, hold on. First things first. You've an appointment with ectogenesis, in case you've forgotten. I've allowed you two days to play catch-up with Paris. Any longer than that, according to the medics, and you'll start feeling ill again. So don't prevaricate. I know your emotions are all over the place, but just switch your brain back on for a second or two and stop thinking with your hormones. This handover will be here before you know it. We don't have to wait till *our* Christmas to access Christmas *there*. If we can accelerate the baby's development we might have her out of the chamber in three months. Conversely, although it appears to you that Shelley's death-day's advancing remorselessly, we're in a position to take as long as we like over planning his rescue." She paused reflectively. "I only spoke with him briefly, but I do see why you're so protective of him. Exquisite manners, head in the clouds. Out of step with his time, as you said."

"Exactly, and I'm sure we've been making that disaffection worse. I noticed small changes in his speech patterns. And he didn't even ask how I knew I was expecting a girl. He just accepted it."

"We'll get him sorted," promised Despina, endlessly patient. "How was the sex, by the way?"

"Better. I created a fantasy for him and he enjoyed the roleplay."

"I'm intrigued," Despina said.

***

Elvira and Paris spent the next two days at home with the communicator system off. They reminisced, made plans, exchanged trivia and wondered how long it would be before they could marry.

258

"Oh, I almost forgot," Paris said. "Albie called to book a building safety inspection, and wanted to chat as usual. He can't marry Lelza yet, obviously, so he's going to turn that old cinema into a wedding venue and intends being the first to use it. He thought we might like to be the second."

"If the design matches his previous work, I'd definitely be tempted," said Elvira. "That Parthenon imitation that Saranna recommended was cold and austere. I didn't say anything at the time but it just wasn't me."

"Nor me."

They were lounging on the futon, Pari's fingers tracing little circles round Elvira's baby bump. "You're going to miss that, aren't you?" she teased. "I never though you'd go all broody."

"Neither did I."

"The next one will be yours. Promise. I think we'd better steer clear of Astrolabe Babes, though."

"Too right."

They fell silent. Elvira knew what he'd say next but didn't prompt him.

"Do you love Shelley?" he asked eventually.

"What I feel for Shelley isn't love as you and I understand it. As soon as you walked into my life -"

"Fell into it."

"- it was as if I'd always known you. You made room for yourself in my past."

"And you became my future."

"I'd say that makes us inseparable. Shelley makes me want to cherish him, the way one would cherish a rare work of art or a beautiful flower. I want him to be happy and I know he never will be, not in that era. Always running away from himself. Permanence just isn't in his vocabulary."

"Will you see him again?"

"Not unless the scriveners agree we can extract him. He and Despina had a talk before we came home, and he maintains that whoever brings the baby to 1818 – even if it's me – he shouldn't be present. A lawyer should deal with it."

"That sounds a bit impersonal."

"It sounds as if she nudged him toward that decision. It means she doesn't have to search on my behalf for times when he'll be alone. It'll have become a GTC matter by then, anyway. My part in it will be over." She sighed. "Speaking of which, you do realise I'll be out of circulation for a while? I don't just mean the op. They want to keep me in a bubble while I'm healing, so I won't know anything about any of it. They're already growing my bio-weft culture so they can start the procedure as soon as I check in."

Paris looked disappointed. "I was hoping to visit."

"They don't want anxious husbands hanging around. If there's not enough going on at Construction then let Saranna take you to be measured for your bridegroom outfit. And, you really should message Eva, just out of courtesy."

"Can't you think of anything *pleasant* for me to do?"

"There's something very pleasant you can do immediately, but only if you promise to perform one of the tasks I've just set you. If I come out of stasis and find you haven't done either, there will be consequences."

"I promise," he said, trying not to grin.

He was as good as his word. Of the two options, recording a message to his mother seemed the least onerous. He even invited her to the wedding. The rest of the time he worked cheerfully at TTI Construction, again impressing Cyprian with his easy efficiency.

In precisely a fortnight and two days, he was on hand to assist the newly-awakened Elvira from her bubble. She looked so tranquil in her induced sleep that his thoughts instantly fled back to his first morning in Hampstead when he'd watched her slowly awaken. This time she woke with no trace of languor and directed a bright smile at him. In her gown and slippers she sat with him at a side table and drank some essential nutrients. Then, leaning on him, she slowly walked to inspect the ectogenesis pod where her child now rested. Disappointingly, there was little to be seen, as the sphere's walls were as opaque as the womb whose function it replaced. A diagnostic panel showed stable life-signs.

"The membrane conducts sound to some extent," one of the technicians said. "Some of the mothers talk to their offspring, or even sing to them. Say hello to her. She'll hear you."

Elvira turned aside. "Not today. My voice is still shaky. When can I go home?"

The tech consulted her notes. "We'll give you some physio and a final once-over. I'd say another day and a half. You also need to book your appointment with the aesthetician. They get very busy." She looked more closely at her screen. "It says you've nominated a guardian, Agent Psamathe. Is this correct?"

"Quite correct. She'll take charge of the infant when it's delivered, and I'm fine with that. Come on, Paris, I need to get dressed."

Her tone was several shades too brittle. Paris knew she wasn't as detached as she appeared. But she'd decided how best to handle the situation, and he'd do what he could to support her.

Meanwhile the legal disputes dragged on, and an annulment seemed as far away as ever. House Dawn had requisitioned a full breakdown of the DNA results and were now having them analysed by a specialist of their choice. Eva, via Aurelia, was weighing up her chances of suing Astrolabe Babes for misrepresentation.

While they disputed and argued, Elvira's aesthetician eradicated every trace of her scar and restored her torso to its previous svelte shape. Not content with that, Elvira returned to her MMA sessions with single-minded dedication, saying she'd allowed herself to get slack. No-one challenged her motives.

Paris received a certificate of merit for his innovative work on streamlining and product presentation.

Albie showed Saranna the designs for his wedding venue. In a complete break with tradition he'd envisaged a ceremony "in the round" with holographic effects to order. "There'll be a domed ceiling," he explained, "with an oculus in the centre."

Saranna was sceptical. "What? So the guests can get rained on?"

"It won't be open to the elements," Albie explained, "but to an additional floor above, housing the laser equipment. With so many angles at my disposal I can create new and exciting patterns. Or familiar ones like the Mandelbrot Set."

In the midst of all this creativity, Despina's final visit to 1818 passed almost unnoticed. Shelley was now residing in Naples. She even had an address for him, though she knew better than to use it. She caught up with him at an art gallery.

"Shall we be seated?" she began in her usual peremptory manner. "We've things to talk about. Just remember to keep your voice down." She paused momentarily. "Your daughter's now ready to be transferred. Obviously you can't take her home so it's time to engage foster parents. Accredited ones. Once again it's fallen to me to choreograph your movements, so pay attention."

"Choreograph. Just as you did with Elvira."

"Not me personally, airhead - the GTC. Just don't give me a hard time over this. I know how stubborn you can be."

"I want to do my best for the child," he said more quietly. "Talk me through it. If it's humanly possible I'll honour your wishes."

"Hmm. Rule number one is, don't over-dramatise. This is in your own best interests, whether you think so or not. So, choose who's to foster the infant. Of course I know who you'll choose but you still have to *do* it. As we discussed in Venice, you must also hire a lawyer as a go-between, to pay the carers on your behalf. He is not to reveal your identity to them. He can say that you're English, nothing more. He'll need a pseudonym for you, so choose one. You needn't tell me what it is."

"I shall ask my expatriate friends to recommend someone efficient and discreet," he said. "I assume that's what I did?"

"Yes it is. So put him to work and I'll take temporary charge of the child. And Shelley – for everyone's sake, don't try and see her."

"Do I attempt to?"

"So far there's no evidence of it. I like to think there's a chance you kept your head."

"Your faith in me is second to none," he remarked. "Am I permitted to ask how Elvira is?"

"She gave birth while in a controlled sleep and fought her way back to health. As yet, she hasn't asked to see her baby and I don't believe she'll change her mind. It would make the separation too painful."

"And Paris? Did she have to give him up too?"

"He's still married but we've good grounds for an annulment. It's being processed."

"Surely you already know if it will succeed?"

Despina frowned suddenly. "We never look at our own futures, Shelley. Now, don't you think it's time your little girl had a name?"

"You *know* her name!"

"I still need to hear you say it. You said you'd behave!"

"Very well. Elvira's alias was Helen, but I prefer the Italian version, Elena. Elena Adelaide Shelley." He stared at the floor. "Forgive me, but this seems like an exercise in futility. Elena doesn't survive, does she? Please grant me the benefit of your knowledge this once. I've already lost one daughter."

"The indications aren't good," Despina said. "But consider: this tiny girl will have a phenomenal influence on a timeline which spans centuries. I predict that even if she dies, her case will remain prominent in the annals of the GTC and will give guidance to romantically entangled time travellers."

"A strange legacy, but beautiful," Shelley mused. "I might include her in a poem, if that's allowed. After all, no-one will read it."

"You're mistaken."

"Mistaken or not, I'd forego all my aspirations just to see and hold Elena."

"Go ahead, if you want to rip your family apart."

"She cried," Shelley said obscurely. "Elvira. On the gondola. I was almost asleep - "

"Understandably."

"- and I felt her tears fall. Like a benediction, I thought at the time. Now, it seems like yet another secret. She was so stoic about our child, so resolved. So, what made her cry? What else does she know?"

Despina was quick to hijack this train of thought. "You've given me an idea. There's just the smallest chance of bringing you and Elena together for a few minutes. But you aren't going to like how it's done."

"How? Tell me!!"

A few art lovers turned to glare at him.

"Shh! First you need to register her birth, name yourself as the father."

"Her presence wouldn't be required for that."

"It wouldn't, but supposing you wanted her baptised as well? Could you countenance such a thing?"

"A difficult choice for someone like me."

"Then I suggest you think it through. I'll know which you decide." Despina sighed gustily. "I must go. We should leave separately."

"Will I see Elvira again?"

"That depends. On a variety of factors."

Despina glanced back as she left, knowing he was watching her. The image of his profoundly sad azure gaze remained with her longer than she intended.

***

Her work was far from over. On returning to the GTC's Ops in Progress section she promptly engaged a spotter team to obtain historic co-ordinates for the Parish Church of St Joseph at Chiaia. An essential move, considering the number of churches in Naples. Shelley had decided in favour of the baptism but had dithered over it until the day before he and his entourage were due to leave for Rome.

She barely made it to 45 Via Vico Canale in time to collect baby Elena for the service. The foster parents greeted her effusively and she tried to respond with suitable familiarity. Difficult, since from her point of view Elena was still in the post-natal unit. In agency parlance, this was a "carousel" op.

Shelley was outside the church waiting for her.

"Cutting it a bit fine, aren't you?" she remarked.

"Well, aren't you going to pick her up?"

He hesitated.

"What's with the guilty expression? No, wait, don't tell me. You tried to salvage the situation and made it worse."

"I ... tried to persuade Mary to adopt her," he confessed. "I said she was a foundling."

"She didn't believe you, and you had a massive row," Despina concluded. "Whatever happened to all that free love? Come on, let's get this over with. I'm the godmother in case anyone asks."

They did, more than once, as if repetition might have lent it some truth. Despina maintained her usual hauteur. Shelley read from a cue sheet and kept his head down. Elena yawned several times and didn't react to the cold water.

At last they were outside again. The weak sunlight seemed dazzling after the grey gloom of the church. Despina found a bench to sit on. Shelley carried Elena inside his overcoat. After a tactful moment or two of silence, the most she dared allow him, Despina reclaimed his attention.

"I assume your lawyer Del Rosso has started paying the foster family, since they didn't mention money when they saw me. I'll need to drop in on him at some point."

"Why?"

"Because you're going to give me the birth and baptism certificates, and I'll lodge them with him for safekeeping. Or do you want Mary to find them in your pocket? If you thought this morning's quarrel was bad, what do you think she'll say if she sees herself named as Elena's mother on those documents? *And* they've spelt her name wrong. Come on, hand them over."

He obeyed resignedly. "Tomorrow was supposed to be a fresh start," he murmured, almost to himself.

"You and your fresh starts!" Despina scoffed. Then, more gently: "We can't stay here much longer. Say goodbye to her."

Shelley lifted Elena from her cocoon of warmth and dropped a tiny kiss on her forehead. "She's still so small. How old is she now?"

Despina made a show of counting on her fingers. "I'm not exactly sure," she confessed. Which was true. Elena had been in ectogenesis for months, while the team had tried without success to sustain her growth. Her return to her own time was having little effect either. She'd been in the future too long.

"Take her before she gets cold," Shelley said. Despina returned Elena to her bassinet and placed a tiny recall bracelet round her wrist.

"Why are you putting one of those things on her?"

"To facilitate a fifty second relocation. I don't intend dragging her round the city when I don't have to. How do you think I brought her here from 2585?"

He continued to look uneasy.

"From now on, this will simply be an ordinary gold bracelet. A gift from her doting father. It will never work again because I'll delete her profile from the GTC database."

"Whatever that means. Do what you have to do, Despina. Thank you for today, and my apologies for having been such poor company." He walked away, displaying the unconscious dignity afforded him by his upbringing.

Despina began to see him in a new light. Carefully she transported the now fractious Elena back to her foster parents, emphasising how well-behaved she'd been hitherto. Then she absented herself, promising to visit whenever she was in the city.

***

There was no-one in the secretarial hall, the actual time being 2.15 am. Despina made e-copies of the two certificates and left them in a restricted folder. Then she went to the post-natal unit, selecting a Moses basket which would pass for a carry-cot in any era. Since she'd been lugging the same basket around with her for hours, it had already fulfilled that role.

Traci, the ectogenesis tech whom Elvira had been so abrupt with, was on duty.

"Don't ask," Despina said with a weary smile. "It's been one of those days."

"I knew you'd be here, so I waited to see this through," Traci said. "I didn't know Elena was a time-bound child. We don't get many. I realise now why Ms Jones was so dismissive. It must be heartbreaking, having to give her up."

"Which is why *I've* got the job," Despina said wryly.

Traci fetched Elena from her cot. "She's been irritable all day. Maybe she'll settle once she's in her own century."

"I've just come from her christening – yes, it's a carousel op – and she was suspiciously drowsy throughout. I suspect the foster-mother had been giving her opiates."

"Par for the course back then," Traci said neutrally.

The foster family welcomed Despina, whom they were seeing for the first time, and assured her that they'd been paid for a month. "Is her mamma no longer with us?" asked the woman. "Signor del Rosso does not say in his letter."

"I believe that to be the case," Despina said.

"Such a shame. She's the prettiest bambina. Beautiful skin."

After five more minutes of baby talk Despina made her escape. Her penultimate time trip, not part of the carousel, could wait until the morrow. She hoped it would be the last time she had to suffer Regency fashions for a while.

Her destination was Livorno, and the office of Shelley's urbane, capable lawyer Frederico del Rosso. The date was May 14th, 1819. She handed over Elena's birth and baptism certificates and in return was shown a ledger entry of payments made to the family at 45 Via Vico Canale, Naples, on behalf of an Englishman named only as Mr Jones.

Despina smiled whimsically when she saw this. "There is one more related matter. I believe Mr Shelley has given you a poste restante address, so you may contact him – or should I say Mr Jones – if any need arises regarding the child."

"That is correct, Signora."

"Unfortunately," Despina went on, "he is too trusting with people in his household, and I fear one of them will betray that trust. Should this occur, you may possibly see me here again."

271

"Are you godmother to the child or to the man?" Del Rosso asked shrewdly.

"I sometimes ask myself that," Despina said.

***

She had one more loose end to deal with. Elvira, she'd decided, shouldn't be involved, having only just accepted that Elena wouldn't live beyond June 1820. There was still no word on Paris' annulment, but he and Elvira had simply ignored the legal bickering and were steadfastly together. Their twenty-ninth birthdays were marked only by affectionate hand-holding across the table at La Chanson d'Amour.

Having assured herself that she could take her eye off her proteges for a while, Despina visited the scrivener interface at Ops in Progress. Again, she was surprised at how quickly she was seen.

"Despina Psamathe, you are currently working the case of the timebound child Elena. How may the scriveners assist you?"

"I am monitoring the infant's last days and am about to close the case. However, a miscreant is interfering in the life of Elena's sire and threatens to destabilise the final stage of my work. I'd like to raise a person of interest profile for this individual, allowing me to access his location at certain times. It is a minor matter but one which would allow me to resolve the Elena case swiftly and efficiently."

"How often would you require access?" asked the scrivener. Despina had the impression that she was only half listening.

"Three sessions, three separate days," she hazarded. "Non-consecutive."

"And the name of the ... miscreant?"

"Paolo Foggi."

That produced a reaction. "Agent Psamathe, are you working alone? We have already logged a profile request for this man."

"I'm not aware of anyone being co-opted, but I've been in the field almost non-stop. Who made the request?"

"Norvus Maysson."

"Ah. That makes sense." Despina was annoyed and tried not to show it. "We've worked as a team many times. I'll liaise with him."

Norvus had been discharged from the medical unit. Rather than bespeak his apartment, she went there in person. He wasn't surprised to see her.

"What gives?" she demanded. "Trying to steal my thunder?"

"Dial it back, D. I've been surveying your op but you were too engaged to notice. You've been brilliant, but you don't want to botch the resolution due to your justifiable outrage. If you'll permit it, I'll join you for the coup de grace and take some of the pressure off."

Despina sighed. "You're right as usual. I've been too immersed in this case. Time for a review. What have we got?"

Norvus tapped the info screen. "Paolo Foggi, liar, thief and extortionist. Manservant to the Shelleys for several years, let go after consistently pilfering household funds. Manages to insinuate himself into the Livorno expat community and begins to spread scandal about baby Elena, now dead. He's reinvented the old lie that's been kicking around for some time, namely, that Shelley was the lover of Mary's step-sister Claire, and Elena their child. Del Rosso, acting for Shelley, manages to get Paolo thrown out of Livorno. End of."

"But that won't stop him talking," Despina objected. "Gossip doesn't have to be true, it only needs people to *think* that it's true. Paolo still believes that Shelley will pay up."

"And you were going to silence Paolo how? Threaten him? Beat him senseless? You don't have leave to *do* that. It would impact on your career and you'd probably lose the chance to help Elvira rescue Shelley."

"I know."

"So, we need a lighter touch. History shows that Paolo just vanishes off Shelley's timeline, and here's how we'll arrange it. Is your language status in order? Good. We're going to stalk Master Foggi and scare him into keeping quiet."

Norvus elaborated his scheme, and Despina began to smile.

***

Paolo, small and shifty, stared belligerently at his two visitors. "Who *are* you? Did Del Rosso send you? I still have four hours before I have to leave."

Norvus ignored the questions. "Did it never cross your mind that an aristocrat like Shelley would have some powerful friends in England? Friends in secret organisations? We look after our own, and it occurred to us that you'd be tempted to continue your slanders at a distance."

"We are here to ensure you do not," said Despina.

"Proceed with your change of residence," Norvus instructed. "Be inventive. Go wherever you please – the coastal towns or this delightful countryside. We do not offer violence where it can be avoided, but know this: one more slanderous utterance regarding our esteemed friend, and things will not go well for you."

"You'll have to find me first," Paolo said rather weakly.

"Rest assured, we will *always* find you," Despina promised. "Hide in a wine cellar or run for the hills. We'll enjoy the chase."

Subsequently, after he'd relocated to Pisa, he found them seated in his vettura as he was about to pick up a fare. A day or two later they walked into the inn where he was drinking and stood either side of him. And finally they arrived at a nameless shabby apartment where he was about to bed his latest inamorata. She promptly ran off, and for the first time he showed apprehension.

"How is this possible? Ten minutes ago I didn't know I'd *be* here!"

"I think he's got the message," Norvus said, sounding bored. "We've disrupted his business, his leisure and his sex life. He can expect worse things if he doesn't mend his ways."

"We'll always be watching you, Paolo," Despina said softly. Then she picked him up with one hand and sat him on top of the wardrobe.

The Ops in Progress staff were surprised to see them in raucous good humour when they emerged from their cubicle, but they quickly regained their usual professionalism when submitting their final report on Elena Adelaide.

"I'll be available for debriefing tomorrow," Despina added.

Norvus fell easily into step beside her as they left the department. "Back to mine?" he asked.

"Why not? I could use the company."

"Likewise. And tomorrow, once the debrief's over, we can rough out a plan for Shelley's extraction. We'll need the scrutineers on side, initially."

"It's the scriveners we have to convince, surely?"

"Eventually, yes. But we need more evidence than those ancient memoirs Elvira's been poring over. We can't approach the scriveners until we've seen exactly what went on in the Gulf of La Spezia."

Chapter Nine

"It seems to me," said the scrutineer, "that you wish to squander an inordinate amount of GTC resources on this matter."

"I was under the impression that anomalies had to be resolved," Despina returned. "Here we have an event variously described as a shipwreck, or a capsized vessel, and yet it sank upright with all the goods neatly in its hold exactly as they'd been stowed prior to departure. On being salvaged, there was evidence that the Ariel had been holed below the waterline. And yes, I know the crew cannot continue to live in their own time. But there's no valid reason for them to die in it."

"Once more, we see the influence of Ms Jones at work. A woman who was granted the uncommon privilege of a lifetime relocation. Why does her name feature so often in our overview?"

"Because the scriveners recruited her to take part in an 1818 reset, at considerable risk to her health. She had no knowledge of this assignment until she found herself living it. Prior to her participation she'd carried out extensive research into the sinking of the Ariel."

The scrutineer sighed. "Very well. We will grant the use of an airborne device for the purpose of obtaining a visual record. Duration, one hour only."

"And am I also granted permission to intervene if it proves to be necessary?"

"If foul play is discovered, I will recommend taking steps to suppress it – subject to scrivener approval." The scrutineer green-lit Despina's petition. "Next case, please."

***

A group consisting of Despina, Norvus, Elvira, Paris and Saranna assembled in the TTI's little-used packet dispatch unit to view the all-important drone footage.

"I can't believe we're *doing* this at last," Elvira said breathlessly.

"I hope I'm not going to regret this," Despina muttered to Norvus.

"Too late now," he replied philosophically.

Paris carefully retrieved the drone and disengaged the mini-brace which had protected it from turbulence. "Right, let's see what we've got."

They all craned forward to look at the tiny image.

The storm was about to break. Every other leisure craft was heading rapidly for the coast, but the Ariel sailed blithely on. The drone could see what its crew could not: a dilapidated fishing vessel following at a distance. An argument was in progress between Shelley and crewmate Edward Williams. There was no audio but the gist was obvious – Williams wanted to take in sail, Shelley objected. Charles Vivian, their boat-boy, tried to intervene and they both told him to shut up. Meanwhile the fishing boat came alongside, and the

Ariel was boarded by its crew of three. Their speed and agility suggested this wasn't the first time they'd waylaid unsuspecting amateurs.

Shelley drew a pistol, attempted to fire at one of the ruffians, slipped on the wet planks and stumbled backwards. At the same moment, the boom swung round and hit him. He fell overboard. Williams grabbed an oar and tried to fend off a second pirate, who promptly disarmed him and struck him round the head. As he lay motionless his attacker divested him of his fashionable jacket, put it on and pranced about. The other two raiders had disappeared into the hold in search of booty. Charles Vivian dived overboard in an attempt to reach the landing tender, which was bobbing along at the end of its rope. He might have reached it, but a heavy wave broke over him and slammed him back against the Ariel's hull. He didn't resurface.

The fishing boat slipped its tether and was swept away by the suddenly turbulent sea.

Then a two-masted felucca, of the type favoured by customs patrols, approached out of the sea fog and, with no attempt to alter course, smashed into the Ariel. Damaged below the waterline, it filled up rapidly and went straight down. The customs boat made no attempt to come about and was soon lost in the distance.

The recording ended.

"Well, that was unexpected," Norvus remarked.

"Why didn't that patrol boat try to save anyone?" asked Saranna indignantly.

"I've read about that," Elvira said. "It's to do with quarantine. I'll still have the info on file."

"Ethics apart," said Despina, "this just got very complicated. We'll take the drone to Analytics, get an enhanced version of events and make a thorough study. Paris, your good standing with the TTI will come in useful. We're going to need some quarantine facilities of our own!"

Once the drone evidence was in the scriveners' possession, they had little choice but to approve the op. Despina, unsurprisingly, was put in charge, subject to an edict that no pirates, actual or potential, were to be brought forward. No-one in TTI admin would have allowed that in any case. The crew of the Ariel would be granted provisional residence, and a volunteer citizen would be assigned to each of the trio to supervise their resettlement. The three mentors would be held fully responsible for any misdemeanour committed by the person in their charge.

"I suppose I'll be looking after Shelley," Despina sighed. "What was it I said about regretting this?"

"Can't *I* do it?" asked Elvira.

"You're not eligible. You can probably help me, though."

Saranna surprised everyone by offering to mentor Charles Vivian. "The scriveners would love it if we could line up careers for the newbies," she explained. "I think I may have just the thing for young Charles."

Norvus offered to mentor Edward Williams. "Army man, isn't he? Sensible? Shouldn't be a problem. And, we'll be able to keep him and Shelley in close contact. I think they'll benefit by that."

Paris went to confer with the Arrivals team leader and explain the situation. "I know this sounds bizarre, Rollo, but it's essential you follow these instructions to the letter."

"You don't want much, do you?" said the foreman jokingly. "Run that past me again. Three newcomers for permanent relocation. Got that. You only have the requisite DNA profile for *one* of them - "

"A GTC agent is acquiring the data as we speak. We can't wait for gold bracelets to be etched so we'll have to use custody bands. I *told* you that!"

"So you did. Just checking. And, once these by now confused travellers are here, we're to pretend to be hygiene officials, make noises about quarantine and introduce them to a communal particle scrub unit."

"Precisely. The one you use for Mud Olympics contestants will do nicely."

"All completely spurious."

"Not according to the GTC. If we separate the extractees too soon, they'll be frightened. They're from 1822!"

"And just to put them at their ease," said the foreman, his smile growing ever broader, "we're to confiscate all their clothes and give them back to your team."

"What's so amusing? The clothes are artefacts. They don't belong here."

"If you say so."

"I *do* say so. Just ensure they're returned in their entirety, including contents of pockets."

"This doesn't suit you, Paris," said Rollo. "All the messy stuff we get as soon as we bring people into the equation. You like everything neat and organised."

Paris sighed. "If only life were like that. I'm glad I'm not running this op – not that I'm qualified to."

"It's one of Despina's?"

"Yes. She's trying to save three key individuals and keep the timeline intact. I don't envy her. Anyway, Rollo, just give our guests something contemporary to wear and then let Despina take over."

"With pleasure. I don't want my department involved any longer than necessary."

***

Norvus sauntered through a quayside tavern in Livorno, making little attempt to look inconspicuous. Ned Williams and Charles Vivian were seated near the entrance, trying to make two beers last as long as possible. Charles fidgeted. He wanted to be underway before tempers got frayed.

Norvus saw his chance. "Everything to your liking, signori? Your beer seems to be flat. Allow me to replace it, on the house."

He whisked the glasses away before anyone could object. Halfway down the cellar steps he paused and said: "Ready for recall. A smooth one, if you please. I'm carrying breakables."

Shelley raced up to his shipmates in barely suppressed panic. "We have to leave, now. I'm being followed."

"By whom?" asked Ned disinterestedly.

"The man who was speaking with you."

"He works here."

"He was bringing us more beer," Charles added helpfully.

"Where is it, then? And where's *he*? He was lurking on the quayside earlier, observing Trelawny and me. He's a government informer. My pamphlets, my Irish campaign – they've had eyes on me ever since."

"That was *years* ago!"

"I first saw that spy years ago. In Secheron!"

"I told Trelawny we'd wait," Ned objected. "He still doesn't have port clearance for the Bolivar."

"Well, we'll have to go without him." Shelley was in no mood to change his mind.

"Are the provisions loaded?"

"Yes, and the money. Fifty pounds. So if we don't *sail* the Ariel out of here, we'll have to sleep on board tonight."

"You win," Ned conceded. "I'll tell Trelawny we can't wait any longer."

They thankfully quit the airless confines of the tavern.

On the horizon, black clouds gathered.

***

"What in Hades were you *doing*, Norvus, letting yourself be seen?"

"Doing my homework, Despina dearest. They'd decided to wait for their friend Trelawny, an experienced sailor with a much bigger boat. If they hadn't set sail by 4 pm, *alone,* the entire timeline would've been trashed. Fortunately, thanks to Elvira's tireless research, I knew Shelley was convinced the Home Office was tailing him. I merely reinforced that belief. So, now that I've stabilised the timeline, would you care to join me in this errand of mercy? Shelley knows you, so he's not likely to throw a fit when we arrive."

"You think? He loves that boat. He won't want us to take him."

"I suppose I can't be there?" asked Elvira.

"Sorry again. GTC only. What's that you're travelling with?"

"A bound edition of Trelawny's memoirs. It'll help Shelley understand why we did what we're about to do. Here's the passage I remembered about the quarantine laws. Take a look."

Despina took it and read: "If you render assistance to a vessel in distress, or rescue a drowning stranger, on returning to port you are condemned to a long and rigorous quarantine. The consequence is, should one vessel see another in peril, or even run it down by accident, she hastens on her course, and by general accord not a word is said or reported on the subject."

"Hera's tits," muttered Norvus expressively. "Come on, D, let's get this done."

"We'll reconvene at Arrivals," said Elvira. "Has anyone given any thought to lodgings for them?"

"Leave that to me," said Saranna.

Norvus and Despina headed for GTC Dispatch, with its highly skilled tech team who could select the most difficult destinations with pinpoint accuracy. They would need to be at the top of their game, as the Ariel was a diminutive target in a sullenly heaving ocean.

"Initially, the brace will protect you from the elements," said Zyra, acting Tech Harmost. "Here's the schematic from the drone. The best chance of your materialisation being unobserved is during the argument about the sails. We've used the drone footage to sync the timeframe to the exact nanosecond. As you can see from these heat signatures, all three crew members are in a cluster at one end of the boat."

"The end one steers from, presumably," said Norvus. "Or maybe not."

"The sails will obscure you from view, but only momentarily. Take care when orienting yourselves after the brace disconnects. Once we have the signal from all three custody bands we'll initiate the transfer to Arrivals. You, of course, will be returned here to make your report. So, shall we expedite?"

"Ready," said the agents.

"On my mark."

The sharp-eyed boat boy was the first to spot them. "Mr Williams, Mr Shelley – we've got stowaways!"

Norvus, suave and smiling, advanced toward them. "Hello again!"

"*You*!" Shelley drew his pistol and, unlike his recorded self, kept his footing.

Despina marched forward and shoved the weapon aside. "Really, Shelley, you're a mite too handy with that thing. Give it here. Is this any way to greet an old friend?"

He stared. "Despina?"

"You *know* her?" Ned gaped at her in astonishment. Her hair was coiffed into a businesslike pleat, and she wore an emerald bodysuit and tabard.

"I do indeed."

"Another of your lady friends? Why didn't you just invite her along instead of secreting her away? And as for you - " His gaze swivelled to Norvus – "I'd like you to explain yourself, sir. What are you? Waiter? Brigand? Spy?"

"None of those. We're your rescuers."

Despina took Shelley's suddenly nerveless hand and clipped the custody bracelet round his wrist. He made a vague attempt to remove it, knowing he'd be unable to. "Be careful what you say," she murmured in his ear. "Your friends don't have your insider knowledge."

286

The expected protest didn't happen. Instead he was calm, *too* calm. "Make an end of this," he said evenly.

"What do you mean, rescuers?" Williams demanded, still addressing Norvus and cutting across her reply.

"You'll find out if you don't do as you're told. See that sail in the distance? They're pirates. I heard them plotting to kill you and plunder your vessel. We're from Maritime Crime Prevention - "

"Never heard of it."

" - and we've only just managed to catch up with these villains. We intend to take you to safety and lie in wait for them." He seized the opportunity to slap a bracelet on Ned while he was still pondering the announcement. "You'll have to be quarantined of course, and these bands will identify you to my onshore colleagues. Your turn, young one."

Charles obediently extended an arm.

"Take us to safety in *what*?" Ned demanded.

"You'll see." Norvus caught Shelley's eye. "Sorry about your boat."

Thunder rolled overhead.

***

They found themselves in a room with featureless white walls and ceiling. A soft pearly illumination, with no visible source, made their skin look unnaturally pale.

287

"Strip, and enter the stalls," said an authoritarian voice. "Place your discarded clothes in the receptacle nearest your stall. Remove any rings and accessories and place them with your clothes."

They did so, expecting to be dunked or drenched. Instead, a warm breeze enveloped them, along with a gentle pattering like fine rain. But their skin remained dry.

Ned and Charles hardly noticed how sleepy they were feeling. They certainly didn't realise that the hitherto solid floor covering was now like featherdown. Shelley, however, was awake and alert. His metabolism, accustomed to copious amounts of laudanum, was unaffected by the gentle sedative administered by the Arrivals team. And thus, when two women arrived to wheel away the clothes baskets, they were confronted by an irate, stark naked but completely unselfconscious young man.

"Where do you think you're going with my books? Give them back!"

"What books?" asked the elder of the two workers.

"The ones in my pockets, of course. I didn't realise you'd be taking everything."

"I'm sorry. We have our orders," said the younger woman, finding her voice. "Books can carry disease and have to be fumigated."

Her colleague whispered to her.

"Or, since they may not survive the process, we can replace them with current editions. Your new clothes will be delivered momentarily."

Outside, they conferred. "Well, Pola, that was a nice surprise. Who's mentoring him?"

"Despina, I think."

"Lucky her. Have they chosen his work placement yet? He'd make a great model."

"Bit skinny, surely?"

"Oh, Pol! Don't you follow Nimue Pamina's vlog? Thin is *in*. Leisure 4 Lovers would snap him up."

Pola shook her head. "Paris says this is a timeline reset, a major one. The GTC will have his future all mapped out."

"Oh. Shame."

***

"What if the pirates don't put the clothes on?" Elvira asked.

"No such thing as what if. Detailed study revealed the threadbare nature of their own attire," Norvus said airily. "But, I left nothing to chance. We had fifteen minutes' drone allowance left, so I sent it back. And, the very accomplished Zyra added a translator AI which interpreted most of their conversation."

"Only *most*?" Despina inquired sarcastically.

"I couldn't invite them to face the camera," Norvus said imperturbably. "Watch."

The pirates boarded the deserted Ariel cautiously, weapons at the ready.

"Where are the English milords?" asked the youngest.

"Does it matter? Let's take what we can while we can, starting with their laundry. Good expensive stuff. Here, Tomasso, put these stripey breeches on. You might even *look* like a sailor for once. Then set a course for Viareggio. This boat's been going in circles."

"Si, Papa."

Tomasso Senior, grey bearded, donned Ned's frock coat, necktie and cavalry boots. The coat fitted but the boots were too small, and the left boot resisted all his efforts to remove it.

The third pirate, tall and taciturn, ignored his gyrations and continued to put on Shelley's clothes. They might have been made for him.

"Oh, well done, Lofty. Someone's as tall as you are."

"Papa, our boat's gone!"

"We don't need it, do we? Hold your course. I'm going to see what's stashed away. Lend a hand, Alto. And help me off with this boot."

"Any second now," Norvus murmured. "And here she is. One customs vessel, right on cue. Collision imminent. Has everyone seen enough?"

They all assented, and Norvus cut the feed.

"Why the long faces?" It was Paris who uncharacteristically spoke up. "Those ruffians murdered three people before we changed the timeline. And more before that, probably."

290

"The GTC has to make decisions like this every day," Despina confirmed.

"Moving on," said Norvus. "Arrivals just reported that Ned and young Charles took the sedation without incident, and they've been kitted out with leisurewear and sent straight to history and language processing. They need to make sense of their environment before we can help them further. That leaves Shelley. The sedative had no effect on him and he's now asking to see you, Despina, and of course you, Elvira. It's not clear how much he understands, but certainly more than we expected. And apart from a spat with the clothiers about losing his books, he's been remarkably pragmatic."

"He seemed that way in Naples, too," Despina reflected. "But very, very unhappy. We need to work on that."

"Let me see him now," Elvira begged. "Please."

"Isn't it time I met him too?" Paris asked.

Elvira gave him a gentle hug. "Not quite yet. He may think he knows where and when, but that's not enough. He needs to know *why*, and I should be the one to explain. Once we've overcome that hurdle, I'll gladly introduce you."

"You know best," Paris said mildly.

"Take copies of the drone recordings to our flat," Elvira continued. "It's the quickest, most efficient way to back up written evidence. He'll understand. He knows about photography."

"Oh yes, so he does. Great Russell Street, 1818. I wonder why he burnt that photo?"

"Because I told him to."

"And why was that, exactly?"

"Enough, you two!" Despina said wrathfully. "Paris, get the footage. Elvira, you're with me."

The Arrivals department had some short-term hospitality rooms, for travellers waiting to be picked up by distant contacts. Shelley, unresisting but uncommunicative, had been placed in one of them.

"I hope you're going to take him with you," said Zyra. "He won't engage with us, won't eat, and will drink only water. We've tried telling him he isn't a criminal so there's no need to act like one, but all he does is ask for you two."

"I'm not surprised. We're the only ones he trusts," Despina replied tartly. "Our colleague Saranna has booked him and his shipmates into the Spaceport Hilton, so he'll soon be permanently off your hands. We'll see him now."

Accordingly, they were shown into Shelley's temporary abode. He sprang to his feet when he saw them, but didn't smile. "At last. Would you please explain yourselves? I want to know why we were kidnapped, where this place is, and why I find myself dressed in this peculiar manner."

"I've looked forward to this moment so much," Elvira said unhappily. "I thought it would be joyous for both of us. But once again, time has us fooled." She handed him the vintage book she'd kept at the ready: 'Recollections of the Last Days of Shelley and Byron.' "This will tell you why we acted as we did. I borrowed this from a museum, incidentally, because our reading methods would only confuse you at the moment."

The full implication of his capture was suddenly made clear. "What year is it?"

"2585. So, if you'd turn to page 79, you'll find the section I'd like you to read. It's an account of your death, written by your friend Trelawny. Sit down. Take as long as you want."

Shelley read swiftly, holding the book close to his face. Despina made a mental note to get his eyesight corrected along with his other scheduled procedures. She and Elvira stood silently until he'd finished the chapter.

"How can this be true?" he asked eventually. Then, more accurately: "How did you arrange it?"

"After our affair, I campaigned ceaselessly for the GTC to authorise your rescue," Elvira said. "I believed Trelawny's account. For centuries, the whole world believed it. But when we investigated, we found something very different." She glanced at Despina. "Shall we proceed?"

"I think he's ready." Despina brandished Shelley's custody bracelet, which a somewhat relieved Zyra had returned to her.

"Not again," he protested.

"Oh, stop complaining. Did it hurt last time? No. Did the sky fall in? No. We're taking you to Elvira's and Paris' home so you can relax in the company of friends and hear the rest of the story." She activated her bio-communicator, while he watched curiously. "Paris, while you're out and about, could you bring us something to eat? Shelley's vegetarian, don't forget."

"Fine. I'll bring some Vegi-sim."

"Don't you dare. On second thoughts, why not? He might even like it."

"I'll stick with Italian." Paris signed off.

"Elvira told me you could speak over distances," Shelley said. "Could I see the instrument? May I have one?"

"No," Despina said emphatically. "What did I tell you, Elvira? Once we get him started on the science, he'll stop being peeved at us."

"You hope," Elvira retorted.

Despina requisitioned a couple of extra chairs and a folding table to make their dining experience less crowded. Paris wasn't back yet, and Elvira couldn't help feeling slightly edgy at the thought of possible jealousies. She was also sorry that today was probably the last she'd be speaking historic English. From tomorrow everyone would default to the 26th century equivalent, Shelley included.

When Paris arrived, bearing a huge pizza, Shelley immediately rose to greet him. As soon as he walked forward, he had effortless command of his surroundings. Elvira recalled a comment, probably Byron's, that "no finer gentleman ever crossed a drawing-room." She confiscated the pizza and took it into the kitchen, leaving the men to formally shake hands.

"It's a pleasure to meet you at last, Mr Evason," Shelley said. Then, as Elvira reappeared, "You are indeed fortunate, sir."

"Fortunate that you don't challenge me to a duel?" Paris responded with an impish grin. "I'm afraid I can't match your prowess with weapons or words."

"Save the verbal sparring for later," Despina advised. "Did you bring chips?"

While the women condescendingly set the table and divided up the pizza, Shelley and Paris politely swapped details of one another's backgrounds, and soon discovered they had one important thing in common: distant, undemonstrative mothers. This broke the ice, and by the time coffee and biscuits were served, Paris was telling stories about his finishing school and Shelley was doubled up with laughter.

"Well, that went better than I expected," said Despina, just before her communicator buzzed. It was Saranna. "I'd better take this outside in case there's a problem." About ten minutes later she returned, frowning.

Elvira shut the kitchen door and waited.

"All's good with the sailor lad: he hadn't been working for them all that long, so hadn't formed any real connection. He's quiet and biddable, and Saranna already has a work interview lined up. He's currently devouring some Errol Flynn movies. Ned, on the other hand, wants to see more of MetroLondon."

"Then why the frown?"

"Because Saranna's made a move on him. He reciprocated."

"Damn it!"

295

"I shouldn't worry too much. You know Saranna. Her affairs only last until the next piece of exotica drifts through the spaceport."

Elvira sighed. "I know, but … I wanted to keep everyone together for a while. I still don't know how Shelley's going to react to his posthumous fame."

"Can't *you* be around to deal with any histrionics? Paris won't give you grief over it."

"I never told Paris how I felt when I first arrived here. So much history, so much unfamiliarity. It's one thing to have all the knowledge in your head, but quite another to have your roots torn up. At least I had Paris with me and I knew he'd love me no matter what. Shelley only has you and me."

"You were the one who pressed for this extraction," Despina said unhelpfully. "He's alive, isn't he? And now would be an ideal moment to show him that drone footage."

They made more coffee and returned to the living area. Paris caught Elvira's eye and put on a serious face.

"More science for you now, Percy. We're going to show you what really happened to the Ariel."

"Photographs?"

"No, moving picture images."

"A magic lantern?"

"You're getting warmer. This isn't hand-cranked, it's real, or it was. We sent a drone – a mechanical bird – to fly above your boat and record its last moments. Ready? Watch the wall!"

Shelley remained motionless, gripping the arms of his chair. When the playback ended he uttered a word Elvira never thought she'd hear him use. In mitigation, he *had* just witnessed his own demise.

"So, in order to save you three, we had to make changes but keep the timeline intact," Paris went on calmly. "Trelawny's version had to ring true. So I'm afraid all that garbage about fumigating your clothes was just to get them off you. Now, observe. Along come the pirates once again – and of course they have no recollection of their previous enactment. It's been erased. And here comes the felucca. Bam. History is saved, and so are you."

He waited for Shelley's reaction. It wasn't the one he expected.

"So you don't know who was in the customs boat?"

"Well … no. We didn't think it mattered."

"Of course it matters. That collision was deliberate."

"Who'd *do* that?"

"Castlereagh's lackeys, of course. Spies, trying to silence me."

"Oh, not that again," Despina muttered.

"Can you not fly the drone again, photo-illumine the crew?"

"Not without permission. We've used our allocation," Paris explained, none too clearly. "And even if we could, what would we see? A bunch of customs officers in their uniforms, assuming they have them. No-one's going to be wearing a t-shirt with 'I am a spy' on it."

"You're not likely to be on anyone's hit list after several hundred years," Despina put in.

"Probably not," he agreed. "But I'll reserve my own opinion on the matter. I was targeted. Excuse me, my friends."

He disappeared into the hygiene unit.

"Shouldn't someone …?" ventured Elvira.

"He'll be fine," Paris said. "The ablutions at Arrivals have framed instructions on the walls. With diagrams! We were laughing about it earlier."

Shelley emerged looking unconcerned, but didn't sit down. "Is it not time for our after-dinner walk?"

"Walk? Why?" asked Paris.

"That might have been the custom for you nineteenth century landowners," Despina remarked, "but most of us have work in the morning. Anyway, what do you think is out there? Fields? Hedgerows?"

Elvira activated the feed from the nearest city-cam. "Look at that sunset! Despina, why not take Shelley to see Paris' favourite view over Hampstead?"

"Great idea. It'll help him orient himself. And then, my troublesome poet, I'll round up Norvus and convey you to the Spaceport Hilton. Because tomorrow …" She paused for effect. " … you'll be a new man. Come on. No bracelets this time. You won't need a coat either – it's a warm evening."

"And you know this because …?"

She pointed to the temperature display on the city-cam. "Oh, sorry. Universal measurement. Only in use for the past three hundred years."

"I don't even *have* a coat."

"I'll put it on the to-do list." She ushered him into the corridor.

As they walked, she noted his easy, energetic stride, and the sinews in his arms when he prised open a door which failed to open automatically. She would, of course, have had no problem forcing the door, but enjoyed the display of chivalry. As Elvira had once commented, his Victorian image – the ethereal, otherworldly doomed youth – was far from accurate. He was too thin for his height, certainly, but his every step spelt resolve and determination. Not to mention obstinacy.

He hated the multi-cubes, detested being shut in, but recovered as soon as he set foot on the level close to La Chanson d'Amour. The glorious sunset was reflected off the grain towers surrounding the vast city.

"Hampstead," said Despina, pointing down.

"I had some good friends there," he said, almost inaudibly. Then, in an apparent change of subject: "You confiscated my pistol just before we were taken from the Ariel. I suppose I'm not allowed to have it back?"

"MetroLondoners aren't permitted to bear arms," Despina said. "But I didn't follow procedure and give your weapon to the GTC artefacts collection. If I had, it would have been on a one-way trip. I appreciate that you're accustomed to

299

being armed, and after seeing your face just now I suspect you won't want to stay in MetroLondon. When the occasion's right, I'll return your property. I might even rustle up some spare ammunition."

"Thank you." He paused a moment. "Paris told me about yonder towers and how he'd never seen a cornfield till he met Elvira. Is it all like this?" He made an expansive gesture.

"You'll have all the answers tomorrow," Despina promised.

"So you keep saying. Perhaps we should go to the hotel now. I've seen more than enough."

***

Charles Vivian met Prince Agarad the Second of Altair 3 in a spaceport reception room. He moved to shake hands, then took a startled step back. "Sir! Are you a merman?"

"Sadly, no. Webbed fingers and toes, but no tail."

"Agarad has a local job offer for you," said Saranna. "But first, here's a short video of his home world. Only one main land mass, but many islands and boats, boats, boats. Experienced sailors are always needed. I think you'd do really well there."

"I should like the opportunity," Charles said eagerly. "What work are you offering, Prince?"

"My people have an oral tradition, and I have a photographic memory. I tour libraries, memorise tracts of ancient books, then recite them to an audience. But I'm unable to wear the obligatory gloves when handling old documents. I need a page turner. You."

Charles looked crestfallen. "I cannot read."

"I think you'll find you can. You've not yet accessed your new memories. Would you consider a trial run? Starting today?"

"Yes sir. Most certainly."

Agarad turned to Saranna. "As well as modern English, I'd like him taught Latin and medieval French. Then we can get to work. Well done, Saranna Sefora. And remember, young man: as my apprentice, you'll be mostly free to pursue your own occupation, here or on my homeworld. My book tours only take place once a year."

"I'll set up the extra language programmes," promised Saranna.

"Assuming the Prince employs me," Charles said, "would you please tell Mr Williams and Mr Shelley my news? Altair 3 looks amazing."

"I'll tell them," Saranna assured him. "They'll be pleased for you."

"For a day or two," Charles said astutely.

***

Even in the economy suites, the Spaceport Hilton was beautifully appointed and traditional enough to please Shelley. Norvus had been waiting for them, and he and Despina promised to stay the night in the adjoining bedroom. Inevitably Shelley had inquired after his fellow castaways, only to be informed that Charles was on his way to a new life and that Ned was involved with a spaceport hostess.

Shelley was genuinely surprised to hear about Ned. "Already? He was so devoted to his wife Jane."

"So were you, by all accounts," said Despina, resisting an urge to elbow him in the ribs.

"Your alias, while a guest here, is Percy Jones," Norvus continued. "You're hoping to join the GTC. I've endorsed your presence, so no-one will question it. You look like a man whose head's on fire, if you don't mind me saying so. We can get you something to help you sleep."

"The Arrivals tranquilliser didn't work, Norve," Despina reminded him, " and he doesn't want any heavy duty substitutes. He has to be clear-headed tomorrow for his induction."

"Laudanum?" Shelley suggested hopefully. "It focuses the mind beautifully."

"No can do. It's been banned," Norvus told him.

"I'm sure that detail wouldn't deter *you*," Shelley smiled.

"I'll pretend you never said that."

Despina scowled. "Oh, Norve, lighten up! Let him keep a handle on familiarity, just for tonight. We'll be here to ration the dosage."

"See how she leads me astray?" Norvus remarked to Shelley.

"If you've read my report on the Great Russell Street incident, you'll know exactly where to find some," Despina went on. "Off you go!"

302

Norvus departed.

"You didn't have to do that, Despina," Shelley said gratefully.

"It's exactly what I had to do, while you're still betwixt and between," she replied. "I'm officially in charge of your welfare. Now, let me outline your timetable for tomorrow. First, I'll take you to the Orientation Suite to update your English and give you an outline of recent history. Then we'll pop into a Making Eyes parlour and make a booking to correct that longsightedness of yours. And finally, Elvira will take you shopping for clothes. She insists."

"I've no money!"

"Details, details. Don't worry about it. Fancy some hot chocolate?"

"I'd like that very much. And perhaps I should shave now? To save time in the morning?"

"Er ... right."

"I noticed some accessories in the bathroom, but nothing that looks like a razor. Would you show me what to use?"

"I think we'd better wait for Norvus. I'm sure he won't be long. Shall we see what's on television? Or, we could just spy on people in the lobby."

When Norvus returned, she bundled him into one of the bedrooms. "Oh, D, this is so sudden!" he exclaimed in mock alarm.

She kicked the door shut. It wasn't a prelude to passion.

"What's up?"

303

"Shelley's asking about … *shaving*. You need to give him the talk."

"*Does* he shave?"

"He says he does. I know! I didn't think he did either. Skin like a girl. Just show him the instruments, if you don't mind. And then book him into a gentleman's salon for a haircut and perdurable epilation. You'll have to go with him."

"Be glad to. Don't be mad at him, D. He wasn't to know."

Norvus gravely beckoned Shelley into the bathroom and demonstrated some depilatory products retrieved from a concealed cabinet. "Always bear in mind that shaving's never mentioned in mixed company. To do so is vulgar and often offends."

Shelley shrieked with laughter. "That's beyond absurd. It's priceless! Maybe this century won't be so bad after all."

***

Elvira met Despina in the Regardez Café, prior to her shopping trip with Shelley. "Lost him already? Where is he?"

Despina explained about the shaving faux pas. "Norvus has taken him to one of those sordid men-only places to get seen to."

"Did the rest of the morning go well?"

"Very. That dreadful Arrivals leisure suit was actually pure cotton, including the underwear, so he wasn't required to wear paper pants during his orientation. Pity. It seems everyone's seen him strip off except me."

"You went into the chamber with him?"

"Just peeked in the door. I thought he might panic. Anyway, I needn't have worried. He was obedience personified, followed all the instructions without demur, and called the AI 'madam'. So sweet! And he was astounded when the staff at Making Eyes promised perfect reading vision in half an hour."

"Is it done?"

"No, tomorrow. And, they offered a generous price reduction if he allowed them to use a close-up of his eyes in their ads."

"Did they realise who they were talking to?"

"No, absolutely not. He's using the alias Percy Jones, courtesy of Norvus. As regards the ad, he just said 'if you like'. He's used to having his eyes admired, so didn't think it an odd request. Ah, here come the menfolk. Which means I must love you and leave you as I've a stack of admin to catch up on. Here's the key fob for his hotel suite. He'll have to add his palm print of course. The new memories take a while to settle, so be patient."

"I can't wait for the history module to embed. He'll be amazed at how famous he became. Any news of Ned and Saranna?"

"Only that it's still on. Nuisance! I didn't want Shelley to be alone just yet. You're the next nearest thing to a contemporary, so be vigilant."

"It's OK, Despina, I've got this. If I know Shelley – and you have to admit I *do* – he'll want to read, read, read. I'll demonstrate e-readers to him and ensure he has a plentiful supply of the written word. That should keep him out of mischief till Ned returns."

Despina digested that, and conceded that Elvira was probably right. "One more piece of advice. The staff of Leisure 4 Lovers will doubtless assume you're a couple. Watch how you handle it. Above all, don't deny it. That's guaranteed to get Nimue Pamina's attention, and we certainly don't want that."

At length Despina departed, first planting a kiss on Shelley's cheek and exclaiming: "Oh, that's so much better!" There was, of course, no difference, although a more obvious attempt had been made to discipline his hair. Elvira ushered him in the direction of Leisure 4 Lovers, noting his casual acceptance of his surroundings. The acquired memories were taking effect.

The Romantic trend in men's outfits – all crushed velvet and diaphanous sleeves – looked exquisite on Shelley's hologram, but he declared them impractical. He seemed just as disinterested in buying clothes as Paris was. To please Elvira he chose one item from the collection, featuring an open-necked shirt, jacket and hose in autumnal colours. Thereafter, Elvira mischievously guided his attention toward items that suited Paris, such as form-fitting jeans, traditional t-shirts and sneakers – not forgetting see-through undershorts and a fashion pouch or two.

"That's enough for now, I think," she announced at last. "Just a moment while I pay." She waved a small disc at an anonymous section of wall. "There. All done."

"That's paying?" he asked, then almost immediately added: "Citywide ID. Connects with your bank, favourite stores, entertainments, travel …"

"Right first time. Still a bit of synaptic lag, but that'll correct itself. Does it still feel as if there are two of you?"

"Exactly. Like someone whispering in my ear."

"It'll soon pass. I've had the upgrades myself, remember. Now, I'll just round up a live human to ensure these purchases go to your address and not mine."

"Elvira, I cannot keep imposing on you like this!"

"It isn't an imposition. I'll tell you a story about that later. In the meantime, would you promise me something?"

"Name it."

"Please don't lose sight of your Regency English. It's so much a part of you."

"Then I shall retain it, Miss Jones. Always."

Over lunch, she told him about Vivette, the wonder fabric Vivlar, and the shares in House of Plessis bequeathed to her by her friend. "So you see, I've done nothing to earn my wealth and I'll achieve nothing by hoarding it. I was instrumental in bringing you here, so I'll continue to support you as long as you need it. And still on the subject of finance, we need to make one more visit before we go back to the Hilton."

The visit, unsurprisingly, was to the Thetamora Sol UK bank. There, she briskly gave orders that her cousin Percy was to have his name and ID linked to her account. Hopefully the staff wouldn't look too closely into the background Norvus had set up.

The deception held, and soon Shelley had his own debit disc. Once in his suite she ensured he was able to use the interactive consumer services, with particular regard to literature.

"Can I still borrow books?" he asked.

"I'm not sure. But why go to that trouble? The British Library has everything, and you can access their terminal from here. Alternatively, if you just like to have books around you, there are still second-hand suppliers. I'll set up a few links. And I've ordered you a connected e-reader so you aren't forever staring at the wall. When's your eye appointment?"

"Ten, Despina said."

"They might tell you not to read too much for a day or two. Don't ignore their instructions. Shelley? You're very quiet. Too much information? Should I stop?"

"For a moment. My mind's still chaotic." He managed a wry smile. "Maybe it always has been. I scarcely know who I am anymore."

"If you value my opinion," Elvira said carefully. "I believe you won't have a stable picture of what you *are* until you're thoroughly acquainted with who you *were*. You didn't believe me, nor Despina, when we said you'd be famous. When I was with you in your time, you constantly undervalued yourself. Once you discover how the world sees you now, you'll be elated."

"But I can never continue that life, can I?"

"That goes without saying, but you can carry your beliefs and ideals forward. And you'll always have friends who know the truth." She finished configuring the info screen and came towards him. "Do stop pacing. Settle down."

"Miss Jones – Elvira – I've no claim on your affection any longer. You should send me away."

"Oh? What's brought this on?"

"Paris is a fine, honourable gentleman and you'll soon be married. How can I continue in a menage a trois?"

"Aren't you forgetting something?" Elvira inquired gently. "As a woman, I have the deciding voice. Paris and I have a robust relationship which has survived the most adverse circumstances. It was nearly ended by time itself until his mother, of all people, requested my relocation from 2023. Then we had an arranged marriage to free Paris from. Then I fell pregnant with your love child, having been set up by the GTC. I told you, when we met again in Venice, how close I came to miscarrying. To save the child I was kept in an induced sleep."

"Despina told me."

"Did she also tell you that she and Paris had a rip-roaring sexual encounter to ease his frustration?"

"No." A smile tweaked the corners of Shelley's mouth. "Were you angry?"

"Not in the least. They don't even realise I know – at least, I don't think they do. Paris and I did have a heart to heart, though, about our future. He's decided he wants children. We talked about you, too. He asked if I loved you."

"To which you replied ...?"

"Not in the same way as I loved *him*. With you, it's love for someone unique and brilliant, but unhappy. I want to see you happy."

"And what then?" he asked.

"Then you won't need me anymore."

"No. You're wrong about that."

"I don't think I am. Time will tell, as it always does. But first, I want to watch your journey of discovery. Where shall we start? There are so many downloads - "

Impulsive as always, he kissed her. His kisses were as beautiful as ever.

"I'm beginning to think you deserve your bad reputation," she murmured.

"Oh, I do hope so," he replied.

Chapter Ten

"Where have you *been*?" demanded Paris in a rare show of irritation.

"Spaceport Hilton. Installing everything Shelley will need when researching his own past."

"Where was Despina?"

"GTC work. She asked me to stand in for her." Elvira hoped she didn't sound guilty. She hadn't intended to prolong her liaison with Shelley, especially not when he was still so fragile. "What's the matter, anyway? Bad day at Construction?"

Paris took both her hands. "Sorry to be ratty just now. Aurelia Neve's been trying to contact us all day. She couldn't locate you, and Cyprian still doesn't allow electronics in the workplace. There were half a dozen messages when I got home." He paused, smiling broadly. "The annulment's through. It finally is! We can be married any time we like. Hey, careful with the hugs. Tungstron oil!"

"I *love* the smell of tungstron oil!"

"There's more news. Albie and Lelza are also free to marry, of course, and they don't want to wait. They're marrying at the weekend and they want us to be guests of honour."

"Where? The imitation Parthenon?"

"No, much further off. Le Jardin de la Javeliere."

"Lelza's picture window," Elvira murmured. "They're actually *going* there? What will that cost them?"

"House Dawn's paying. It's a peace offering from her family, Elvira. We have to accept. And, diplomacy apart, who else does that isolated pair have to invite?"

"Albie must have co-workers at the spaceport, surely. He might even ask Saranna, if he can find her." Elvira suppressed a frown. "Why is nothing ever straightforward? I'm still mad at her for disappearing with Ned. It's too soon to ask Shelley to fend for himself."

"He'll have to stand on his own two feet sometime," Paris said dismissively.

Elvira didn't comment. Instead, she tried to summon enthusiasm for the wedding – which, under more settled circumstances, would have delighted her. "There's another problem," she said, pulling a face at herself in the mirror. "For me, at any rate. I'd never intentionally overshadow Lelza on her big day, but how do I avoid media tattle?"

"Dress down," Paris said, and laughed. "Don't worry! I doubt that Nimue Pamina's tentacles reach that far. Lelza's mother will take care of the photo shoot."

"How do we get there?" Elvira was envisaging some form of localised time travel. "Can you set it up from here? We'll need travel to the venue, and a two-night stay for the wedding and reception - "

"The reception's three days long. A feast, a concert and a shopping trip. It was in the message."

"Five days, then," Elvira amended. "We'll programme the return for, say, a couple of hours after we've set out. Duty discharged there, commitments taken care of here."

Paris shook his head. "Sorry, my angel, time travel doesn't work like that. I can't believe we've been together all this while and not had the subject come up."

"What subject?"

"Lateral relativity. One of the most – if not *the* most – important restrictions time lays on us. Put simply, you only have one existence. One only. You can't occupy the same time twice. So, if we stay in France for five days, that same five days must elapse here."

Elvira wrestled with the concept. "So we're free to move about spacially, but we can't return to a time we've already been in."

"Correct."

"So I'll never come face to face with my younger self?"

"Afraid not."

"How long ago did the TTI find this out?"

"Lifetimes ago. Probably the first time someone tried to pay themselves a visit. Don't worry, there are numerous failsafes to guard against neglect or inattention. Nobody wants a temporal implosion."

"This," Elvira declared, "is getting scary. To go back to my original question: how do we get to the wedding?"

"Short range hopper, probably. I haven't checked."

"Then check. Have you replied to the RSVP?"

313

"Not yet."

"Well, do it then. For all five days. That's if Cyprian will give you the time off."

"It's only three days. Weekends don't count."

"Fine. I'll make some tea and then I'll call Despina. She'd better step up!"

Paris followed her into the kitchenette and put his warm arms about her. "I hope my less than perfect explanation's made you aware that when Despina isn't always around when we want her, it's due to a time clash with her other GTC work. She tends to take on historic cases because they're easier to chart, but if she *has* to take work in the here and now, various lacunae tend to crop up. It's often a juggling act for agents. I've seen it over and over."

"Is that why agents so often form relationships with other agents?"

"That's exactly why. Their lifestyle doesn't suit the majority."

While Elvira finished getting the tea, Paris contacted Albie, as the invitation had come from him. "I'm so glad you've accepted," he enthused. "Lelza wasn't sure if you would. She's at her mother's, of course. You know how it is with women and weddings. Primping. I'll send you a hard copy of the service right away. I was hoping to be married at the cinema makeover – I really must invent a better name for it – but it isn't quite finished and Lelza wouldn't wait. It's just a matter of weeks now. Will you and Elvira be the first to marry there?"

"Of course we will," Paris said. "We also have a few things to sort out, so hopefully we'll be ready when you are. I still don't know if my mother's going to be present. Procyon 4 is a bit of a hike!"

Despina assured Elvira that she'd keep a close watch on Shelley during their absence. "*You* were the one who said he'd only want to read," she pointed out. "Once his eyesight's fixed, he'll doubtless do just that. In spades. What's the betting he tells me to clear off and stop interrupting him? Now put him out of your head and make your travel plans."

Elvira did so, first gently raising her concerns with Albie about keeping a low profile. He gratefully shared the hologram image of Lelza's outfit, which he'd helped design. Rather than underplay her waif-like qualities, he'd emphasised them. She wore a white shift dress with a bodice decorated with seed pearls, plus a pearl tiara. Her bouquet was of white peonies. Her two child attendants, girl cousins, wore short bell-shaped dresses, also in white, with a leaf-green trim.

Albie suggested a pink two-piece suit for Elvira, with a fascinator and clutch bag. Paris, they decided, would wear a traditional linen suit, thus excusing him from a fitting-room session.

"I didn't know you were a fashion expert, Albie," Elvira said. "Is there no end to your talents?"

"No," he replied, deadpan. "And, I should very much like you to wear a golden gown for your

315

wedding. When you see the décor and lighting in the, er, ex-cinema, you'll know why I suggested it."

"I'll have Leisure 4 Lovers run off your designs," she promised.

"We'll see you in a day and a half," Albie said. "Don't worry about accommodation – House Dawn has booked an entire hotel, the largest in Montbarrois. So all you need do is buy your hopper tickets."

"I'm really looking forward to this now," said Elvira.

***

The day after Shelley's visit to Making Eyes, Despina received an unexpected and irritating call from the GTC closed case section.

"We're sorry to disrupt your week's leave," said Freenish, the head of department, "but the City Enforcers are calling on you to justify your role in the arrest of Araminta Grace. They're saying it was an enforcer matter rather than a GTC one, and that you should have turned the case over to them."

"An enforcer matter? When illicit use was being made of our packet transport?"

"I agree, it's a ridiculous claim. And since the GTC outranks them, the outcome's foregone. But, to maintain our quasi-cordial relationship with them, you'd better go through the motions with their representatives."

"Waste a day on pointless questioning?"

"At the speed they move at, it's more likely to be two."

"Dammit, Free! I still haven't resolved the La Spezia mission to my satisfaction."

"I know that, otherwise I'd have seen your report. But are a couple of missed days really going to matter?"

"They might."

"Don't you have a stand-in? What about Norvus Maysson?"

"He'd comply, but he lacks empathy with the situation. Can you give me one more day?"

"A half-day. No longer."

***

Shelley seemed grateful to see her. He looked as though he hadn't slept.

"How's it going?" Despina asked, although she already knew and was troubled by it.

"It's … daunting," he replied. "I've assembled diaries and memoirs from 1822 onwards, and had to buy to more e-readers as their memory stores keep filling up. I've found so many sad things, poignant things. I wanted to see what had happened to my contemporaries …"

"Maybe that wasn't such a good idea," Despina remarked.

"I started with Byron," Shelley continued undeterred, "and found he'd died only two years after I was … taken. Two years! He seemed so unassailable."

317

Not quite, Despina thought, remembering La Fornarina.

"And then there's Trelawny," Shelley was saying. "Young, flamboyant, with his tales of the sea. Suddenly he's eighty-one, in a portrait, his daughter holding his hand while he dreams of past exploits. And my one surviving son, Percy Florence, said the only recollection he had of me was of being lifted from his cot by two capable arms."

"That's life-affirming, in a way," said Despina.

"Hardly, when they're all dead."

Despina sighed. "You shouldn't have started with friends and family. We all have to live with such reminders, but we're used to it. Time travel's a blessing and a curse."

"There's one exception," Shelley went on more quietly. "My daughter. My little Elena. She lived in the here and now, *and* seven hundred years ago. I find that almost comforting. And you can add to that."

"How?"

"That day in Naples, after she was christened: I was handing her back to you and I noticed a stray sunbeam glancing off your emerald ring. Only it wasn't the sun, was it? It was the light-emission from a miniature camera. You took Elena's picture."

"I did," Despina said. "I intended it for Elvira, in case she ever wants to see her."

"She won't. It's her coping mechanism. I wish I had her strength." He turned the full entreaty of his gaze on Despina. "May *I* have the photograph?"

"If it will help you acclimatise. I'll put a copy on your e-reader. Have you eaten lately?"

"No, I - "

"I thought not." Despina went to the hotel intercom and ordered two English breakfasts and a plentiful supply of coffee. "Now listen, Shelley. I'm going to be absent for two days – some stupid bureaucratic meeting I have to attend – but I'll detail Norvus to call on you. What I want you to do, and I'll ensure he checks on this, is to stick to respected biographers and literary critics who'll give lengthy appraisals of your poetry and once-removed commentaries on your life. Promise me you'll do that."

"I promise," Shelley said, and meant it.

He accordingly began his studies and was suitably amazed when his lasting fame was incrementally revealed. He kept reading. Norvus looked in twice, and left after a few moments, reporting to Despina that their excitable, emotional guest was bemused but gratified.

He and Despina were both wrong. Shelley was neither gratified nor ecstatic, merely piqued that recognition had come too late. And as he read on, every respected biographer and learned critic had one subject in common: the diligent, devoted way Mary had kept faith with him, ceaselessly promoting his legacy. He was increasingly remorseful, berating himself for his coldness toward

319

her in what she believed to be his final days. Eventually, wracked with guilt, he vowed she had to know how conscience-stricken he was. There was only one way to achieve that: via the TTI.

At last, after much rifling through ancient books and online reproductions, and after careful cross-referencing of dates, he had a plan. First, he drafted a letter.

"Dear Mary, my best girl, I write in haste. I hope to deliver this in person but I suspect this privilege will be denied me. Whilst in Livorno I found that Home Office spies were following my every move. Ned and Charles were witness to this. I later discovered that Trelawny was refused port clearance and thus our return to Lerici will not have the protection of the Bolivar and her armaments. I fear, therefore, that our journey will not be completed. Perhaps this will mean exile, incarceration, or even death. If the latter, be assured it will not have been an accident. Forgive me, dearest girl, for taking you so much for granted. You are, and always will be, my one true love. I have lost my way so often and now seek to return after many cares and sorrows. From your penitent S."

It was his intention to visit Casa Magni, briefly, in the interval before the various bodies were washed ashore. He had from July 9th, 1822, to the 17th. If he bought one of the TTI's fifteen minute economy trips, he could hand his letter to the first person he saw, and maybe obtain more than Mary's forgiveness. He was hoping that the householder reaction to his presence would convince the GTC that he truly belonged in the past.

Next he made a fair copy of the letter, using a quill pen, ink and parchment sourced remotely. Whatever he took with him had to resemble a prop rather than an anachronism, or it would be confiscated by the Dispatch staff. He dared not write Mary's name where it would be seen, either. After a little hesitation he inscribed the nickname he'd given her: the Maie, c/o Casa Magni, San Terenzo.

Clothing was less of a problem. If he wore the quasi-Regency garb from Leisure 4 Lovers, there would be no need to make a lengthy detour via the wardrobe department. Apparently, habitual time tourists preferred to purchase their own attire. It was all part of the experience.

With extreme care he located the TTI booking site and reserved a fifteen minute slot for early afternoon in two days' time. Lerici showed up obligingly, but the date settings were displayed only in years, and would not budge. Rather than risk a system crash – his tentative use of the machine seemed to invite them – he left the date incomplete. The check-in clerks would doubtless sort it out. Finally he reached the payment screen, outraged when a £300 bill presented itself. Guiltily he proffered Elvira's disc. A courtesy acknowledgement popped up. He deleted it.

On an impulse he started to read one of Mary's novels, The Last Man. Its apocalyptic theme suited his mood, but he almost stopped reading when he realised the character of Adrian was based on *him*. It didn't assuage his guilt. If anything, it contributed to it. No matter how many times she rewrote him, he and his conscience were immutable.

Later, the book half read, he was interrupted by a subdued chime from the entry phone. A smiling employee wheeled in his evening meal – a mixed vegetable bake which Despina had ordered for him on her way out. He ate it gratefully, but wondered how long it would be before she tired of ministering to him.

He was prompted, then, to inspect her photo of Elena. He'd expected something grainy and indistinct, but instead, a bold bright image dazzled him. Baby Elena's blue-green eyes were half closed against the winter sunshine, her sleepy face upturned. On camera, his own expression was a mixture of tenderness and sadness. For several minutes he remained as immobile as his onscreen self; then, carefully setting the e-reader aside, he fetched two large scatter cushions from the corner sofa and placed them on the floor. He dimmed the overhead lights and lay down, his arm around one cushion, his head on the other. The e-reader, with its benign image of a moment long past, shone steadfastly.

"Everything I touch turns to dust," he murmured softly. Eventually, curled up like a tired child, he slept.

***

He was lost. Not just psychologically, but physically, indubitably, stupidly lost in MetroLondon. He thought he'd memorised the way to TTI Dispatch. From the hotel he'd retraced his steps to the orientation suite, then remained on the same level and headed east. The upper storeys of the TTI were solely concerned with admin, wardrobe and executive tourist suites; the central areas staff accommodation, the physics lab, the generator hall, repair units and spares storage. Beneath all these, in the basement, was transport by rail. Level Two, where he needed to be, was home to Construction, the Stats department, the staff canteen and Dispatch. And that, he now knew, was where he'd gone badly wrong.

Those infernal multi-cubes, with their omnidirectional touch controls, were to blame. He'd keyed in up-down instead of left-right. The cube had disgorged him onto an open-air level, with ground and air traffic hurtling past on invisible lanes, anonymous many-storeyed buildings everywhere and a miniscule patch of sky far above. There were very few pedestrians and those he did see were hurrying past in a way which brooked no interruption. Then, almost in his ear, a soft voice said: "Hello, pretty! Lost your way?"

"Yes," he began thankfully. "Could you direct me to - "

The girl, wearing a black bandana and a loose-fitting black dress, inelegantly stuck her fingers in her mouth and gave a piercing whistle. "Hey, gang! Look what I've found!"

Several other young women, identically clad, appeared from doorways and dark shadows, slowly but purposefully closing in.

"Careful now, don't scare him," he heard one say. They drew closer.

"Where were you going, angel face?"

"Into cosplay, are you? Can we join in?"

"Come along with us."

"Whatever your game is, I'm in no mood for it." Shelley tried to sound dismissive. In fact, having read about MetroLondon's feral girls, he was close to panic.

"Now that's not friendly," said the girl who'd whistled.

"Definitely antisocial," said another.

"Relax, blue eyes."

"You've got to be *friendly* when you're in this part of town. Got the stuff, Milly?"

A small cylinder was passed around. They dabbed the contents on their pulse points.

"This isn't Priap-sin. It's odourless. You've been ripped off."

"*We* can't smell it, dimwit!" Milly retorted. "But *he* can, or he will any moment."

Shelley remembered an anecdote Paris had shared when they'd both had a little too much to drink, and smiled mirthlessly to himself. Aphrodisiac perfume. The irony was, he'd remembered too late.

"Get ready. Don't let him fall."

"*Sophia. Emilia. Jane …*"

"If that's what you want to call us, go right ahead."

"Sophia. Your hands on the harp strings. I crave the touch of your hands ..."

"Well, now you've got them, sugar plum."

"Emilia. Run away with me."

"All in good time."

"Jane. Together we will solve the great mystery. Kiss me. Kiss me ..."

Milly, the most daring, decided to kiss him. "Oh, wow," she said eventually. "Wait up, gang. He's an adept. Some rich woman's sex toy, I'll bet. We'd better leave off. We don't want trouble from the Houses."

"No, we go on," said the self-appointed leader. "Let's get him into the cloisters. Everyone grab a piece. And quick march ..."

"Stop!" A sharp command halted the girls and partially awakened Shelley from his trance. An aircar, its canopy raised, sat by the kerb. An older woman in a yellow uniform approached the group, stun-gun at the ready. A few of the culprits tried to slip away and were peremptorily called back. The enforcer scrutinised the girls narrowly, then walked round them with a small recording device.

"You should be ashamed," she pronounced at last. "Attempted kidnap in broad daylight. I've bio-scanned the lot of you and if you reoffend, you'll get more than just a caution. Now beat it!"

They vanished, and the woman turned to Shelley in professional concern. "All right now, sir?"

"I ... think so."

The bio-scanner was at work again. "Priap-sin, was it? I'm detecting a trace. You were lucky. Someone sold them an adulterated version. Take deep breaths. You'll be fine."

"Thank you. I'm obliged."

"You shouldn't have entered this district unaccompanied. It was asking for trouble."

"I know. The ferals -"

"*Ferals*? Is that where you think you are? This is Level Two, not Level Minus Two. These are the hallowed precincts of academe. Women's universities, forbidden to men. Those girls are science students, fresh from their graduation. Didn't their gowns tell you anything? They were celebrating, and you got in the way. If I hadn't happened along they'd have had their fun and left you tied naked to the nearest lamppost."

"Graduates?" Shelley was still bemused.

"With distinction, most of them. I accessed their results. Milly Francesca, reading hyperway enhancement, author of an award-winning paper on applied Boolean fractals. Germaine Hazel, the ringleader of your thrill-seekers, researching quantum variants in overstrung brace transmission."

"I've no idea what any of that means."

"Neither have I. Now, where are you in from? Centauri? Which tourist spot were you heading for?"

"The TTI. I had an appointment at ten past two. I've probably missed it."

The enforcer consulted her wrist database. "No, you've fifteen minutes yet. Come on." She secured her car, and with an unintentionally ferocious grip on his arm, hurried him back to the multi-cube interface. "Hold the door open while I programme this. So, here's what will happen. This cube will now travel non-stop to TTI Dispatch, ignoring any customer attempts to flag it down. I've entered my badge number as authority. You'll get there with five minutes to spare. On your way, Percy Jones."

***

"You're late," said the TTI dispatch clerk.

"I'm sorry." Shelley wished she'd look at him. That always made things easier. "I was held up."

"Palm print here, please. Validated. You can proceed to cubicles."

"Just one moment, if I may. The destination date's incomplete. It only says 1822."

She looked at him then, or rather, *through* him. "You bought a fifteen minute economy trip, accurate only in years, not days or months. If you wanted an exact date you should have bought economy plus, at £500."

Shelley felt a keen disappointment and a sudden sense of danger. But the girl had already processed his ticket, so he had to follow the other tourists into the lattice hall.

"Face away from the entrance," said another dispatcher, clipping a bracelet on him as he entered a cubicle. "Move forward when directed."

A moment later he heard the instruction but could see only mist. Was this Lerici?

Suddenly he was back in the cubicle. "Sorry," said the girl over the intercom. "It stalled. Reprocessing."

Again, he moved forward when told. The mist was back.

***

Casa Magni, June 1822

Jane Williams rushed to the window. "Good Lord! Can Shelley have leapt from the wall?"

"Whatever do you mean, Jane?" asked Trelawny. "Shelley isn't here."

"He *is*! I just saw him walking along the balcony. Twice, in the same direction!"

"Without turning around? Look, there he is on the beach with Ned, near the Ariel."

"I swear I saw him," Jane insisted.

***

"What's wrong with these machines today?" the dispatcher muttered to her friend. "One more try. If this doesn't work we'll have to offer him a refund."

This time Shelley sensed someone staring at him through the shifting air. He was annoyed now.

The fifteen minutes were counting down and he was squandering them by letting himself be stared at. Who was that fellow anyway? An Italian? One of the servants?

"Siete soddisfatto?" he demanded. "You are impudent, sir. I wish to see - "

For the briefest moment, the mist was gone. The sentence was never finished. He was staring into his own face.

Chapter Eleven

At the same time as Shelley was being tormented by the neo-grads, Despina, Norvus, Elvira and Paris were gathered outside the poet's hotel suite, taking turns to shout through the intercom and hammer on the door.

"Why didn't you call me, Norvus?" Despina remonstrated.

"He was fine yesterday. He said he was busy working on a new poem and that he'd see me later. He sounded cheerful."

"But he didn't let you in."

"Well, no. I put it down to artistic temperament."

"You should have called me," Despina reiterated.

An employee arrived with a pass key.

"Finally!"

The door swung open to reveal a litter of books, expired e-readers, discarded clothes, cushions and dirty plates. A half-eaten loaf lay on the floor along with a bag of raisins.

"Looks like he's been channelling his inner teenager," remarked Norvus.

Despina searched the bedrooms. "He isn't here."

Some sheets of parchment lay on the suite's one table. Paris picked them up. "This must be the poem he was working on. Here's the finished copy."

Elvira peered over his shoulder. "What's happened to his handwriting? That looks almost legible!"

"I gave him a boxful of ballpoint pens," said Paris laconically. "Oh, Hades. Whatever he told Norvus, he isn't in a good place. Listen."

To Elena: An Invocation

Elena, child of my heedless past, hear me!
Cast your brave life-spark through immensity
And guide lost lovers, though they love no more,
Across time's oceans, endless shore on shore.
For I am now adrift, as lost as they,
Without your tiny light to steer my way.
I am a shadow, neither old nor young.
The Earth is stilled, its melodies unsung.
Elena, with thy mother's eyes, awaken!
Descry me now! Together we will seek
The world of the unloved and the forsaken,
And sleep forever in the wild and bleak
Embrace of time; while one who bears my name
Basks in the joy of his belated fame.

Elvira dabbed a tear.

"Some of these jottings are addressed to Mary," Paris went on. "Why would ... no. Oh no. Elvira, check your bank statements."

She complied. "He paid £300 to the TTI yesterday."

"Three hundred. Not five?"

"Three. Why?"

"Despina," said Paris urgently, "call this in. I want a fifty second emergency relocation to Dispatch. I don't *care* if there's no bracelet, just get me there! The rest of you, follow any way you can. We have to stop him!"

The vertiginous, gut-wrenching fall into Dispatch was strongly reminiscent of his panic flight into Hampstead 2023. Suppressing an urge to throw up, Paris scrambled to his feet. "Percy Jones, which cubicle?"

"Twenty-five," responded several of the startled team.

Paris hit the nearest alarm button. A klaxon sounded. "Paris Evason, voiceprint alert. Imminent lateral breach at Dispatch unit two-five. Brace brace brace, execute!" Then, at considerable risk to himself, he reached into the cubicle, hauled Shelley out, threw him to the floor and shielded him with his own body. The triple strength brace, hastily cast around the structure by the physics team, resembled a heat haze.

Precisely seven seconds after Paris' announcement, a temporal implosion wrecked the cubicle's interior. The brace contained most of the recoil that followed, but a spattering of small fiery fragments landed on Paris' back, burning minute holes in his new jacket. Oblivious, he stood up and stormed across to the dispatch desk.

"Diagnostic! Now!"

Wordlessly they turned the screen toward him. The results suited his purpose.

"You had two misfires – *two*! – and you didn't abort?" he demanded in his angriest tones.

"We didn't think they *were* misfires," objected the more senior of the dispatchers. "Just glitches."

"You ignored the most basic aspect of your training – always err on the side of caution. You then got yourselves a potentially lethal implosion. Well done!"

"Are you putting us on report?"

Paris looked across to Elvira and Despina, who were helping Shelley to sit up. "Not if he's unhurt. He won't want any publicity. But several other people saw what happened, so I'll leave you in their hands."

Elvira hurried across and began patting at his singed jacket. "I'm so proud of you. You saved him!"

"My name would've been mud if I hadn't."

Despina came up. "I'll have the medics check Percy over to ensure there was no damage at molecular level. Paris, will you stick around and keep an eye on him? We've got a hotel room to put straight."

"Yes, I'll stay. I'd like to talk to him."

"Hasn't he been through enough?" Elvira asked indignantly.

"I promise I won't tell him off," Paris said. "Just this once, could you step back? There's always such a frisson between you two and I'd like him calm and settled, if such a thing's possible."

"Let them talk, Elvira," Despina advised. "It'll do them both good."

Shelley understandably thought he was due for a tongue-lashing, but soon found he was mistaken.

"Today must have been quite an adventure for you," Paris said affably.

"You could say that. I suppose I have to answer to the TTI?"

"No, you don't. I convinced them their machine was faulty."

"Thanks for extricating me."

"Just don't make a habit of it." Paris massaged a wrenched shoulder. "You're heavier than you look."

"So are you. I hope you don't throw yourself on Elvira like that."

Paris grinned. "Not without saying please and thank you."

Shelley was silent for a moment. "What *really* happened, Paris?"

"The machine tried to send you to June 1822," Paris said, and carefully outlined the principle of lateral relativity. "It's specialised knowledge, so it wouldn't have been included in your orientation. I *have* to know, as I work here."

"What about the habitual time travellers? Aren't they at risk of running into themselves?"

"No, because the TTI keeps a data profile on every client. *We* remember, so they don't have to. Elvira didn't know about lateral relativity till just the other day, so don't blame her for not sharing." He paused. "I wanted to see you for two reasons.

334

Firstly, to thank you. Yes, you heard aright. Having read the rough draft of your letter to Mary, it was obvious that you'd exercised great care in maintaining the timeline we'd devised. The only person potentially in trouble would have been you. You were so nearly successful. What a pity you didn't read our website more thoroughly."

"A pity? No. I was destined to make that mistake because I already had the memory of confronting myself." He shivered a little. "I thought it was a hallucination. We'd all been on edge that week. Even dear down-to-earth Jane saw two of me on the balcony. Anyway, it's over – another failure to chalk up. What else did you want to see me about?"

"A proposition," Paris said.

"Oh?"

"I don't dare send you back to the correct date in 1822, however briefly, but I could send your letter by itself. I assume you have it?"

"It's here; I sewed my pocket up. But how - "

"Time travel started small. Little packages, not people. And that facility's still operational, though most of my colleagues think it's obsolete. I'll show you what it can do, but not until you've ditched that Leisure4Lovers romp suit. You'll need a TTI uniform. Then you'll need to defer to me as my assistant, as we could well encounter GTC staff who *don't* know about you."

"Are there such beings?"

"Plenty. So, nice and quiet does it. Give me the letter."

Reluctantly Shelley broke open the loose stitching and handed it over.

"Right, uniform next. And remember to stand up straight!"

As Paris had anticipated, some young but officious GTC recruits were idling around the single packet relay unit. Paris showed his pass. "This work's restricted so you'll need to leave," he said brusquely.

"Restricted? *Here*?"

"Yes, here. I have a missive for Coherence Co, back where it all started. Now are you going to absent yourselves or do I have to call Clovis Trell?"

Her name had the desired effect.

"Dragon lady," Paris supplemented.

"Oh. I've known a few of those."

"First, we send our receptor," Paris continued, positioning a small lidless box on some floor markings and activating a nearby panel. "I copied the Lerici settings from Dispatch," he added. "What exactly did you put on the destination form?"

"That I wanted to see Casa Magni before it became a tourist attraction and memorial. I pointed out that the ocean level had receded since 1822, and that in the days of the poet the ground floor was often flooded. I advised the programmers to avoid high tides and bad weather."

"So you got yourself a balcony, residents included. Just the kind of dim-witted logic I'd expect from an economy-based AI," muttered Paris. "I'll keep that error if I can, and make it work for us."

The receptor, with the letter in it, vanished in a gentle wash of air. A moment later, it returned empty.

"Is that all? Did it get there?"

"It did. I can't guarantee that Mary will find it, but there's a good chance."

"Why are you helping me, Paris?"

"Because I can. Because Elvira would want me to. And because you're struggling."

"I don't deny it."

"So, I'm not sending you back to that soulless hotel. Come to the flat with me. We'll round up the others and have a confab."

"Paris of the many fathers," Shelley said formally, "I owe you a debt of honour and I shall repay it. I don't yet know how, but should an opportunity arise, I shall be ready."

Over a vegan take-away, they talked seriously.

"There's one thing I must re-emphasise," Paris began, "just to ensure there can be no misunderstanding. You can never ever resume your old life, and neither I nor anyone else will assist you in such an attempt. Elvira has already told you this, very gently I imagine, and since you raised the subject with her yourself, I think you're well aware of the situation."

"You went to a lot of trouble to persuade everyone I was dead. That seemed fairly one-way to me. I'll abide by it, but that doesn't mean I approve. Convince me."

Paris marshalled his arguments. "Your case is virtually unique, as a link to this time was formed via Elena – a link initiated by the scriveners, who doubtless had reasons they didn't vouchsafe to us."

"Maybe they thought I'd be too much of a menace where I was," Shelley said, not quite jokingly.

"There's probably some truth in that," Paris agreed soberly. "Let's consider what you might have done. You'd have written more poetry, obviously, and literary history would have been changed. Upon the death of your father you might have gone into the House of Lords, and Britain in the Victorian age was a powerful country. Whatever you did, however slight your political influence, you would in some degree have changed the world, and the timeline, irrevocably. And frankly, I think you'd have hated every second of it."

"I think you're right."

"You now know," Paris said more quietly, "that your poetry's revered, your radicalism is admired and embraced, your life-style emulated and envied. Of course you still have your detractors, but any celebrity does. So please, try and draw a line under all that, and move on."

"I suppose I must."

"Don't just suppose. Act. Be honest, now - you were in difficulties before we ever came on the scene. Elvira said you were always running away from yourself. It's time to stop running."

Shelley lapsed into one of his silences, regarding Paris intently over the rim of his brandy glass. Eventually, changing the subject completely,

338

he said: "When I was with Despina in Naples, she suddenly declared – nervously – that neither she nor anyone else looked at their own futures. At the time I didn't, of course, know about lateral relativity. I now realise why she, you and just about everyone avoids travelling to the future, whether as tourists or scientists or just because it's there. Supposing you want to put that machine over yonder, the Hope, through its paces. You try relocating to next week. It won't let you as you're there already. The same applies to next year, next decade, thirty, forty, fifty years ahead. And then, suddenly, you're free to travel. On one unremarkable day, the way is open. But you don't go, because the preceding day was your death-day and you don't care to venture near. And that's why, aside from a few brave, nihilistic or stubborn people, you leave the future to its own devices."

Paris exhaled slowly. "You amaze me, Shelley. In the course of one day you've been lost in a strange city, got yourself roughed up by rampaging neo-grads and almost vapourised by a temporal implosion. And you're still able to calmly sit there and apply that daunting intellect to one of the last taboos of our time."

"Am I right?"

"Of course you're right, and you know it. One could add that the far future is malleable, just as the past is, and for safety's sake we decided not to set up receptors."

339

"Why not? There might be all kinds of tyranny and oppression at work there, which you have a duty to suppress."

Paris began to see why Shelley would never settle into 2585. He thrived on adversity, living as he had in a time when there were many causes to espouse and wrongs to be tackled head on. Here, his thoughts would turn inward even further than they had already, and there'd be nowhere to run to. Elvira wouldn't be able to help him this time.

While he was pondering whether to air his dour conclusions or keep them to himself, some cheery voices sounded in the corridor leading to the flat, and the door opened to admit Despina, Elvira, Norvus – and Ned Williams.

"We found this one skulking around the hotel," Despina explained.

Shelley's face lit in a broad smile. He was out of his chair in an instant, slapping his friend on the back and then hugging him. "It's wonderful to see you! Where have you *been*? I thought you'd gone for good!"

"After five days? Didn't Saranna get word to you?"

"Yes, with no contact details."

"Oh, sorry. I didn't realise. Did I miss anything?"

They told him, over more drinks.

"Always getting into scrapes, Percy," grinned Ned. "Can't I leave you alone for five minutes?"

"Where's your paramour?" Shelley asked pointedly.

"I know how that must have looked, but I completely misread your situation. All I knew was, you had history – silly choice of words. You'd had a romance with Elvira, and there was a baby, and after what happened on the Ariel I thought you were involved with Despina too. I naturally assumed you'd want to stay here. I also thought, wrongly as it turned out, that you lived so much in your own head it wouldn't matter where you settled. After the induction, and having divested me of my whiskers, Norvus showed me MetroLondon and I was astounded. Not in a good way. It was like being in a huge cage. I asked Norvus - " The two men exchanged friendly nods - "if it were possible to relocate somewhere closer to my own century. He said no, because if I'd done that we'd already know about it. It wasn't the answer I was hoping for. And then, suddenly, there was Saranna – laughing, bouncing with life. I swear she saved my sanity. More importantly, she told me about young Vivian and his aquatic world, and said there were frontier planets out there, worlds with a lower level of technology than ours, which were always on the lookout for colonists. Then Paris called this group meeting and I didn't have a chance to learn more."

"Those other worlds won't disappear," Norvus said. "Neither will Saranna. Girls, I presume you'll be happy for these two shipmates to live at the Spaceport Hilton a little longer, since we've managed to conceal Percy's depredations from the hotel staff? He and Ned have to decide how they want their lives to go."

"I'm OK with that," Elvira said. "Paris and I have a wedding to organise. Firstly, we'll need to touch base with Albie and see how much longer he'll need to finish that cinema. I wonder if he's found a name for it yet?"

***

Back at the hotel, Ned lost no time in giving Shelley a dose of much needed common sense.
"Ye gods, Percy, you have to stop raking over the past. Look what it's doing to you! As far as I was concerned, we were finished with that life as soon as the Ariel went down. I've seen all the versions – the storm itself, the pirates, a customs boat full of spies – and it always ends the same way. I did take one look back, to see what became of Jane. We weren't legally married, as you know, and with me gone I worried that she might again fall prey to the husband she ran from. But, sensible as always, she found another protector in your friend Thomas Jefferson Hogg. I needn't have worried. Now you and I should begin to plan ahead."

Shelley wasn't persuaded. "Apart from its cage-like properties, pray tell me what's so wrong with MetroLondon. It's well run, clean, and scientifically advanced."

"It's culturally stagnant. Every stage performance and every note of music is a homage to its history. And then there's time tourism, when the past of the whole world is on offer. Ask Norvus who's writing new music and new literature."

"Well, Norvus?"

"I was never one for the arts," he said evasively.

Ned sighed. "I don't wish to be sequestered or cocooned, or gossiped at by images on walls. There has to be more to life than that, and Saranna was about to tell me."

"Then go see her. Take Shelley along as well. Now, can I leave you two alone for the rest of the day without either of you doing anything stupid?"

"You can indeed," Ned replied.

"Shelley?"

"I think I've learnt my lesson."

"Good. If you want some entertainment, why not take a look at the twentieth century movies that your young friend Charles found so fascinating. They're still on the e-drive. I viewed some myself a while back, when I was convalescing."

"Convalescing? From what?"

"It's classified. But since it involves someone you used to know, try asking Elvira and Despina."

"Stop hedging and tell us!"

"Not going to happen. I'm needed elsewhere. Watch your films."

Later, they had to admit that the American West had its appeal.

"Prairies, big skies, tumbleweeds, cacti - " recited Ned.

"All gone. It'll be spaceports, more spaceports, adventure parks and vertical wheatfields."

"Steam engines?" continued Ned.

"Don't get me started on those. I knew they were the future of transport on land and sea, but I couldn't raise the finance."

"And what about those guns, those Colt 45's? Wouldn't you like to get your hands on one? Don't bother answering – I know you would. And that's another irksome thing about MetroLondon – we don't have the right to bear arms. Does Despina still have your pistol?"

Shelley frowned. "She does."

Ned was silent for a moment or two. "Do you recall your days out with Lord Byron? Thundering along deserted beaches on a pair of thoroughbreds? No-one could keep up with you two. That's one memory you should cherish."

"I shall. It was exhilarating."

"And the shooting parties? Target practice with gold coins and playing cards? You were easily the best shot among us."

"No, Byron was."

"He took too long taking aim. And his hand shook, whereas you aimed and fired in one seamless movement. I envied you."

"And your point is?"

"I never saw you look so well, so animated, before or since. You were born to that life and

344

there's a very strong argument for getting back to a semblance of it."

"All in good time."

"You're thinking of Elvira, aren't you? Percy, you have to let her go. She'll be married soon."

"I tried to end the affair just the other day. She wouldn't hear of it."

"Then she's toying with you."

"No. She said there'd come a time when we didn't need each other. She's not being deliberately evasive – we leave that to the GTC. If they're keeping things from her, it's a sign our love hasn't yet run its course."

Ned gave a wry chuckle. "Nothing's ever straightforward with you, is it? Now you may not have noticed, but it's late and I'm tired. I'm going to my bed, and I don't want any interruptions such as sleepwalking, nightmares, yelling, climbing the walls, or other tricks you may have learnt. I'm under orders not to let you wander off, so if that seems likely I'll have to lock you in. And yes, I can do that. Norvus demonstrated. Sweet dreams, if your fevered brain will allow it. Tomorrow I'll introduce you to Saranna."

***

"Hello again," said a mischievous voice.

"Again?" Shelley was puzzled.

Saranna, her uniform cap back to front in blissful disregard of the spaceport dress code, grinned at him. "We did meet, for a few seconds.

You, me and Elvira were all at Secheron, briefly, on a certain day in 1816. I caused a commotion by kissing Byron, the invigilators rushed to sort it out and that gave Elvira a chance to speak with you. Your first meeting."

"Then, indirectly, I owe you my life, " Shelley replied. "Am I not allowed a kiss too?"

"Sadly, no," Saranna said, wagging a finger at him. "I've been warned your kisses are addictive. Now, if you'd both follow me to a very small and very basic lecture room, I'll display various line drawings, not to scale, of the Consortium of Worlds and how it's maintained. And, to save you asking a question that's never far from everyone's psyche, these ads for colonists are purely work and economy related, not a marriage brokerage."

Images came and went in quick succession.

"According to Ned you'll be looking for a colony with a level of development similar to 19th century Earth. Transport of the four-legged kind at local level, no domestic electricity, possible communication by telegraph. A more leisurely way of life. I'll maintain a search of the new postings and let you know the moment anything suitable shows up. You, my friends, will be a very desirable commodity. You're not just seeking a less evolved society, you've grown up in one!"

"How much information do we get in advance?" asked Ned.

"As much as you want. There are virtual tours, of course, and you could even have a trial run if you're still not sure." She handed him two

346

embarkation tags. "Here. Two tickets for the Polar
Orbiter. Three day stay. It'll help Shelley get things
into perspective."

"You're not coming?"

She gave him a surprisingly gentle smile. "Not
this time. But you might find some friends of mine
up there. Right now, I've promised to help Albie
with some final embellishments to his cinema. He
says it'll be ready in four days, so don't be late for
the preview. This wedding's going to be really
special!"

***

"I've called it the Electroscope," Albie said
proudly, "based on a junior school experiment with
two tiny gold leaves and some static electricity."

"What planet did you say you were from?"
called a jocular voice – one of his hired crew.

"Pimlico!" he shouted back.

The rest of his audience, a casual straggle of
acquaintances – mostly Saranna's – listened
indulgently. Lelza and her mother looked on
benignly.

"If I may continue," Albie went on, beaming,
"the Electroscope was also, I'm reliably informed,
the favourite cinema of Elvira's great-grandmother.
As you can see from the seating arrangement, I've
placed the audience in the round, to give everyone a
better view. The oculus, directly above, is *not* open
to the weather but houses the holo-emitters, plus a
spotlight if required. The rectangular wall panels,

presently lit in the lower right corner only, can depict sunrise, sunset, moonrise ..."

Shelley and Ned had not arrived. Saranna, on spaceport reception duty, briefly hurried in and explained that the Polar Orbiter shuttle had gone technical and another had been sent to pick them up. "They'll be along," she promised. "A flitter's waiting to rush them here the instant they touch down."

Albie was explaining that the holo-emitters could reproduce popular backdrops such as woodlands, gardens, beaches, the cosmos, etcetera. But on this occasion, because of the TTI's association with gold – the gold brace tether, the gold leaf of the receptor casings – he'd gone with sunbeams to play round the couple, holographic wedding rings to encircle them.

"As you'll all have noticed," he continued," where the screen was is now an art deco tree, which can display all four seasons: spring blossom, summer in full leaf, russet autumn, even winter snow if requested. The autumn version has gold leaves which shimmer constantly, gently stirred by the air-conditioning inlets. Paris will be escorted to the central dais by his mother, or her representative if she can't be present. Immediately before, Elvira will enter via an archway and proceed alone to the dais. A celebrant has yet to be appointed, but since the ceremony has no legal status, the couple can nominate anyone they choose. They will already have attended the nearest registry and obtained the marriage certificate." He cleared his throat. "Here, now, is the gold-bedecked sequence as we'll see it on the day."

Daybreak slowly brightened each of the wall panels. Two larger than life holographic rings hovered over the dais. At the same moment, Ned and Shelley were ushered into the back of the hall. They hastened forward to find seats, but two thirds of the way down the narrow aisle, Shelley suddenly froze. Sunbeams danced round the archway where Elvira in her gold dress would step radiantly into view. Music played discreetly.

"Percy, what ails you?" Ned demanded as loudly as he dared.

"This can't be real." Shelley's reply was scarcely audible. "Ned, tell me this isn't ..." Then his long limbs folded gently under him and he collapsed to the floor as lightly as one of Albie's gold leaves.

Ned knelt and shook him. He would have called for help but Elvira, Paris and Despina were already at his side. A small inquisitive crowd seemed about to join them.

"Don't worry, everyone, he'll be fine," Despina announced in her best authoritarian tones. "He's just had his first trip to the Orbiter and the shuttle pilot's re-entry was a bit enthusiastic."

The onlookers drifted away.

With a strong sense of deja-vu Despina performed routine checks, this time with a mini-medpack to assist her. "Just like last time," she said to Elvira. "He's deeply asleep. Not even REM sleep. I'll call it in." Then, to Ned: "Did he say anything before he took a nap?"

"Nothing that made sense. He said *this* – " he waved an arm to indicate their surroundings – "couldn't be real, and he wanted me to confirm it wasn't. Now you know as much as I do."

"We'll take him to the GTC medical unit," said Despina briskly. "I assume this isn't the first time he's had these presentiments? I'd like to know more, and you're the one to tell us. Norvus, would you oblige?"

"Certainly. Come along, Ned, let's grab some coffee. Shelley will be fine. Let the women handle this."

"Well," said Despina a little later, "here we are again. This place is beginning to seem like home from home. Sorry to bundle Ned off like that but this matter just became classified and he doesn't have clearance." Then, to the orderlies: "If any attempt is made to separate this exhausted young man from his clothes, other than his shoes, you'll encounter some instant Spartan retribution. He's only just forgiven us for what happened here last time. Put him on a couch, bring him a pillow, a blanket and some purified water, then be about your duties. One of us will sit with him."

"Yes, Agent Psamathe," they chorused.

Five minutes later the trio and their somnolent companion were transferred to a VIP observation room.

"Typical," Paris said. "He's got all of us worried to bits and he just lies there looking like Endymion."

Elvira agreed, a little ruefully. Shelley did, at that moment, resemble goddess bait. He looked deceptively innocent. One hand lay on the coverlet, palm upwards. And across his palm, scarcely visible, were two parallel scratches with a pattern of circles overlaid.

"Now what, I wonder, could that be?" Despina asked, well aware of the answer. "OK kids, fess up. You first, Paris. You know what this is."

"I should. I configured it."

"And Elvira? You recognize it too."

"It's the design on my recall bracelet," she said reluctantly.

"From the top, please. Great Russell Street?"

Elvira looked awkward. "We were having a play-fight. He said, 'you shall not escape,' seized my wrists and pinned me down. Then there was a spat of static, he passed out and I called you for help. While I was waiting I noticed indentations from the bracelet across his right palm, but they'd gone before you arrived. I didn't think there'd be a residual effect."

"Another time, think," said Despina tersely. "Paris? Something more to add?"

He sighed. "Elvira wanted a slender bracelet, not the usual chunky sort, so I put some of the circuit conduits, shielded, on the outside. I disguised them as stems and flowers."

Shelley stirred restlessly.

351

"He's all yours, Elvira," said Despina. "Paris and I need to talk shop."

***

Despina's change of locality was minimal, but she'd chosen an interview room with recording facilities. Paris was instantly suspicious.

"Don't fidget," Despina admonished. "We wouldn't be here if it wasn't important. I may need to upgrade your security clearance. First, answer me this: who taught you to make those conduits?"

"I ... don't know. Someone must have."

"Think again." Astoundingly, she had a synapsyn gun and seemed about to use it.

"What? No! Despina, this is unethical!"

"This isn't an interrogation," she returned. "This is an ... advanced health check, I suppose. My colleagues at GTC Forensics have made an in-depth study of your DNA, based on new evidence collected from Araminta Grace and Astrolabe Babes. It seems you were given a set of genes selected to boost your IQ when you came of age. Which means they're active now. Eva Mariosa wanted you to have an uncomplicated youth, as we both know, so she concealed your marriage pact and, apparently, your full career potential. One of the male donors matched our profile of Esquisse Polson, renowned polymath. We've obtained a statement from Eva, confirming her choice. Whatever your profession, she wants you to excel at it. Don't worry, you won't suffer any personality changes. You'll still be the same Paris we know and love. It was this burgeoning awareness which almost certainly drew you to your work in Construction and earned you kudos from Cyprian. So, shall I use this synapsyn or will you provide the answers we need?"

"Eva never did know anything about science," Paris said with a mirthless chuckle. "Esquisse hardly ever completed his grand projects. So, if anything brilliant comes of this, it will all be down to my diligence."

"Nerd," said Despina. "Tell me more about the magic bracelet."

"What more can I say, other than I always fear for Elvira when she travels? I wanted a failsafe, and it occurred to me that if her bracelet malfunctioned and left her stranded, she could trigger a recall by giving the exterior detail a good squeeze. I didn't realise Shelley would grab it, nor did I realise the imprint would reappear. Since I'd no idea why it would *do* that, I kept quiet. Sorry."

"And what about Shelley's visions?"

"Oh, come on, Despina, you're taking this way too seriously! First you think he's seen the Hope, then he keels over after a two-second glimpse of Albie's cinema. And as for the sleeping sickness, try looking at Hogg's memoirs – that's his college friend who appropriated Ned's wife. Shelley was *always* asleep! On the floor, under a table – to say nothing of the wreckage we found at the Hilton."

Despina sighed. "Doubt me if you must, but I still believe he's strayed into scrivener territory.

353

Which of course means I wouldn't get a straight answer even if I demanded one. You know the drill by now: the character in play must have no guidance. Free will is essential."

"But *Shelley*, Despina?"

"I admit he seems an unlikely choice. Let's hope the scriveners know what they're doing. I think they just might. I think they'd designated him a character in play even before we'd extracted him."

"Unbelievable!"

"Quite. Let's leave it there, shall we? Just don't assume you're off the hook. My bosses are still going to want those conduits. You've been honest, but I suspect you don't realise the extent of your nascent abilities."

***

"A lovely lady, garmented in light from her own beauty," Shelley said hazily. "If it brings you to my bedside I'll faint more often."

Elvira hugged him. "This is all my fault. I'm so sorry!"

"Sorry? Why?"

"For not listening to you. When we were in Byron's gondola you described Albie's cinema down to the last detail. Because I was expecting to hear about the Hope, having misinterpreted your poem, I didn't believe a word you'd said. Just another of Percy's hallucinations. I didn't even tell Despina! And now she's down the corridor ranting at Paris, blaming him for my negligence. I'm supposed to be taking care of you. And what have I done so far? Had your baby and abandoned her. I've made us both miserable. And when I saw those striations on your hand today, I thought I'd killed you!" She wept profusely then, clinging to him.

He stroked her hair. "If I thought these tears were for me, I'd be immeasurably flattered. But I suspect this is merely a bout of pre-nuptial nerves. Please stop crying. You'll make your lovely face all blotchy."

"It isn't even my face!" she sobbed, then proceeded to explain, shakily, what she'd had done to it and why Paris had been so upset. "You've seen the *real* me. Remember our first meeting at the Hotel d'Angleterre?"

"Yes. Vividly. I thought you looked tired, maybe from a long journey. But still beautiful." He paused. "Why not change it back? Your beauticians could do that, surely? It would make the perfect wedding present for Paris."

"So it would," she said with a watery smile. "I've been wondering what to get him."

"Have you named the day yet?"

"If everyone's in favour, May 4th. Obviously we have to get Beltane out of the way first."

"And when's that again?"

"April 30th. Less than a week. And you're going to stay right here, under observation, till it's over. No arguments."

"There won't be," Shelley promised, trying not to envisage an entire city full of predatory neo-grads.

"What did you think of the view from the Orbiter?" Elvira asked, drying her eyes and changing the subject.

"It looked much better in my imagination," Shelley said candidly. "But I can understand why Saranna wanted me to see it. Endings and beginnings for you and me. I promise you, my dear Miss Jones, that on the occasion of your wedding I shall comport myself in a calm, clearheaded manner with no fits nor fancies."

"I'm glad to hear it," Elvira said.

***

GTC headquarters, MetroLondon, was – unsurprisingly – the safest place to be on Beltane night. The staff had a rota system to accommodate those wanting the evening off, but not everyone took advantage of it.

As midnight approached, Elvira, Despina, Shelley and Paris were relaxing in the diner. Norvus and Ned had disappeared on a training exercise, as Norvus described it. "I'm nominally in charge of you, and if your plans for a new life hold good, I need to know that you can handle yourself," he'd explained. He'd then led the way to a hastily arranged bare-knuckle fight – the only day of the year scheduled bouts could be held, as the enforcers were too busy to interfere. "I've no real doubts about your suitability for life on a frontier world, but proof's always useful. Wait until you see how these pampered townies perform. I'd put money on you any day."

Saranna was on duty at the spaceport. It was closed to passengers until morning, but unmanned transports could still arrive with their cargo, including recorded greetings and news from the Consortium.

Paris was astounded to receive a real-time call from Eva. "Is that you, boy? Well, speak up. I'm here at your invitation. We've been stood off for tonight but should make landfall

tomorrow. I shall be staying at the Hilton, of course, Tell Elvira I look forward to meeting her."

"I ... I ..."

"Is that all you have to say after ... how many years has it been? Never mind. I understand you haven't yet hired a celebrant. Fortunately my good friend Rayah-Nova will be delighted to step in. You can depend on her to bring the correct gravitas to the role."

Paris stammered something incoherent. The call ended.

"Well!" said Despina, raising an eyebrow. "One of the Morii conducting a wedding. Nimue Pamina will be intrigued."

"She'll try and take over," Paris muttered.

"Of course she won't!"

"Not Rayah. Mother."

"I'm curious to meet this martinet," said Shelley.

"You will."

357

Midnight arrived and someone accessed the live feed from the streets. Shelley listened for a few moments, then shrugged. "The locals outside Casa Magni made more noise than that. Might I have everyone's permission to retire now? I'm still weary."

"Not quite yet," Despina said. "Now that it's the first of May, it's traditional for ladies to give their gentlemen friends gifts."

"But yours will have to wait until I've been to the shops, Paris," said Elvira. "It'll be worth it."

"It'll have to be spectacular to beat last year's," Paris declared. Then, to Shelley: "That was when I discovered I didn't have to marry Lelza."

"Paris has something for you," Despina went on, still addressing Shelley, "but in the interests of tradition I'll make the presentation for him. I have a little something for you too, but, gentlemen first." She produced her e-reader. "I know all about yours and Paris' trip to the single packet relay department, and I imagine the scriveners did too. Because less than one per cent of the timeline was impacted, no preventative action was taken. This is a typical example of what I found." She began to read aloud. "Much has been written about the authenticity of Shelley's last letter to his wife, delivered by courier when the Ariel had already set sail, and reputedly found among Mary's effects after her death in 1851. The original then disappeared for over three hundred years before discovery in the hands of a private collector. The handwriting has been studied at great length by experts and appears to be genuine, but recent analysis of the paper shows that it is of modern manufacture and has recycled components. The ink, too, is of similar origin, and we must therefore conclude that the letter is a forgery. However, the fact that Mary kept it suggests she may have believed otherwise, and derived comfort from it in the long years she successfully promoted her husband's work."

"I hope that was the result you wanted," Paris added.

Shelley turned away, fighting back tears but keeping his dignity. Elvira wanted to hug him, but sensibly forbore. Despina left momentarily and returned with a brand new carrying case.

"And, here's your pistol. I've had it cleaned, obtained more ammunition and provided a fresh supply of black powder."

Shelley, still wordless, accepted the return of his property.

"This comes with new instructions, so listen carefully. As soon as is convenient, go and see Albie. He's cleverly obtained permission to have the Electroscope designated neutral territory along with the rest of the spaceport. This means you can legitimately bear arms there. Albie intends to launch a helium balloon loaded with confetti, and it will be your task to shoot it down at the end of the ceremony. The confetti, of course, will sprinkle prettily over everything and everyone."

Just then, Norvus made a noisy entrance. "Well, come on!" he called over his shoulder. "They won't eat you!"

Ned appeared, bedraggled and apologetic. His knuckles were red raw and he had the beginnings of a black eye.

"Look!" said Norvus proudly, throwing handfuls of paper money onto the table. "Pugilist of the hour!"

"He's not coming to my wedding looking like that!" Elvira declared. "Norvus, I'm surprised at you."

"Elvira, sweetness," Norvus responded equably, "couldn't you find time tomorrow to escort him to one of those face places and get him spruced up?"

"Fine. I'll get it sorted," Elvira said, trying not to look pleased. It was the perfect opportunity for a quick confab with cosmetic sculptress Adelaide, and she took it while Ned was being cosseted by Ace My Face's junior staff.

Adelaide was reassuring. "Of course we have your template. Some of our clients change their faces all the time! And even if we hadn't kept it, your face would revert to its default appearance as soon as we removed our work. If that's all you need at present, we can do it tomorrow afternoon – which will give your prospective bridegroom time to view the result before you marry. He doesn't know you're doing this?"

"No. But it *is* what he wants. I didn't consult him originally, which I should have done."

"Why?" countered Adelaide. "He's just a man. They can be so silly at times. Right: you're booked in at 2.30. See you then."

Elvira decided to say nothing to Saranna, thinking she'd probably try and talk her out of it. Surprisingly, the remaining tasks were progressing smoothly. Tomorrow morning she'd take delivery of her gown, and Paris would collect his white suit. Then they would together visit a leading jewellers to pick up two white-gold rings. Finally, they would attend the nearest registry to legalise their union ahead of the public ceremony.

Everything else was in the hands of the planners – everything but the music for the service, which Paris had insisted on choosing himself. Before Albie's rehearsal, and not included in it for the sake of surprise, he'd asked Shelley's permission to use one of his short lyrics.

"Why trouble to ask?" had come the weary response. "It's all in the public domain now."

Paris would have tried to lighten Shelley's mood but assumed he was moping after Elvira and decided he wasn't the best person to offer a pep talk. Besides, time was of the essence. He called on Petra, still a talented musician, and asked her to compose and perform an up to date setting of Shelley's Bridal Song. She was delighted to accept, and swiftly produced a warm, gentle arrangement for soprano and piano. Paris loved it.

"From what you tell me," Petra said, "a piano wouldn't suit the Electroscope's acoustics, aside from the hassle of installing one. I could borrow a zither and add amplification."

"I'd no idea you played the zither."

"When I sing in public I need something portable and a little unusual. I think Albie will approve."

During the reception at the Hilton, a string quartet would accompany cocktails and snacks. Lavish wedding feasts with formal seating arrangements were a thing of the past; 26th century guests had typically travelled vast distances and were looking to circulate and catch up. It was no longer de rigueur for the married couple to remain for all the socialising, and Paris in particular was hoping for a quick getaway.

His anticipated confrontation with his mother hadn't yet taken place, as she'd promptly disappeared into Rayah's quarters and remained there. Subsequently she'd gone to inspect the wedding venue and met her match in Albie, who refused to change a single second of the Spring Blossoms presentation, and proceeded to out-talk her.

From the spaceport Saranna made an enthusiastic call to Shelley and Ned via Norvus' bio link, forestalling the trio as they were about to pick up their hired outfits. She'd found something intriguing amid the recent data messages she'd been sifting through. Prior to its stopover at the Procyon system, the Morii hyperway liner had paused at 82G Eridani, nineteen light-years from Earth, to collect freight and recordings from one of its three planets.

"The world's known as Lambency, and New Montana is its largest continent," she continued excitedly. "One of those Old West frontier colonies we talked about, only with a more temperate climate. Shall I go on?"

"Please do," replied Ned. "You've got our interest."

"The principal industry's gold mining. There aren't any gold-based currencies within the Consortium but it's still in constant demand."

"Mostly from the TTI," Norvus commented.

"Inevitably, on worlds like Lambency," Saranna went on, "there's small-scale bullion theft and illicit trade, and therefore there's always a need for security staff and standby militia. That sounds like a job for *you*, Ned. More to the point, there's currently a vacancy for a newspaper editor in the town of Constantia. The successful applicant will have unlimited access to a printing press and help run the telegraph office. Interested, Shelley?"

"A printing press?" he echoed. "That does sound tempting."

"Well, if you two will kindly get your cute little backsides down to the lecture room asap, I'll treat you to an immersive video about the planet. Then you can decide if you'd like some work experience."

***

"Paris? Are you home?"

"In the shower. Won't be long."

"You've been at *work*?"

"Yes, why not? It was either that or spend hours with my mother. Where have *you* been, anyway?"

"Getting your present."

He emerged, pristine and smiling, towel round his waist. "Where is it, then?"

"I'm wearing it."

His expression suddenly changed from mild curiosity to pure joy. "You crazy, wonderful girl! Come here!" He gently kissed the face he loved: both cheeks, her forehead and the tip of her nose. "Thank you for doing this. Now I can fall for you all over again."

"And I you," she answered.

They made love as tenderly and lingeringly as they had the very first time after their hesitant courtship. Elvira teasingly reminded him about his fleeting indignation when she'd stared too long at his face rather than his other attributes. They laughed reminiscently. Somehow the thought of having to entertain Eva had ceased to be so daunting.

"We'll take her to La Chanson d'Amour," Elvira said. "To show her my origins. Just one more day, Paris. One more day till we're married for all to see. We need never be apart again."

Chapter Twelve

May 4th dawned bright and sunny.

"All present and correct?" inquired Despina.

"More or less," Shelley answered, trying to smooth his unruly hair. Otherwise he looked presentable in a grey suit, white silk shirt with lace cuffs, and a lightweight scarf loosely knotted about his neck. No amount of cajoling had induced him to wear a collar and tie.

"Let's have a look at you," Despina continued. "You were right to choose a loose-fitting jacket. Makes you look less skinny. Lots of pockets, as we agreed. Plenty of room for the pistol. Have you got the accessory case, spare ammo, powder horn - ?"

"I'll only need one shot."

"Take everything anyway. Why are you dragging your feet? I thought you'd be glad to leave the convalescent ward."

"I've enjoyed hiding from the world."

"No more time for that. Ned and Norvus are waiting at the hotel. I've ordered a continental breakfast for us all, and then we'll wander down to Albie's at half eleven. Just one more thing before we leave: I'm obliged to tell you that the scriveners have designated you a character in play. That means - "

"I know what it means. Elvira explained it all to me in 1818."

"Then you know I can't give guidance. Not that I've a clue what's going on. Just try not to do anything weird."

"I don't intend to. I promised Elvira."

"That's good enough for me. Now come on."

She noticed that he only picked at his breakfast, but didn't nag him. He was edgy enough as it was.

They arrived at the Electroscope just before 11.30. Most of the guests had yet to show up. Near the dais, Albie was fussing over last-minute details. Ambient music played quietly.

Shelley took time choosing a place to sit, glancing several times at the dais, the entrance arch, and the columns – each on its own plinth – that supported the domed ceiling. Ned silently allowed him to make his choice.

"Ned," he said at last, in a sudden rush of words, "please hear me out before you censure me. There's danger here."

"I'll take heed, I promise. Norvus said I must give your premonitions more credence."

"Oh?"

"He wasn't supposed to explain why, but I insisted. Paris was concerned about Elvira time-travelling alone, so he put – what was it again? – intuitive circuitry into her recall bracelet. Not a true intelligence, Norvus was at pains to point out. Just a safety feature linked to her timeline. And then you laid hold of the bracelet. The supposition is, it sees you and Elvira as conjoined. You received its alerts, she didn't. When you panicked, it sent itself into sleep mode and you along with it."

Marise Morland

"Back in 1818 I tried to warn her there was a threat," Shelley said tonelessly. "I could see the disbelief in her face. The other day she apologised for doubting me – but I know she still does. That first time, I saw little; this time I saw much more – and said nothing. I didn't know what to believe." He paused, squaring his shoulders. "Now I do, thanks to you and Norvus."

"What did you see?" Ned asked patiently.

"Elvira's death. There's a killer here, Ned. She steps through that archway, some orbs of lightning strike her and she just vapourises, like a moth in a candle flame. But now I've a chance to save her. I'm resolved on it." With familiar ease, he loaded and primed the pistol.

The auditorium was filling up.

"What can I do to help?" asked Ned.

"Two pairs of eyes are better than one. The assassin will already be in position, facing the arch. Look for anything, *anything*, that will reveal him."

The service began. A spring sunrise. Rayah-Nova took her dignified place as celebrant. First Eva, then Paris, joined her. And then, an incongruity. A flash of silver amid the omnipresent gold.

"There!" whispered Ned. "Did you see that?"

"Yes. He's by the second column on the right. That silver's the barrel of a weapon."

"He can't get a clear shot from that angle. He'll have to move away from the plinth, towards us."

"I know." Shelley was suddenly very calm. "I'll be ready."

Thirty seconds later, a smiling, radiant Elvira made her entrance. The gunman stepped swiftly into position. Coolly, his hand rock-steady, Shelley aimed and fired.

The explosion set up echoes in the enclosed space, punctuated by a wail of pain as the would-be killer stumbled forward, dropping the laser rifle he carried. The lead ball had smashed into his shoulder. Incredibly, he tried to retrieve the weapon with his left hand.

Despina was there first. She kicked the rifle away and punched the assailant to the ground. Norvus appeared at her side.

"Oh, there you are," she said casually. "Got a med kit? I need some coagulant for his wound. Don't want to get my new outfit messed up."

Paris and Elvira, drawn forward, stared at the injured man neither of them knew.

"All right, the drama's over," yelled Albie. "Everyone stay in your seats while the agents finish their work."

The audience seemed disinclined to obey him. Then a new voice cut across the anxious mutterings.

"Wedding guests! Gentlemen, ladies. I am Eva Mariosa, mother of the bridegroom, and I've travelled ten light-years to see him married. I for one would like this ceremony to proceed, and I'm sure you would too. In the meantime, we can witness tomorrow's news in the making, as our ever-vigilant GTC agents interrogate the sad individual who tried to bring tragedy into our midst. If Nimue Pamina or any of her acolytes are here, I hope you will join with me in thanking the quick-witted young man with the antique pistol, who believed his only task would be to shoot down a confetti balloon. Music, please, Albie."

Albie put on some country dances.

Despina readied a dose of synapsyn. Paris wondered if she ever went anywhere without it.

"Shouldn't we take him to HQ?" asked Norvus.

"No, he's fit to be interrogated. The synapsyn will dull the pain. We do this here."

"At least put him where the guests can't see him."

"Agreed. Back to his hiding place, then."

They dragged him, none too gently. Despina then wielded the synapsyn canister and a sprinkle of crystals was absorbed by the captive's skin. "You failed, miscreant. Now tell us your name."

"Nicholas Peregrine Bridgenorth. Nick for short." He grinned vacantly.

Paris gasped. "The receptor box in the museum. The initials. They're his!"

"Is he right?" Despina inquired. "Speak. We're waiting."

"I am the true inventor of time travel," declared Nick. "My uncle bankrupted me and stole my work. Clive Brightlingsea took the credit. But none of that would have happened without your interference, Paris Evason."

"We had no idea you existed!" Paris exclaimed.

"Don't engage with him," Despina ordered. "Not until we have the whole picture. Nicholas, were you responsible for the Point Nemo murders?"

"I wanted to bring the TTI into disrepute. Jenufa got greedy."

"Despina," Elvira whispered urgently, "ask if he had an accomplice in 2023. The receptor box couldn't be operated by just one person."

Despina put the question. Amazingly, Nick began fighting the truth drug. "No. No accomplice. I acted alone."

She applied more crystals. "You need to give me a name. "You're really sorry for what you did. You're remorseful. Is your accomplice with you in this time?"

"I … can't." Nick's eyes brimmed with tears. "I'm so, so sorry …"

"Not sorry enough. Name your co-conspirator. Where are they now?"

"Despina, you can't give him any more," Norvus advised. "Let's hand him on."

"One more try." Despina adopted a beseeching tone. "Nick, this is making me very sad. We only want to help. Why won't you confide in us?"

"Because … I love her." Nick gave an anguished sob. "Gwen … forgive me - "

There was a minor commotion in the auditorium as a small, slight figure made a dash for the exit. Eva barred her way and seized her by the hair. "No you don't, madam."

"I'm nearly out of synapsyn," Despina said, hurrying up with Elvira at her heels.

"No need for it," said Elvira. "I know who she is. Her name's Gwen Morrow. Clive romanced her and stole her research."

370

"Ah. The woman scorned. And Nick's evil genius, if I'm not mistaken."

"Nick is weak," Gwen snarled. "And easily controlled." She turned to Elvira. "Why did I target *you*? Easy. Killing Paris would have been too swift a punishment for sabotaging our future. I wanted him to suffer real loss, and to go on suffering."

"One question before we take you in," said Despina. "With or without synapsyn. It's up to you."

"Ask," Gwen suggested.

"Why could we never find you?"

"Because you didn't reach far enough into the past. We took refuge in the disused railway tunnel at Chipping Norton, where Clive had run his silly little experiments. Every time CoherenceCo sent or received a package, we used their signal to mask our trips into the future."

"I assume you left evidence of your stay?"

"We didn't bother to clean up before we left, if that's what you mean."

"Good." Despina spoke into her bio-communicator. "Send a squad to this location. Two arrests, one injury. Maximum security."

In less than a minute the officers arrived. Bronze bangles were affixed to the criminal couple's wrists and ankles. Nick received sedation and was stretchered off. Gwen refused to look at him. Then, instantaneously, all were gone, including Norvus. Only Despina remained.

"What will happen to them?" asked Elvira.

"That will be decided at the highest level," Despina said. "We'll keep them on ice till then."

Elvira surveyed the auditorium, trying not to frown. "Do we go on with the wedding, or not? Everyone's getting restive."

"Wait," Despina advised. "Rayah-Nova and Paris' mother had their heads together a while back. They're up to something."

As if in response the lighting changed to the palest aquamarine. The music ceased. Then Albie's amplified voice said: "And now, the Electroscope is honoured to present Rayah-Nova's masterclass, the Novettes."

Six young Morii women paced into view and began an a capella chorale. Their voices were extraordinary – high, ethereal, hypnotic. In analysis the vocals were wordless vowel sounds, yet each listener heard something different and meaningful. The atmosphere became calm again.

Rayah beckoned to Elvira. Despina gave her a shove and she found herself walking with the utmost poise to the dais where Paris waited.

The spring landscape returned and Rayah began an invocation to the Spirit of Nature and the four elements. Albie's lovingly constructed holographic rings, many times life-size, hovered over the dais. At the conclusion of the anthem Elvira and Paris put on their own rings, and Rayah then looped a white sash round their linked hands. On cue, Petra readied her zither and began to sing.

"The golden gates of sleep unbar

Where strength and beauty meet together.
Hence, coy hour! and quench thy light,
Lest other eyes see their delight.
O joy! O fear! What may be done
In the absence of the sun?"

Shelley, further back, moved round to take a better look.

"Night, with all thy stars, look down,
Darkness weep thy holiest dew,
Never smiled th' inconstant moon
On a pair so true ..."

The blaze of sunlight slowly faded from the wall panels, leaving a many-hued sunset.

"Elvira Jones and Paris Evason, I declare you matriarch and spouse."

Despina intercepted Shelley just before he reached Petra. His iridescent eyes were half closed, his lips slightly parted. "Percy! *No!*"

"Her voice is like a shower of diamonds," he murmured.

"Maybe. She's also a mathematician. Didn't your friend Byron warn you about those? Now shoot the damn balloon!"

"Oh. Yes. Sorry." The gun roared. His aim was as true as ever. Confetti fluttered gently down.

"Nice to see your libido back in working order, but this is neither the time nor the place."

The music system played "The Air that I Breathe" by the Hollies. Paris and Elvira, entwined, slowly walked toward the exit. Rayah and Eva followed.

"Rayah wants to thank you for your prompt action today," Despina said, picking some sprinkles of confetti out of Shelley's hair. "And I suspect Nimue Pamina might be next in line." She bundled him into Albie's workshop. Presently Rayah appeared, serene as always.

"I know who you really are, in case you're wondering," she smiled. "I simply wish to thank you for your timely intervention. If the attempt on Elvira's life had succeeded, Paris would have been dealt a blow from which he'd never have recovered. Neither, I suspect, would Eva."

She held out her hand. Shelley took it and raised it to his lips in Regency tradition.

"You will be listed in the Morii Hall of Merit," she continued.

"Under which name, Lady Rayah?" he asked.

Despina never heard the reply, as at that moment a camera flash lit the gloom. "Nimue!" she yelled, and hurtled after her.

She caught up with the reporter just outside the reception room. A hubbub could be heard from within. "Nimue, what in Hades? You *know* we don't allow photos of the Morii!"

Nimue, agile and birdlike, stood her ground. "She's a teacher and she works among us. Cut me some slack, Despina! This is *my* scoop. I got here before Percipient UK. Who was Elvira's saviour? Come on, give!"

"I'll give you something you can use but you *must* be guided by me on this. For a start, the attempted murder was not a crime passionel by a jilted lover, but a would-be revenge killing. The couple we arrested were responsible for the Point Nemo murders."

"I thought you'd solved that!"

"We didn't get the architects of it. When we're finished with them there'll be a press release, so till then it's all sub judice I'm afraid. But City News won't get anything either. What you *can* say is that the perp had a work-related grudge against Paris and targeted Elvira out of spite."

"And what about the pistol-packing hero? I know him from somewhere."

"Probably from Making Eyes' latest ad."

"Oh, of course! Those beautiful blue peepers. Good thing he got them fixed beforehand, eh? Can I say that?"

"If you must. If anything else goes on your vlog it'll be shut down within the first few words, either by the Morii or the scriveners. The young man's been a character in play, though I think his role has ended now. He's had a stressful, difficult past and if I'm not mistaken, will relocate to a frontier world once the case is closed."

"Pity. He sounds interesting."

"If there's any chance of a statement from him later, I'll see that you get it. But for now, you have to leave him alone."

"Was the ceremony recorded?"

"Of course, and I'll supply an edited version as soon as it's ready."

"You drive a hard bargain, Despina."

"Don't I just. Now, off you trot."

Despina saw her as far as the nearest cube, then went back to retrieve Shelley. She found him sitting patiently at a work table. Rayah was no longer there. "Come on, nature boy. The happy couple will be leaving soon."

"I didn't realise. I need to see Paris." He hesitated. "The Lady Rayah said that once I have the GTC's clearance, she'll erase my vision of Elvira's murder. If I wish it. You do realise why I couldn't trust myself to speak of it?"

"Of course. I can imagine what you saw. He had a pulse-laser repeating rifle. Totally illegal for centuries. What alerted you to his presence?"

"A reflection. Silver."

"A muzzle-mounted parabolic mirror. It focuses the beam." She took his arm. "Let's go. This will all be over soon."

A ragged cheer went up as he entered the crowded venue. Despina waved an arm to shut everyone up. Paris, suffused with gratitude, caught both his hands.

"Would you agree," Shelley intoned quietly, "that my debt to you is paid?"

"In full," Paris said. "What you did was amazing."

Despina went to find Saranna. "Not like you to skip a celebration."

"Someone had to do the catering. Anyway, I didn't miss a single second. It was live-streamed up here."

"Good. So you'll understand why both our extractees need a distraction. Can you set up the Lambency work experience as soon as possible? I want them on the next liner, whenever that is. If it's soon enough we can have them there and back before their citizen status needs finalising." Her bio-communicator peremptorily delivered a migraine-inducing squawk. "Uh-oh, here we go. It's fall-out time."

"Headquarters?"

"Afraid so. Let them wait. I'd like a cocktail or two before I report to the presence."

"What do you think will happen?"

"Happen? Nothing, apart form the GTC chewing the fat with the scriveners. Both parties will be only too aware that there's no resetting this particular timeline without bringing down the entire TTI edifice. And if I were a betting person, I'd put money on the probability that the City Elders will forego the expense of a trial. After all, there were multiple witnesses and confessions from both offenders."

"And their sentence?"

"Exile; what else? The Morii will say it's more humane than locking them up."

"Exile *where*?"

Despina shrugged. "It's a big universe. I know what *I'd* do: stick them on an uninhabited planetoid, put a force barrier round it and let them drive one another mad. But, that's too knee-jerk for the Morii. They can do things to one's psyche that make synapsyn seem like sugar candy." Her communicator shrilled again. "Next time I'll have to answer it."

"Nick wouldn't last a day on your planetoid," Saranna declared. "Gwen would kill him."

"And you believe that because -?"

"Nick's a loser. There's no way he'd have escaped after shooting Elvira. I reckon he intended to turn the gun on himself. And Gwen, a stranger to us all, would simply have vanished into the city."

"When you're not playing the social gadabout," observed Despina, "you've a good forensic mentality. Well, would you look at that!"

"What?"

Despina pointed. Eva and Paris were hugging one another. "Time for bridges to be built, I think."

Saranna logged into the nearest booking point with her spaceport ID. "They won't have much time together. Eva will be on her way back to Procyon tomorrow."

"I don't think she'll stay away as long in future."

Saranna's fingers danced nimbly over the screen. "Hey, we're in luck – Eva's taking the same liner she came here on. It's the return journey: Procyon first, 82G Eridani second. And, there are still a few seats left. Can our two heroes rise to the occasion?"

"Well, Shelley's over there, talking to Elvira. Provided there's a convenient transport back to Sol, suggest it to him."

"There's a stopover via Epsilon Eridani a fortnight later. We do a brisk trade with the Eridanus worlds."

"Fine. Go ask. And since Elvira will be paying, be transparent about the fares!"

Shelley was acquiescent for once. "Do please make the arrangements. I'm still interested."

"And now, Saranna," Elvira said sweetly, "would you kindly round up Ned? He's at the bar with some of Paris' cronies. I don't intend picking up *their* tab!"

Saranna gave her a mock salute and skipped off.

"You still have that lost look, Shelley," Elvira ventured.

"It's a lot to take in."

"Well, don't let Saranna bamboozle you into emigrating. You don't have to go offworld. You don't have to stay in MetroLondon either. What about Italy? You were very fond of it once."

"And I'd rather remember it as it was, rather than see it futurised." He took her hands. "Space travel, Elvira! I never dreamt, when I was describing it in Queen Mab, that I'd have a chance to *do* it. This is only an exploratory trip, remember. I'll send you a bulletin while we're there. First impressions."

Paris had appeared at her elbow. "Sorry, Percy. It's time I took my bride home before someone asks one of us to make a speech. I refuse to make an idiot of myself in front of Mother!"

***

The flat looked comfortingly mundane. Without a word the newly-weds exchanged their formal attire for loungewear. Elvira made hot chocolate. They chose the couch rather than the mezzanine. The info panel was displaying Elvira's favourite screensaver: a hearth, a mantelpiece and an open fire, all glowing coals and dancing flames.

Elvira spoke first. "Well, husband, do you have a confession of your own to make?"

"Confession? I don't know what you mean."

"Oh yes you do. I know your every mood, and right now you're wondering how to tell me you've let me down."

Paris sighed. "I've let us *both* down. Remember our dream of going back to the 2020's, permanently?"

"That was *your* dream," Elvira corrected him gently. "But a flying visit could be tempting. You, me, a cornfield ..."

"My thoughts exactly. So, I asked for a feasibility study. I was hoping to be told that a short sabbatical was possible, if we were vigilant. That would have been my present to you."

"When was this?"

"Just before Albie's and Lelza's wedding, when I told you about lateral relativity. I suddenly realised how compromised our timeline was. The scrutineers ran a simulation, and it didn't look good. Remember the complete absence of data on you – media, finance, everything – that they found prior to your extraction? We'd have had no proof of identity, no money, nowhere to live, no ability to rent anything or even hire a car. If we'd happened to see Vivette we'd have risked creating a worse dichotomy than Norvus did. And now, after what we learnt today, there's no point in even hoping. Not with Nick and Gwen in residence at Chipping Norton. We'd be looking over our shoulders the whole time."

"So we're screwed, basically. I get it."

"There's something else too: these additional genes of mine. The GTC were *very* interested in those conduits, which I didn't even know were special. I think it'll soon be *my* turn to be the lab rat. They won't want to let me out of their sight."

"Well, you did once say that time travel terrified you and you weren't going to do it again."

"True. You could still participate, though. And they're bound to have something in mind."

"Hopefully not yet." Elvira kissed him. "So, what are we to do with ourselves tomorrow?"

"I – er …"

"Not something else!"

"I promised Albie we'd help tidy up the Electroscope, get rid of the confetti, spilt gunpowder, etcetera. The GTC haven't cleared him to bring contractors in, and meanwhile he's had availability enquiries."

"Already?"

"Notoriety breeds popularity."

"Did you tell him about our timeline trouble?"

"Not without your say-so. But he did wonder why I was less than happy."

"He's a good friend." Elvira snuggled closer. "And what about Lelza? Is House Dawn's finest going to wield a mop and bucket?"

"She will if you will."

"This I must see. Tell Albie I'm looking forward to it."

***

A week and a half had elapsed before Saranna brought the all-important mail message from Lambency. She, together with Elvira, Paris and Despina, assembled in the flat to play it. Ned, who'd made the recording, started by saying that as he'd always kept a journal, he felt best qualified to speak. "Percy's head's all over the place, as you can imagine," he continued. "Sorry for the delay in getting this dispatched, but there's been so much going on. After we made landfall, Percy insisted on driving us to Constantia himself. I'd forgotten what a speed freak he is when he gets near anything horse-drawn. I thought we were going to lose a wheel. But, we arrived at the newspaper office in one piece, if somewhat shaken up. The typesetter and chief reporter are husband and wife, a pleasant couple. They showed us some recent copies of the Constantia Courier and we both thought it needed more photographic content. Something for the future, perhaps.

382

Percy learnt Morse Code in about three hours and has been busy tap-tapping out messages and transcribing incoming ones, although Mr and Mrs Vanderzee found his handwriting a challenge. Our paper delivery boy is called Beau, about eleven I'd say, and very bright. He'll make an excellent reporter one day. He's keen to visit Earth.

What else? We went on the railroad, inspected the steam engine and admired the scenery. It's so unspoilt – mountains in the distance, cloudless blue sky. The railroad track runs alongside a lake, with boats for hire. I'll do my best to keep Percy away from them. I briefly visited the nearest gold refinery and they do need security staff and outriders. I told them I was interested.

Our lodgings are with Beau's mother, Kesiah, who runs the local saloon. She's an ex-feral girl from MetroLondon! Small and thin but tough as whipcord, and totes a gun almost as big as she is. She says she was ejected from the sisterhood after conceiving a male child. That's against their code, apparently. And Mrs Vanderzee, who's a mine of information, gave us the lowdown on the ferals. The Consortium of Worlds has renounced war, as we all know, but further into space there are worlds which have not. And so, the Morii maintain a defence. Those girls are soldiers in waiting! They may be uncivilised but they genuinely love their homeworlds. If triggered by the Morii, they'll remember the subliminal skills they were given and become a dedicated fighting force. Oh, nearly forgot – Keziah says she knows you, Paris, from years back. You may remember her as Kizzy.

The device is signalling me to stop. This world seems to be all that was promised. See you next week!"

"Right", said Despina briskly, "now we've all heard the good news I must take this clip to HQ and start the formalities. There'll have to be a cooling-off period of course, but if the Sheriff of Constantia can put in a good word, it could all be done and dusted in three weeks or so. Do you know the date of the next transport, Saranna?"

"I can find out when I'm back at work – which should have been twenty minutes ago."

And, scarcely pausing to say goodbye, they were gone, unmindful of Paris' sudden silence. Elvira laid a gentle hand on his arm and waited for him to speak.

"I never expected to hear that name again," he said at last. "Kizzy. How old did Ned say her son was?"

"Eleven."

"The date fits. You do realise that boy could be *my* son?"

"Don't get in a state about it. She's never contacted you, has she?"

"All the same - "

"Stop right there. The enforcers saved you from being ransomed, she still had your specimen so she used it on herself. It was a means of escape and she took it. That *is* what you're imagining, isn't it?"

"It's feasible."

"It was kidnap. You owe her nothing." Elvira marshalled her arguments. "She's doing all right for herself. She doesn't have a man around and probably doesn't need one. Leave things be, *please*."

He hesitated.

"It's just a supposition, Paris! He's obviously a happy kid. How's he going to feel if a bunch of enforcers turn up demanding DNA tests? You were right to keep your escapade to yourself all those years ago, and you need to keep it that way. Do you want to jeopardise your reconciliation with Eva before it's hardly begun?"

Paris sighed. "You know best, as usual."

"In this case, yes. There's a clever way of dealing with this but I'm not seeing it yet."

***

Three days later, Elvira, Paris and Norvus were at the shuttle terminal to welcome Ned and Shelley. Despina was on a case, but left word for Shelley to contact her on a matter of some importance. Ned had brought Norvus some export packs of local hooch, and promptly volunteered to help him sample it.

"My digs, I think," Norvus said. "This needs to be done properly!"

Elvira and Paris escorted Shelley to his newly valeted hotel suite. "You kept my books," he said, a little surprised.

"All your belongings are here," Elvira assured him. "Despina thinks it'll be at least three weeks before the legalities are sorted."

"Am I still Percy Jones?"

"Unless you want to change it."

"No; I'll keep your name, if I may."

They ordered refreshments. Elvira had intended to be circumspect about the Kizzy situation, but the atmosphere was so strained that she found herself blurting out the whole story as rapidly as she could. Paris, embarrassed, said little.

"Well," Shelley declared when she'd fallen silent, "I never thought you two could be such numbskulls. Thank providence you came to me first!"

Elvira had never heard him sound so severe.

""I'm sorry," he continued more quietly, "but don't you remember my history? I had two children taken from me by the courts. If you make any move, however well-intentioned, to acknowledge Beau, who do you think will complete his upbringing? An ex-feral girl, alone, working in a rough environment on a frontier world? You, Paris, happily married, the pride of TTI Construction, about to reveal new horizons in space-time? Or, Eva of House Mariosa, diplomat, friend of the Morii, eager to secure the future of her first grandson, already past the irritating brat stage and ripe for admission to finishing school? Ah, you see it now, both of you. House Mariosa would gain custody and Beau would be uprooted from his own journey of discovery."

"Ever though of joining the scriveners?" asked Paris acidly. "So, why did Kizzy announce herself if she doesn't want to lose him? What does she want?"

"Money," said Elvira.

"The local school's useless." Shelley spared them the details. "I offered to tutor Beau until he's ready to sit the entrance exam for Gramercy College. They accept pupils from the age of thirteen. Only – there are fees. My salary will hardly keep me in shoe leather."

"I'll sponsor him, when the time comes," Elvira said.

"You don't even know he's mine!" Paris protested.

"We can find out. But whether he is or not, I'd like to give him this chance."

"There's something else," Shelley said. "I almost didn't accept the Courier post. I felt it would tie me down when I wanted to explore this panoply of worlds. But Beau needed some help with his English, and was such an apt pupil I agreed to stay. So, Elvira, your offer of sponsorship seems all the more befitting."

Paris smiled dolefully. So this strange triangular situation was set to continue. The psychic link between Shelley and Elvira, which he'd unwittingly engineered, was still unbroken. She'd contrived to save the poet's life and shortly after, Paris had saved him in turn. Then, spectacularly, Shelley had rewritten Elvira's timeline. And now, philanthropic as ever, he would mentor Paris' son.

And Beau *was* his son; proof would surely follow. And lastly, presiding over everyone like a benign cherub, baby Elena, whose short life had been documented over and over in centuries past, but hadn't existed until the scriveners had sent Elvira to conceive her.

Time, despite conscientious attempts to manipulate it, often preferred its own agenda.

***

"Well!" said Despina. "Thanks for sparing me the time of day. What happened to yesterday? I did say the matter was urgent. I did *not* say it was GTC related."

"My apologies," Shelley replied a little too formally. "Paris and Elvira engaged me in a rare philosophical discussion. I'd never heard Paris speak so eloquently."

"What about?"

"Time."

"How dull. I was hoping you were enjoying a fun threesome."

"You mean intimacy?"

"Yes, my fine-worded friend. You missed a great opportunity there. Paris is quite phenomenal."

Shelley smiled uncertainly. "Elvira did mention that you'd – how shall I phrase it – sampled his delights."

"She *knows*? And she never said a word, the sly minx. Anyway, enough. I've a once in a lifetime opportunity for you, in heartfelt thanks for

388

your courage and gallantry. How would you like one final voyage on the Ariel?"

"Before it was wrecked? I was there for the whole two months it was mine. How does that equate with lateral relativity?"

"It doesn't. I'm referring to a time well after your extraction. 1827, to be precise. Captain Roberts, your boat-builder, located the Ariel on the sea-bed, salvaged and restored her. She was sold to a small English regiment on the isle of Zante. One day – I have the exact day and time in my dossier – the lads went off to the nearest taverna and left one of their number to keep an eye on the boat. Eventually he got bored and went to join his pals. The Ariel slipped its moorings, found its way to the open sea, and was finally dashed to pieces on the lee shore. I'm wondering – did that mooring rope untether itself, or did it have some help?"

Shelley's eyes shone. "Oh, Despina! Could we?"

"I reckon so."

"But what about Ned? We always sailed together."

"Ned's still hung over. No-one at TTI will let him travel like that. I did ask him, though. He said the boat was jinxed and he'd rather stay where he was."

"So it's just us, then."

"Now do you realise the urgency? However long we stay there, lateral relativity dictates that we'll have to move forward by that same interval on our return. The emigration department will want to see you in two days, so, I'm afraid we only have *one* day with the Ariel. No touring the Greek islands."

"Then I'll make the most of that day."

"Good. Now the official line is, we're locating authorised artefacts for the Greenwich Maritime Museum, and you're a leading authority in such matters."

"What do I wear?"

"I'll find you something suitable. I'll be half an hour or so. Are Elvira and Paris likely to turn up before me?"

"I don't think so. They're with Albie."

"Right. See you soon. We'll be leaving from GTC Dispatch. How would you prefer to transfer to the depot – by bracelet or cube?"

"Neither."

"Bracelet it is then. I'm really looking forward to this."

***

"Well, there she is, Shelley. My team were spot on; no-one about. Shall we?"

Delighted, he untethered the craft, then scurried from one end to the other, hoisting sail. In no time the persistent breeze had filled the canvas and the Ariel skimmed lightly and rapidly across the waves, almost as if it were under power.

"Did you notice she still bears the name Ariel?" Shelley asked. "*We* painted that, Ned and I. Lord Byron had our beautiful boat delivered to us with Don Juan blazoned across one of the sails. Mary

390

said it reminded her of a coal barge. We couldn't scrub the lettering off so we patched the sail."

"Didn't anyone tell you it's bad luck to rename a boat?" Despina asked. Then, leaving him to reacquaint himself with his property, she went to inspect the hold. She found half a dozen or so flintlock rifles, wrapped in sacking. Her first thought was that the Zante lads meant business, but on closer inspection found the weapons were rusting and in one or two instances downright dangerous. The seabed was the best place for those, and sooner rather than later, before a certain meddlesome poet caught sight of them. Despina swore under her breath. She'd assumed his timeline was secure: had she just opened it up to more risk? She picked up the weapons in twos, lobbed them over the side, then checked the sacking to ensure it held no more surprises. It didn't. Not even a bottle of booze.

When she emerged, she couldn't see Shelley anywhere. She noticed the tiller was unattended, called his name, then mounted a more vigorous search, irritably shoving her way past the noisily billowing sails.

Then she found him. He'd climbed onto the prow of the boat and was balanced, arms outspread, just an inch or two from disaster. His mop of hair streamed in the breeze. Fey, capricious creature, still eager to embrace all that Nature could throw at him.

"Get down here!" Despina yelled. "Do you know how difficult it was to create that fake drowning story – how many people were involved, how many favours called in? How would it make me look if you drowned a second time, five years later? Get *off* there!"

When he didn't, she seized his jacket and pulled him backwards. They both ended up in the hold on top of the sacking. "Bloody idiot! Well, since we two are so usefully juxtaposed, I might as well sample the amazing kisses I've heard so much about. And for your sake they'd better be worth it!"

She kissed him, and went on kissing him. There was sea-spray in his hair and the taste of salt on his lips. "By Hades, those stories didn't exaggerate. No, don't move. This will be all about *you*."

In her usual peremptory fashion, she threw open his jacket, undid every other button she could find, peeled off her costume and straddled him. As she'd always known, there was nothing of the delicate flower about him. His body was afire with sensation and she delighted in the responses she was evoking. He was in awe of her sexuality, and she found that unexpectedly poignant. Before his pleasure could become torment she released him and gathered him to her.

"I wanted to please you," he murmured.

"And you did. You're a connoisseur. Now rest."

They sat, she holding him, while the sails billowed and the timbers creaked. Then she suddenly realised that given the Ariel's rapid progress and the distance to the lee shore - as calculated by the spotter team – they only had minutes left. She threw on her dress and looked out. And just as hastily returned to pummel Shelley into wakefulness.

"Get respectable, *now*! We've got about a minute. Rocks dead ahead!"

He complied, fumbling with the assortment of buttons. The rocks were very close.

"We'll be retrieved in twenty seconds!" Despina shouted above the breakers. "Say goodbye to your - "

And they materialised in GTC Arrivals, she marginally presentable, he dishevelled with most of his clothes hanging off him.

"Well," Despina said casually to her colleagues, "you know how it is."

***

Spring evolved into summer, and life moved on. As everyone had assumed, Shelley was excused from giving evidence to the GTC. Just before he and Ned returned to Lambency, he was again visited by Rayah-Nova.

"Would you now like me to take the memory of Elvira's assassination?" she asked gently.

"As I'm sure you already know, my lady," Shelley replied, "I have decided against this. I've seen murder committed in Naples, and half a year later held my beloved son in my arms while he was dying. I cannot shield myself from such events and at the same time call myself a commentator on the human condition."

393

"I commend your resilience," said the Morii.

"I shall continue to write poetry," he went on. "I'm permitted to write in the style of Percy Shelley, and when I do so I shall call myself Shiloh Jones, in wry homage to the nickname Byron once gave me. Otherwise I shall be Percy Jones, newspaper editor and part-time author. And, once I've seen young Beau safely into college, who knows? Tomorrow, the stars. I'll go on until I'm stopped, Lady Rayah. And I'm *never* stopped."

***

"Hey," said Paris. "I think I need to say sorry and imbue it with more meaning than one of my finishing school specials. I should never have got myself so wound up over the Kizzy situation."

"Every married couple's allowed a few tiffs," Elvira replied, accepting the cup of tea he'd just brought her.

"And before that," Paris continued quietly, "I was too self-centred about losing Hampstead 2023. It wasn't your dream, as you said. Anyway – I've some news that might put a new spin on our life here. Albie's found some more subterranean sites near the Electroscope. According to the historic street plans, there was a restaurant and a ballet school. He's going to turn them into two luxury flats, and he'd like us to have one."

"This year, next year ...?"

"He'll have plenty of help. People are falling over themselves to work for him now."

"Oh, Paris, I don't know," Elvira said doubtfully, looking around at their customised home. "I like it where we are."

"But it isn't ours," Paris reminded her. "Despina might suddenly need it back."

"She wouldn't evict us without warning. And what about the Hope? It wouldn't work if we moved it away from the brace generators."

"Cyprian says we can house it in the Construction shop. It'd work just as well there."

"You've already asked him?"

"Contingency plans."

Elvira smiled indulgently. "OK, you win. Tell Albie I'd like to view the schematics." And that, she thought to herself, was as good as a done deal. When did Albie Nellison's work ever disappoint?

***

Thanks to Albie's newly-acquired workforce and a generous hand-out from House Dawn, the flat conversions were completed by early November; but his trademark holograms weren't yet installed. No-one seemed to be working on them. Elvira and Paris were content to wait, as there was still plenty to do prior to the move. The relocation and performance testing of the Hope kept Paris and Cyprian busy for weeks, during which Elvira – inevitably – was hustled off by Saranna for a shopping marathon. The new flat was substantially larger than the old, and required tasteful furnishing. This did not include Albie's unfinished project. The home theatre, which he'd commandeered, remained locked.

"But where *is* he?" Saranna wanted to know. "Lelza's not saying. And he missed your birthday!"

"Yes, and Paris forgot it too. It's just a day, like any other. I really don't mind. The TTI was overrun with outgoing tourists at Christmas, and as soon as that was over, the GTC started banging on about his new IQ. I gave them a roasting over that. He needed rest." Elvira paused, then continued more quietly: "If Lelza isn't worried then Albie's doing nothing dangerous. Didn't he promise to have everything sorted by Paris' thirtieth birthday? Well, let's give him the benefit of the doubt. It's less than a month away."

***

"Hello, you two! said Albie. "And happy birthday to you, Paris. Sorry about all the mystery but I didn't want anyone spoiling the surprise. Ready for the big reveal?" He overrode the security system on the home theatre. "This will take five minutes or so to activate fully, as it's, well, sizeable. Not like Lelza's little gardens. Here we go."

The interior of the room filled with a different daylight. Abstract blue and gold patterns swirled and settled.

"Oh, Paris. Look. Look! It's Fingest Lane!"

"You time-travelled, Albie?" inquired Paris. "A novice? Alone?"

"Not quite. Despina supplied the coordinates and was monitoring me, but lateral relativity stopped her from participating more fully. So I was indeed a one man band, and that's why it took so long. I was determined to incorporate a skylark and I had to go back three times before it put in an appearance. Which meant, of course, several shunts forward this end. I shall have to make it up to Lelza now!"

They walked slowly into the achingly familiar landscape, both beginning to see the true extent of Albie's genius. Every sight, sound, breath of wind and pattern of light had been sampled, replayed, analysed and reconstructed.

"Two things to remember," Albie went on. "Firstly, this is *not* a simulation. It's micro-sampling from real-time, GTC approved. And secondly, there won't be anything as amateur as a repeating loop. I've included a randomiser for authentic continuity. When I heard you couldn't return to your cornfield, Paris, I decided to bring it to *you*. Enjoy yourselves. Oh, and this is a present. Won't cost you a thing. The exit programme's embossed on the stile. Bye!"

The wheatsheaves swayed imperceptibly in the August afternoon. Above, invisible, the skylark twittered joyfully. Elvira gazed lovingly at her confident, smiling husband, so different from the scared, anxious boy who'd stumbled into her life through the tangles of chance and time. Taking his hand, she led him deeper into the corn.

"You've dreamt of this," she reminded him. "So, shall we?"

"Nothing would please me more," he replied. "I'm still your thrall. Command me!"

THE END